JUST US

Previous Works by K. R. Lugo

Schism
Prey for the Soulless
Dream Kill

Schism

In Lugo's debut mystery ... the creepiness factor rises when the dolls start talking back to their "mother." Readers with a fear of dolls beware. A bloody savage soap opera.

—Kirkus Review

Prey for the Soulless

Lugo poignantly explores themes of human nature, the depth of evil, reality television ... while spinning a horrifying tale ... and the cover of this thought-provoking book may make readers fall prey to its message.

—Foreword Clarion Review

In a nightmarish, alternate world ... A thrillingly orchestrated tale of America's ultracorrupt future.

—Kirkus Review

Editor's Choice Award
iUniverse Publishing

Dream Kill

A supernatural thriller in which the heart of evil seems to beat in the chest of a righteous man ... A fast-paced psychological thrill, with a vivid overlay of old-fashioned good versus evil ... Lugo counterbalances this spiritual struggle with a parallel cast of venal, grubby characters led by the book's wonderfully melodramatic main villain ... and the author takes care to lace his narrative with both sharply authentic dialogue and touches of wry humor.

—Kirkus Review

Editor's Choice Award
iUniverse Publishing

Dream Kill

For readers who relish gore and want to sink their teeth into a fantasy story that raises deep questions about the origins of evil, its evolution over time, and the means of vanquishing it. Lugo expertly weaves together two parallel story threads ... Extreme good and evil battle for supremacy ... a fantasy novel by K. R. Lugo about unconditional love, loyalty, and revenge in the present day and across time.

-Foreword Clarion Review

Editor's Choice Award
iUniverse Publishing

Dream Kill

K. R. Lugo takes a gritty, true-crime approach to *Dream Kill,* a fantastical tale about ancient monsters and supernatural peril. *Dream Kill* hinges on a battle straight out of the most twisted kind of fairy tale. The balance between realism and fantasy recalls themes and plot structures from Stephen King and Peter Straub ... promising work packed with genuinely creepy moments in these pages.

—BlueInk Review

Editor's Choice Award
iUniverse Publishing

JUST US

K. R. LUGO

iUniverse®

JUST US

iUniverse books may be ordered through booksellers or by contacting:

iUniverse
1663 Liberty Drive
Bloomington, IN 47403
www.iuniverse.com
1-800-Authors (1-800-288-4677)

ISBN: 978-1-5320-1255-6 (sc)
ISBN: 978-1-5320-1256-3 (e)

Library of Congress Control Number: 2017900520

Print information available on the last page.

iUniverse rev. date: 3/24/2017

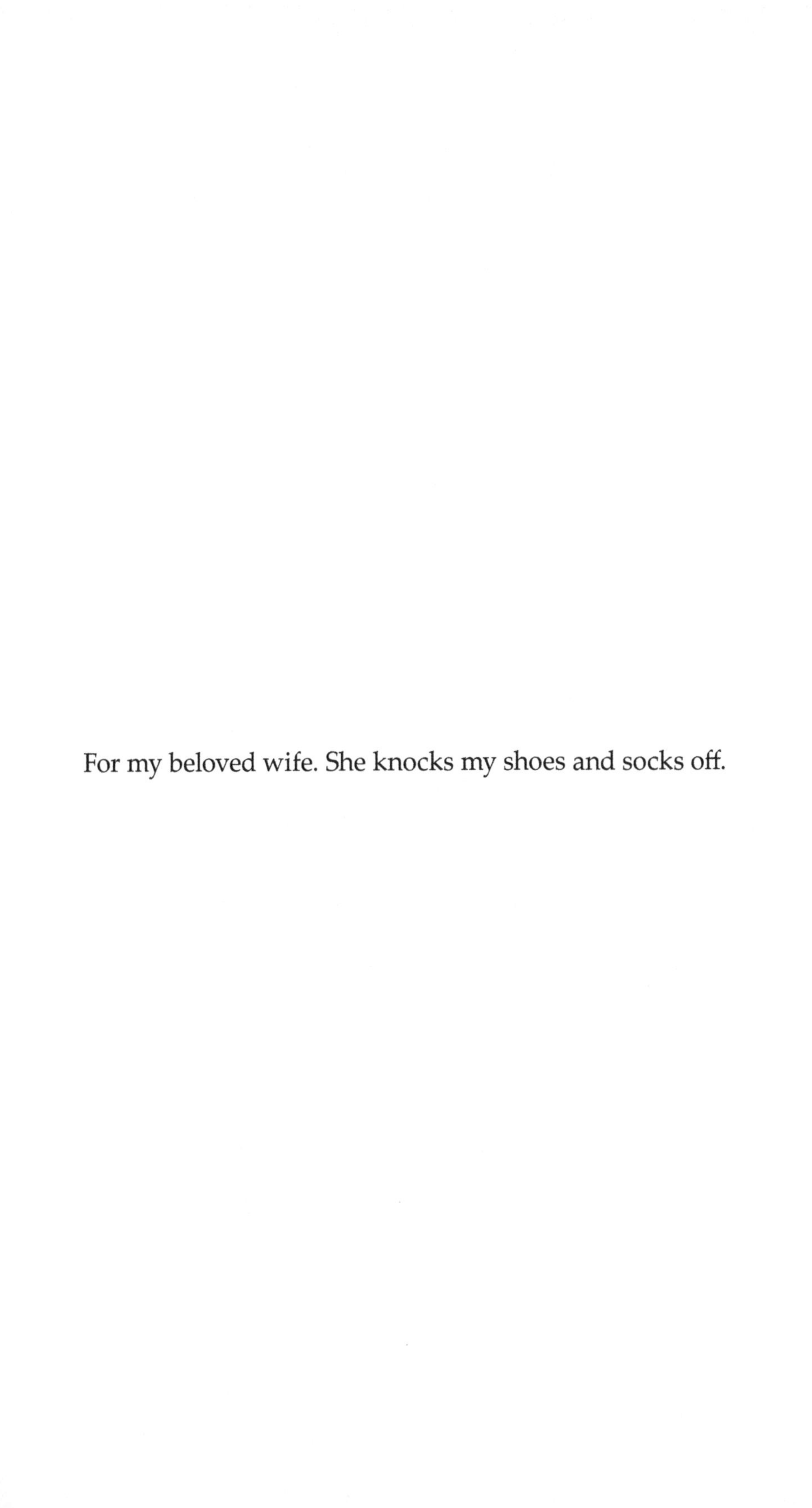

For my beloved wife. She knocks my shoes and socks off.

October 1, 1996, twenty years ago

Seated behind the same bench for the past fifteen years condemning men to miserable lives spent in prison, the Honorable Judge Terrence Harper cleared his throat and leveled a pair of steely eyes on defendant Trent Varus. A sneer of contempt marked his face and made it clear to anyone in the courtroom that he detested the man standing behind a wooden table next to defense attorney Gary Kirkpatrick.

Trent refused to cower or avert his eyes from the judge, though he accepted the fact that Harper had the power to destroy his life. Instead, he stood proud and defiant, resolute on maintaining his claim of innocence.

Although the evidence presented at trial by Deputy District Attorney Walter Callahan was overwhelming, his devoted wife, Connie, remained standing by him in her belief that he was innocent. She now served as his only refuge, his only advocate, encouraging him to stay strong and trust that everything would eventually turn out in their favor. However, to his unspoken shame, he did not share in her blind faith that bad things only happened to the deserved.

On the day of his arrest, reality had come crashing down on their sheltered lives and threatened to wash away everything they had built together.

Now, only the soft sound of Connie's muffled cries coming

from the other side of the bar interrupted the otherwise deafening silence in the room. Ostracized by all her friends and neighbors, she sat alone, dabbing daintily at her bloodshot eyes. Their lives were in complete shambles. The television news, which had dubbed her husband "the Pinstripe Killer," only increased the number of accusations from the public.

Against his attorney's advice, Trent had refused every plea offer made by the prosecution, along with every urging his attorney made to just surrender to public pressure and beg for mercy before the court. He was innocent. No force existed on earth that could make him admit to a crime he did not commit.

Spectators from every corner of the city filled the seats in the courtroom. The gleam in their eyes told the tale of how anxious they felt about this true-life court action. Some were dressed in suits, others in casual wear. The press from every local network had the best seats in the courtroom and held the tools of their respective trade at the ready. Competition in the field was fierce. Reporters on scene held their fingers eagerly poised over the send buttons of their laptops and cell phones. There was little doubt that the race was afoot. Everyone present was hungry to be first to report the sentence handed down by the hanging judge against defendant Trent Varus for the crime of first-degree murder. Those in attendance sat content in stony silence, waiting for the scythe of justice to fall on the neck of the guilty.

Judge Harper snorted derision at the convicted murderer standing emotionless in his presence and shifted his eyes to the prosecution's table. "Before I pronounce sentence on the defendant, do the people have anything to add?" he said with a guttural growl.

Deputy District Attorney Callahan shot a quick leer at Varus and shook his head. "The court has already received the recommendations from the probation department, Your Honor," he said with a note of hostility. "Since probation is not applicable in this case, and there is nothing in the record to support a single factor in mitigation, the people assert that the statutory maximum is a foregone conclusion." A savage grin creased his face. He then continued without missing a beat. "With that said, the people have nothing further to add. Thank you, Your Honor."

Judge Harper craned his neck and locked eyes with Detective Mike Johnson, who sat behind Callahan with a smug expression of victory etched across his face. His cruel eyes danced with humor. Harper gave a faint nod at the detective and then brought his attention on Varus.

"Very well," he said gruffly. "Mr. Varus, a jury of your peers has found you guilty for the heinous crime of murder in the first degree of a Mr. Morris Stokes, a human being. You have demonstrated no remorse or contrition during any of these proceedings for your terrible crimes against this great state and the people who reside in it. In addition, you have failed to take any responsibility for your crime, giving this court no reason but to believe that you are anything but a cold-blooded reptile that should spend the rest of its life in prison, and die there. It is the duty of this court to protect the public from such monsters."

Trent's wife continued to weep behind the bar. "It's all a lie," she whispered through strangled breaths. "He's a good and gentle man."

Judge Harper rolled his eyes and continued. "Is there anything you wish to say to this court and to the people whose lives you've destroyed?" He practically spat the words—disgust dripped from his tone.

Trent wrinkled up his nose at the stench of the judge's words. "What can I possibly say to you or anyone else that could matter now?" he said, keeping his voice calm, cool, and controlled. "This is not over, and it never will be until everything is set right."

Judge Harper's jaw set. "Bent on staying stoic and chilling to the end, huh?"

Trent craned his neck and smiled at his wife. "I will love you forever, Connie," he said.

Connie stood in a dignified manner; tears rolled down her cheeks. "I love you too, Trent," she said bravely. "And I am right here waiting for you, no matter what it takes."

Strengthened by her resolve and the love in her unshakable

devotion to him and their marriage, Trent faced the judge, proud and defiant. Nothing could defeat him nor wear him down. He stood on uncompromising principle, refusing to bow before the corrupt set of eyes leering down at him. His wife loved him, and that was all he needed to sustain him. "Let's get this circus over with," he said, prepared to face whatever nightmare might lie ahead.

Judge Harper picked up the gavel. His hand was trembling in anger. "Trent Varus, this court sentences you to the term of twenty-five years to life in the state prison." He brought the gavel down on the hard wood with a thunderous boom.

In the heavy stillness of uncirculated air on the first floor of the lavish two-story home, directly below the upstairs master bedroom, the mercurial temperature inside the robust television area infiltrated every square inch with a miserable stickiness. The slow approach of evening shadows brought on by nightfall did very little to lower the triple-digit degree or diminish the uncomfortable conditions normally found in forgotten marshlands.

Shadows in the fading light slowly crept across the carpeted floor and stretched over a pair of expensive boots worn by Trent Varus, who sat comfortably in an ergonomic chair with his legs crossed. One booted foot bobbed up and down in rhythm to music only heard by his ears. The tune was a beloved one he had listened to during the drive over, which had left a lasting impression on his mind. He had not spoken a word since turning the dial to the off position on the CD player over an hour ago.

After sixty agonizingly slow-moving minutes, satisfied that he'd maintained a level of practiced patience long enough—a learned discipline that had taken years to master under the worst conditions imaginable by the human mind—Trent finally surrendered to the aching temptation that had tugged at him since he'd broken into the residence. He tilted his head back and gazed up at the tiny tendrils of smoke curling upward from the burning cigarette he held pinched between his fingers. Thin swirls of diaphanous gray slithered like phantom snakes and dissipated before they touched the fourteen-foot ceiling. The ghostly dance of smoke reminded him of how easy the trick had been that had allowed him to circumvent the district attorney's outdated security system without leaving any trace evidence that an intruder had breached the electronic sensors. He now marveled at how useful the men incarcerated in the worst prisons of his home state had proved. Over his long years of incarceration, he had made friends with many of the country's notorious cat burglars and bank robbers willing to teach him the best ways to bypass security alarms—and all for the modest price of legal assistance, a small bag filled with individually wrapped Top Ramen soup, and a sixteen-ounce jar of Folgers coffee. The idea that a bizarre twist of fate had resulted in such a perversion of poetic justice brought great pleasure. Manipulating the woefully antiquated alarm system inside the plush residence had proved little more than child's play to a professionally readied cat burglar.

Trent snickered. *Time to play with my old friend, I guess.*

He lowered his head and leveled unsympathetic eyes back on the district attorney securely bound to a chair no more than a few feet away from where he sat. The cloak-and-dagger escapade he had planned for so many years, to his surprise, did not quite measure up to everything he had predicted. Something critical was missing. He furrowed his brow, wondering why the expected euphoria rumored to accompany revenge did not trigger anything that might erase his pain. The more he dwelled on things, the less satisfying his desire for revenge felt.

Disillusioned about the rush of anticipated vengeance finally fulfilled, Trent pressed his lips into a fine line and sighed. His sworn commitment to set things right decades earlier now seemed so far away, and he could not deny the emptiness that still filled his heart and mind. *What is wrong? Why am I not thrilled over this? Shouldn't I be tickled friggin' pink?* No matter how hard he searched his mind to answer the nagging questions that now plagued his thoughts, nothing of meaningful substance came to mind.

A guttural groan slipped from his lips as the specter of doubt raised its thorny head. His nerve to follow through with his preconceived plan started to falter, and he had to shake his head to rid his conscience of the voice attempting to dissuade him from completing his long-awaited mission.

"Grant no mercy; receive even less," he said.

His focus returned to the nightmarish suffering he had endured at the hands of the man seated only a few feet away. He weighed the magnitude of the man's crimes against that of granting him any semblance of forgiveness. He needed no more than three ticks of the second hand on a watch to reach the only conclusion. It was too late to simply back out and go home. Revenge had demanded its pound of flesh decades ago, mercilessly haunting all those years spent in a concrete cage. If he did nothing, no one else would, and the destroyer of lives would continue to do to others what he had done to him.

Trent narrowed his eyes, his revulsion for District Attorney Walter Callahan pumping anew in his veins, rekindling his true purpose for coming in the first place.

Don't punk out now! Trent took a deep breath. *So, let it begin.*

Trent then reached out and removed the blindfold that covered Callahan's frightened eyes. His blood ran cold and deadly in his veins. "Do you remember me?" he said.

Callahan moved his jaw to speak, but the gag taped over his mouth muffled his attempt to form words. He started to struggle against the restraints on his legs and arms, but then he stopped his futile fight when Trent snubbed out his cigarette and slid the butt into his front shirt pocket. He returned to working his jaw against the gag.

Trent cleared his throat. "You seem a little distressed," he said. "I wonder why that is, Mr. Callahan. Now, answer my question."

Callahan nodded. His wide eyes spoke volumes of terror. Sweat beaded his forehead.

Trent withdrew an enormous hunting knife from a hidden sheath tucked behind his back. "I'm impressed," he said. "Good to see you, I suppose." He cut away the gag with a precise flick of his wrist.

Callahan jerked his head forward. "Please!" he blurted. "I'll give you anything you want—anything. Just don't hurt me. Just name it, and it's yours."

Trent sneered at the disgusting offer made by the sadistic coward, and Callahan's attempt to weasel his way out of paying for his past sins only added fuel to the fire that had burned in his heart for years. He chalked up the bribe to the predicted actions of a typical bully.

The district attorney's eyes sparked with life, and he ran his tongue over his lips. "Name your price," he said. "I have money, a lot of it, if that is what you're after, Varus."

Trent shook his head, sickened. He had never found another human being more repulsive. "You have nothing I want or need," he said. "That is, except for your miserable, bloodsucking life."

Callahan jerked in the chair. "I don't understand," he said. "What are you saying?"

Trent leaned toward Callahan's now pale features. "You will forfeit your life to me, or I shall kill your entire family," he said, "one by one, right in front of you. I will end them, cruelly, sadistically. First your children will fall and then your wife." He held up the knife and twisted the blade to punctuate his point.

Callahan swallowed hard, his Adam's apple moving up and down. "You c-can't just ask me to agree to let you murder me," he said. His voice cracked on the last two words. Tears pooled in his eyes.

Trent chuckled. "Who said anything about asking?" he said. "I'm demanding, and it's not open for debate." He pointed the tip of the blade at Callahan. "You will sacrifice your life, or I will throw your family tree in the damn furnace. At least I am giving you a choice, unlike the one you denied me in another lifetime."

Callahan's mouth fell open with a whimper.

Trent walked over to where a black medical bag rested on a small end table. He opened it and then removed a pair of surgical gloves, a Polaroid picture, and a hypodermic needle. He placed the needle on the table and donned the gloves with two sharp snaps.

Callahan twisted in the chair. "What's that for?" he said with a tiny squeak. His eyes widened at the sight of the syringe.

Trent held up the items, smiling with cruel intentions. "That depends on the choice you make here today," he said. "Like I said, it's not open for debate. One way or the other, you are going to die today. The only question is whether you're taking your family with you." He moved toward Callahan on catlike feet and set the picture on his lap for an unobstructed view.

At first, Callahan appeared confused as to why the man would bother showing him a picture, but then a look of crystal clear understanding seeped in once he lowered his eyes and realized that it was a recent picture of his wife and two little girls lying on their marital bed upstairs.

"Do you hear what I'm telling you, now?"

"You filthy bastard!" He glowered. "Do you have any idea who I am? Do you know what kind of people cater to my every whim? I have real power, and I will destroy you and everything in your lousy convict life."

Trent gave a snort of derision at Callahan's feeble threat and snatched up the picture. He waved a nonchalant hand through the air. "That's the word on the street," he said humorously. "Save your false bravado for someone who intimidates." He then backhanded the DA across the face. "I don't want to hear your empty threats. You are not in charge here. I am. You have nothing with which to threaten me. I lost everything a very long time ago, and all I have left in this stinking world is my revenge."

Callahan ran his tongue over his sore lip. "Please. You don't have to do this," he said. His demeanor changed in an instant, and he looked around the room, his face stricken. "They're innocent. I'm responsible, so blame me."

Trent grinned at the man now begging for mercy. "You're embarrassing yourself and wasting your time," he said. "The time has come to take your medicine."

"But my family needs—"

Another hard backhand across his mouth stopped him from finishing the sentence.

Trent turned livid, his hands shaking in fury. "Don't you dare finish those words," he said. He retrieved the syringe and slid it into his shirt's front pocket. "I remember a time when I made a similar claim, back in another life—before I became the creature you now see standing in front of you."

"There's a big difference." Callahan's features pinched.

He looked down at Callahan. "Not to me," he commented dryly. "You knew that I was innocent, that I never committed a crime in my life, and you didn't care. It was just business as usual. Am I right? Just doing your lousy job, and I'd wager that you never lost a wink of sleep over what you did to me and mine." Bitterness swelled inside of him. Single-mindedness had driven him to this very day, to this homicidal moment, and he glared at the evil serpent that had destroyed his Eden. "You will be held accountable. Of that you can be certain."

Callahan cringed back in fear. "I'm sorry," he cried. "Okay? I'm sorry for what I did to you."

Trent moved his face within inches of Callahan's. "Not yet you aren't," he snapped, spittle flying from his mouth. "You killed my wife. You murdered my son. My mother and father are gone because of you, you disgusting maggot." He straightened up and took control of his pent-up hostility before it boiled over.

Callahan winced. "I can—"

Trent placed a finger under his chin and tilted his face upward. Trent narrowed his eyes. "Save your apologies for God," he said, "because you will receive nothing from me. I am not your father confessor."

Callahan's eyes turned wild in fear. "You're crazy," he said. "I don't know what you're talking about. I've never met your family, and I certainly didn't murder anyone."

Trent removed his finger. "Shut up!" he said. He turned and walked over to the medical bag. He retrieved a long, rubber tube; a legal tablet; and a pen. He tucked the tube in the back pocket of his pants.

Callahan wriggled against the restraints. "What's going on?" he said.

Trent sauntered back over to Callahan with the pen and paper in hand. "Any last words?" he said.

"Like what?"

He shrugged. "I don't know and don't care." He set the items on the table and then pointed at them. "You're going to write your suicide note, and you're going to make it credible. I've studied your writing style, so don't even try anything funny, or, in this case"—he chuckled with mirth—"stupid, because I will know."

"What makes you think I'd ever agree to do this?"

Trent looked down into his eyes, savoring the coward's feigned courage. "If you don't, then I'll just hippity-hop upstairs and slit all three of their throats. After that, I'll come back down here and start chopping pieces off your body, starting with your toes and working my way up." He shrugged. "It makes no real difference to me. I have no plans for tonight."

Callahan pursed his lips, no doubt mulling over the words. "How do I know you'll keep your end of the deal?"

"You don't," Trent said bluntly. "However, I would not have gone through the rigorous effort of drugging them to make certain they were excluded from our personal business if I intended to kill them. As far as they will know, they merely fell asleep on the bed. I took great measures to make sure they were not included in any of this." He pushed the table closer to the chair and plucked the syringe from his pocket. He popped the cap, dropping the orange piece of plastic in his pocket.

His brow knitted. "And if I refuse?"

He tightened his grip on the knife. "You won't," he said matter of fact. "Now, I'm going to cut your right hand free so you can write. Don't be a false hero."

Callahan watched his every move, clearly looking for some way to sneak his way out of the situation.

Trent moved behind him and gently slid the knife between the Terry cloth towel and zip tie—he had used the cloth to avoid any incriminating evidence of bruising—and then cut it loose with a sharp tug of the blade. "Very good," he said when Callahan offered no resistance, keeping the blade poised at the ready.

Callahan raised his wrist and checked it for any sign of

redness. There was no sign of trauma. "It's still not too late to call this off," he said, reaching for the pen.

Trent pointed the tip of the knife at the tablet of paper. "Write!" he ordered. "You have nothing to say that I want to hear. As far as I'm concerned, you're getting off light." He swished the knife through the air. "Come on, hurry up. We need to wrap this up. I'm a busy man, and you're the first on a long list of people I intend to visit." He gave him a shove. "Write."

Callahan placed the tip of the pen against the paper. His trembling hand failed to move. "This is so twisted and demented," he said in a shaky voice.

Trent remained stoic, unfeeling. He accepted the fact that one man extorting another to jot down his eulogy was monstrously sick. After all, how could any man explain to his wife and children why daddy was about to kill himself? What could any man hope to write that would suffice? How could any woman ever hope to explain such a selfish act to their children? He smirked at all the empty answers and poked the back of his victim's neck with the point of the knife.

Callahan wept softly. Tears dripped across the paper. Another poke at the back of his neck got the pen moving and the ink flowing.

"Oh, that's good," he said with a sinister giggle. "Try to spill a few more crocodile tears on the paper. It will do wonders for overall effect."

"You're a cold-blooded bastard," he said, "pure evil incarnate." His writing hand picked up speed. More tears struck the page and smeared some of the ink.

Trent tapped the side of his neck with the blade. "Good boy," he said. "You just might save your family after all."

After Callahan finished writing his final farewells, Trent quickly snatched the pen and paper.

"This isn't right," Callahan said.

Trent shook his head. "Nothing ever is," he said.

Callahan tilted his head back and glared up at him.

Trent read the letter, nodding his satisfaction as he walked over and set the materials on a matching table. "It's a good letter," he said, placing his hand over his heart. "I'm all choked up, and there might even be tears."

"Screw you!"

"Yeah, you wish." Trent removed the rubber tubing from his back pocket. "Like I haven't heard that a time or two before, old buddy."

"What now?"

"I'm afraid to say that our business together is about to reach its inevitable conclusion." He held out the tools of the drug trade. "I want you to tie off and shoot up with the morphine in this rig. There's 4 cc's, so that will be plenty to take care of the deed." He gave a wink. "I'm aware of your prior tangles with chasing the dragon, Mr. District Attorney, so everyone will buy a severe backslide. In the end, dope fiends never change."

Left with no chance to escape his fate, Callahan wrapped the rubber tubing around his bicep and made a fist. He slapped at his arm several times and then looked up at his executioner. Hatred burned in his eyes, as he rested the point of the needle against the thick vein in his arm. "Do you promise not to hurt them?"

Trent nodded. "That is the deal," he said. "Good-bye, Callahan. I hope you burn in hell."

Callahan pierced the vein. "I'll see you there."

"Probably," he said.

He depressed the plunger.

The effects of the Class A narcotic were instantaneous. Callahan's head lolled side to side, twisting on his thin neck. His eyes rolled back, just as his body sagged in the chair. With three quick flashes of his wrist, Trent severed the remaining zip ties and watched his sworn enemy crash onto the floor in a near lifeless heap.

Trent held the knife at the ready and stared at the syringe still embedded in Callahan's arm. He nudged him with a foot. "Are you dead yet?"

There was neither sound nor movement.

He went to a single knee and placed two fingers on Callahan's carotid artery, finding no pulse. His grin faded. He was not entirely certain as to what he should feel, but he was relatively sure there should have been something more, a whole lot more. He furrowed his brow as he contemplated. Did he feel true satisfaction? Not that he could tell. Had murder quenched his desire for revenge or changed anything at all? Nothing he had done had cured one damn thing.

Again, he nudged the body with his foot. "Hey, this isn't cutting it, pal," he said with a disgruntled growl. Stunned by the unexpected revelation, Trent sat down on the floor next to the now dead Callahan. For the first time since bypassing the alarm system, he looked around at the plush decor of the room. *All bought with blood money,* he thought grimly. He shook away the reverie.

He then peered into his victim's vacant eyes. "Time to go, sport," he said. He gave him a pat on the head and stood up.

He quickly gathered up all the evidence that could possibly allow the crime scene experts to infer anything except suicide. Only after he had double-checked everything did he head upstairs to where the rest of the family lay in a heavy, drug-induced sleep.

CHAPTER 2

Benny Maldonado—ex-con and three-time loser—had been involved in the sexually tantalizing world of exotic dancing since he was just a punk kid, starting at the ripe age of seven. Like many children from broken families with missing father figures, Benny had spent most of his youth knowing his mother was twirling around the stripper pole under the hypnotized eyes of the lowliest drunk and drug-addled minds the town had to offer. His mother could only on the rarest occasion afford to pay for a babysitter to watch him in the run-down tenement in which they lived, so she had little choice but to drag her impressionable son to work, where he fraternized with the immoral customers no one else welcomed.

Fifty years later, nothing much had changed in Benny's world. The only real difference was that time had moved on without him. Now it was too late to expect anything pure out of life. He was sixty years old, he felt a lot older than his actual age due to the hard miles traveled on the road to hell, and the bitter pill he swallowed each morning only seemed to grow worse with resentment. Times were different, he was different, and all his hopes and dreams had died long ago, left to stink on a stretch of rotten highway that defined his life as a total failure.

The only bragging rights he had to anything, if such could be deemed as an accomplishment, was that he had become the owner of the infamous strip club the Mousetrap after he had served his last prison term of five years.

Benny was still reminiscing over his disappointing life when he heard the familiar squeak of the back door, which led to the filth in the alley, shoved open. He turned and sucked back on his lower lip. The last thing he needed today was another headache. His tax returns for the year were proving migraine material.

Contrary to his best prayers, he did not need a second guess to know who had just entered, unwelcome, his place of business. His morning had started out with a broken jukebox, and nothing since the repair person refused to come and fix it had improved.

He stole a quick glance at the clock hanging on the wall and rolled his eyes, knowing his day was about to take a huge dip in the sewer. It was still too early for any of his regulars to show up, and only two types of people ever sneaked into the strip joint before the noon hour. His uninvited visitor was either one of the local riffraff that had wandered in from the street in search of something to eat—usually still on a drunken bender or completely whacked out on drugs—or a dirty cop bent on abusing his authority and blackmailing Benny into forcing one of his girls to have free sex with him. It was a vicious circle, one in which he had been dancing around for years in order to keep his liquor license valid and his doors open to the public.

With a nasty grunt of malcontent, Benny sauntered over to a round table, where his twin nephews sat across from each other drinking a bottle of his best bourbon, and slid into an empty chair equidistant between them. He looked to the left and then to the right. A groan of despair slipped from his aged lips. He had never known a lazier pair of brothers.

James set his glass on the table, wiped at his mouth with the sleeve of his shirt, and burped loudly. His bloodshot eyes sparked with humor. "What's up, Uncle Benny?" he said in a slightly slurred voice. "You don't usually come and sit with us. You say we're nuts and disgusting." He snickered.

Benny ran an impatient hand over his pate. His unwanted patron would enter the main room in a matter of only minutes, and he had to think fast. "Look, you idiot, I don't have a lot of time to explain the particulars to you, but I need for you and your brother to move behind the bar, give me a little room, and relieve Tabitha." He pointed in her direction.

"Can we ask why?" James said.

Benny shook his head in irritation. "No, you can't," he snapped. "Just do what I say, and don't ask me any stupid questions. I'm running this thing here."

Jim brought an open hand down on the table with a loud smack. Wood cracked beneath the power of his arm. "That ain't fair, Uncle Benny," he said with a sneer. "We're always getting screwed and disrespected. We were here first. Why can't you go and sit somewhere else? I don't see your name on this table."

Benny flashed out a knife from his back pocket and held it firmly against Jim's neck. "What did you say to me?" he said angrily. "I don't care how big you boys are. I'll cut the two of you open like a couple of trout if you don't watch your mouths and the way you speak to me."

James threw up his hands and motioned for his brother to calm down. "He didn't mean nothing by it, Uncle Benny," he said. "But you do kind of treat us bad at times. The three of us, we are supposed to be family, but you treat Tabitha a whole lot better than us. She ain't even blood."

A malicious grin formed on Jim's face. There was no fear in his eyes, only a strange sort of pleasurable gleam at the feel of cold steel pressed against his throat. "Are you going to cut me or let me finish my drink, Uncle Benny?" He tightened his fingers around the glass and lifted his chin a little higher. "Do it ear to ear and make me a pumper."

"Now who's acting nuts?" James said dryly. "This is ridiculous."

Benny ignored the comment and applied a little more pressure. "Do you think I'm kidding, Jim?" he said with a hiss. Nothing either one of his nephews did ever surprised him. He sometimes wondered if demons possessed them. "Family or not, I'm not the one to screw with, kid."

Jim turned his head to the left and to the right several times. His throat seesawed against the blade, drawing thin trickles of blood. "I know you're not kidding," he said. "I'm not kidding either, Uncle Benny."

Benny narrowed his eyes. *You are one crazy bastard!* He thought back to his misspent teenage years and all the trouble he had gotten into.

James threw the rest of his drink in Jim's face. "Shut up, Jim!" he snapped. "We're not impressed, you dumb-ass." He got up from the table and placed a hand on Benny's hand. "We'll do what you say."

Benny met James's eyes, nodding. "Good," he said, relieved that he did not have to force the issue of respect on his nephew. He withdrew the knife and slipped it back into his pocket. "But don't you two wander off. We need to talk after I take care of our guest. We got some business to discuss."

A greedy look for some much-needed action to earn easy money suddenly crossed Jim's face as he slowly got up from the table. "What kind of business?" He picked up a tablecloth and dabbed at the spots of blood still dripping from the thin incision on his neck.

Benny offered him a knowing wink. "Later, boys," he said. "Now, go behind the bar and clean yourself up."

Jim and James picked up their glasses and walked over to the bar.

Benny motioned for Tabitha, who was standing mute and obviously disinterested behind the bar, to come over. Always preferring to take the role as the queen of wit for the less appreciative, she gave a quick flash of her pearly whites that looked more like an unscrupulous sneer of discontent and poured herself a large coke. Only after she had taken a hefty gulp did she finally sashay around the end of the bar and head in Benny's direction. Despite the feigned smile that remained plastered across her ruby-red lips, she did not look pleased with Benny summoning her to the table like some sort of lackey. She took Jim's vacant seat and shot a pair of light blue lasers that struck Benny right into his heart.

Benny pulled a cigarette from his shirt pocket and lit it. He knew all too well what the constipated look on her face meant. He rapped his knuckles on the table for good luck. "I think your boyfriend is coming here today, babe," he said, struggling to keep a straight face. He hoped his first guess about their visitor proved inaccurate.

A look of instant nausea shadowed Tabitha's face. Her forced smile vanishing completely, she rolled her eyes and then made a gagging noise of disgust in the back of her throat. She snatched the cigarette out of his hand and took a quick puff on it. "You know better than to call him that, you ass," she warned in a harsh-sounding voice, eyes glaring none too gently. "The guy is a total creep, and he makes my skin crawl." She visibly shivered to punctuate her point and then added, "And not in a good, fashionable way."

Benny gave a grunt in agreement. "He makes everyone's skin crawl, babe," he countered. "You're just better at handling his rather peculiar appetites."

"You mean gross and grotesque," she corrected.

He shrugged, grimacing. No one had spoken truer words.

She handed the cigarette back and took another drink of her coke. "His poor wife must be a wreck," she offered. "My heart really goes out to her." She squirmed in the chair, as if something revolting had just occurred to her. "Hell, he's not even a decent screw."

Benny choked on the smoke from her complete lack of couth. He threw a hand over his mouth, smoke billowing out of his nose.

She extended her pinky finger, wrinkling her nose. "His pickle is about the size of my little finger, and he can't even use that much right ... and he cries after he gets his squirtsy done. It is embarrassing. I'm a good actress, but I'm no Meryl Streep."

Benny broke out in laughter. Tears filled his eyes. He grabbed her by the finger and shook it, laughing even harder when she frowned at him. "That isn't much, babe," he said. "No sirree, Bob. His getting shortchanged in the deal might explain his bizarre appetites."

She waved the smoke out of her face. Nothing on her face

showed a hint of humor. "No, it's not," she said. "And he's weird, Benny, creepy weird. He always wants me to put his hat on, hold up his friggin' badge, and then order him to lick my butthole." He stopped laughing, and she continued. "And that's far from the worst of it. His breath smells like the end of a pigmy goat on the rag, and his stupid nightstick is a whole nother kind of thing. None of it is good. I don't get that trip at all."

Benny grimaced from shock at the use of butthole and nightstick in the same breath. He did not know the details, and he never wanted to know. Some things were just better unsaid. Ignorance in this case was indeed bliss. Far too many images had already come to mind, none of which he wanted poking around in his head.

He held up a hand for her to stop talking. "Uh … y-yeah, okay then," he stammered uneasily, swallowing with difficulty. "Come on, babe, just humor the freak show a little longer. A few more encounters on video of him doing the nasty with you in the back room will give me the leverage I need to kick him to the curb." He snuffed out the cigarette in an overflowing ashtray.

Her brow knitted. "How much longer do I got to do this?"

"We almost got everything we'll need, babe."

"We better," she said. "I'm getting real sick of this stuff. The dude is getting stranger and stranger."

Benny looked over her shoulder and waved at the topic of their conversation. He faked his best smile.

Tabitha blanched. "What?"

"He's here," he whispered.

"No way," she said.

He nodded.

"Already?" she grumbled.

"Yup," he said, amused.

❦

Tabitha did her normal routine and mentally prepared herself for one of Officer Barry Markinson's inevitable hand gropes, but nothing she ever did to ready herself seemed to work. Today was no exception.

Stuck in the middle of an impossible situation, she had no choice except to play along with the sham. She would do what she always did—grin and bear the humiliation.

Barry embraced her from behind, rubbed his member against her body, and then cupped her right breast in his greedy hand. He pinched her nipple hard enough to make her wince. Then he snaked his other hand down into her crotch, roughly rubbing her sex. Her entire body tensed, and she looked like every fiber in her body wanted to erupt into one gigantic dry heave.

Benny would have sworn on a stack of Bibles that her complexion had actually turned a sickly green.

Tabitha played along to entice him even more. "Oh, baby, you know what I like," she said with an overdramatic purr of pleasure.

Barry lifted her heavy breast and bounced it up and down, while bobbing his head in rhythm to a beat only his sick mind heard. "Hey, baby," he said in his best husky voice. "How's my girl?" He leaned down and licked her long neck.

She wrinkled her nose and stuck out her tongue, as if volunteering it for a medical scrape. Her eyes flashed with pure revulsion.

Benny was all smiles, grateful that she was willing to go along with their charade a little longer. However, for a split second, possibly less, he thought she was going to lose all control and attack the rogue officer with murderous intent. Nevertheless, like a real trooper in the business, she held it together and let the vile pervert fondle her oversized boob like a kid playing with a large water balloon.

She nuzzled his stomach with the back of her head. "You sure know how to make me meow," she teased.

Benny widened his eyes to show her that he understood how she felt. *I really do need to give her a raise,* he thought, knowing deep down that he never would offer one without her coaxing him into it. *He really is a damn weirdo.*

Barry gave her breasts a final squeeze. "Now that's what I'm talking about."

Benny showed a mouthful of teeth. "How're you doing, Barry?"

Barry straightened up, ran a hand over the front of his uniform, and glared at Benny. His mouth curled up in a vicious snarl. "That's Officer Markinson," he said sharply. "I'm on duty." He tapped his chest with a finger. "Can't you see the badge?"

Benny raised a hand of innocence. "My bad, Officer Markinson," he said. "How does a round of drinks on the house sound, officer? You know, before you go out and bust some bad guys." He started to get up from the chair, but Barry lifted a hand and stopped him.

Barry took Tabitha by the hand and practically pulled her out of the chair. His face beamed. "Thanks, Benny," he said, "but I know exactly what I'm in the mood for." He gave her butt a playful swat. "Isn't that right, Busty?" He licked his lips. "And you need some true blue man meat, don't you? Big Barry is in the house now."

Tabitha craned her slender neck and fluttered her long eyelashes at him. "Oh, love stud, you are going to ruin me for all other men." She ran her tongue over her front teeth, purring softly.

Barry snapped his teeth together with a growl, gnashing them at her. "That's right, baby," he said.

She turned on her heels and headed toward the back room, where VIPs held private parties. The click-clack of her stiletto heels faded as she disappeared around the corner. Her intoxicating perfume lingered in the air like a diaphanous cloud of heaven.

After Tabitha vanished from sight, Barry walked around the table and patted Benny on the shoulder. "I gotta go and make her feel like a real woman, sport." He slapped his hands eagerly together. "You might want to turn up the music, because I'm going to make her sing like a bunch of fanatical women at a church choir."

He spun and followed her steps.

Physically repulsed by the degenerate cop, Benny watched him leave. Barry was already removing his shirt. "Pig!" he muttered with a hiss. A shadow of guilt raised its ugly head for placing his surrogate daughter in such an unsavory position. However, he knew she was a survivor, and she would always come out on top.

What Tabitha lacked in formal education, she more than made up for in street smarts. Benny had known very few people nearly as intelligent, and her ability to read men was unparalleled. She had always thought men in general were like hot shaving cream. They were big on appearance, but with very little substance inside all the fluff. All a woman had to do to own them was compliment their sexual prowess in the sack and the enormous size of their package. Gullible and insecure, the blood flowing in their one-track brain could not travel south quick enough to suit their need for instant gratification. She had told Benny on more than one occasion that cops were the easiest to manipulate. It was the same old, tired story. Their wives did not understand them and offered no moral support for the dangerous job they did. Their jobs were stressful.

"Jeez," she often commented, "who doesn't have stress these days."

He got up from the table and headed toward the bar to fetch a needed drink. *The things my girls have to do to keep those vultures off my ass,* he thought, *but not for much longer, freak show.*

His nephews grinned at him from behind the bar as he moved toward them. He watched James fill a glass with his favorite brand of Scotch and push it toward the opposite edge.

Benny offered them a friendly nod of thanks and quickly downed the drink in a single swallow. He set the glass down and tapped the rim to signal for a second shot.

James tilted the bottle and filled the glass for round two.

Benny shifted his gaze from one nephew to the other. "I hope the two of you aren't still sore at me," he said offhandedly. "I may have been a little harsh on you boys. I got a lot on my mind, and business could be better."

Jim waved a hand through the air, shrugging. "Naw, Uncle

Benny," he said earnestly. "Sometimes we need a good ass chewing, especially me. I can be a little over the top at times, like when I get a little pissed off at something or someone. I got no hard feelings." He patted his enormous chest with a hand. "I got nothing but love for you. You're our Uncle Benny, and we got no one else. For better or worse, we are all the family we got left."

Benny gave a satisfied grunt. "How about you, James?" he said. "Are we square?"

James took a healthy swig of whatever he was drinking and finished the rest off. "We're right as rain, Uncle Benny," he said. "Family can never have a beef so bad that it can't be fixed with a few shots and a nice score for some money."

"That's good to hear," he said.

Jim pursed his lips. "Tabitha doing that piece of crap in the back?" he said. "That girl must have the willpower of I don't know what to lay down with that cop."

Benny nodded.

"I don't know why you just don't let us drag that guy out in the desert and off his ass," Jim said. "I mean, she may not be family, but still—"

"She's as loyal as the day is long," Benny finished for him.

James nodded. "She is that," he admitted. "But still, wouldn't it be better for you if me and Jim just dumped that cop in a ditch somewhere out in the desert? We could find a mineshaft, toss him down it, and then throw a stick of dynamite to cover him up." He and Jim snickered. "The only people that would ever find him are archaeologists a few hundred years from now."

Jim and James gave each other a high five.

Benny rubbed at his temple. "It's just not that easy, knuckleheads," he said. "A missing cop like that draws attention, and I don't need anything like that." He held up a hand. "I'm working on cutting him loose."

They exchanged quick looks. "Okay," they said in unison. "It's your call."

Benny tapped on the edge of his glass for another refill. "I got a deal set up with this guy by the name of Tinker for some dope and guns," he said. "Are you two interested? I'd feel better if the two of you were with me."

"We know Tinker," Jim said, filling the glass. "He's sort of a buster kind of dude, real sneaky and slimy. Are you sure you want to deal with that dude?"

Benny raised the glass to his lips, paused. "It sounds like a pretty sweet deal," he said. "He's got some silencers that I could resell for triple the amount."

James reached for a bowl of corn nuts. "What're you going to cut us in for?" he said. "We get something for the trouble, right?"

Benny grinned. "Don't you always?" he said. "Don't worry, I'll treat the two of you right."

They nodded at each other. "We're in."

Benny took a healthy gulp. "Good," he said. "Now, go away. I'll call when I'm ready to take off."

They left the club.

Trent opened the closet's folding doors and removed a hard leather gun case that sat atop the second shelf. The natural surface of the case felt masculine and inviting in his hands as he walked over to the desk five feet away. As if cradling a tiny infant child in his arms, he gently laid the four-foot case on the hard mahogany. Next to it sat a blue and gray gym bag that contained a change of clothes more fitting for the area he planned on venturing into in a few short hours—along with an eclectic assortment of material necessary to accomplish his next goal.

The news that his personal private investigator and loyal bodyguard had already loaded the other required materials into the back of his newly purchased jeep several hours earlier helped put his mind at ease. Trent had only to make a few last-minute arrangements to make certain he had taken care of everything related to housekeeping. Loose ends had never been part of his vocabulary, inadvertent or otherwise. Wisdom of a different animal thrust upon him, he had long learned how to remain patient when everything around him screamed for action. This art of discipline had instilled in him the uncanny ability to command total control over his emotions, and Trent neither hurried nor acted rashly for any reason. Proficient plans created desired results. In all of his vast experiences, Trent had come to obey effectiveness and efficiency, as revered kings, at all cost. Nothing positive had ever come from a sloppily executed endeavor, and there was all the time in the world to follow through with what he'd come to consider as a foregone conclusion. No one and nothing had mastery over him, simply because he refused to allow it. He now dictated the future with an iron fist, and no force on earth could stop him from keeping the promise he had made to his wife. He always kept his promises, no matter what.

The arduous years he'd spent in a concrete cage had taught him many valuable lessons. The first at the top of the list was not to invest personal feelings into anyone's psychological drama. More people translated into more drama. More drama automatically led to serious consequences, most of which could get a person killed with a sharp piece of steel. Trent needed no brushup courses to keep his personal feelings suppressed. Key to overcoming the insurmountable odds of all life's drama was to learn and maintain emotional detachment. Some wounds just cut too deep, far too penetrating for any amount of elapsed time to cure. Time had defeated him. The once kind and tender man from happier days had died in a prison cell a very long time ago, which left only a new creation born with a heart of stone. All Trent had left in his empty life was his revenge. All things, he knew and accepted, good or bad, had to come to an eventual end.

His next target, on whom he planned to exact long overdue justice, probably still believed that he had gotten away with his betrayal and had nothing to worry about, least of all a homicidal blast from the past visiting the present.

Trent smirked at the thought of seeing the horrified look on his brother-in-law's face when they met eye to eye for the first time in decades. He imagined the power he would have over Sam when he looked deeply into his eyes and saw it register in Sam's mind that the sands of time had finally run out, that the grim reaper had reached out from the shadows to snatch the residuals of what remained of his pathetic life. Trent could hardly contain his enthusiasm about showing up unannounced at the front door of Sam's run-down trailer anchored in a desert not located on any map, after refusing for so many years to search for the last member of his extended family. The priceless error the government had made in sending Jerry Smith's—a.k.a. Sam

Herd in a former life—1099 tax statement to his wife Connie's last known address had served as a stroke of luck.

Trent looked up at the atomic clock mounted on the wall of his private office located on the fifteenth floor of the Barnabus Building, in downtown Century City, while unsnapping the dual locks on either side of the gun case. His heart felt dead and cold in his chest, having abandoned any memory of warmth and love, which left only scars of mental and physical torture caused by those under the color of authority.

Often, while lying in the dark atop a urine-stained mattress, he had wondered how much pain and loneliness a man could endure before insanity finally pushed away the purity of a soul from the body. What constituted the measure of a man's true essence when cast into the darkness with no hope of light ever returning? Could the man survive without the mind's subterranean monster rising from that evil spot tainted by original sin? If not, then what became of a good man turned into something terrible, hideously grotesque and murderous? Was it too late for saving? Trent closed his eyes against the horrific memories that still haunted his every thought, hopelessly condemned to wander through life and never find strength enough to banish them.

Trent shook his head and chased away the webs of despair still clinging to his mind, grinding his teeth together. *Shiver in fear and pray in supplication for forgiveness, my old friend, for I shall release you from all pain and sin.* He slowly opened the case and grinned at the instrument of delayed destruction.

Safely hidden inside the tailored gun case, a high-power tranquilizer dart rifle lay tucked against a perfectly sculpted mold covered in black velvet. A large scope for the rifle rested perpendicular to the butt, and a dozen tranquilizer darts sealed in clear plastic tubes lay on the other side of the case, aligned in similar fashion in front of the barrel. The weapon's nickel plating shined with polished brilliance.

He ran a long, manicured finger along the weapon's fine oak stock. "I've waited a long time to finally put you to good use, girl," he whispered to the gun. "You are going to help me set a lot of things right. At least as right as they can be set."

Trent plucked the individual tubes containing the darts and checked them for potential defects.

Satisfied that everything was in perfect working condition, he closed the gun case with a snap and fastened the locks with simultaneous clicks. He ran a hand over his head and smoothed out his jet-black hair. "Now, I just—" His cell phone rang and interrupted his train of thought.

He checked the caller ID and answered the phone. "Varus here," he announced. "What can I do for you, Lenny?" While waiting for an answer, he continued to survey the room to make sure he had not inadvertently overlooked anything crucial to the mission.

"Hey, boss." Lenny's voice was a deep baritone and all business.

Trent rechecked the time. "Everything all right?" he said. "You're calling me a little premature, aren't you?"

The slight growl coming from Lenny over the phone conjured up the same embarrassed look that showed up on his face whenever he was being lectured. "I'm just checking in," he said. "I've finished that follow-up on our mutual friend from the desert."

Trent nodded out of habit. "Excellent work," he commented. "What did you learn? Is there anything new? Am I still on schedule?"

"There are no changes, boss," he said in a firm voice. "Everything is the same, unchanged. I did verify that he is still working at that crappy gas station and gets off from work every evening around five, late afternoon, give or take an hour, depending on how busy that dump might get. The owner also runs a half-assed towing service from that armpit. Some old derelict-looking dude by the name of Gus Stevens owns the festering eyesore."

An exchange of heated words erupted from the front end of the law office, on the other side of his locked office door, and distracted Trent from the conversation. *Now what?* He grumbled deep in his belly. *I don't need more damn drama today. Everyone has a bug up his or her butt this week.* He cocked an eyebrow and looked at the door, frowning. He hoped that Janet would be able to handle the problem without a glitch.

"Are you still there?" Lenny's voice snapped him back to the present. "Everything went dead."

Trent pressed the phone against his ear. "Anything else I might need to know, Lenny?" he said, still somewhat distracted. "I don't like surprises. Is our backstabbing friend still holed up in that metal coffin of a trailer?"

"Yeah, that vermin is still there, stinking up the place," he said. "A piece of junk generator on its last leg runs the power in the mobile hovel. The interior looks like a damn hamster cage, and it smells like rotten cabbage. The guy is a total pig."

Trent offered a slight chuckle of appreciation at the vivid description of the man and his nasty habits. *Some things never change,* he mused. His brother-in-law living in squalor brightened his overall outlook now. "Does he have a girlfriend or someone else in his life that means anything to him? You know," he paused to think, and then finished, "anyone that might miss him and later report him to the authorities as missing."

Silence filled the air between the phones. "Not really, Trent." Lenny's gravelly voice finally cut through the quiet.

"What does that mean?"

"Our bum has an on-again, off-again, canker sore girlfriend by the name of Angela Hanley," he said with a mild grumble. "She's some kind of middle-age lot lizard that takes off her clothes for peanuts at a local titty bar a few miles down the dirt road from the gas station. Apparently, according to her, at least yesterday, she is pissed off at him for ditching her to play poker with a bunch of losers she not so delicately labeled as potential pedophiles. There seems to be no love lost between them. She's already screwing some other pustule that works at the bar."

"Are you sure about your information?" he said. "Did you believe her?"

Lenny made his patented groan of feigned insult. "Come on, Trent," he said. "This isn't my first rodeo, and you know me better than that. Five hundred bucks works miracles on some drunk and stoned slut. He stole her rent money the last time they were knocking boots behind his trailer."

Trent knitted his brow. "Did you say behind the trailer?"

"That's right," he said.

"In the dirt?" he said.

"I guess," he said. "I kind of stopped my questioning right then and there because she started to touch and hit on me and ..." His voice trailed off with a groan of disgust.

Trent let the words drift off and focused on the related topic. "And what did you learn about the other person in question?" he said. "Do you have a status report on him?"

"Everything appears unchanged, but I'm going to verify everything and everyone involved one more time just to be sure. Nothing exceeds like excess. Isn't that right?"

"Do you think anyone suspects anything?"

"No way in hell," he said, his words spoken with conviction. "I know everything and everyone is in the dark."

"Excellent job," he said sincerely. "I want some pictures for the usual reasons."

Lenny grunted into the phone.

Trent sighed. "I hope that's not going to be a problem."

"No, Trent," he said. "It's not a problem, not exactly. Do you want me to hire an outsider to spy and click the flicks, or would you prefer that I personally take care of it?"

"I'd prefer to keep everything in-house for now," he said. "We can always subcontract later. Besides, you enjoy snapping pictures without people's knowledge. Whatever happened to that sense of power, your self-indulgent mantra that you see them but they cannot see you?" He gave a hearty chuckle.

"Whatever you want," he said. "But I'm sure Snapshot wouldn't mind the work."

"Maybe later," he said. "Perhaps you should touch base with him and see if he's still in town."

"I'll do that."

The verbal disturbance coming from the other side of the door grew louder, more intense. His legal secretary Janet Simpson was now arguing with a man whose voice he did not recognize as one of his regular clients. Nothing about the conversation sounded friendly. The stranger was now hurling rude and belligerent insults at her.

Trent got up from the chair. "Hold your next thought for a minute, Lenny," he said with an irritated grumble. "I got a slight situation here." After he set the cell phone on the desk, Trent returned the gun case and gym bag to the closet and sealed the doors shut. Annoyed with the unwanted raucous outside his office door, he turned an ear toward the door and listened more intently to the heated exchange of words.

"Sir, if you would please just step away from my desk, I'm quite sure I can help you with whatever you need," said Janet. The dull thud of struck wood followed her words.

"Look, lady," said the stranger's voice. "I need to talk to my law-yer." He drew out the word slowly.

"I understand, sir. As I said before, I am happy to make you an appointment?"

"Screw that, bitch!" snapped the stranger. "Do your damn job and tell him to get out here right now, before I start making a whole helluva lot of trouble for the two of you."

The sound of papers hitting the ground followed the threat.

Janet squeaked in fear. "What's your name, please?"

"Blink!"

"Excuse me."

"My name is John Robinson, but everyone calls me Blink."

"I see."

"You don't see shit, bitch!"

The intercom connection on Trent's desk sprang to life, followed by his legal secretary's strained voice over the small speaker.

"Excuse me, Mr. Varus," said Janet, "but I have a gentleman out here demanding to speak with you."

Trent opened his office door and moved into the doorway. He crossed his arms over his muscular chest. "What in the hell is going on out here?" he said sharply, moving on silent feet into the reception area, darting his eyes about the room like a snake in search of food. "I was on an important call with an employee doing research for this firm, for crying out loud." He narrowed his eyes at the paper-littered floor, and then he shifted his attention to the stranger dressed like some sort of homeless reject. "Janet, would you please be so kind as to tell me who this … this, um, person is."

Janet quickly regained her composure at the sight of her employer. She cleared her throat, her eyes now glassy and frightened. "Of course, Mr. Varus," she said demurely as she ran a nervous hand down the front of her simple print dress to smooth out invisible wrinkles. "Hey says—"

"Hey!" Blink made several indecipherable gestures with his hands. "I don't need a dumb bitch to talk for me." He turned and faced Trent. "I'm Blink, and I need a good lawyer, not one of them dump trucks at the public pretender's office."

Janet gasped aloud.

Trent stared at the man, feeling only revulsion. "Blink, huh?" he said. "What's your real name?"

Blink snarled and took two aggressive steps toward him, balling his hands into fists. "What's that got to do with anything?" He swayed drunkenly on his feet, eyes bugging. "I need a lawyer, and Benny Bones says you're the top dude in the business, that you know what it's like and don't take no shit off some punk-ass DA."

Trent forced a deep, calming breath, remembering the man from his past with mixed emotions. "Ah, I see, Benny Bones," he repeated in a faraway voice. "I haven't heard that name for a time. But that does explain a lot."

"What's that mean?"

Ignoring Blink for the moment, Trent walked over to where Janet stood visibly shaking and laid a tender hand against her elderly face. Her eyes were watery, her body still dangerously tense from the ordeal. He pressed his lips together, thinking how much she reminded him of his mother.

"Are you all right, Janet?" he said.

She forced a weak smile and nodded. Tears fell from her eyes and caressed her cheeks.

He reached up and wiped the tears away with his thumb. "My dearest Janet," he whispered softly, his heart pained by such unnecessary abuse. "Why don't you take off the rest of the day and go home." He then added, smiling, "With pay of course."

"Hey, I need to talk to you today, homey," Blink interjected. "I got big trouble, and you can take care of Grandma Moses later."

Trent shot an angry look at Blink and shut him up. He reached into his pocket and pulled out of small wad of fifty-dollar bills. He peeled off several and stuffed them into her hand. "I got a better idea. Take a day at the spa, dear, and just relax," he said affectionately. "It's okay. It's on me, my treat. You don't need this kind of nonsense in your life today."

She bit down on her lower lip, no doubt on the verge of shedding a storm of tears. "Are you sure?" she stammered. "I can stay and finish the interrogatories for you."

Trent pulled out the desk drawer and grabbed her purse. "I'm sure, dear," he said, pushing it at her. "I can finish them, and we'll just go over them tomorrow. How does that sound?"

She clutched the purse against her bosom. "Thank you, Mr. Varus. You are such a nice man. If my Harold was still alive, he would have loved to have a son just like you."

"Thank you, Janet," he said. "I appreciate that."

Janet hurried out of the office, closing the door on her way out.

After Janet left the office, Trent turned and looked at the lowlife called Blink. He motioned with the sweep of his hand, wondering how people ever sank so far down in the gutter. He had spent decades surrounded by the same sort of filth, and subsequent freedom had done nothing to lessen his distaste for ex-cons. "Well, come on in, Mr. Blink," he said, moving into his office. "You were in such a hurry to see me, so let's get on with it. I see no point putting it off any longer." He looked over his shoulder. "Let's get what you need."

Blink nodded in apparent victory and shoved his hands into both pockets. "You got that straight," he said. "It's about time I got some friggin' respect 'round here." He followed Trent through the door.

At the soft click of the office door, Trent spun on his heels and sent a wicked blow to the irritant's unprotected stomach, which dropped him to his knees spitting and sputtering in pain. Blink wheezed like a stuck pig drowning in mud and collapsed face-first on the floor. His body curled up in a fetal position, and he groaned deeply. Trent inched a little closer to the fallen man, moving his Italian loafer only inches away from the back of his head. He glared down, utterly repulsed by the human excrement drooling on his freshly shampooed carpet.

How dare you come into my house and treat my staff with such rudeness, you festering little cockroach! Hatred riddled his thoughts. *Prison forced me to tolerate garbage like you for years, and now I do not have to put up with it at all.*

Blink opened his mouth as if to say something, but Trent viciously kicked him in the kidney. A small shriek of pain fell from the uninvited client's lips, and the blow stopped him from uttering a single word. Trent was in no mood to listen to just another lie from a piece of former prison trash.

"Puhlease," Blink mumbled with a moan.

Trent used his foot and rolled him over onto his back. "Shut up!" he said. "I don't know who the hell you think you are, you little butt plug." He placed a tasseled shoe on the man's chest. "But in what world do you think I'd ever allow you to speak to such a sweet woman with such disrespect? She is worth more than ten thousand of you, and you are still alive only because I permit it."

Blink peered up with terrified eyes, grimacing. "I didn't mean—"

A second kick shut his mouth.

Trent hissed. "Shut up, dirtbag," he said with a sneer. "I don't want to hear it. Do we understand each other?" He leaned over, feverish hatred burning in his eyes. His heart pounded in his chest. "You have no idea with whom you are dealing. I do not like cons or ex-cons. In my book, they're all cut from the same cloth, a shit-stained one that has no use whatsoever."

Blink nodded. "Yeah, dude, it's cool." His eyes widened with realization that his attacker was not kidding, that he was deadly serious. "I read ya, Mr. Varus. No sweat."

Trent smiled without a hint of humor. "That's good," he said, jerking his chin at the exit. "Now, get the hell out of here and don't ever come back. Next time, I will not be so charitable." He shook a fist at the retreating scumbag. "And don't you even think about telling anybody, especially the authorities, what happened here today. I would hate to tell Benny that you're causing me issues. Somehow, I doubt he would react well to that bit of news. He needs me, while I do not need him. Get the picture?"

Blink's face blanched at the threat. Everyone on the street knew Benny was crazy, homicidally so. Rumors about his past still caused caution about crossing him, and his nephews were far worse. "I won't say a word to no one." He struggled to get off the floor. "I'm sorry for what I've done, sir."

Trent pointed a finger. "Get out!"

Blink left without looking back.

After Blink closed the main door to his office, Trent told Lenny that he'd call him back later, left his office, and walked into the reception area to begin the chore of gathering the paperwork still scattered across the floor. He stopped beside Janet's desk, surprised to find a lone woman seated on the couch with her head bowed. Since he did not recognize her and he was fairly certain Janet had not scheduled an appointment with a new client, the thought to ask her to leave did cross his mind, but then he realized that he did not have the stomach to act so apathetically.

Something about the way she sat bothered him deeply.

Finally, Trent cleared his throat. "Excuse me, miss," he said softly. "May I help you?"

The woman looked up at the sound of his voice. She was

a natural beauty, stunning in fact, with deep blue eyes; high, aristocratic cheekbones; and long, flowing hair the color of midnight. Her features might have appeared flawless, if not for the large black-and-blue bruises she had unsuccessfully tried to cover up with thick layers of makeup. She shook her head, pursing her lips like a scared schoolgirl. She lowered her head. She reminded him of a little bird with a broken wing.

Deciding to give her a silent moment in peace, Trent kneeled and collected the papers. He quickly perused them to make sure he had placed everything in proper order, occasionally stealing a curious glance at the unmoving woman, and then he set the collated stack back on the desk. He stood up, contemplating what to say or do. "I'll be in my office most of the day, miss," he said softly. "Please, feel free to stay as long as you want." He made a sympathetic smile, wishing he could do something else for her. She looked so helpless, so lost in pain. "There's coffee on the table, and I think a couple of doughnuts with sprinkles are stashed in my secretary's minifridge, if you're hungry. Help yourself to whatever might look good." He turned and started to walk back into his office. A faint whisper from behind caught his attention. He craned his neck and looked into a pair of the saddest eyes he had ever seen. "I'm sorry. I didn't hear you."

She sniffed back tears, miserable. "My husband hits me," she stammered. Tears now streamed down her cheeks. Her hands were trembling. "He hurts me a lot, real bad sometimes." She dropped her face into her hands and wept.

He remained still and patient, allowing her to take the initiative to speak again. It took a lot of courage for any woman to admit such a thing to anyone, especially another man, a stranger the same sex as the victimizer. Her face served as proof that she was a battered woman. He had seen if often enough in recent times, along with hearing the ridiculous excuses made by men that beat the women they claimed to love.

She continued to weep, her shoulders shaking.

Trent took several steps toward her and went to a single knee, making sure to keep a respectable distance and not touch her. "I don't understand, miss," he said. "Would you like me to call the police?"

She shook her head.

He moved to stand back up, but she suddenly lashed out a hand and grabbed him by the wrist. She squeezed tightly. "Don't go," she pleaded. "Please."

He settled back down and placed his hand over hers to offer reassurance. "I won't." He wondered how many times a man had to hit a woman to cause the level of mental anguish seated in front of him. A surge of anger pulsed through him.

Lousy wife-beating coward!

She lifted her face with a wince. "He hits me all the time and calls me cruel names." Her eyes fluttered several times. "I need to get away from him before he kills me."

"So, it's a divorce you want," he said. "Correct?"

She nodded.

Trent took a deep breath. He had to keep her talking. "Okay," he said. "Have you filed any complaints with the police? You know, like a restraining order."

Her eyes went wide, horrified.

He squeezed her hand to try to reassure her that she was safe. "May I ask why not?"

She just stared at him.

He offered her a friendly grin to coax the reason out of her. "Everything is okay, miss. We're the only ones here. No one will hurt you while you are here, with me."

She pressed her lips together. "He's a cop." The words spilled from her mouth like liquid poison.

Trent nodded his understanding. "I see." Her behavior now made more sense to him. Cops protect other cops. "You do realize that my practice revolves around criminal defense, maybe a little civil work, and that I don't practice family law." For reasons he could not quite grasp, he felt ashamed the second he finished the sentence.

Her shoulders dipped. "I don't know what any of that means," she mumbled, wiping tears away with the back of her hand. "You are a lawyer, aren't you?"

"Well, um, yeah," he said. The words rolled clumsily over his tongue. "But family law, divorce, and child custody stuff is not really my field of expertise. I would be remiss if I didn't tell you that. But I do know a couple of excellent divorce attorneys who are well acquainted—"

"No!" she interrupted in an abrupt and demonstrative inner strength. "I want you to be my lawyer." She reached down and grabbed her purse that rested next to her leg. She dug through it with purpose. "I can pay. I have some money."

Trent rose to his feet. His thoughts went in a thousand different directions. He wanted to help her, but he could not get around the fact that he lacked the requisite knowledge in that particular field of law. He ran an open palm over the top of his head, apprehensive and uncomfortable with the situation. "Miss, really," he said. "It's not about the money." He wondered if the words sounded as pathetic as he felt. "I just think there are other attorneys better suited for you in this kind case. I've never practiced a divorce proceeding." He raised his hands into the air. "I don't have a clue."

She beamed at him for the first time, standing up from the couch and holding out her pixie-like hand. "That's good," she said spiritedly, "because I've never been divorced. So, we're both a couple of first timers." Her attitude melted his heart. She was doing everything to put up a fortified front. "Do we have a deal?"

Disarmed by her infectious charm, Trent groaned aloud and rolled his eyes. He knew he should have provided a reference for a qualified attorney and pushed her in that direction. Ethically, a referral was the right thing to do. He was not a divorce attorney. Then she smiled with trusting eyes and wriggled tiny fingers aching to seal the deal. Everything she did projected faith that he could help her, save her from a life of misery.

Trent let out a conquered breath. *I'm such a sucker for a pretty face,* he thought, embarrassed that a hundred and twenty pound woman had just taken him down. *But how can I not even try?*

"Well," she prodded unrelentingly, her eyes sparkling in perceived victory. "Do we have a deal?"

Trent accepted her hand. "I guess we have a deal."

"Great!"

With an exaggerated sweep of his hand, coupled with a chivalrous bow, Trent motioned for her to join him in the privacy of his office. "If you will please follow me," he said, "together we can draw up the contract and discuss your new future, Mrs., um—" He knitted his brow.

She stepped across the threshold. "Markinson," she finished for him. "Lisa Markinson."

Trent closed the door behind her. "Okay, Lisa Markinson," he said. "Let's make some plans to shake that rat from your neck, so you can finally breathe easy."

Lisa giggled.

CHAPTER 4

Detective Erik Lomax flopped down onto his tattered recliner and started to dive into his favorite lunch—a bucket of chicken and a supersized soda—when the phone resting on a nearby stand unexpectedly sprang to life. He craned his neck and glared hatefully at the noisy contraption that had ruined countless meals over the years. It was his day off, his first in several weeks, and he wondered if he should just let it ring until the caller finally gave up trying to reach him. Since everyone at the precinct, in particular Captain Mike Johnson, knew that he'd had no personal life whatsoever since his last wife had died years earlier, dispatch kept his home number on speed dial for all emergencies.

Detective Lomax had served in the police department for the past twenty-five years, his last thirteen spent in the homicide division. A constant professional, divorced three times, his entire life revolved around the only thing he had left in life—his career. He had seen everything the underbelly of life had to offer—from brutal pimps beating prostitutes with coat hangers to domestic squabbles that ended with entire families butchered beyond recognition—and nothing had surprised him in a very long time, especially the irrational reasons behind such egregious acts of unmitigated cruelty.

He had come to believe that, with very few exceptions, people were born inherently self-destructive and selfish, looking out for only number one. Despite his misanthropic views of men and women in general, he harbored no particular malice for criminals, at least not in the orthodox sense of the word. He thought there were only two kinds of criminals. The first type of criminal was a person who just made a mistake, sometimes a horrible one, while the second type was a person who chose crime as a lifestyle. Everyone made mistakes. He had made plenty over the course of his many years on the planet. It was the repetition he found inexcusable. Lomax even tolerated some lawyers, though he often voiced to anyone within earshot that most were bottom-feeders in a society of laws and belonged in a category right next to the lowest form of pedophile. However, a dirty cop, he considered without question, sank several fathoms below the collective bottom of the bunch.

If asked his position on the country as a whole, Lomax would say that America was on its way to darkening the back pages of a history book, much in the same way as the once great Roman Empire had. Decadence and debauchery had indeed prevailed over good sense. Chaos and anarchy would soon follow. Such was inevitable; such was the proverbial circle of corrupt government.

Lomax tore off a large piece of meat from a leg with an animalistic snarl. *Go away, and leave me to my dead bird.* He chewed slowly, savoring the greasy flavor that sparked his taste buds to life.

The phone continued to ring.

Lomax shook his chicken leg at the phone. A hint of guilt for ignoring the caller tugged at him. *Come on. It's my day off.* His conscience started to win the battle. *I got chicken.* He looked into the bucket filled with more pieces of dead fowl resting on his lap, burped into his other hand.

The caller persisted.

Lomax finally dropped the half-eaten chunk of dead bird into the bucket. "Damn it to hell!" he cursed, reaching for the phone. "What?"

"Lomax?" It was Captain Johnson on the phone, his voice grim.

"Yeah, Captain," he said. "This is Lomax."

There was a pause over the phone, and only the faint sound of heavy breathing let Lomax know that it was still an open line.

"We got a problem, Detective." Captain Johnson's voice sounded strained, worried.

Lomax shifted in the chair uneasily. He hated politics, and the man he had known for years tripped over words only when departmental politics were involved. Nothing good had ever come from getting between rival powers. "A big or small one?" he said, preferring to tread lightly until he learned more details. "I'll settle for the bullet points right now."

"It is potentially huge."

"I don't like the sound of that."

"You won't like most of it."

"You know how I feel about the spotlight, Captain."

"If you do this one for me, I will owe you big-time."

Lomax bit down on his tongue, thinking. He rubbed at his eyes. "Then let's hear it."

He listened intently as Captain Johnson briefly explained the situation and subsequently ordered him to report immediately to a specific address, keeping everything in the process official. He assured Lomax that he would be glad to provide the grisly details after his arrival, ordering him to speak to no one except him. The hairs on the back of Lomax's neck bristled. The two of them had known each other over the course of their careers, and Lomax could not recall a single scenario when Johnson had allowed his personal involvement in any case. However, to his trained ears, trouble now filled the surrounding air. Something serious had definitely rattled his longtime friend.

"I'll be there within the hour, sir," he said, following the end of the condensed story.

Johnson gave a grunt, and the line went dead.

Lomax tore the remaining meat from the bone, stood up, dropped the stripped bone in the bucket, and then headed for his car. He tightened his hold on the bucket, holding what remained of his meal.

Twenty minutes later, Lomax turned left on Citrus Drive and groaned aloud at the circus down the street, which was going to make finding a parking spot for his clanking jalopy next to impossible.

Pandemonium filled the area for a hundred yards in either direction.

Uniformed officers scurried about the street, barking orders at one another and pointing fingers at several groups of gawking spectators trying to get a bird's-eye view of what was happening in their otherwise quiet neighborhood. Two ambulances parked in the middle of the street still had lights flashing atop the roofs. Paramedics and other medical staff stood off to the side of their vehicles, apparently interested only in talking to one another with animated zeal. A few news trucks from the local networks lined the street, haphazardly parked alongside the curbs. There was no sign of any television personnel nearby.

Now wishing he had simply ignored the phone and finished his meal in peace, Lomax honked his horn at the people standing in his path. *Get out of the way you lousy, good-for-nothing parasites!* He grumbled under his breath when no one moved out of his way. *What in the hell is wrong with all of you!* His blood pressure skipped upward a notch. *Screw it!* He ran the car up the nearest curb, barely fitting between two squad cars, and parked. With a heavy grunt of exasperation, he climbed out and walked the rest of the way toward a long walkway that led to the residence located in the center of the storm.

A young man dressed in civilian clothes met Lomax at the front door. He held up a yielding hand, stealthily moving a little to the left to block the entrance of the house. His eyes swept over Lomax with a distinct air of superiority. A hiss of disapproval fell from his thin lips.

Lomax pulled up short. His thoughts focused more on the man dressed in plain clothes, who he was and why he was there at all. He had been led to believe that he was the only detective who'd been summoned to be on scene, so there could be no plausible reason for such a joker standing like a gargoyle at his crime scene. Homicide was not in the habit of hiring pimple-faced punks to run high-profile investigations, and the man standing in front of him was far too young for such an honor. Lomax smelled a rat, a big, fat one.

The young man raised a critical eyebrow. "Detective Lomax, I presume," he said snidely.

Lomax tried to steal a look over the man's shoulder to see what was going on behind the scene, but the man rose up on his toes and blocked his view. "Yeah, I'm Lomax," he said gruffly, leveling cool eyes on the amateurish gatekeeper. "Captain Johnson called me about a half hour ago. Said there was some trouble of some sort, that he wanted me here." He shrugged. "Something like that, anyway. Who're you?"

The young man removed his wallet and proudly flashed his credentials. "I'm Officer Biggs, Internal Affairs." His features turned hard, eyes intense.

Lomax furrowed his brow, surprised that IA had gotten involved so quickly. "Internal Affairs," he repeated, saying the words intentionally slowly, mocking the man and his department. "What's going on in there?"

Biggs slipped his wallet back into his pocket. "Well, detective ..." His words trailed off, and an air of uncertainty as to how best to finish the sentence seemed to envelope him.

Lomax pushed past Biggs. "Get out of my way, kid," he said, without apology. "I have more important things to do than play stupid games with you."

As soon as Lomax cleared the doorway, Captain Johnson disengaged himself from a small group of officers and walked toward him. He was waving for him to come over. The expression on his face was tight and uncommonly nervous. Dark bags sagged beneath his eyes.

Lomax held out his hand. *This can't be good.*

Johnson slid his hand into Lomax's and shook. "Glad you got down here so fast, Erik." His voice now sounded more tired than he looked. His grip felt weak and damp as he pulled his hand free. "I really need you on this one, pal."

Lomax did a quick visual of the area. "What's with the zoo, Captain?" he said. People everywhere were aimlessly traipsing all over the carpeted floor with no apparent purpose. "Why is the dill hole from IA here? They usually come after cleanup."

Johnson placed a conspiratorial hand on his shoulder and leaned forward. He seemed afraid that someone in the room might overhear him. "We got ourselves a dead district attorney, Erik," he whispered only inches from Lomax's ear. "It looks like a suicide, but I just got this weird feeling about the whole thing. His wife is in the next room."

Lomax jerked away as if stung. He eyed his friend. His survival instincts kicked into overdrive. Now he was certain something was amiss. "Captain, if it's suicide, then why did you call me?" he said. His stomach growled, and the abandoned bucket of chicken still in the front seat of his car entered his mind. "I'm homicide, not suicide." He jerked his chin at Biggs. "And why is the rat squad interested in a DA's suicide? Those vultures primarily hunt cops."

Johnson threw his hands up. "Keep your damn voice down," he warned. "I called you in because something is just askew here. I spoke to the wife, and her story just doesn't make any sense. Biggs is here because IA was investigating our dead attorney for trafficking drugs—heroin and morphine." His face blanched. "It looks like he died of an overdose. The damn rig is still stuck in his arm. The son of a bitch has track marks."

Lomax ran a calloused hand over his pate. So far, he did not like anything he had heard. "Lord have mercy," he muttered. "How long do you think it will be before someone rips the cat out of the bag? This has stench written all over it, and if IA gets a whiff ..." He whistled and let the words hang in the air.

"Tell me about it."

Now, more worried than ever about getting tricked and used as someone's patsy inside a case of warring politics, which was never a good place for an unpopular detective, Lomax took a step back. He had never liked the limelight, certainly not one so bright and hot. "With all due respect, Captain, I'm not vice or narcotics," he said lamely, wanting nothing more than to distance himself from a tabloid disaster. "I still don't see how this involves me. It's out of my jurisdiction." He knitted his brow. "Do you suspect his wife? Do you think she killed him or something in that vein?" He paused to look for any avenue in which to extricate from the situation. "Now, it's you not making much sense."

"I'm not sure what I suspect, all right," the captain said in a dubious tone. "I just want you to check it out, poke around here and there. Talk to the wife, see what she knows, or might know and doesn't know it. Treat it like a hobby case from a dead file."

Lomax straightened up. His curiosity sparked with an incongruent mixture of dread and excitement. "You think this guy is dirty, don't you?" He smirked, taking out a pen and paper from his back pocket.

Johnson's face changed into one of queasiness, eyes widening in horror. "Let's just say that I have some real doubts about this guy's character," he said with a croak. "My spidey senses are tingling."

"Fair enough," he said, placing the pen to paper. "What's the vic's name?"

"His name's Callahan."

Lomax's hand froze. "Walter Callahan?" he said, stunned by the revelation. He put the pen and paper back into his pocket. "The victim isn't a deputy. It's the actual DA, in the flesh?"

Johnson nodded. "Yeah, that's what I said," he said. A befuddled look marked his face. "Walter Callahan is his name. Why?"

Lomax crossed his arms over his chest. His face turned hard. "If Callahan was under IA investigation, I would say that there is a damn solid basis for it."

"I was afraid of that, damn it." Johnson scratched his head. "Look, Erik, I want you to dig into it and see what you can find. I want to try to save the department from scandal." He looked around at the expensive furnishings.

The house and everything in it exceeded a district attorney's salary by a large margin.

Lomax heard warning bells go off in his head, and he suddenly grew wary of the direction his captain seemed interested in taking the conversation. Johnson had said more to him in the last five minutes than he had in the previous six months.

Johnson brought his eyes back on him. "If we—"

Lomax raised a hand to stop him from finishing. He was the last man on earth willing to take a leap of faith for another person. His career had remained relatively spotless for only one reason. He did not trust one damn thing, especially people trying to rub elbows with him. "Now, wait just a minute, Captain," he said calmly. "I hope you're not suggesting that I sabotage or curtail an IA investigation. If so, then I am not the one."

The blood drained from Johnson's face. He shook his head at the numerous implications involved. "God, no, Erik," he said. "Internal Affairs has some sort of agenda to hang Callahan's reputation. I do not know why. A bunch of damn cowboys run the narco department. You have no loyalties or love for any of them. You are about the only independent I know in the entire precinct, and I would just like to have a heads-up if Callahan turns up dirty as mud. Nothing more, I swear. I don't want you fudging anything." He held out his hand as a peace offering. "Are we clear?"

Lomax studied the man's face for several silent minutes before daring to say a word. Johnson was a captain, his captain in fact, but Lomax knew that the man patiently waiting for an answer with his hand outstretched was also a seasoned politician inside the department. No one rose to the level of captain without skills to finesse the upper brass and status-climbing mayor. Everyone above his pay grade who worked in government made deals daily. Such was the nature of the beast, which served as his main reason for never throwing his hat into the ring. He did not like entanglements, definitely not as a spy. Politics ultimately interfered with competent police work.

As will a scandal inside a dirty DA's office.

"Come on, Erik. Help me out on this. I need you, buddy."

Stuck in the middle of an impossible dilemma, Lomax somehow knew that he was going to live just long enough to regret forging an unofficial relationship and going out on a limb for something that mattered very little to him. Against everything screaming for him to turn around and run away, he accepted Johnson's hand. "I'll look into it, sir," he said, already feeling like the world's biggest sucker.

"Thank you, Erik," Johnson said with a sigh.

He slipped his hand free. "Don't thank me yet, sir," he said. "Where did you say the wife was?"

Johnson pointed to a door at the opposite end of the room. "She's in there, past the doors that lead into their private library." Johnson then turned and walked toward Biggs, who was still standing in the doorway and staring daggers at him.

He made a grunt of irritation and went to speak with the widow, figuring the sooner he started, the sooner he would be out of the fray.

Lomax found Julie Callahan seated on a brown leather sofa—her eyes bloodshot and watery, her face puffy, making it visibly obvious to anyone within thirty feet that she had been crying. An attractive woman in her late forties, her auburn hair pulled back in an extreme bun, sat beside the grieving widow. Her arm draped protectively over the disheveled woman's shoulder, she watched an elderly man with silver hair seated in a chair against the adjoining wall of the library. His features were drawn tight, expressionless, and his eyes stared blankly at nothing of consequence. A dozen others stood scattered across a floor covered with Persian rugs. No one in the room spoke. Only the sound of people sniffing back wet tears proved life existed inside the room that smelled of old leather books.

Lomax stood unmoving just past the door. Even after all the years he had faithfully committed to hundreds of murder investigations, he still loathed the aftermath of such a heinous crime. It was the worst part of his job, which came in the form of questioning the victim's loved ones. There was no icebreaker or words to console those left behind. No matter the circumstances of the death in question—accidental or deliberate—he always walked away from the interviews feeling like some sort of morbid vulture that had just finished pillaging the sanctity of a person's most private and vulnerable moment.

He took a deep breath. *I might as well get this over with,* he thought with dismay. *She's going to hate me anyway.*

Lomax slid his hands into his front pockets, put on his best smile, and approached the two huddled together like a pair of old friends. He needed cooperation, not outrage or indignation and certainly not closed mouths.

He cleared his throat. "Excuse me, Mrs. Callahan," he began softly, maintaining his award-winning smile. Her husband may have been a total sleaze, but she was an innocent, merely a loving wife mourning the loss of her husband and the father of her children. It wasn't her fault that she'd trusted a turd.

Julie Callahan looked up. Tears streaked her face. "Yes," she stammered, her lower lip quivering. "I'm Julie Callahan." The woman next to her pulled her closer and glared up with hostile eyes.

The silver-haired man leaned back in his chair a little farther and continued to stare off into space.

"I'm Detective Lomax, Mrs. Callahan," he announced sincerely. "I am sorry for your loss."

Julie sniffed back tears and wiped her nose with the back of her hand. "Thank you." A pained smile of gratitude crept across her face.

He pulled his hands free from the pockets. "I realize this is a terrible time for you, but I would like to ask you a few questions," he said and then tactfully added, "If that's all right with you? It's important to get answers while everything is still fresh in the mind."

As if protecting Julie from a verbal assault, the woman shot Lomax a piercing set of angry eyes. Her jaw set. "Can't this wait until tomorrow, Detective?" She adjusted herself so that she served as a barrier between him and Julie. "The other officers have already taken her statement."

"I'm sorry, Miss ..." he began, forcing himself to remain calm.

One rude step, and he might blow everything. "I'm sorry, but I didn't get your name."

Her face hardened like tempered steel. "Brenda Beltag, attorney-at-law and personal family friend of the Callahans." Her voice was like toxic venom.

He shifted his feet, searching for a way around a sticky situation. His smile faltered. *Great,* he thought miserably. *Now I got a damn lawyer and family friend in the mix.* He cringed inwardly. *That is not a good combo.* He folded his hands together and tried to portray a positive image. "Ms. Beltag, I understand your pain and concern for your friend," he began diplomatically, "but I have only a couple of questions. The rest can wait for tomorrow." He raised his hand and extended two fingers side by side. "I promise."

Beltag narrowed her eyes, now seeming even more suspicious. Her body language screamed her hatred for cops. "I think it would be best to just—"

Julie pulled away from the safety of Beltag's arm and rested a hand on her friend's leg, interrupting her.

Julie met his eyes. "No, Brenda," she said. "It's okay. I'm sure the detective is just trying to do his job and find my Walter's killer." She lifted her chin to shore up her courage. "Go ahead and ask your questions."

He flashed a toothy grin. "Thank you," he said. "I'll take only a few moments of your time and leave you to your loved ones."

Julie folded her hands and laid them gently in her lap. "I appreciate the sentiment."

Beltag straightened up, eyes mistrustful. If looks could kill, Lomax would be dead on the spot.

He retrieved his pad of paper and pen from his pocket. "Did you and your husband have any personal problems in your marriage?"

"No," she said. "We didn't have any problems, Detective." Her eyes wandered off for a split second, as if searching her memory, and then came back to him, continuing. "Our relationship had no more issues than any other couple. We loved each other very much. The long hours his job demanded sometimes made a sticking point for us, but that's to be expected with a workaholic."

Lomax frowned at the expected answer. Nothing in the woman's demeanor offered any reason to think that she was anything but a loving wife. "I see."

Beltag shifted her body. She looked ready for an old-fashioned brawl. "Next question," she quipped.

"I understand," he said amicably. He then dabbed the end of the pen against the tip of his tongue. "Do you know if Walter, um … I mean, your husband was using drugs again?"

Julie's shoulders slumped forward, her face falling much in the same defeated way. The light in her eyes faded to a dull gray.

Beltag's body went stiff. Her lips curled up. "Be careful, Detective," she warned with a throaty growl. "Tread lightly, and keep this civil. My client is cooperating as a courtesy, so don't overreach."

Lomax pressed his lips together to feign innocence. There were things he had to know if he wanted to serve justice. He scribbled the statement down and then flipped to the next page. "Mrs. Callahan, if you'd be patient enough with me so that I can rule you out as a possible suspect, I'd appreciate it. It's a little personal."

Julie gave a faint nod, and Beltag looked about ready to pounce on him.

"Let's keep this pleasant, Detective."

Julie raised her chin to show that she was ready. "Ask your question," she said.

"Where were you at the time of your husband's death?"

Despite his implied warning, the subtle accusation rocked Julie back on the sofa, her mouth agape, eyes wide from the verbal impact. "What?" she cried. Her whole body shuddered. "I've already explained to the others that—" She dropped her chin to her chest and wept anew.

Beltag nearly flew off the sofa, her face twisted in burning rage. "All right, Detective," she spat. "This is an outrage, and this interview is over. I do not like stinking cops sandbagging me with underhanded tactics. My client is a victim in this tragedy, and you're treating her like a damn suspect."

He shrugged, damned if he was going to apologize for something in which he took no joy. Questioning a spouse who had just lost a loved one made his skin crawl. "I'm only trying to figure out what happened, Counselor."

She sneered at him. "Oh, I'm quite aware of what you are trying to do, you heartless parasite." She shook her head. "And it's not happening today, not on my watch."

Lomax held the pen up in the air. "That's fair enough," he began, pausing for the count of three, and then added, "Well, as you know, if I can rule out the wife as a possible suspect to any involvement, and I mean any, then that unsavory situation can be officially concluded."

Julie lifted her face from her hands. "I was upstairs," she said abruptly.

Beltag placed a hand on her shoulder. "Be quiet, Jules," she said firmly. "This interview is over, so if you will please excuse us, Detective." She took Julie by the arm and moved to escort her from the room, no doubt away from Lomax.

Politely stepping aside to allow ample room for them to pass, Lomax slid the paper back into his pocket and made a slight bow. "I understand, ladies," he said in a professional voice. "Once again, Mrs. Callahan, please accept my deepest condolences."

Beltag glared over her shoulder, a scowl crossing her face. "Good-bye, Detective," she said. "Do not come around here again, or there will be consequences, severe consequences, which I promise will not be pleasant."

The women disappeared behind a side door.

Ignoring the malevolent stares of those standing on the sidelines, Lomax stood alone in silence for several minutes and contemplated his next line of investigation. He supposed that he could have handled the situation with a little more finesse, but he also knew there was nothing decent about murder and the broken pieces he had to collect in the aftermath.

With no one else to question in the immediate vicinity, he finally decided to find the body.

Perhaps I can glean something of value from it, he reasoned with a shrug. *Probably not.* He gave a snappy wave to the glassy-eyed man with silver hair and headed off to find the recently deceased Walter Callahan.

Five minutes later, while standing over the dead body of the former district attorney Walter Callahan, Lomax discovered nothing mind-blowing about the body's condition or the surrounding area. The crime scene looked no different from that of a typical junkie with a syringe crammed in his arm—no big whoop. Callahan's physical appearance was gaunt, like he had not slept in a year. Lomax remembered the man from the previous year when the "powers that be" had forced him to attend one of Callahan's sycophantic fundraisers and speak on the DA's behalf to the doe-eyed anticrime advocate groups gathered together. Callahan's face—young and vibrant then—had aged a decade.

Nevertheless, the pale and emaciated cadaver was Walter Callahan all right, in the flesh.

Lomax let out a small snort of derision. "Not looking so hot now, are ya?" he mumbled, ignoring the uncomplimentary stares of the forensic team standing off to the side. He reached out and accepted a pair of surgical gloves from one of the team, a pimple-faced kid, and then got down on a single knee. "Hmmm." He searched for any evidence that might undermine or refute suicide. "Come on. Talk to me."

A team member cleared his throat.

Lomax peered up at the rude interruption, cocking an eyebrow when he found the senior crime investigator Harper Collins now looming over him. "Do you have any opinions on our stiff, Harp?" he said matter-of-factly.

Harper frowned at him. "You already know that I prefer to reserve any opinion as to cause of death until after my office concludes its official investigation." His words came out mechanical and rehearsed. "We need to run a full tox screen, an autopsy, and—"

Lomax grunted his disapproval and lifted an impatient hand to stop the man from reciting the coroner's playbook. "Yeah, yeah, yeah," he repeated with irritation. He was well acquainted with the avoidance tactics implemented by such departments. No one ever wanted a superior to box him or her in and hold him or her accountable upon later finding it necessary to revise a preliminary finding. Defense attorneys rallied at the prospect during cross-examination for impeachment purposes. "All I'm asking is whether you and your team found any reason to believe this guy's death is anything but suicide."

Harper fidgeted. "Well, I'm afraid … This is not conclusive, of course," he began apprehensively. He seemed to search for some way to hedge his answer.

Lomax nodded in hope of encouraging him to finish. "Off the record," he added.

Harper sighed his resignation. "My initial findings are that the subject died of a massive overdose, probably an opiate." He cupped his chin with his right hand, as if in deep thought. "We will need to get the body and surrounding paraphernalia back to the lab and run prints and tissue analysis to confirm." He took a deep breath. "Simply stated, Detective, he was taking no chances for recovery or resuscitation. He died quick and painless."

Lomax mulled the words over in his mind and looked around the room. He wrinkled his brow. "I see," he mumbled. "Is it possible that someone could have done it for him?"

Harper blinked. "I don't understand your question," he said. "Done what, exactly?"

Lomax got to his feet with a heavy grunt. "Shot him up and killed him," he offered. He pretended to jab an invisible needle into his arm.

Harper's eyes sparked to life. "You mean, murdered the district attorney by lethal injection?" His lips curled up and formed a strange grin. "That is an interesting theory. He who lives to deliver death by lethal injection dies by the needle is your inference from all this? How morbidly poetic is that? It's something right out of Edgar Allen Poe." He rubbed his chin. "I like it. It's just so grandiose, sinister, and a savage twist of fate."

"I didn't ask you if you liked it," Lomax snapped.

Harper guffawed. "I see no evidence to support that scenario, Detective," he said snidely. "I deal only in facts, not fairy tales."

"Is it possible?"

Harper shrugged. "Sure, why not," he said. "Hell, anything is possible." He looked back at the body.

"But there's no sign of physical struggle—no trauma, cuts, or bruising—and the position of the body is consistent with suicide."

Lomax peeled off the gloves and stuffed them into a nearby plastic bag. Johnson was right. The unexpected mystery now intrigued him. *Something just doesn't feel quite right. Something about this whole thing stinks. It's just too tightly wrapped for my taste.*

Lomax knew Callahan was as dirty as they came; about that he had no delusions. Still, it just seemed a little unnatural for any man to kill himself where the first people to find him would be his wife and children. That kind of selfishness went far beyond dirty. Callahan's act was downright cruel to those that loved him. Perhaps Callahan was that kind of man. One way or another, Lomax soon realized that he no longer had a choice but to learn the truth. He had to know the facts, because that was just the kind of detective he was.

Filled with a new sense of purpose, Lomax stepped outside and took a deep breath of fresh air. It felt good to be back on the hunt.

Here I come, killer, he swore. *I will find you no matter where you are hiding.* A flash of reflective light came from somewhere on the roof of the house across the street and distracted his thought process.

He shielded his eyes from the sun overhead and looked across the street. "What in the hell was that?" he whispered.

Nothing moved or seemed out of place.

Lomax gave a grunt and headed toward his car.

Trent hunkered down and lay prone in the softest spot of sand atop a small dune under the blistering torment of the desert sun, elbows planted firmly in the ground with the rifle held at the ready in gloved hands. His cell phone suddenly vibrated to life. Unbearably hot, stiff, and uncomfortably cramped after lying in wait for the past two hours in the heat, Trent squinted; nothing for as far as his sun-scorched eyes could see offered any form of comfort. Sweat stung his eyes. Even though the sun had already passed over him, the temperature remained at a steady 115 degrees. He had watched the fiery orb since his arrival, which seemed in no hurry to move toward the horizon just beyond the shimmering metal that had served as his next target's home for the past twenty years. He had waited decades for this moment in time.

His cell phone continued to vibrate.

Trent grunted his discontent at the unwanted interruption and lifted the flap covering the camouflage jacket's arm pocket. He removed his phone and held it up to his ear. This time he did not bother with checking the caller ID. He was in the zone, and he preferred no distractions. "Yeah, Varus here," he said grumpily, wiping at the sweat peppering his brow with the sleeve. "Who's calling?"

Lenny's familiar laugh came from the phone. "Hey, boss," he greeted with a spark of humor. "Nice way to answer your phone.

Your signal is a little weak, so if we get cut off you know why. How many bars do you have?"

Trent grumbled deep in his throat. He supposed the ungodly heat was finally getting to him, practically cooking his brain from the inside out. Normally, he would be angry, but only on the rarest occasions did his right-hand man, Lenny, break routine and make unscheduled calls. He kept his eyes focused on the long stretch of dirt road that lead to the bulbous trailer two hundred yards away from where he waited with purpose. He balanced the rifle in the crook of his arm. "Forget the bars, Lenny," he said. "I can hear you fine. I'm a little busy at the moment. What's up?"

"Do you remember our new client, the one married to that dirtbag cop?" His voice sounded pinched and uneasy. "You know who I'm talking about, don't you? She's the good-looking brunette."

Trent nodded. "Lisa Markinson. Sure I remember her," he said. "She's the cute little thing married to that ultracreep. She's something any guy would remember, cute as a button."

"Yeah, that's right."

Trent raised his head and squinted at the barely perceptible puff of dust in the distance. The image of Lisa's kind and vulnerable face as she sat crying in his office came to mind. "Why are we talking about her, Lenny?" he said. "Is she okay? That creep hasn't tried anything weird, has he? After all, she is now under our watchful eyes, and I don't want that cop bothering our client."

"Not yet, boss." His voice was an uncommon stammer. "But I do have my concerns. Since he is a cop, other things come into play. He has resources the regular run-of-the-mill husband just doesn't have on hand."

Trent furrowed his brow at Lenny's tone. "Explain."

An audible groan came over the phone. "I made a few rounds in the neighborhood officer creepo patrols." His voice still sounded uneasy. "You know, to get the lay of the land and a feel for the guy from some of the girls who hustle the street. I had a couple of long discussions with a few of the longer term pros that walk the street on his beat." His voice had taken on a darker tone. "All of them had some very perverted things to say about our boy in blue."

The dust cloud grew larger as it narrowed the distance from where the trailer sat.

"Like what?"

"Real sick kind of stuff, Trent," he said.

Trent brought the rifle to bear and peered through the high-powered scope to confirm the model of car.

"Just spit it out, Lenny," he said testily. "I don't have all day for you to tell me all the gory details of what goes down while Officer Markinson is on the job, so trust what I say when I tell you that I doubt there is anything you can say that will surprise me. I've seen some pretty gross things in my lifetime."

"Are you sure you want to hear the details about how the creep burns the girls with cigarettes and cuts them with razor blades if they get out of line?"

Finally, Trent confirmed the model of car that drove toward the trailer. His thoughts drifted from the conversation. He smiled in satisfaction. *One down, one on the hook,* he thought triumphantly. *There is nowhere for any of you to run and hide any longer.*

"Are you still there?"

The sharpness in Lenny's voice shook Trent out of his reverie, and he blinked. "Yeah, I'm still here, buddy," he said. "I've got a bit on my mind, so I sort of drifted off for a second."

"So, what do you want me to do?"

"First, tell me why you're so concerned."

Lenny cleared his voice over the phone. "Well, as far as the girls go, Markinson blackmails and threatens them if they don't put out for him." His voice deepened with concern. "In fact, two of the girls I've known since back in the day said he forced them into the car and drove them out of town to a bunch of old, abandoned buildings last year. I think they were talking about the old industrial park on the outskirts of town. I know the place fairly well. I used to bust some of the neighborhood teens out there. They used to conduct illegal races." He paused. "Anyway, they said he pulled a medium-sized gun from an ankle holster and threatened to kill them if they didn't …" His voice trailed off into what sounded like embarrassment.

"Screw him and do other nasty things for free," Trent finished for him. "Am I right?"

"Yeah, I guess that about sums everything up in a nutshell." His voice sounded subdued. "The place is very isolated, and no one really goes out there anymore."

"Do you believe them?"

"Yeah, Trent," he said. "I believe them. They have no reason to lie about it."

"You see, that wasn't so hard," he said softly. "I sort of expected that kind of thing. It goes with the territory. Men are predictable when it comes to stuff like that, especially cops. They are just not that creative."

"I guess."

Trent tracked the car through the scope's lens and watched with growing interest as it pulled in front of the trailer. The strong magnification made it possible for him to see that only one passenger sat inside the vehicle. Despite the painfully slow passage of so many years, regardless of all the terrible things he had seen and experienced during the loneliest years spent locked in a cage, nothing on earth could ever make him forget the face of the man who had sat on the witness stand and pointed a finger of condemnation at him. The driver looked much older than he expected, the sun no doubt having wrinkled his face prematurely. Even his hair had thinned.

Nevertheless, Trent knew he could have identified his former brother-in-law in a lineup of a thousand men. He would know that face, no matter how loose the skin had become around the mouth and neck. Bitter hatred that had lived in him since that day flashed like lightning in an apocalyptic storm. *I'm coming for you.* He clenched his jaw and set the cell phone on the ground, face up.

Lenny's voice coming from the phone was unintelligible.

Trent narrowed his right eye, ignoring the grumbling coming from the phone. "Now, it's time to take your long overdue medicine, you lousy backstabbing son of a bitch," he whispered with a hiss. Lenny's raised voice erupted from the phone's speaker and caught Trent's attention.

"I'll be right there, Lenny."

"Excuse me, boss. Did you say something?"

Trent's brother-in-law—a man he had known as Sam before the federal agents in the witness protection program had supplied him with a false identity under the name of Jerry Smith—opened the car door and got out, slamming it shut hard enough to reach his ears. Sam slapped at his coveralls and knocked loose patches of rogue dirt and what looked like caked grease stains as he walked toward the trailer.

Trent drew a bead on Sam's upper back, right between his emaciated shoulder blades. His finger tightened on the trigger. He took slow, controlled breaths. "I want you to keep an eye on Lisa Markinson, Lenny," he said, "and I want you to keep a close eye on her sister, Maureen. That sick bastard might try to hurt our client by first going after the sister, a sort of diversionary tactic to trick her into doing something desperate. We have an obligation to protect Mrs. Markinson and keep her sister safe from that weirdo, so keep an eye on both of them; sort of go back and forth between them. I want you to keep everything on the QT for now, so do your best and stay in the shadows. I see no reason to scare either one of them unnecessarily."

"Do you want me to follow the creep, keep tabs on him?"

"Only as long as it doesn't place either woman in danger," he said.

"I would never do anything to put either one of them in danger, Trent." Lenny's voice sounded hurt.

Sam was now only twenty feet from the rusted front door of the trailer.

"I know that, Lenny," he said apologetically. "I just want you to focus on the women, not the weirdo. If the time should arrive, then we will deal with him."

"Understood," he said.

The call terminated with a faint buzz.

Sam opened the trailer's door and took a single step inside.

Trent pulled the trigger, grinning widely against the left side of the rifle when the custom-made dart found its target.

Gotcha!

Sam twisted at the waist, instinctively throwing his hands behind his back and reaching for whatever had struck him. His mouth stretched open in a silent cry of pain. He grappled clumsily with his fingers, visibly shuddering from the spasms that had to be rushing through his body from the drug now coursing through his body. His knees gave out within seconds. His head seemed to float about his neck, swimming about in a circular motion, his eyes squeezing shut.

Trent continued to stare through the magnified lens of the scope, savoring every jerk and twist of the man who had helped destroy his life. "There's nowhere for you to go, Sam," he said. "It is over, my old friend. All debts shall be paid in full, including all interest payments."

Finally, Sam collapsed onto the heavily stained, cigarette burned carpet inside the fetid bowels of his home.

Two hours after Trent had shot the tranquilizer dart from a distant sand dune into Sam Herd's back, he reached back with gloved hands and slapped the man he had not spoken to for over two decades to wake him from his drug-induced unconsciousness.

Sam's head snapped backward. A small groan slipped from his lips, signifying that he was now starting to regain consciousness. His head lolled on a scrawny neck. His eyes fluttered several times.

Trent stretched out his fingers. "Ahhhh," he said with a snicker. "How nice, you are finally awake. Rise and shine, sunshine. I was wondering how long the drug would keep your lights out." He pulled up a chair, which squeaked in protest of bearing his weight. "I've waited a very long time for this day to finally arrive, Sammy boy."

His brother-in-law shook his head, as if attempting to shake the pharmaceutically enhanced cobwebs created by the drug from his addled mind. "Where am I?" His voice slurred. His eyes opened slowly. "What did you do to me? I can hardly see much of anything. Everything looks fuzzy, out of focus."

"You are where the heart is." Trent leaned a little closer, studying the man he had once loved and trusted with his life. "Don't you worry one bit; your vision will clear up soon enough. I want you to see your future, or rather lack of it."

"And where is the heart?" He ran a tongue over cracked lips. "Who are you? What do you want? Do you think I owe you money or something?"

Trent made a deep, malevolent chuckle that filled the cramped space of the trailer. "What's the matter?" He let the words hang for several seconds, and then added, "Sam?"

Sam's face wrinkled up. "I think you have the wrong dude, partner." His voice was gruff, almost arrogant. "My name is Jerry Smith, and I've lived here for a very long time. Everyone around these parts knows who I am."

"They know what you want them to know," he said. "They don't know you like I know you." Trent leaned a little farther forward in the chair. "Don't you remember me? I sure remember you. Your name is Sam Herd, and you have been living a lie for a very long time. I'd say about twenty some odd years." He tapped a finger against Sam's forehead. "I'm a bona fide flash from the past."

Sam's head jerked back at the touch, his face paling for a split second. Thick beads of sweat broke out across his brow. Trent saw that his eyes started to show the first signs of clearing. Even the dizziness appeared to fade, now replaced by genuine fear. "How do you know that?" There was a distinct tremble in his voice, and Trent felt the light fingers of vengeance brush across the back of his neck.

"Take a guess."

Sam's head shook. "I don't know what you're talking about. My name—"

Trent slapped him on the side of the head, stopping him

in midsentence. "Is Sam Herd," he finished for him. "How disappointing, but you may want to stop lying to me before I get upset and make this far more personal than it already is." He folded his gloved hands and turned his head to the left and to the right. "Nice place. So, this is the reason you took the stand at my trial and lied to the jury?"

The blood seemed to drain from Sam's face, and Trent saw that the pretended game of cat and mouse had finally reached its end.

"Ah, so you do remember," he said. The age that had laid claim to his brother-in-law's face reminded him of how many years had been lost for nothing. It was clear that time had not been kind. "Am I missing something here?" The situation made his head hurt. "Help me out, because I am just not getting any of this, and it's driving me up the wall. Out of the deal, you got a new hideout, a new identity, and a new life?" He guffawed.

"What you see is what I got, Trent." The words hung in the air like sour grapes.

"But why did you settle for the name of Jerry?"

"It's the name they gave me, Trent." His voice sounded weary and burned out. "I had nothing to do with it."

Trent crossed his arms over his chest. "I'm flattered you still remember my name," he said. "That's something, I guess."

"Come on, Trent," he said. "It wasn't like that, and you know it."

"I don't know much of anything, except that I spent a good chunk of my life in hell because of you," he said. "You stole everything from me and my family."

Sam's chin dipped in shame. "I was weak, and they had me on a hook." His voice quavered. "I was going to go down forever and a day if I didn't find some way out of my mess. It's not pretty, but that is the truth of the matter. You just—"

A hard slap across the mouth cut off his words. His tongue ran across bloody teeth.

Trent rose from the chair. He clenched his teeth together, his jaw muscles writhing beneath the skin. "So, why go to prison when you can send a friend?" He growled at Sam. "Is that what you're telling me? Is that your best defense for what you did? Are you joking?"

"If you'll just—" Sam began, but Trent flashed up a hand and stopped him from finishing another string of excuses.

"Don't you dare try to justify what you did," he said angrily.

"It's all I got."

Trent reached down the left side of the chair and withdrew a large hypodermic needle from inside a black satchel resting on the ground beside the chair. He held it up for Sam to see, staring at him with dark, menacing eyes now devoid of anything that resembled the human compassion that had once lived behind them.

At the sight of the silver needle, Sam's eyes widened in fear. His body twisted in the chair, but the leather restraints wrapped around his arms and legs held him fast. Nothing he did made any difference against the thick leather. "What's that for?" The words came out with a squeak.

Trent brushed off the question with a flick of his hand and walked past Sam, into the small bedroom near the rear of the tiny trailer, where he had stashed a sealed fifteen-gallon container of anhydrous ether commonly used by methamphetamine cooks to manufacture the highly addictive drug.

"What are you doing?"

Trent dragged the heavy container out of the bedroom and across the narrow floor, grunting from the exertion of sore and tired muscles he had used only a few hours ago to move ninety pounds of liquid twenty feet. Sweat broke out over his back, his shirt sticking. Dull thuds and scratches reverberated inside the metal belly of the trailer, accompanied by the sound of chemicals sloshing about inside the blue plastic. He set the large container next to Sam.

Sam started to whimper. "Puh-lease," he pleaded in a stammer, "don't kill me." His struggle against the leather began anew. "You don't have to do this." His eyes filled with tears. "You're better than this, always were."

Trent clenched his jaw at the begging words and removed a

glass pipe, a butane torch, a box of wood matches, and an old-fashioned windup alarm clock from the satchel. He set everything on a lopsided kitchen table.

"Why won't you talk to me?"

Trent took a deep breath. *You better shut up while you're ahead, dummy.*

"Connie would never condone what you're doing."

Trent craned his neck and curled his upper lip at the man he had once loved as a brother. Now, all he felt was disgust. "Don't you dare say her name," he said with a hateful sneer, "and don't beg for what I will never give. In case you are in need of a reminder, you are in a position to ask for nothing, and I am in the position to grant even less. We were friends, the best, and you betrayed me. I called you brother, and you were the best man at my wedding, and yet you stabbed me in the back."

"What was I supposed to do?"

"Hush," he said with a hiss. He closed his eyes and thought about the last time he had seen his wife's face. "I trusted you even as I watched you walk up and take the stand for the prosecution." His voice deepened. "Even when my attorney told me that you were going to lay the blame on me, I told him to shut up. I refused to accept that scenario. I told him that you would never do that to me, that you would rather die than hang me for something I did not do."

Sam sniffed back tears. "But—"

Trent opened his eyes and stared at Sam in fury. "And then you pointed your finger right at me!" he barked. "Your sister was my wife, and you killed her. You killed my whole family, your own family, and I am going to kill you." He straightened up, pulled back his shoulders, and stretched out his neck.

Sam shook his head, tears flying from his eyes. "How was I supposed to know she would get killed?" he mumbled through tears. "Connie was my family too. And I loved her."

Trent moved his face within inches of Sam's. "Is that how you think she saw it?"

A wince tweaked Sam's features. "I swear to God that it wasn't supposed to go down like that!"

"Don't you dare invoke God's name in this," he warned. "This is your sin to carry, not mine, certainly not God's. We all have our crosses to bear."

Sam spat a wad of blood on the floor. "And what about yours?" His voice hardened. "Your hands are not entirely clean either. If you weren't so damn stubborn to force a public trial, none of it would have happened. That DA promised me that you would take a deal if those around you squeezed hard enough and accept a sentence for a whole helluva lot less time. But you wouldn't hear of it. Oh, no, not the great and sanctimonious Trent Varus. Not Mr. Righteous. He bows to no one. You just had to act all holier than thou and push back, letting anal-retentive pride and principal send you straight to the box and then to a prison cell. Your greatest sin in all of this, at the expense of all around you, is pride, the worst of all seven."

Trent smirked at the string of vacuous words, deeply offended and repulsed by such notions. "So, I was supposed to get up in court, in front of friends and family, in front of the whole damn world, under oath, with God as my witness, and falsely admit that I murdered some man who I had never met in cold blood?" he said, incredulous. "Is that what you are telling me? You cannot be serious."

"Yes, damn it!" he exclaimed. "I am serious as a heart attack." His jaw muscles writhed beneath the skin. "It's done every day. That's the world we live in. Unfortunately, nothing about it will ever change. Deep down, no one wants it to change, because change is too much work. Everyone does it, and no one cares if you are innocent or guilty, just that someone—anyone other than himself or herself—pays for whatever crime the government pukes claim. No one in government will willingly admit that it makes mistakes. People must believe that the system is fair and impartial, that authorities in power do not cast out the innocent and downtrodden for no reason. It lets them drown in the false dream through a bogus election process."

Trent's jaw went slack, stunned by what he had just heard.

A maniacal grin creased Sam's face. "That's the system, like it or lump it. It is clear as day, and I thought you understood that much. It's nothing personal, just business as usual. People get busted for whatever, and then they turn in other people in exchange for sweet deals, leniency, and immunity. It's the old-fashioned Hollywood blacklist brought into our new society for everyone on the street. It doesn't matter if anything they say is true, just that the testimony supports the manufactured evidence so the charges stick. A defendant's remorse is measured by how many people he turns over to the government. The higher the number, the more mitigation is calculated into the sentence. Neighbor turns in neighbor. Kids turn in their parents. That is the new American way of life, and you still fight to keep the blinders on from seeing the forest. It is a dog-eat-dog world, and the police love it."

Trent felt his stomach do a sickly flip-flop. He thought he might puke all over the floor any second, wondering how he could have ever been so blind. Something in Sam's words could not be denied, no matter how far he wanted to shove his head into the ground and keep it there until everything foul in his life blew over.

Sam's face softened. The corners of his mouth turned downward. "Oh, you poor bastard," he said in a gentle sounding voice. He shook his head. "Haven't you figured that one out after all these years? No matter what you may think, Trent, no one cares about what is right anymore. I'm not sure anyone ever did. I didn't make the world; I just knew how to adapt so that I didn't have to suffer like so many others." He paused and then added, "Like you."

Trent shook his head, struck numb at words he could never fully grasp, least of all accept as true. He had been so certain over the years that he had just made an egregious mistake in trusting the wrong people, believing with all his heart that not everything in his life was a total sham. But now he looked into Sam's face and saw reality.

Trent felt a thousand tiny deaths pierce his heart.

Trent cleared his throat. "So, I sat in a cage for over twenty years, where I was abused, forced to eat garbage, and subjected to inhumane treatment you could not in your wildest nightmare imagine because you offered me up for legal slaughter to your slave master DA to slide out of your legal problems?" He took an unsteady breath, his thoughts threatening to spin off their axis points. "Is that why my family died? So you didn't have to go to prison for a few short years?"

Sam slumped in the chair, shoulders sagging in what looked like defeat from the verbal punch to the gut. "What do you want me to say?" He sighed. "That I was a coward and sacrificed everybody, that I lied to get out of going to prison?"

"I want the truth," he demanded. "I want an explanation. I need to know why."

Sam dipped his chin to his chest, closing his eyes against the sharp sting of words. He now looked a thousand years old to Trent, spent and useless, just another degenerate that had attempted to attach false integrity onto bankrupt morality.

"Well," he pressed. "Aren't you going to answer me?"

Sam lifted his face. "You're not going to like it."

"Try me."

"That is the simple truth."

Trent furrowed his brow, wondering if he had missed something cryptic in the conversation. "What is?"

"I didn't want to go to prison."

Trent blinked, uncertain he comprehended all the involved implications in such a pithy response. "The DA suspected you were lying?"

"Come on, Trent." His voice sounded exasperated. "You'll drive yourself crazy." He pressed his lips together. "Let it go. Let it all go."

He shook his head. "I already tried to do that," he said. "No matter how hard I tried, no matter how many years I tried to brush away the past, I just couldn't move past any of it. The memories will not let me go; nor will the pain. It pulls at me from the darkness, never letting me go until I exorcise the demons."

Sam licked his lips. "I'm warning you not to go down that rabbit hole. You'll find only darkness."

"Maybe," he said. "But I'm already there."

Sam inhaled deeply. "The DA knew I was lying," he finally said. "Is that what you want to hear?" He licked his lips. "They all knew I was lying through my teeth—the cops, the DA, and even the damn judge in the case. Detective Johnson said you were an easy fish to help cover up something none of them talked in detail about in front of me. That's all that mattered to them. It was something someone said or heard. Whatever it was, all three of them were troubled because it was big and bad enough to bring them all down."

Trent's heart skipped a beat. "Judge Harper was in on it?" he said, eyes widening in horror.

Sam nodded. "From the beginning," he said. "You didn't have a chance in hell. The four of them settled your destiny in a back room. They decided your life in a nanosecond."

"Why?"

"The DA needed something big to stay in office, and the judge needed to stay on the bench." His shoulders shrugged. "It came down to politics, I think."

"You said there were four of them."

"Yeah, that's right."

Anger started to well in him. He narrowed his eyes at Sam. "How?" he said with a grumble.

"The DA met Harper in chambers and discussed my testimony to guarantee a conviction." Sam's voice was matter-of-fact. "It had to be rock solid to withstand appeal, so they coached me in such a way that everything would be deemed as harmless error, or some such thing. I didn't understand all the legalese. But they were the ones keeping me out of prison, so I wasn't about to do anything that might piss them off. There were threats, about what would happen if I tried to back out or hire a private lawyer, someone outside the box."

Trent stared with glazed eyes. He had a difficult time believing the depth of the conspiracy. "What does that mean, 'outside the box'?"

Silence filled the trailer.

Finally, Sam averted his eyes in what looked like shame. "I told you to let it go, Trent." Pain now dripped from his words. "It will only sting deeper."

Trent moved past his last question. "Is there anything else I don't know?"

Sam turned his eyes back on him. "Not really." His voice was weary. "Not that I can think of. It was a long time ago. The only other thing that comes to mind is that Harper somehow arranged to have that public defender appointed to your case. He was a distant cousin or nephew, something in that vein."

"So, they set me up from the get-go."

"Haven't you been listening to me?" His voice was now anxious. "You were set up from the moment you were arrested. It was all planned out. You were fated to go to prison. How long depended on whether you agreed to play ball and take a deal. It was that damn simple."

Trent's body trembled. "But why would they do such a thing?"

"I already told you that," he said. "I was just one of the means to your end, the snitch they used to put you away."

"What about the jury?" Trent's nostrils flared. "Were they in on it too?"

Sam shook his head. "Trent, I realize that it may seem impossible to you, but you have to just let it all go and start over," he urged. "You are still young, and you can live a full life, be happy. Besides, you can do nothing about it. They're too tactically positioned in the system, too powerful for you to touch. You'll end up back in a cage or worse."

Trent sneered at him. He now found new reasons to justify everything he intended to do. "Oh, no?"

"What can you possibly do to such men?"

Trent turned his lips up and made a wicked grin. "I can kill them," he said. His voice was cold and calculating. "I am going to kill all of them, one at a time. To let you in on a little secret, I've already started."

Sam's eyes flickered in rapid succession. A small croak slipped from his throat. "Then you are really going to kill me?"

"Yes, Sam, I am really going to kill you," he confirmed with relish in his tone. "The old adage of 'in for a penny, in for a pound', undoubtedly rings true in this instance. And it's true what they say about the first one being the hardest."

"But I told you what you wanted to hear," he stammered and then added, "no, what you needed to hear."

"And I really appreciate that, Sam," he said. "I really do." The grin vanished from his face. He was no longer amused. "But you have to pay for what you did."

Sam's body sagged in the chair, as if his will to live had drained from every muscle.

Trent wasted no time and quickly went to work on his project. He taped a striker onto the bell of the alarm clock and two wooden matches to the arms that would beat a flame to life when they sprang alert in thirty minutes. He placed the clock on the run-down kitchen counter. He then unscrewed the plastic plug on the container of anhydrous ether and splashed the strong-smelling chemical on the walls; the floor; and, lastly, Sam, until he had successfully emptied the volatile chemicals from the container. He knew fire investigators called on the scene would automatically detect the chemical commonly used in producing methamphetamine and conclude that another drug manufacturer had gone up in flames after mishandling flammable material—an end many so-called bathtub chemists met—at which point everyone involved would lose interest and place the case on a back burner.

Satisfied that everything was in proper order, Trent slapped dust from his gloved hands and then snatched up the black satchel. He turned and looked at Sam, who refused to meet his eyes.

"Well, old friend, that's about it for now," he said with morbid calm. "This one is definitely a wrap." He stole a look at his watch.

I got ten minutes left to go.

Sam lifted his chin and looked forward, appearing numb and detached from life. "Seems like," he mumbled. His lips barely moved to form the words.

Chemical fumes grew thick in the air, slowly infiltrating the confining space of the trailer.

Trent peeled off the gloves and dropped them to the floor. "Good-bye, Sam." he said. He opened the door and took a deep breath of fresh air.

"Hey, Trent," Sam whispered from behind his back.

Trent craned his neck and looked at Sam. Sorrow filled him as he briefly reminisced over the fond memories they had shared in common from another life. "Yeah, Sam," he said. "What is it?" His voice cracked.

Tears now streaked across Sam's face. "I know it doesn't mean anything now—" His voice caught in the tremble of his chin. He then added with a wince, "But I am really sorry you and everybody else had to pay for my selfish weakness."

For the first time since he had spied him from the sand dune through the magnified lens of the scope, Trent felt compassion for the man who had destroyed his life. The hatred and anger he had harbored over the years for the person now crying at his mercy seemed to float away like dust on the wind. It was now clear to him that the tortures of life had possessed a much further reach than he had anticipated, having claimed more victims than he'd previously considered, in a treacherous trek of deceit and betrayal that allowed for no winners. In near countless ways, he estimated, nothing of the old Sam had survived the carnage. Time had indeed defeated him, broken him down into little more than an ostracized desert gnome with no future, leaving nothing but an empty husk of emotional damage in its wake.

Trent lifted a hand. "I know you are, Sam," he offered sincerely. "You are and always will be my brother." He cleared his throat. "And I forgive you."

Sam straightened his back, lifting his chin in a demonstration of pride. He appeared at peace with his deserved fate. "Then let's do this, Trent." His voice was bold. "Good-bye, my brother. If God forgives me, I will tell Connie that you love her."

Trent stepped out of the trailer, shut the door behind him,

and began his short journey across the desert to where he had parked his jeep.

Five minutes later, the clock sprang to life and ignited a blast of fire that gutted the silver hull of Sam's final resting place.

CHAPTER 6

Seated across the dilapidated motel table from his antisocial nephew James, Benny set down his cell phone and carefully slid free a single card from the six fanned out in his left hand. He tossed it in the center of the table, partially covering his nephew's last play. A sour expression touched his face as he silently counted off the number for no points. His attitude had slowly worsened since James had incessantly nagged him long enough to wear down his resolve about playing a game of cribbage while they waited for their connection—a low-life dealer with the creative moniker 'Tinker'—to arrive with two kilos of pure cocaine and a cache of military hardware adorned with professionally machined silencers.

Contrary to his nephew's assertions, Benny believed that the only card game that truly tested a man's mettle and intellectual skill was five-card stud, one-eyed Jacks wild. All other games conjured up by the so-called gambling aficionados, in his semiprofessional opinion, did not come close to holding a candle to the father of all games of chance.

As Benny looked over the top of the five cards still gripped in his hand, regret started to tug at him for deciding to make a personal appearance at a motel he had once vowed never to visit again. The last time he had conducted business in a room four doors down, and gunfire had broken out between two men trying to renegotiate a deal Benny had brokered. His reputation for making clean deals for others had taken a hit on the street, which had created a problem in maintaining a constant cash flow.

Under normal circumstances, Benny would have simply sent James and his wayward brother, Jim, alone to handle things for him, but hard times had fallen on him, and he was in desperate need of an easy way to earn some fast cash, something in the neighborhood of at least $10,000, to pay off increasing debt. The bank was really leaning on him, threatening to close his doors if he didn't cough up something quickly to stave off overdue loans. The economy was circling the drain, and most cheating husbands had little choice but to stay home and save what little cash they could after paying their bills. Benny could not remember the last time a big spender had darkened the door of his withering business, his beloved Mousetrap. Everything he had worked for now hung in the balance, and he was damned if hard times were going to make him lose his business, force him to forfeit what little remained in his bank account, and push him out to live like a bum on the street without a fight.

In addition to his growing anxiety, coupled with his slow descent into financial destitution and eventual bankruptcy if he didn't do something industrious within the week, Officer Markinson had chased off several of his most popular girls—four avid professionals who could dance the money out of any man's pocket—and six more of the city's dirty cops had apparently sniffed him out as easy pickings in recent days. Like a pack of wolves prepared to pounce on a wounded deer, the six officers had first showed up in his club nearly a month ago, boldly demanding heavy donations to their wallets to supplement their income, in what they had not so jokingly referred to as "Personal Indemnification against Illicit Fire Insurance and Closure."

Benny had tried to protest their ridiculous demands for him to hand over more money than he was currently making, but the officers had only held out their hands, wriggled their greedy fingers, and laughed at him and his failing prosperity.

Now, to his increasing shame and humiliation as he sat across the table from one half of his troublesome relatives, Benny's successful career as a profiteer in the flesh-peddling trade under the stage lights inside his nightclub was on the verge of tanking in the worst possible way. Any semblance of pride and dignity as a semisuccessful businessperson continued to dwindle with each passing day, which made his regretful return to the unsavory element that dealt its wares on every street corner and sleazy motel in the lower part of the city stink to the nth degree.

He looked at the pair of coffee cups that sat atop the table. *Oh, how the worm has turned.*

Benny lifted his tired face and peered at James with half-lidded eyes. The mind numbing game had accentuated his boredom tenfold in the last twenty minutes. His nephew leered over the top of his cards and made a sneered gasp of malcontent at him, plucking a center card from those in his hand.

Benny lowered his hand, making sure to keep the face of his cards down because James would cheat without hesitation. "What's the problem, now?" he said grumpily. Tinker was now running fifteen minutes late, which only worsened his mood. He locked eyes with James. He had a hard time believing James was the smarter of the two. He had to question the logic of comparing the two. If James was dumb as a bag of hair, what did that make Jim? His failure to find the appropriate word to describe the actual degree of Jim's idiocy brought a faint tug at the corners of his mouth.

James pointed down at the card he had just played. "You have to call out the count, Uncle Benny." His voice was dead serious, eyes cold and deadly. "That's the rules, and I can't play my card until I know how much you count."

Benny guffawed at such a ridiculous expectation, grinning. "You're shittin' me," he said. "You can see the cards right there." He pointed at the cards. "They're in clear view, unless you're blind as a bat."

The corner of James's right eye twitched. "I don't joke when playing cards. This is serious business, and counting out the number is the rules."

Benny rolled his eyes. "Can't you just—"

James shook his head. "No!" His tone was adamant. "Those are the rules, and we follow the rules, or the game doesn't mean anything."

Dumbfounded, Benny stared at his nephew with his mouth agape. *No one can be this thick in the head,* he thought. He knew their alcoholic father had beaten Jim and James within inches of their lives since they could crawl, many times having broken several bones and caused head trauma that might have killed weaker boys, but now he had to wonder if Patrick Maddock had actually caused severe brain damage during one of his countless fits of drunken rage.

The testimony during the boys' youth trial after they had killed their father with a butcher knife still resonated with a bizarre pattern of grotesque imagery that sometimes kept Benny awake at night. The way his nephews described how they had chopped their father into tiny pieces after he stopped fighting back far surpassed most forms of sick cruelty, particularly since each boy had laughed during his testimony. Benny still wondered which of the twins was more vicious. Even after the passage of so many years, he had not found an answer to this barbaric question that no uncle should ever have to ask. No father should ever do the terrible things Patrick had done to his twins, but then nothing had seemed more unnatural to him than two brothers celebrating patricide with such unadulterated splendor. It was the first time Benny had seen them act like normal, well-adjusted boys during play. Both had survived the impossible, and the matching tattoos of bloody daggers with the words that read "Father Killers and Proud" over their hearts served as their immemorial reminder that fate had cut them from the same crimson-colored cloth, forever tying them as one.

James stretched out his back and placed a hand behind his ear. "Are you going to count it out or what?" His voice was sinister sounding. "I'm getting tired of waiting."

Benny shook away the memories of finding his nephews covered in blood on the back porch of his missing sister's house. "Twelve," he finally said.

A look of gratitude suddenly appeared on James's face. His

eyes sparked with renewed humor, his mouth curling up in a grin. He tossed out a three of spades. "Fifteen for two points." Pride dripped from his words.

A long-awaited knock on the front door of the motel room interrupted their game just as James reached out for his cup. His eyes darted at the sound. He did not appear in any hurry to answer the door.

Benny grumbled his irritation at Tinker's blatant disrespect for making him wait so long. He checked his watch and growled. It was already fifteen minutes after eleven o'clock that morning—over half an hour late. *Stinkin' bastard! I ought to cut off his balls and feed them to the alley cats in the back.*

A second round of knocks, louder and more insistent this time, shook the hinges on the door.

Benny grinned. He found ignoring Tinker and having him wait outside sort of evened things out. He had not slept very well for the past few days, and his disposition was not exactly marked by goodwill.

"Aren't you going to answer the door, Uncle Benny?"

Benny smirked, holding up a hand. "Just give it a minute," he said. "He deserves to stand out there for a minute or two. Let him see how it feels."

A foot kicked the door.

James got up from the chair. "I'll get the door, since you don't seem to give a crap," he said. "I want to get this done and over with. Jim's going to get tired of waiting pretty soon and come in here all bitchy and whatnot."

Benny flicked a hand in the air. "Go ahead, kid," he said. "Handle it."

James turned and walked toward the door. "Hang on. I'm coming."

Deep heavy thuds came from the other side of the door. Dust sprang from off the wood.

Benny prepared himself for anything. Tinker had a reputation for going sideways on people. He grinned when James balled his hands into fists.

"I said I'm coming," he said. "Stop banging on the damn door."

"You tell him," Benny said.

James flung the door open and stood in the center of the doorway, keeping Benny partially blocked from prying eyes. A stranger not included in the original agreement stood next to Tinker. "Who in the hell is this? You were supposed to come alone, by yourself. You never told Uncle Benny about some new guy we don't know, and don't want to know."

The stranger stepped forward, and James moved a little to the left and blocked his way. He placed his hands on either side of the doorjamb.

Benny leaned over to the left to get a clearer picture of the stranger's face. His thoughts raced when he saw a briefcase held in Tinker's hand.

The stranger made a thin line with his mouth. "I'm his partner," he announced in a challenging tone of voice. "They call me 'Barbed Wire' in the hood."

James's whole body seemed to tense up. "I wasn't talking to you, homeboy." His voice was sharp. "Talk to me, Tink. You know you're not supposed to show up with someone we don't know."

Tinker lifted the briefcase and made a lopsided grin. "Come on, James." His voice pinched on his name. "He's my partner. I'll cosign for him. Right here, right now, if that's what you want. He's cool." He looked over James's shoulder, into the room, and nodded. "Are we going to do some business or what? I'm a busy man. I have places to go, people to see."

Benny rose from the table and studied the mannerisms of the new arrivals. Something about Barbed Wire bothered him. He was shifty, a little too quick to play along, as if they were old friends. He ran a hand over his chin. "Where are the assault rifles, Tinker?" he said guardedly. "I know you didn't fit them in that case."

Tinker jerked his head over his shoulder. "I got them in the trunk, Benny. You didn't think I was going to bring everything in here until I saw the money, did you? We go back a ways, but not that far."

Benny motioned James with a hand. "Let 'em in," he said. His survival instincts went on high alert. He could almost smell a rip-off coming. He did not like surprises or last-minute changes in any plan. Changes created complications, always dangerous, always reckless.

"Are you sure?" James did not sound convinced.

Tinker shifted his feet, appearing a little more eager than usual. "Are we going to do this thing or not?"

"Yeah, James, I'm sure," he said. "Let them in, so we can do some business."

James moved to the side and let the two men pass.

Benny greedily rubbed his hands together. "Whatcha got for me, Tinker?" he said.

Tinker walked over to a small table and set the briefcase down. Barbed Wire took a seat on the bed.

Benny waved for James to check the case. "You better not be trying to dump your trash on me," he warned. He pointed at the case. "Top of the line, I hope."

Tinker unlocked the snaps. "Damn, Benny, you're getting more like your nephews." His voice raised an octave. "All of you are paranoid."

Cocking his head as if listening for any noise that did not belong in a tiny motel, Tinker craned his neck and did a quick survey of the area. His eyes came to rest on James. "So, where's your brother, Jim?"

James narrowed his eyes. "Why?"

"I'd like to say hi."

He shook his head. "No, you wouldn't."

"Sure I would."

"Why?"

Benny sensed the tension increase in the air. If Tinker was asking questions, then there was a definite reason. Everyone in the neighborhood who dealt drugs and guns knew that one brother did not do business without the other nearby. They had always functioned as a team. Individually, they were extremely dangerous, but together they were lethal nightmares.

Tinker shrugged. "No real reason, bro," he said. "I'm just trying to be friendly, that's all. After all, we're all friends here."

The left corner of James's face curled up. An aura of dangerousness surrounded his face. His eyes turned dark and menacing. "We ain't friends, dude." The words came out with a growl.

"Damn, homeboy, that's harsh," Tinker said. "If you don't want to tell me, that's cool."

Benny balled up his hands when he saw Tinker and his partner Barbed Wire exchange quick glances.

His old connection to the street's wholesaler was up to something, trickery and deceit mounting with each passing second. The tension in the air was unmistakable. The mood inside the room had grown thick and intense with mistrust, and Benny knew he had to sweeten the pot and make Tinker and his partner believe it was just the two of them at the motel. Treachery was the nature of doing illegal business with the criminal mind. No matter how long or how many times people dealt guns or drugs, the novelty of trust evaporated at the sight of cold hard cash. Greed instantly became the dealer's choice of drug, and snitches trying to set up others for the police in exchange for leniency on a pending case were worse than locusts at harvest. However, rip-offs remained a constant concern for those working the street, something for nothing serving as the lyrics of their favorite mantra.

Tinker opened the briefcase and turned it around to give James a clear view of its contents. His eyes shifted to Benny. "Just as we agreed, Benny," he said firmly, patting two bags stuffed with white powder. "Two kilos of Peruvian flake, four professionally modified Colt .45s, eight perfectly machined silencers, and three pounds of C-4 explosives. I've even added four boxes of special loads to keep the speed down for efficiency. Everything is clean and untraceable, which is not easy these days. That Patriot Act is really screwing everything up for the private businessperson." He removed one of the handguns and held it out for James's inspection. "Here, check it out, bro."

James stepped forward to accept the gun and broke the criminal's most treasured commandment. Benny recognized the rookie mistake his nephew had made in an instant and started for the man James had stupidly taken his eyes off. He opened his mouth to shout a warning.

Barbed Wire rose from the bed and withdrew a small caliber handgun hidden behind his waistband. He brought the gun around with expert precision and trained it on James's head. His mouth formed silent words of sayonara, before curling into a murderous-looking smile.

A thunderous roar came from outside the motel door and startled Barbed Wire enough to throw off his aim just as he pulled the trigger. The shot went wild and shattered the front window. The door exploded into a thousand splintered fragments and flew off its hinges. Benny felt his heart stop in his chest, the eruption of violent chaos far more than he was prepared to handle. His simple deal had turned into a complete mess in just a matter of seconds.

Shouting like some kind of futuristic storm trooper on a crazed rampage, Jim rushed into the room, a sawed-off shotgun gripped in his meaty hand. He yelled for his brother and Benny to drop to the ground, to get out of the way, and smiled at a terrified Tinker, who threw up his hands in surrender and screamed for the confirmed murderer not to kill him, that he was unarmed.

James dropped to his knees, grinning maniacally at his brother. "Kill that bastard, bro! Blow them off the map!"

Benny fell facedown and covered his head with both arms. *How in the hell did I get trapped into a bloodbath?* He then tilted his face to the side and sneaked a peek, waiting for another loud explosion.

Barbed Wire turned in an attempt to fend off Jim's attack at the click-clack of a chambered twelve-gauge shell. "Son of a bitch! Where did you come from?" He swung his gun around.

Another burst of gunpowder filled the air.

Barbed Wire's head blew apart with the visual of a popped party balloon stuffed with red confetti.

Jim stepped over Barbed Wire's headless body and pointed the shotgun at Tinker's head. "You tried to rip us off and kill my brother and uncle, you sack of shit!" He chambered another shell, his face now marked with murderous wrath and vengeance. "Now, you pay."

Tinker fell to his knees and pressed his hands together in what looked like devout prayer for divine intervention. Fresh urine pooled around his knees. "No, Jim. I swear to God I wouldn't do anything like that." His mouth pulled down at the corners in horror. Tiny red chunks of his former partner's head stuck to the front of his shirt. "I didn't know he was going to do that."

Benny climbed to his feet and stared wide-eyed at the bloody mess in the room. Despite his criminal lifestyle and the awful things done by him over the years, a few even close to unspeakable, only now did he fully grasp the insanity shared by his twin nephews. He had a difficult time believing they could sink so far down the homicidal tunnel without batting an eye of care or remorse. He stood in shock, unable to do anything but watch the grisly scene play out to its inevitable end. Murder was one thing, but this hit at a completely different kind of level. His boys seemed to take genuine pleasure from the act. He then realized just how far their father's abuse had driven their sickness.

With a grunt that sounded similar to that of embarrassment, James got to his feet and brushed pieces of gore off his shirt. He slapped Jim across the shoulder. "You completely messed up my favorite shirt." He then flicked a lump of bloody tissue off his shoulder. "This really sucks. I love this shirt—makes my biceps stand out."

Jim craned his neck and grinned. "You missed a spot."

James huffed irritably. "Screw you, bro." He continued to search and pick at the human debris clinging to the shirt. "This will never come out. I need some club soda or something, maybe Tide."

Jim let out a belt of laughter.

Benny made a wince of disgust and wondered just how far off the map his boys' minds had gone. He looked around the room and then at the man on the floor. *What am I going to do about this? I can't just make this go away.* He shuddered at the lack of plausible answers at his disposal.

Tinker remained on his knees with his head bowed, silent and unmoving as the two psychopaths joked and poked fun at each other over a worn-out T-shirt.

Jim tapped Tinker on the head with the barrel of the shotgun. "I hate to disturb all your fussiness and whatnot, but what do you think we should do with homeboy Tinker here?" The look on his face made it clear that now that the action was over he was bored. "Want me to blow his dick off? You know, for shits and giggles." He pointed the gun at Tinker's crotch. "How about a two for one shot?"

James picked up the guns Tinker and Barbed Wire had dropped on the floor, placed them in the briefcase, and snapped it closed.

A soft whimper slipped from Tinker's lips. His face was deathly pale, his eyes bloodshot and watery.

Benny took a step forward and started to intervene on Tinker's behalf, but something in the eyes of his nephews warned him to stay out of the situation and keep his opinion to himself. One wrong move just might be his last if he did anything to interfere with the natural course of expected events. Compassion and mercy were for the weak, and Benny was not certain enough that Jim and James would not turn on him, as they had their father, if he showed any sign of weakness.

James leered down at Tinker. "I got no use for him," he said in a malevolent hiss. "Kill the lying traitor."

Jim nodded his approval at such a deserved sentence. "Buh-bye, Tinkboy." With a giggle on his lips, he pulled the trigger and sent Tinker into the afterlife.

James sniffed at the air. "God, I just love the tangy smell of blood in the air."

Nausea churned violently in Benny's stomach. He pinched the bridge of his nose. *What have I gotten myself into?* For the first time in his life, the idea of family made him feel ill. His bloodline now trapped him in a world without logic. *How am I going to keep this away from Tabitha?*

Jim chambered another shell and walked toward what was left of the front entrance. He held the shotgun at the ready and did a quick check of the parking lot, no doubt looking for any sign of witnesses.

Since the sleazebag motel was located in the worst part of town, infamously known as being nothing more than a low-rent crack house for those who couldn't afford to stay at a better dive, open gunfire and screams for help were nothing out of the ordinary. In fact, both were daily expectations. Years ago, even the cops had given up their efforts to maintain any semblance of law and order in the area. No one had seemed to want either. All the police had ever received for their trouble was potshots taken at them from broken-down balconies. Eventually, "No thanks" evolved from the mouths of every officer working in precincts around the city. "Let the scum kill each other off." Society in general certainly would not spill a single bitter tear over a dead street urchin overdosed from dope. Even strung-out hookers willing to give a blow job for a pack of cigarettes had more self-respect for themselves than to hang out at such a rat hole.

Benny found that he could do nothing but stare in shock as his nephews prepared to leave the room.

Finally, Jim motioned him and James with a jerk of the shotgun. "Come on, you guys," he said gruffly. "Let's beat feet and put some distance between us and this dump." He took a step out of the room. "It's all clear, and I'm getting might hungry."

James snatched up the briefcase and playfully hopped over Tinker's body. "Thanks for the stuff, homeboy," he said in a high-spirited voice. "See ya, wouldn't want to be ya." He headed out the door. A skip was in his step as he hurried to catch up with his brother. "Hey, you owe me a shirt."

Benny walked over to the destroyed doorway and stopped

at the threshold. He had never felt so helpless, lost in an abyss where life and death made no sense. His nephews were monsters, and he wondered how he could ever hope to keep the promise he made to his sister to look after them. Just watching the two of them goof around on the way to the car after murdering two men in cold blood made his skin crawl. He could still hear the banter between them.

Jim made a loud belch. "You're welcome."

James flipped his middle finger at him. "Welcome? For what, bro?"

"What do you mean, for what?" Jim repeated in an incredulous-sounding voice. "For saving your damn skin back there, that's what!"

James blew childish kisses at Jim. "Then I guess that makes you my hero."

Jim nodded. "Damn right I am."

The brothers climbed into the car, still arguing back and forth with each other. James stuck his arm out the driver side window and waved for Benny to hurry up.

Benny took a deep breath, took a tentative step out the door, and then started to head toward the car. A horn honked, and Benny jumped back just in time to avoid being hit by a pizza delivery truck. The driver craned his neck and looked with eyes wide as dinner plates at Benny and the shot up door behind him.

Oh, hell no, Benny thought. He committed the license plate to memory. *I am not going down for this.*

The young man driving the truck snapped his head forward, as if trying to pretend that he had not seen anything.

Benny shuffled across the parking lot, though he knew the truck would be too long gone to catch. Tomorrow was a completely new day to fix things.

The truck's engine roared to life seconds later. The truck bounced over the curb and raced around the nearest corner, disappearing from sight.

Trent entered the front doors of the city's public indoor shooting range with an anxious skip in his step, upbeat and ready to shoot up a roll of figures drawn on paper. A man born possessed with many hidden talents, a few of which he took great pride in, his skill as a sharpshooter easily surpassed that of the majority of people raised around guns. Even though he had dabbled in countless hobbies, no other activity filled him with the same sort of grandiose satisfaction or palpable sense of personal security than the empowering feel of a handgun gripped in his hand as he fired a perfectly placed bullet in the heart of a paper silhouette target hanging forty feet away.

The front doors closed behind him with a faint *whoosh* of air, followed by the single click of doors snapping together as they aligned.

Trent tightened his fingers around the ivory handle of the gun case that contained a Smith & Wesson .357; a Glock 9 mm, and his pride and joy, a Colt .45 Gold Cup. He had qualified as an expert in all three calibers the previous year. A slow grin touched his lips at the soft pops of other gun enthusiasts firing their weapons of choice from behind sealed doors built to suppress the loud report of all firearms permitted for practice in the building. For reasons he had not yet come to understand, the sound of discharged weapons always brought him a sense of peace.

A familiar warmth filled him, and he picked up his pace down the carpeted floor of the hallway that led to the reservation desk located in the center of the large structure, which served as the nexus for the other six hallways fanning out in different directions.

He grinned at the friendly face of Gloria, who sat in the center of the half-moon-shaped counter, as he narrowed the distance separating them. She rose from a chair hidden behind the height of the desk and returned his grin, waving her hand for him to hurry up. The visor of the hat atop her head, adorned with an NRA patch stitched across the front, did little to shade the spark of light behind her pale green eyes. Her brown T-shirt had the same three letters stenciled across the right pocket, which left a clear and distinct message of her position on the Second Amendment.

Trent stopped at her desk just as a patron of the range opened a door on the left side of the counter and exited the hallway marked section E. The roar of guns blazing from the cubicles on either side of the hallway that stretched for twenty-five yards erupted inside the reception area. The door then shut and muffled the noise with a resounding click, not unlike the one that came from the front doors. He had frequented the shooting range every Thursday for the past twenty-four months, having never missed a day since his first, so he was mildly surprised to find Gloria working on a Saturday morning.

He placed the case on top of the counter, unsnapped the clasp on either side, opened the lid, and then turned it to allow her to inspect the contents. "Nice to see you, Gloria," he greeted warmly. "I wasn't expecting to see you today." He made a thin line with his lips. "Are you normally weekend staff?"

She cast her gaze downward toward the three guns inside the case. "Good to see you too." Her eyes ticked back and forth. "One of the girls got sick last night, probably partying too much, and so here I am." She closed the lid and pushed it toward him. "I'm not complaining though. We can use the overtime pay. Things at home are getting a little tight, with all this economy stuff circling the drain."

Trent snapped the clasps closed. "So, how are the kids and Burt?" he said. "I haven't seen him for quite some time now."

"They're doing pretty good, thanks for asking." A hint of relief emanated from her voice. She continued. "Ever since the quarry reopened and rehired him, he's been in high spirits." She rapped her knuckles softly on the wooden top of the counter, and her face softened. "Burt wanted me to thank you for drafting that codicil thingy for his mother's estate. We would never have thought about needing something like that to protect her from those insurance parasites had you not reviewed it for us."

Trent nodded gravely, treading lightly into a delicate subject. "How is your mom?"

She took a deep breath, sighing. "As well as can be expected, I guess," she said softly. "The chemotherapy isn't really working all that great anymore, and I think she's just tired of living in pain, ready to move onto greener pastures." Her shoulders lifted. "That's what she likes to say, anyhow. I guess I see her point. This is the fourth round of them, and she knows the hospital bills are not slowing down. I have made my peace with everything, and the doctors are not very optimistic. They estimate she has only a few more months left. It has been coming for quite some time. She's a tough ol' bird, but I think she has lost the will to fight something she cannot beat. I don't blame her."

"I'm really sorry to hear that," he said. His history with personal loss surfaced with a sharp sting. "If there is anything I can do, please do not hesitate to ask."

"We appreciate that, Trent."

He looked around at the empty section of the building, deciding to change the subject. "You don't seem to have much traffic for a weekend," he commented. "Are you normally this slow on a Saturday?"

"We get a few here and there." Her voice had lost its spark. "More will show up after lunch."

He made a wry grin. "Is there anyone I should keep an eye on for the upcoming competition?" he said. "I plan on winning the club championship this year. I'm tired of taking second and third." He looked at the club's trophy case pressed against the wall. He had coveted the club's 'Best Shot' cup sitting atop the top shelf, in between several small honors plated in gold, since he'd first seen it.

A mischievous smile slowly crept across Gloria's face. She tapped her chin with a single finger. "As a matter of fact, we do have a member who would give anyone a serious run for his or her money." Her voice was an awed hush. "Today is the first time I've seen the gentleman in question for several months, and he has never actually competed in any of our members only competition. I don't know why he doesn't compete in any of the contests. If he ever did decide to throw a cartridge into the hat, I doubt any of the trophies would stay in our possession. My Burt is good, but this guy makes him look like an amateur."

Trent furrowed his brow. He was unaware that any member with such skill belonged to the club and soured at the idea that another member might steal his glory for a third time. "Is he really that good a shot?" he said, dubious. People often exaggerated. "What's his target percentage?"

Her lips puckered, whistling at his question. "Through the roof," she said in a firm voice. "The guy doesn't seem to pay attention to accuracy results. He once told me that they don't truly measure a shooter's skill. I asked him what he meant by that, but he merely smiled at me with the strangest gleam in his eye." She placed a hand over her heart. "Personally, I have never seen him miss. The man is lethally accurate with every class of handgun."

Trent licked his lips at the intimidating assertions she had just made. She had made the man sound more like a machine. "Every class?" he repeated numbly. "How is that even possible? No one is that damn good with a gun, certainly not all of them."

"I don't know what to tell you, Trent." She held up her hands. "The guns just seem like extensions of his body, part of his hands."

"His hands?" He repeated.

She nodded. "He's just as good with his left as he is with his right." Her voice was firm. "I've watched him switch hands in the middle of firing off a single magazine. I've watched him fire two guns at the same time with perfect accuracy."

"You're kidding."

"As I've said, you just have to watch him in action." Her voice was dead serious. "He is hell on wheels with a gun, and it is very humbling to see anyone shoot the way he does, even the way he practices. Everything he does is very unorthodox."

Trent knitted his brow. He wanted to know more about the stranger. Practice was simply practice, in his opinion. "What do you mean?"

"It is something you just have to see for yourself." Her voice stammered. "I cannot really explain it. He does some kind of quick draw thing from off the counter, where he does this—" She flashed out her right hand and slapped it against the counter to demonstrate.

Intrigued by the mystery that seemed to surround the unnamed man with lightning quick reflexes, Trent placed his elbows on top of the gun case and leaned forward. He looked her straight in the eye. "Who is this guy?" he said. "What's his name?"

"Dominique Cieo."

Trent straightened up at the mention of such a notorious name in the city. Very few weeks passed without a mention in some byline of his name. The government had been after Dominique Cieo for years, attempting and failing to get an indictment on twelve separate occasions, and there was little doubt that any criminal defense attorney did not know the name that belonged to the chief enforcer for Antony Viscotti—the most powerful crime boss in the United States. In just the past few years, many unconfirmed rumors had circulated about the organization's chain of command, which supported the idea that Antony Viscotti had finally stepped down from running the vast criminal empire, while strategically placing the reins in his protégé's capable hands.

Despite the savage stories that surrounded Dominique Cieo's meteoric rise in the criminal underworld, ripe opportunity knocked at the back of Trent's head. *I could really find a connection with him helpful.*

A light sparked in Gloria's eyes. "So, I see you recognize the name." She reached under the counter and produced a green tablet.

"Who wouldn't?" he said, incredulous. "The man is practically a celebrity in this town. He's like Teflon, and no one in the prosecutor's office has been able to touch him. He is supposed to be some kind of genius—a Harvard graduate who chose a life of crime. He's an interesting character."

"I suppose." She seemed unimpressed. "Be careful about the company you choose to keep, Trent. He and his kind bite, and they bite hard. The papers have called him a ruthless killer."

Trent shrugged his indifference. "The papers write a great many things," he said with a snort of derision, "most of them lies. They do not report news. They make it."

"Perhaps," she offered drily. "I don't really read or listen to the news."

"Is he receptive?"

"He's not impolite, if that's what you mean?"

"You got me curious."

She opened the green tablet. "Shall I give you a nearby cubicle in the same hallway?" Her voice was almost teasingly playful. "It's clear on your face that you know exactly who he is. I rather figured you would. You sure do act like some kind of danger junkie at times. It's kind of odd for an attorney."

"I'm a little surprised that someone like that, with so many enemies in the world, would risk coming to a public place like this," he said. Her shoulders shrugged, and he continued. "It just seems a little dangerous for him to come out and expose himself to someone who might try to kill him."

A tiny laugh fell from her lips. "Someone kill that guy?" She practically choked on each syllable. "Trust me, Trent. No one is going to screw with Dominique Cieo at a place where there are guns everywhere. That would be like attacking a damn shark in the warm waters of the Atlantic Ocean. There is just something about the man when you look into his eyes. There is something dark and severely dangerous in them. You will know what I am saying when you see him face-to-face and talk to him. I swear there's the devil in him."

"So, what are you saying?" Trent now felt confused by her words. "Are you saying that he's aggressive and mean—that he'll try to hurt me here?"

She shook her head. "Not at all," she said. "He's very cultured, polite, and extremely soft spoken, all of which seems to only make the air around him feel that much more lethal. Believe me when I say that you will see what I mean, if and when you meet the man."

Trent slid the gun case from off the counter and turned. He was now more anxious than ever to meet the notorious gunslinger.

"Go to hallway F." Her voice remained gentle, friendly, and partially amused. "I'll buzz you in. Take cubicle nine, two squares away from where he is now practicing. I'll hit your lights from here."

Trent shuffled over to the door and pulled it open at the sound of the buzz.

Inside the inner sanctum of hallway F, Trent heard the familiar *whoosh* of air and click of the door locking closed behind him as he strolled down the corridor. Odd numbered cubicles were located on the right, the even numbered on the left. Bright overhead lights lined the ceiling, allowing no shadows to hide from such brilliance in any corner. The loud report of guns rang out in differentiating volumes, depending on which caliber of gun the individuals were firing. Other than people practicing with their weapons, nothing out of the ordinary sounded from any of the spaces tucked to the sides of the hallway, hidden away from anyone traveling toward his or her assigned area until he or she reached it.

On the left, Trent passed a woman in cubicle three who was inexpertly holding a Raven .25 and missing most of the silhouette target hanging near the far wall. Standing opposite, an overweight man was firing a Smith & Wesson .38 with little more success than the woman firing the Raven.

Trent paused behind cubicle six and watched a petite brunette fumble with a speed loader on what he believed was a .41-caliber Smith & Wesson. She could not have weighed more than a hundred pounds, and he wondered which unethical gun dealer had duped her into buying such a monstrous weapon. The recoil was something he had experienced only once before permanently swearing off such a beast.

As if she sensed someone was watching her from behind, she suddenly whipped her head around. Her eyes narrowed at him, shooting daggers at him. Bullets slipped free from the cylinder and hit the rubber mat on which she stood with six dull thuds.

Trent shifted his feet and grimaced with embarrassment for getting caught staring at her.

"Look at what you made me do!" Her voice matched her tiny body. Her lips pulled back into a snarl. "Don't you have something better to do than stalk women from the shadows and stare at their butts?"

Trent tipped his head with an apologetic grin. He had come to the range to help unwind his frayed nerves, and he certainly did not intend to create a scene at one of his favorite places. "I am sorry," he said sincerely. He tried to think up a quick cover story and then continued. "I did not mean to interrupt you. I was impressed with the speed in which you were moving when changing cylinders." He wondered if his phony compliment sounded as lame to her as it did to him.

She straightened up immediately, removing the hearing protection headphones from her head. She tossed them on the counter. "What did you say?" Her voice was sharp.

"I said that I was sorry for disturbing you," he said. "I was just watching you try to handle that cannon. That is a .41, isn't it?"

Her head moved up and down, mistrustful. "Yeah, that's right."

"I thought so," he said conversationally. "I tried to fire one of those calibers just once, and I never gave it another chance to break my elbow off again."

Her lips curled up into a faint smile, and the corners around her eyes softened. She set the enormous gun on the counter, next to the headphones. "No. Please accept my apologies for barking at you." A note of regret touched her voice. "I was frustrated long before you showed up, and I dropped everything because I can be such a klutz. This gun has driven me crazy. The jerk at the gun shop said it was the homemaker's best tool for home protection, but I am starting to think the guy lied to me. It kicks like a mule, nearly pulled my shoulder out of joint, and I cannot hit the broadside of a barn with it. Do you know anything about guns? This is my first one."

"I know a little about them," he admitted. "I'm far from an expert, but you don't need a professional to tell you that the jerk who sold you that gun lied through his teeth. A better fit for you would be something more like a .380, maybe a nine millimeter. You have no need for more firepower at home. Both guns have enough knockdown impact, and you will be able to hit what you are shooting at. I don't think it does any good to have a cannon if you can't hit anything with it."

An embarrassed, lopsided grin replaced the original smile on her mouth. "You got that right." She picked up her gun. "If you will please excuse me, I need to go have a little talk with the guy who screwed me over."

"I hate it when that happens," he said with a faint chuckle as she headed for the exit.

"Me too," she called over her shoulder, pushing the bar that released the auto lock on the door.

Trent turned and resumed his short journey to cubicle nine. *I would not want to be that guy.*

Having reached his destination without further delay, Trent set his gun case on the counter. He slid free the acoustic earmuffs from a hook on the wall and draped them around the back of his neck.

He then opened the lid. He removed the Glock, enjoying the feel of it in his hand as he admired the expertly engineered piece of weaponry. In his opinion, there were few guns made as well, and he would challenge anyone to show him a better all-around gun. He slid a magazine home and had started to raise the headphones over his ears when he heard rapid fire erupt from a different cubicle on his left. He could not be exact on the number, but he was relatively sure the shooter had just fired eleven consecutive rounds. Three seconds later another volley of rounds exploded inside the area. Then in half that time, a third series of rounds exploded. Each set of rounds sounded like different calibers, smallest to largest. The first face and name that entered his mind after hearing the repetitive blaze of gunfire belonged to his childhood hero "Wild Bill" Hickok.

Trent's curiosity about the identity of the shooter refused to let go, which made it impossible for him to concentrate on his own practice so that he could clear his mind of the last few days. The stress of what he had done only seemed to escalate with each passing hour. Even his now deceased brother-in-law's face had visited him on several unwanted occasions, leaving a permanent black mark on their shared memories. The more he tried to convince himself that he did not care, the worse his conscience niggled at him.

After several unsuccessful minutes of trying to exorcise the demons unwilling to loosen their stranglehold on his mind, Trent finally laid the Glock back into the molded cradle inside the case and went to find Dominique Cieo to see if he actually lived up to the reputation Gloria had built. Trent considered his skills near the level of a professional, and the only member who had beaten him consistently for the past two years was the resident professional, who had competed against the best in the world for the past twenty years.

Trent found a well-dressed Dominique Cieo standing alone in cubicle eleven. His back was turned, shoulders firm, and legs apart a foot and a half. Although the ensemble he wore appeared in juxtaposition to the environment inside the shooting range, Cieo wore everything with a definitive style of confidence. A strange kind of raw dangerousness emanated from the way he stood with his back ramrod straight. The exotic Anaconda boots on his feet only added a feral quality to the fashionable designer pants and sport coat. An assortment of handguns, a few Trent did not recognize as commonly sold to the public, were spread out across the counter like fanned cards on the green felt of a poker table. A bleach white handkerchief was held almost daintily in his gloved hand as he gingerly wiped down the blue steel barrel of a gun Trent assumed he had just finished emptying.

Cieo shifted his feet, his hand stopping its action.

Trent looked up at the silhouette still hanging in the distance, near the back wall and widened his eyes at the impressive grouping of bullet holes in the target. Cieo had shot out three distinct patches with diameters of one inch with undeniable precision. Trent had never seen such consistent accuracy.

"Are you going to simply stand there, or are you going to properly introduce yourself?" Cieo's voice was deep and menacing. His back remained turned to Trent. "I consider it bad form to stare over another's shoulder without proper introduction." His voice paused. "Do you not agree? I do not and cannot abide by bad form."

Trent cleared his throat. "Indeed," he said. "I meant no offense, Mr. Cieo. My name is Trent Varus."

Cieo gently set his gun down on the counter. His movements were uncommonly graceful, sleek, and something else Trent could not quite describe. "I have heard of you, Mr. Varus." His voice remained cold, apathetic. It was the voice you might imagine coming from the bottom of a tomb. "Your reputation as the defender of the persecuted precedes you."

"Thank you," he began, "I think."

"You are welcome." Cieo turned and faced Trent. His eyes were black as midnight, eerie and depthless, a perfect match for his voice. His features were hard, as if carved from granite. "As you apparently already know, my name is Dominique Cieo." He held out a hand gloved in lambskin. "It is a pleasure to make your acquaintance, Mr. Varus."

Trent accepted the outstretched hand, surprised by the strength in the man's grip. "The pleasure is all mine, Mr. Cieo," he said. "So, how did you happen across familiarity with my profession?" Cieo's hand relaxed, and Trent slid his free.

Cieo's mouth formed a cruel smile that held no humor. "I have a great many friends who tell me many important matters involved with our fine city." His voice held no warmth. "I do not necessarily want them, but I do nevertheless have them." His shoulders lifted. "Sometimes they are useful; most times they are not." He brushed his fingers across the front of his jacket.

Trent could not help but to chuckle at the sly play on words. "What are useless," he said and then added slowly, "the friends or the information?"

The corner of Cieo's right lip curled up, giving his face a creepy veneer. "Touché, Mr. Varus. You are a clever man, and I think I like you. You say what you mean and mean what you say. That is a refreshing change for me. I believe my employer would like you as well."

Trent decided to take a chance and test the depth of dangerous waters further. Dominique Cieo intrigued him. There was little about the man that struck him as usual, far different from what he had been expecting. He also felt an odd sense of kinship with him. "By employer, don't you mean, Mr. Viscotti?"

Cieo's eyes now sparked with genuine humor. "I see you have some similar friends." He chuckled. "I find such coincidences very quaint and curious."

Trent returned his attention on the silhouette. "Gloria was definitely right about your skill with a gun."

"Was she now?"

Trent nodded, pointing at the silhouette. "Bullet holes don't lie," he said with conviction. "But why don't you compete in the tournaments? From the look of things, you would sweep all of us."

"I do not find sport in shooting targets for trophies or the adoration of dizzy fans."

"So then that makes you a hunter. Am I right?"

"A hunter, you ask." He said the words with inflection and then paused as if contemplating an appropriate answer. "Yes. I suppose that such an inference might be drawn, Mr. Varus." He tapped his chin with a finger. "What about you?"

Trent furrowed his brow. "What about me?" he said.

"Are you a hunter as well?"

He shook his head. "No. Not really."

"Are you sure?" His voice turned almost playful. "I'm quite certain you have hunted one type of beast or another. You have that look in your eyes."

Trent blinked. He was surprised Cieo had switched roles in the conversation so smoothly. He had to retake control or risk estrangement. He now suspected Cieo held intelligence in high esteem, in fact respected it above most other things. "What kind of game do you hunt?" he asked.

"I hunt a great many things, depending on the circumstances." Cieo's voice was smooth as glass. "Perhaps, if at all possible, we might schedule a hunt together and see if we mesh well in the field." He peeled back the edge of the left glove and stole a quick glance at his wristwatch. "Well, it is getting late, and I have an appointment that must be kept. Please excuse my bad manners for leaving so hastily." He gathered up his weapons and placed them in a pair of matching gun cases stacked beneath the counter.

Trent removed a business card from his pocket and held it out. Cieo politely accepted it, studying it for several silent seconds before slipping it into his pocket. The man was definitely an anomaly, someone who seemed completely out of place, out of time. Something deep down in Trent's gut told him that it would be good to have such a powerful friend. "I really enjoyed speaking with you, Mr. Cieo," he said. "I would definitely like to pick up from where we started." He grinned. "Besides, I could certainly use some pointers from an expert shot."

"I just may take you up on that." Cieo's voice was amicable. He closed the lids. "But please, call me Dom. All my friends do."

"I'll do that, Dom," he said. "But only if you call me by my first name."

His head tilted. "Agreed. Trent it is."

Trent stepped aside and allowed plenty of room for his new friend to pass unencumbered.

The minute Detective Erik Lomax received the call reporting the discovery of two dead bodies in the eastern part of town, near the off-ramp of Euclid Avenue, he had no reason to second-guess the place and circumstances before dispatch revealed the next grisly detail. In the course of his career, the underlying reasons for most killings in that area rarely varied, whether he bothered to scribble down the supposed motive on a report.

The city's murder rates had skyrocketed so that murders were as commonplace as taking out the trash.

Either a drug robbery ended in murder or an act of revenge was behind it; neither scenario was worthy of much attention from the media, or anyone else for that matter. Deep down, no one actually cared about some dead junkie or poison peddler. Good and decent people were struggling just to make ends meet. With crime the new American pastime, bad people shooting other bad people barely warranted a footnote at the bottom of page thirty in the local rag. As far as the public was concerned, it made no real difference if the authorities made an arrest, particularly since every decent, law-abiding person in the city knew instinctively to avoid, at all cost, that section of town. Nothing positive had ever happened on the east side.

With a grunt of irritation, Lomax hung up the phone and leaned back in his chair. His investigatory plate was already abundantly full, not to mention that he now unofficially worked for the captain as some sort of mercenary mole burrowing into the secret machinations of the life of the recently dead Callahan. He stretched out his neck to rid it of a cramp, grumbling under his breath at the unsavory thought of getting up.

He rubbed his meaty palms into weary eyes. He harbored little doubt, no matter what he discovered, that his investigation would naturally equate to a huge waste—of both his time and his already scarce resources—probably at his expense as well. He had little chance of having the department reimburse him for incurred expenses, not when his spy routine fell off the books.

He scratched his head, dreading another day spent fishing in the cesspool of dirty politics. *Aw, shit,* he thought wearily. *What'd I get myself into now?* He knew that he did not require the use of a Magic 8 Ball to know why the captain had covertly assigned him to go spelunking around the former district attorney's business.

There could be only one reason—to gather enough ammunition to cover his ass and get out from under suspicion if Internal Affairs uncovered evidence that proved Callahan's office guilty of corruption.

Finally, Lomax gave his stomach a last rub and stood up from the chair. He took a quick look around, before heading off to pay another visit to the armpit of his once proud city.

Fifteen minutes later, Lomax steered his car into the hotel parking lot. He was not the least bit surprised to find only a skeleton crew of police officers present at the scene of the crime. In contrast to the circus that took place at the Callahan residence, the handful of officers standing around with their hands shoved down into their pockets looked bored and lifeless. The looks on their faces made it clear that none of them wanted anything to do with a couple of homeless stiffs lucky enough to get their brains blown across a feces-covered wall. Even the raggedly dressed homeless people milling about the street acted as if they had better things to do than gawk at another blood-spattered room. If they had seen it once, no doubt they had seen it a hundred times. The death of one of their own was no big whoop, just another miserable day of their lives spent in a brave new world that spat them out like giant phlegm balls.

Lomax parked his car, struggled to get out with another heavy grunt, and then lit a cigarette without wasting a beat. He smiled at the all-inspiring flavor. Warm smoke filled his blackened lungs with all the sensual pleasure Joe Camel had always promised in long restricted ads. *They are even picking on you, my cylindrical friend,* he thought. *Now, that is a real shame.* He took another heavy drag, flicked the cigarette away, and walked toward the room.

Outside, a uniformed officer sat on the hood of a squad car. Lomax recognized him from the precinct.

He stopped a few feet from the car. "Hey, Pete," he said. "What do you have for me today?"

Pete threw a thumb at a room. "Two vics, boss." His tone was causal, disinterested. "It looks like both were shot with a cannon." His shoulders shrugged. "My guess is it's a soured dope deal—nothing new, same old crap." He yawned. "But it is messier than the norm."

"What makes you think it was over a dope deal?"

His hand moved across his mouth. "We got an ID on one of the motel dregs." He spoke through another yawn. "Darnel Washington. He goes by the name of Tinker on the street. I've busted him once or twice. He has a long sheet on everything. We're still checking to ID the other lowlife."

"Do you have any witnesses?"

His head shook. "Not a single one. Imagine that." He smirked. "A cannon booms, and no one hears a damn thing. Apparently, everyone sleeps like the dead around here. A lot of them are off visiting their mommas and whatnot."

Lomax glanced around at the cracked-out looking faces peeking around the side of stained curtains inside the other rooms and then ducking back into the shadows of their holes like scared rabbits. "I see," he mumbled. "No one ever sees or hears anything around here." He craned his neck. "What about the checkout office guy? Have you spoken to him about who rented the room?"

"We decided to leave that up to you, Lomax." His voice turned dull. "This is homicide's turf, not ours. I am just window dressing. We secured the scene and the manager on duty for you. We figured you would want first crack at him. I'm just a regular beat cop dispatch redirected for garbage pickup. I guess I should not cruise so close to this rat hole. Now I know."

Lomax patted Pete on the shoulder. "You did good," he said. "Thanks."

Pete climbed down from the car and brushed at the front of his pants. "I aim to please, Detective." He checked his watch for the time. "Not to be a stiff on the job, but do you need me for anything else? I ended my double, and I'm pretty damn tired."

Lomax raised a hand. "I'm good, Pete," he said. "Go home and get some z's. You've earned them."

Relief covered his tired face. "G'night then, Lomax."

Lomax turned and withdrew a pen and a pad of paper. He walked into the motel room, stopping after taking only three steps. Pete had not been kidding about the mess. The room inside looked as if a red tornado had swept across the floor and walls. Blood was everywhere, and he did not need a forensic report to determine that both men had died by close-range shotgun blasts. Conventional bullets did not cause so much mess.

A team of crime scene investigators shuffled on busy feet about the room, taking pictures of the bodies at multiple angles, as well as the bloodstained floor, walls, and ceiling. They acted like emotionless robots on a mission, each contributing a special skill to fulfill a common purpose. No one on the team spoke a single word, enraptured only with documenting and collecting evidence relevant to solving a puzzle. One by one, each investigator systematically tagged evidentiary exhibits with a yellow cone adorned with a specific number. So far, at his count, they had laid thirty-four individual markers across the floor. Lomax recognized only one investigator inside the room, a fiery redhead by the name of Becky Swanson who epitomized professional competence.

Thank God for small favors, he thought, relieved to find at least one familiar face in the crowd, someone who exuded genius in forensic science.

Lomax stepped to the side. He knew that it was best to stay out of the team's way until after the investigators had finished noting and processing crucial evidence from the scene. Although science had evolved into an invaluable tool in solving crime, Lomax still believed it would never serve as a viable substitution for years of on-the-job experience and wisdom. Forensic evidence did not reveal motive, and gut instinct about a clue or a suspect were things not found under a microscope.

After five minutes, Lomax finally cleared his throat and shattered the think tank's concentration. "So, who do you think bought it first?" he said, directing his question to no one in particular. "Anyone have any ideas?"

Everyone dressed in white stopped what he or she was doing and leered at him, apparently for ruining the scientific mood in the room.

He grinned as Becky Swanson lowered her clipboard. She then craned her neck and stared at him with emerald green eyes. Her hair blazed fiery red. A Cheshire grin tugged at the corners of her mouth. Two dimples appeared on freckled cheeks. "Although it's inconclusive at this time, Detective Lomax," she began in a professional tone of voice, rising from one knee as gracefully as she spoke, "based on the physical evidence of the door, the trajectory and blood spatter read in conjunction with one another, I believe our first victim was closest to the door." She pointed at the dead body. "He took at least one twelve-gauge blast to the head while in the vertical position. In support of this conclusion, tissue and brain matter splashed the wall. The second victim was subsequently shot while in a lower position to the shooter, likely in the kneeling position." She mimicked the shooter's stance, angling a phantom gun in the downward position.

"So, off the record, an execution of sorts," he said.

She shrugged, noncommittal.

"Do you have an opinion as to how many shooters are involved?"

Her brow knitted. "Not at this time." She appeared disappointed in her inability to answer his question. "It is still premature." She turned to the rest of the team and jutted out her chin. "However, we do expect to resolve it by day's end."

Her team members offered a tight set of constipated-looking grins and nodded.

"Excellent," he said. Lomax was confident in their collective abilities to ferret out all the facts and have them soon delivered. "I have no doubts that you and your team will figure everything out. I look forward to reading your reports, Dr. Swanson."

With a final nod, Becky lifted her clipboard and turned her attention back on the scene to resume her work.

Satisfied that everything was under control and in the right hands, Lomax stepped out of the stuffy motel room and stopped dead in his tracks at the unexpected sight of Pete sitting on the hood of his police car. "I thought you were supposed to go home and get some sleep, Pete," he said. "No offense, buddy, but you look like hell, even worse than the first time I saw you."

Pete's right eye opened. He sat up, stretched out his arms. "The watch commander told me and Judy to hang tight until our relief shows up." His head twisted about his neck to work out the kinks.

Lomax grimaced at him. "Sorry about that, pal." He looked up and down the front sidewalk that ran parallel to the rooms. "Where did you guys store that motel clerk? I forgot to ask you."

His neck craned to the right, pointing a finger in the same direction. "Oh, yeah," he said, his voice now groggy. He scratched his head. "I forgot all about that toadstool. My partner Judy is with that cockroach. They're in the manager's office." He jumped down from the car and started to walk away, toward the far end of the building. "Come on, I'll take you to him. My ass is going numb, and I have to do something to get the blood moving again."

Lomax followed Pete down the concrete path and stopped in front of the only blue painted door in the building. A large square sign with the words 'Manager's Office' sloppily scribbled in magic marker hung crookedly on it.

They entered without knocking.

Lomax found Officer Judith Klein sitting on an old dusty couch. She was reading a week-old newspaper. Appearing equally exhausted and bored as her partner, she looked up at the sound of the tinkling bell that hung from a yo-yo string attached to a metal bar that ran across cracked glass.

On her left, a man dressed in what must pass for motel attire sat on a rusty kitchen chair. His disheveled appearance made it obvious that personal hygiene did not rate at the top of his list of priorities. His fetid body odor filled the tiny office space with a stench strong enough to qualify as one of the seven plagues in ancient Egypt. Lomax felt his stomach lurch, nauseated.

In an instant, the clerk jumped to his feet and moved his arms about the air, pinwheeling them in what looked like misplaced panic. "Man, it's 'bout friggin' time." His voice mixed with a smoker's cough. "I've been waiting here for friggin' ever. I got things to do, and I ain't getting fired from my job over this bullshit. I need this job, or my PO will violate me and send me back to prison."

Judy rolled up the newspaper, shot up from the chair, and then swatted the clerk over the head. "I told you to shut the hell up, Ely, and stay in your chair!" A vein bulged in the side of her neck. "I'm sick of your crap. If I have to tell you just one more time, I'm going to Taser your stinky ass and call it a day."

His eyes narrowed. "You can't threaten me, Five-O," Ely protested. "That's a terrorist threat, a crime against my personality."

She struck him again. "Shut up!" A grimace suddenly covered her face—apparently, she had gotten a whiff of him—and she took two steps back. "Good lord, you smell like shit! There are inventions, stinky, called deodorant, and soap. Why don't you try using them for once in your worthless life?" She then fanned the air with the newspaper. "And brush your damn teeth, for Christ's sake. Your mouth smells like a damn cat box."

"Hey, that's decimation of character, pig!"

"Shut up!"

"I'm a taxpayer," he countered in an angry tone. "You work for me. I'm the victim, and I got fortieth 'mendment rights."

A heavy sigh of weariness slipped from between her lips, as she turned and looked at her partner for help with the man.

Lomax grumbled under his breath. He had just arrived, and he was already sick and tired of listening to the uncontrolled rants of some freebasing crackhead. He watched Pete take four quick steps toward Ely, forcibly shoving him back down into the chair.

"You'll have the Fortieth Amendment right to a coroner if you don't shut the hell up and answer our questions." His nose wrinkled up against the foul assault that defied description. His fingers wrapped around the end of his nightstick, and he sneered down at Ely.

Ely's eyes went wide, cringing away in fear. "It's cool, ossifer." His words came out with a whine. "There's no reason to get all pissed off and vi'lent. I feel ya, and I'll co'perate with you. No problem." His head dropped down into his shoulders.

The officers exchanged humored grins.

Pete's grip slackened on the nightstick, and he backed up. "He's all yours, Detective." Relief filled his voice.

Large beads of sweat broke out across Ely's forehead. Dark pit stains expanded across his yellowish shirt. His eyes darted back and forth, from Judy to Pete and then back to Judy. Fear of the unknown practically dripped from his pores.

Lomax stepped forward. He suddenly stopped as if a truck filled with manure had just hit him head-on. The putrid odor wafting up from the clerk reminded him of a partially decomposed body he had fished out from under a huge pile of soggy garbage tossed in the city dump two years earlier. Unable to bear the stench, he backed up a step. The unwashed clerk may have smelled worse than the rotting corpse. It had definitely smelled fresher. His stomach did an Olympic-style flip-flop.

Judy lowered her face into her hand, muffling a small giggle. Pete did likewise.

Lomax took another step back, moving outside the vortex of stale body odor. "What's your name?" he said.

"I take the Eleventh 'mendment right, the right to discriminate myself." His voice was dead serious.

Again, Judy swatted him over the head. "Answer the damn question, Ely, you stupid crackhead!" Her face turned red, clearly showing her loss of patience with the burnout.

Ely veered away from the newspaper. "Hey, take it easy, lady cop. I weren't dis'prectful to you."

"Name?" Lomax repeated.

Ely's hands shot up. "Okay, okay. Ely Barnes." His head shook. "I didn't do nothin' to no one."

Lomax leveled a cruel set of eyes on Ely, moving closer to him. He playfully slapped him on the cheek. "See, you can help us," he said with a growl. "So, when did you get to work?"

"I got here about six last night." The words came out with a stammer. His head now pressed against the back of the wall.

Lomax nodded approvingly. "Good. Now, we're getting real progress."

"Uh-huh."

"Did you see or hear anything, like gunshots?"

His lips pressed together. "I don't know nothing." His eyes went wide in fear.

Lomax lifted an eyebrow, snickered softly. "That has yet to be determined," he said. "You keep a guest sign-in book, don't you?"

Ely sat up straight in the chair. "Um, yeah, I do." He moved to stand, but Judy flashed out a hand and forced him back down. His eyes looked over at her. "I wasn't gonna do nothin'. The book's behind the counter. I was just—"

Lomax raised a yielding hand and walked behind the counter. "It's all right, Mr. Barnes," he said. "Just sit tight. I'll get the book." He kneeled and searched the shelves, disappearing from the others' sight.

"Second shelf," Ely offered. "It's the big blue one."

"So it is." Lomax rose and placed the book on the cheap Formica top. Yellow water stains covered the front of it. A funky sort of smell drifted up.

"That's the book." A grin crossed Ely's face.

Lomax grimaced, wishing he had saved his gloves from the earlier crime scene. *This is so gross.* He opened the book, flipping through the pages until he came to yesterday's date. He frowned.

"Is something wrong, Detective?" Pete's voice was curious.

Lomax shook his head. "Which room are our stiffs in?"

"Suite twenty-two," Judy offered.

Lomax grunted. *A suite? That shithole. Give me a break.* He ran a finger down the page, stopping at number twenty-two. The name scrawled in what looked like foreign chicken scratch read Joseph Stalin. He snickered. *I thought he was dead. Hmmm.* He then scanned the entire page, smiling inwardly. *How very interesting is this.* He snapped the book closed.

Ely swallowed with an audible gulp. "Did you find what you were looking for?" His voice was a squeak.

"You don't require a driver's license to rent a room, do you?"

His milky eyes blinked. "Um—" His face went slack around the jawline.

Lomax lifted the book and grinned at the dope-addled moron. "I need to confiscate this for evidence, Mr. Barnes," he said. "I will furnish a receipt later."

Ely nodded. "Yeah, sure. Whatever you want. Take it. I don't care. It ain't mine." Panic rose in his voice. "'Sides, I don't read so good anyways." He bit down on his lower lip. "I just don't want those twin br—" His mouth practically slammed shut.

Lomax grinned at him, eyes sparkling with hunger. "Twins, huh?" he said. "Is that a fact?"

Ely's eyes watered in fear of what he had almost said. "Um—" Blood drained from his face.

"Curious," Lomax said.

Ely's chin fell to his chest.

Lomax removed a card from his shirt pocket and walked back around the counter, carrying the book as if it contained secrets to a lost treasure. He tossed his card on the counter. He did not want to risk getting within breathing distance of the foul-smelling man. "On behalf of the police department, I thank you for your time and cooperation, Mr. Barnes," he said in a surly tone. "If you remember anything, anything at all, about last night that might help us catch whoever killed those people in suite twenty-two, I want you to please call me, day or night. My number and extension are on the card."

A miserable look crossed Ely's face. "I will." His voice was that of defeat. "I per ... omise."

Lomax feigned a grateful grin. *No doubt you will, pickle brain.*

A grunt of amusement fell from Pete's mouth, and Judy turned away to hide her face.

Lomax gave a sharp salute. "That's a good citizen, Mr. Barnes," he said, "and the city appreciates your help." He then motioned for the other two officers to follow him.

Outside the office, Lomax faced Pete and Judy in the parking lot. At first, he revealed nothing to either one of them. He merely stared into their eyes, weighing their competence and intuitive abilities to see the situation for what it was. A frown masked Judy's face; an air of confusion surrounded Pete. Both shuffled their feet across the gravel pavement.

He remembered a time, long, long ago when he had been a naive, wide-eyed optimist, brainwashed by his superiors that he was instrumental in saving the world and the innocent people in it. However, over the course of time, he had discovered their words to be beyond ridiculous. No one could save the world, because the world did not want to be saved. Eventually he had evolved into little more than a soured man doing a job no one appreciated.

Life's a bitch, and then you die.

Lomax lifted his eyebrows. "Questions, class?" he said with a smirk.

Pete spoke up first. "I don't understand." His voice was firm. "Why didn't you push that doper puke into a corner and ask more questions? He has to know something. I can feel it. He's just playing dumb."

He chuckled. "Make no mistake about it," he said, "that boy is about as dumb as a bag of hair."

"Then he's hiding something." Pete's voice deepened. "You should have pushed him harder. He almost gave up the names when he made a slip—"

Lomax shook his head, disappointed in the officer. He eyed him critically. "It's too early to push hard, and it would've been counterproductive. He would have shut down."

Judy's lips pursed. "But why wait?"

"Because Ely knows exactly who killed those people, and he is scared to death," he said, holding the book up. "All the signatures in this book are in the same hand—Ely's no doubt. Except for room twenty-two, the one where our mutilated cadavers are getting tagged and bagged. I push too hard; he'll rabbit out of the city." He grinned. "You see, I'm not the one he's afraid of."

Silence filled the space between them.

Pete and Judy exchanged curious looks.

"We need to give him a minute, probably longer, to stew on things." He tucked the book under his arm. "He used the word *twins*, and I know of only one set of them who would instill that kind of fear in a career criminal."

A gleam sparked from Pete's eyes. "So, you know who did this?"

"Maybe," he said. He did not feel comfortable revealing too much information. He feared for the two beat cops' safety, in that they might try to go out and make an arrest. Neither officer was prepared to handle the pair of nightmares he suspected.

Judy brushed a loose strand of hair out of her face. "How long do we wait?"

"Just long enough for stupid in there to figure it out after we leave."

Pete's head turned. "Figure what out?"

"That he's a loose end, and the men that blew those two away with a shotgun will come back to tie things up in a tidy bow."

Slow grins formed on the officers' faces.

Lomax turned on his heels and walked toward his car to wait things out. The chase for a pair of vicious killers was now afoot, and he loved nothing more than a good hunt.

CHAPTER 9

Trent looked up at the clock on the wall for the third time since he first arrived and sighed at the late hour. He still had much to do and many promises to keep, and timing was of the essence. His whole schedule for the day was about to be thrown into a complete tailspin. A flood of hateful memories from his past spiked, as he sat forced to wait for custody staff to discharge its duty.

With a disgruntled growl of irritation after waiting nearly an hour for someone in authority to tell him anything, he started to rise from the discomforts of the prison chair and make an inquiry as to the status of his prospective client's whereabouts when a burly prison guard suddenly appeared on the other side of a large plateglass window. A young man in his middle twenties stood submissively beside him.

He settled back down into the chair. *It's about damn time!* He placed his elbows on the tabletop, interlaced his fingers, and patiently waited for the guard to escort his client into the cramped space the facility utilized as their attorney-client visiting room.

Jimmy Peterson was a twenty-five-year-old man now serving a life sentence for first-degree murder. He was a first termer, never having had a previous brush with the law. Now his life was on the ropes, everything he had known crashing to earth in a heap of destroyed hopes and dreams, which left very little to salvage.

Trent had spent years hardening his heart and mind to avoid emotional attachments that adversely affected his performance and ability to focus on issues of law. There was no place in the legal profession for compassion, and he had come to believe that he'd long grown accustomed to the gaunt and sallow look on prisoners' faces.

Nevertheless, in days like today, times still occurred when that standard of practiced indifference faltered on a grand scale, and the prisoner's vacant eyes and the anemic pallor of his face pried opened the valve of bleeding heart principles and sent his repressed emotions out of control. Trent winced in empathy when the guard opened the door and rudely shoved the emaciated son of Marty and Beatrix Peterson into the room.

Trent shifted uneasily in the chair. *Why do I even come here? All it does is depress me.* He wondered if coming to prison was his subconscious mind's way of reminding him of time spent in hell on earth.

The sickly, bleached-out appearance of Jimmy Peterson's face made it clear that he had already succumbed to the daily stresses found only in the doldrums of pointless prison life. A person did not live in prison; he simply existed along its meaningless astral plane of misery. He had the same tired look Trent had seen many times in the gray reflection of a plastic mirror that had once hung on his cell wall. All dressed in the same drab prison clothes passed out in laundry, those still fighting to cling to any sense of moral decency were soon ferreted out by the unwashed population and made subject to every sadistic whim forced on them by every bottom-feeding lowlife society saw fit to spit from its presence.

A hard leer meant for Trent marked the guard's face. "Fifteen minutes, Counselor." Contempt filled his voice. "You will not be afforded one minute more. This is strictly a courtesy visit." He then shut the door with a loud click.

Jimmy's shoulders hunched at the noise, grimacing as if whipped across the back. He shuffled across the dirty floor, cleared his throat. Fear and nervousness plagued his face. "Mr. Varus?" His voice cracked. He held out a scrawny hand. "I was told that you wanted to see me."

Trent studied the young man's face for several contemplative seconds, wondering if he had ever looked so small and frail during his long incarceration. He rose from the chair and accepted his outstretched hand. "Yes, Mr. Peterson," he said in a professional tone. "My name is Trent Varus, and I am a criminal attorney. Your father contacted me, and he asked me to come and see you about your criminal case."

Life sparked behind Jimmy's eyes, hope springing from their mocha color. "He did?" His voice livened. "So, do you think you might help and get me out of this place?"

Trent sat down, motioning for Jimmy to do the same. "I didn't say that, Mr. Peterson." He knew it wise to tread carefully. The last thing he wanted to do was accidentally give someone so desperate for good news the exact opposite. "Let's not get ahead of ourselves. This is simply a consultation to get a feel for you and the peripherals of your case." He dared a grin. "I like your dad. He seems like a good, hardworking man. I respect that."

His head nodded several times. "Please, call me Jimmy."

Trent squirmed beneath the request. "O-kay," he stammered uneasily. He preferred to maintain personal detachment from his clients. No good had ever come from emotional investments. "Your father retained me to review your case."

His brow furrowed. "Okay."

"My review is now complete."

"And what do you think?"

Trent took a deep breath, wishing he had better news. His prospective client looked as if he was already living on borrowed time. "We have a major problem of timeliness and procedural bars on new claims," he said matter-of-factly.

"I don't understand." Jimmy placed his hands on the table and leaned forward. "What's time got to do with an appeal? What's a procedural bar?"

Trent rubbed his eyes with the palms of his hands. He hated this part of the conversation. The client always grew upset and complained about unfairness. No, it was not fair, he had always agreed, but it was the law. Fair and unfair had nothing to do with law, and neither did personal feelings. He had already tried several times to explain the situation to Marty Peterson, to no avail. Jimmy's father had still insisted that he go speak with his son and listen to his side of the story. Of course, Trent did not fault him. He would have demanded the same thing if he had a son in such terrible trouble.

Jimmy sniffed back tears, his shoulders trembling beneath the prison shirt's cheap cloth.

Trent slid his palms free and stole a quick glance at a pair of the saddest eyes he had ever seen. *Aw, jeez.* He remembered exactly what it felt like on the other side of the table. *Where do I begin?*

"Aren't you going to say anything?" Jimmy's voice came out with a squeak.

Trent sat up straight, exhaling a breath he had not realized he was holding. "You see, Mr. Peterson," he began in his smoothest lawyer voice, "President Clinton signed an enactment into law in 1996 called the Antiterrorism and Effective Death Penalty Act. This act established a one-year time limitation on filing habeas corpus petitions from the time the appellate court denied your direct appeal, and, if you sought review, the State Supreme Court denied your petition. The Supreme Court denied your petition for review over three years ago, so the federal court will bar those issues. We can try to file a state habeas petition in the trial court, but the courts will procedurally bar it for a similar reason." He took a deep breath and then continued. "Basically, it's avoidance and obfuscation. There are only three possible ways we can overcome a procedural bar—by demonstrating that some sort of external factor prevented you from raising a habeas corpus claim within a reasonable time, usually within a one-year period, by proving you were unaware of the facts underlying the claim, or by asserting we can prove actual innocence with new evidence. Due diligence is practically everything."

His nose wrinkled as if he had just smelled something foul. "That's a lot of *or*s and *if*s."

Trent nodded, holding his hands out to the side. "I agree,"

he said. "However, the courts almost always reject any reason offered, even a great one. They just do not give a rat's ass. Judges do not want to upset a conviction. It makes the system look bad."

Tears pooled in Jimmy's eyes as he sat in stunned silence.

Trent shrugged weakly. "I am sorry."

"But my lawyer lied to me." His voice stammered. "And he did a lousy job on my case. Have you seen the appeal that dump truck did?"

Trent fought to remain stoic, professional. "Yeah, kid," he said in a pained whisper. "I read it. It was pure garbage—something done by a first-year law student. But that doesn't matter to the court because the brief is good enough to survive collateral attack on a Sixth Amendment claim."

"But the lawyer lied to me." His voice rose in pitch. "He lied about everything."

"I don't doubt that he did," he said. "I would be surprised if he didn't lie to you, not for a second. But that won't matter either."

"Why?"

Trent sighed. He knew the kid was beginning to suck him back into the misery that defined prison life, the profound feelings of fear and hopelessness. He could not count the number of times he had contemplated suicide. The same shadow of death now flitted across Jimmy Peterson's face, through his eyes.

Jimmy sniffed back a snot bubble. "There must be a reason."

"It is your word against the lawyer's, and the judge will accept his as truth, not the version of a disgruntled malcontent now locked up in a cage," he said. "Even if the judge wanted to believe your version, we'd still have to show that the lawyer's alleged lie contributed to the verdict of guilt."

Jimmy's body folded over as if someone had just sucker punched him in the gut. "But I thought I had a right to a lawyer and a fair trial."

Trent ran a hand over his face. "Define fair, kid," he said. "There is no such thing. It is all false propaganda. You see, the misconception among the public is that you have absolute rights under the Constitution." He sucked back on his gums, thinking about what else he might offer. "Well, that's not entirely accurate. The rights you have, especially when it comes to criminal appeals and so forth, are considered violated only if you can prove that the supposed constitutional violation prejudiced the outcome as perceived by a judge. If you cannot show prejudice, then harmless error attaches, and the claim must fail. Your rights are mere by-products of demonstrative effect on the verdict."

Jimmy's face turned an angry red. "But that's insane!" His hands wildly flew up into the air. "I'm not a damn lawyer. How in the hell am I supposed to know all that legal mumbo jumbo crap?"

Trent leaned back, now exhausted. "You're not," he said, "and that's the whole point of the exercise. 'Ignorance of the law is no excuse' has taken on an entirely new dimension. What you do not know can and will literally kill you or"—he raised a finger in the air and made a sardonic grin and then finished—"get you locked up in a cage for the rest of your life. Most death penalty attorneys consider life without the possibility of parole a win for the client charged with special circumstances."

Jimmy's eyes widened in shock. "You're shitting me."

Amused at the absurdity of his assertions, he shook his head. "Nope," he said. "That's our judicial system, and it's exactly what the government wants. By the time you figure things out"—he slapped his hands together—"bam! It is now too late because the AEDPA is now in full effect, and you, my friend, are up shit creek without a paddle."

"But I'm innocent!"

"So," he countered in a bland voice.

"What do you mean *so*?"

"Can you prove it?"

"Prove what?"

"Prove that you are innocent."

"The witness lied on the stand."

He snorted his contempt at the broken judicial system. "Can you prove the witness knew he was lying at the time of testimony?" Trent paused. "If so, then can you prove the lie caused the guilty verdict?"

Jimmy's eyes opened and closed, making him appear dumbstruck. "Well, I ..." he stammered. "I, um, not exactly."

"I'll take that as a big fat negative," he said. "Just because the witness lied doesn't mean you are not guilty. I advise you to keep that in mind. A judge will most certainly remind you of that little twist of logistical law."

"But that's bullshit."

"Yup," he agreed wholeheartedly.

Jimmy's head shook, his shoulders sagged beneath the invisible burden weighing on him. "So, basically, you're telling me that I'm screwed."

"Yeah, pretty much, kid," he said and then added, "unless you know where I might be able to find some evidence that proves you are innocent."

Jimmy seemed to age right before him.

"I'm sorry, kid. I wish I had better news for you."

"It's not your fault." His voice was faint.

"I tried to explain all this to your dad, but he still wanted me to come see you." Trent felt tears threaten to rise in his eyes. "Your dad loves you, Jimmy, and he really believes you are innocent. You do know that, don't you?"

A forced grin formed on Jimmy's face, and he nodded.

Trent pulled out a business card and tossed it on the table. "I want you to think about what we discussed and talk to your dad," he urged. "I don't take lost causes for just billing purposes. However, if you and your dad understand that the odds of a judge even hearing the merits are long and both of you accept that fact, I promise to bust my ass for you. I will do everything possible to get you out of this hellhole." He stood up and held out a hand. "I know what you are going through."

Jimmy stood up, accepting his hand. "I doubt that." His face appeared forlorn. "Prison isn't even the real punishment. It is the people in here. They are worse than animals."

Trent turned and headed toward the door, stopping only a foot away. He craned his neck. "I know. I was stuck in prison for twenty years before I managed to get my conviction reversed.

I'm telling you that there is always hope—never a reason to ever give up."

Curiosity sparked in his eyes. "Was your case as bad as mine?"

He thought about the question for several seconds before answering. "On its face, worse," he finally said.

"How much is this long shot in the dark going to cost my mom and dad?"

"Quite a bit, Jimmy." Trent grew uneasy with the question and his honest answer. He understood the young man's concern over his family's financial limitations. "There is a lot involved in this kind of case. This is why I told you to talk to your dad."

"Is it more than ten thousand?"

"A lot more," he said.

A frown marked his face. "I see."

Trent gave a final wave. "Good luck, kid." He then left the visiting room and headed to the parking lot, where he had left his car.

Trent had not taken more than a dozen steps beyond the front door of the administration building when he recognized a man from his past sitting on the hood of his car. He had not yet recuperated from his frayed mental state after speaking with a young man who would probably spend the rest of his life in prison, so he slowed his pace down the walkway that led to the visitor parking lot. He certainly was in no hurry to confront a man who had been instrumental in destroying his life so long ago. Questions as to how and why Captain Mike Johnson had come to know that he was visiting the prison niggled at the back of his mind. Hanging out in a prison parking lot just seemed a little beneath a captain's pay grade.

So, now it begins.

Trent shoved his hand in his pants pocket and continued to walk toward his parked car.

Another man dressed in a suit got out of an unmarked car parked next to his and shuffled over to where Captain Johnson sat. Trent had to narrow half the distance before he finally recognized the new addition as the special prosecutor for the city, Sebastian Crue.

"This ought to be loads of fun," he mumbled, wondering whether either one of them had started to figure anything out or whether they were still clinging to the belief that some people are simply untouchable.

Captain Johnson slid off the hood. A vicious grin creased his face. Sebastian crossed his arms over his chest and leaned back against the car. A similar look was on his face.

Trent stopped five feet in front of both men. Hateful disgust filled him as he looked into a pair of faces that had haunted him for years. He slid his hands free, prepared for anything. The last two men on earth he would ever dare trust now stood directly in front of him. He watched Johnson's eyes dip to take a quick look at his hands.

Johnson's head tilted to the side, a sneer replacing the grin. "Are you still trying to save the so-called downtrodden, Varus?" His voice was filled with spite. "You really should let the police deal with such matters of justice. We know how to dole it out appropriately."

Trent faked a humorous chuckle. "I heard that, Captain," he said and then added, "only from you." He did a quick survey of the surrounding area to see if anyone else not involved in their meet was paying attention to them.

Johnson's eyes pinched at the corners. "Did you hear about our mutual friend Walter Callahan?" His voice was tight and impatient.

Trent snorted disdain. "I heard he had some sort of terrible accident," he said offhandedly, "something about him being a junkie who partied one too many times."

The captain's face turned emotionless. "I heard something like that too. I hate it when stuff like that happens. But I bet you didn't lose a wink of sleep, did you?"

"Karma can be a real bitch," Trent said. "What comes around goes around, and we all have to pay the band if we want to dance."

"So, who's your client?"

"That's privileged information."

Johnson ran a hand over his forehead. "Oh, yeah, that's right." His tone was sarcastic. "I forget about all your secrets."

"That's one interpretation," Trent offered. He scratched the side of his head. "Excuse me for being short, but is there something you want from me, or are the two of you in the habit of hanging out in parking lots waiting to pester lawyers trying to help their clients struggle free from the corrupt fingers of the police department? I'm a busy man, and I have better things to do than talk to you."

Sebastian's arms unfolded. "We want to ask you questions about your whereabouts on—" Johnson elbowed him in the side and shut him up.

Trent narrowed his eyes. "Am I under arrest for something?" he said. "If not, then you have no reason to detain me. Like I said, I have appointments."

A deep groan slipped from Johnson's throat. Anger flashed in his eyes. "If I had questions, Varus, you would know it," he snapped. "My colleague and I simply came here as a professional courtesy to warn you to leave the past exactly where it belongs. No good can come from taking matters into your own hands."

Trent stuck a single finger in the air. "First, there is nothing professional about either one of you," he said. "Second, that sounded a little like a threat."

"Not a threat, just a conveyance of concern," he said. His eyes stole a quick look over Trent's shoulder. "After all, we wouldn't want something to go wrong that lands you back into a cage, or maybe something even worse—something gravely permanent. Now, that would be a shame, don't you think?"

Trent smiled at them. "That just isn't going to happen, but I appreciate your concern for my welfare." He placed a hand over his heart. "It just gets me right here in the ol' ticker."

"I'm warning you, Varus." Johnson's voice was now cruelly serious. "Don't push the issue. We are watching you, and I will take you down and keep you down this time."

"I feel safer already," Trent said mockingly. "Now, if you will please excuse me, I am running late."

Johnson motioned for Sebastian to let him pass.

Trent got into his car and rolled down the window. "It is always a pleasure speaking with you, Captain Johnson," he said. "We will have to do it again sometime."

"Maybe sooner than you think, Varus," he said. "By the way, how is that brother-in-law of yours doing these days?"

"I wouldn't know," he said. "I haven't seen him in a coon's age."

Johnson scratched his ear. "What was his name again? Wasn't it something that started with a J, like Jarvis or Jerome?"

"His name is Sam," Trent said firmly.

"Is?" His face appeared to take on a light of innocence.

"Unless you know something I don't know."

The captain stepped out of the way, his shoulders shrugging.

Trent dropped the car in gear and drove away. The game of cat and mouse was among one of his favorites.

CHAPTER 10

Benny had admittedly made many mistakes over the years—some of which he was still paying for—but few compared to the one he had made when he'd brought his homicidal nephews to the motel with him to purchase guns and drugs. That decision had proved an epic error in judgment, one that may result in dire consequences if he did not cure the problem.

While sitting in the back of their recently stolen car—a vehicle the police could not trace to any of them—Benny glanced at his nephews and rued his decision. He scanned the street for the truck driven by the man the girl at the pizza place had so kindly identified as Theodore Stark, adding that he was currently making deliveries. Despite his misgivings about killing an innocent man, he knew he had no choice but to get rid of the only witness who had seen him at the motel. Theodore Stark may not realize the connection between the man he had seen standing outside the motel and the slaughter behind the door, but the police would soon discover his presence in the parking lot at the time of the double homicide once they started going door to door asking questions. Sometimes people did not comprehend what they knew until an outside party grabbed them by the nose and connected the dots for them.

Benny groaned his misery from the backseat, cursing his bad luck and knowing he had to find Theodore Stark before all hell broke loose. Time now worked against him, dangerously so, and he had to stop the tide, not slow it, before it crashed against the rocks of his crumbling life. This was the second time in the last two hours the three of them had circled the area, and he was also fast growing tired of listening to the mindless exchange of heated words between his idiotic nephews. Just the fact that they had argued for nearly ten minutes as to who would drive, even though James had already jumped into the driver's seat with keys in hand, had tested the limits of his patience. Some of the morbid details they exchanged about what they were going to do to the innocent bystander they strangely referred to as soon-to-be "Deadhead Ted" made his skin crawl.

Always true to their barbaric nature, neither brother had ever, to Benny's knowledge, squandered an opportunity to satisfy his ingrained, sick lust to taste the thrill of bloodletting. His nephews may have often bragged about "living fast, dying young, and making a great-looking bullet-riddled corpse," but Benny had never truly realized that their depravity might actually be the death of him. All he had ever really wanted was to make enough money to retire on some isolated beach in the Bahamas.

After his nephews had gunned down the two men at the motel, the money they'd made from selling the cache of weapons and drugs to a special sect of violent gang members had vanished within a day. Jim and James had taken off with every cent, leaving Benny fuming behind in a stink-filled gas station bathroom. In one fell swoop of playing party big shots for the day to those with even less reason to believe in a future, his wayward nephews had happily bragged to him following their return that they'd spent everything on drugs—large baggies of cocaine and an enormous glass bowl filled with hits of ecstasy—cheap women, and even cheaper booze.

Benny had been furious at their new level of stupidity. Nothing they ever did made any sense. And again he found himself wondering if their father had beaten all sense out of their brains.

Now they were broke, bored, and hungry. Their supposed heartfelt apologies meant nothing to him, yet he still refused to abandon them to their own devices. Family loyalty made it impossible to shake them from his neck, regardless of how much they deserved abandonment. As much as it sickened him, Benny did love his nephews, and he still needed them to rid his life of the witness, a man who could send him back to a cage for the rest of his aging life with no more effort than pointing a finger in his direction from the stand during trial.

Benny leaned forward from the backseat and peered at the flashing red "empty" light located just below bold white letters that read "Gas Tank." He ignored James's grunt of hostility for invading his personal space up front, wondering how much farther they could travel on an empty tank.

Shit! This is not good.

"We're going to need to get some gas, Uncle Benny." James spoke as if he had just issued an order.

Benny rolled his eyes and turned his attention on Jim, who sat squirming in the passenger seat of the stolen blue Buick Skylark, scratching at his crotch. His incessant complaints about how his genitals itched, that it felt as if someone had taken a blowtorch to his balls, did nothing to lessen the stress or lighten the mood in the car. Jim's continued offer to bet either one of them that the greasy prostitute they had picked up off the street corner the night before must have infected him with the worst case of crabs known in history only made the time spent with them even more torturous.

"We're running on fumes." James had always possessed a knack for stating the obvious.

A groan of pain fell from Jim's mouth. "Crabs never drove me this insane." An angry growl peppered his voice. "This must be some sort of new breed or strain of jockey bug." His mood had worsened to nearly unbearable now that his bag of cocaine was as empty as the bottle of Jack Daniel's currently rolling around on the floorboard littered with burger wrappers.

Benny rubbed his tired eyes. *Lay down with dogs, and you get fleas, stupid.* He focused on the road.

Jim's hand savagely plunged between his legs, scratching hard enough to tear fabric. "Son of a bitch, this sucks!"

James's head turned to the right. "Quit whining like a little bitch!" His hands tightened around the steering wheel. "It's not like the sausage fleas are eating anything of value, and we're still almost out of gas. I am not pushing this piece of junk, if we run out of gas. That's going to be your job."

"I'm not pushing anything," he complained. "I wish I'd slashed that hooker's no-good throat." He brought a fist down on the dashboard. "I would have if I'd have known this was going to happen."

A deep, resounding laugh slipped from James's mouth. His mouth curled up into a grin.

Jim slapped his brother across the shoulder. "Hey, man, it's not funny. I'm going crazy here. My damn balls feel like someone is roasting them over a damn bonfire or something, microwaved on one of them rotisserie things."

James brought the car to a full stop at a four-way intersection just as a pizza delivery truck passed in front of them. The vehicle's speed announced the driver's hurry.

Benny threw out a finger and pointed at the driver. "That's the bastard who saw us at the motel, boys," he said excitedly. Relief flooded through him. "We got to follow that son of a bitch."

James followed his finger with a spark of keen interest.

Benny chuckled in victory. "Now, we can close the door on any evidence slipping through the cracks."

Jim acted as if he had not heard a word. "Are you listening to me, James?" He was now practically bouncing in the seat.

"Shut up!" James shrieked.

"Don't tell me to shut up. I'm hurting over here."

Benny narrowed his eyes, thinking, trying to do the math on the potential risk of taking the man in broad daylight. "I told you to follow the truck." He did not know if the man by the name of Theodore Stark had already contacted the police, but the longer he waited, the greater the risk. There was no way in hell he was going to risk letting anything or anyone send him back to prison over two scumbags trying to run a scam on him.

James's head bobbed. "I told you she looked nasty, you idiot."

His voice turned calm. "I know a skank when I see one, and she was the harvest queen." He turned left and did as Benny instructed. "Why do you think I passed on her crusty ass?"

"Because you're gay," Jim said with a giggle.

Benny cursed the cruelty of fate straddling him with two of the dumbest nephews on earth. *Dumb shit! One of these days, you are going to shake it over the can, and it is going to drop off in the water.*

The pizza truck traveled down the street another mile with apparent purpose before it finally turned right, popped over a speed bump, and entered an apartment complex. Maintaining a respectful distance to avoid detection, James trailed after it through a parking lot and around a large carport on the corner.

Jim adjusted the shotgun's position between his legs. "She was a sweet ride, bro."

"That's not how it looks from over here."

Jim's nose wrinkled up. "Maybe you are gay or—what is that new word they use?—metrosexual."

"You got me." James's face wrinkled up into a snarl. "I'm your big, fat fairy brother, and I only dip in those with stick. Is that what you want to hear?"

Jim turned and looked out the window. "That flea-infested whore smoked up all my coke—" He banged his forehead against the glass. "And she drank the rest of my Jack. She even broke my favorite pipe by heating it up too much."

Benny slapped his knuckles against the side of Jim's head. "Shut up, both of you, and slow down," he said, jutting his chin. "Look, he's pulling over. Drive past him and stop. Get ready, and we'll take him out."

The deliveryman fumbled with a clipboard as he busily sorted through a short stack of documents attached by a metal clip. He then plucked a couple of sheets from the pile of paperwork and got out of the truck.

Ask and you shall receive. Benny grinned. *This is going to be easier than getting laid in a morgue.*

Again, James did as Benny ordered and slowly drove past the idling truck, parking alongside a concrete retaining wall that separated the apartment complex from an open field. "Who's hungry?"

Jim looked over his shoulder at the truck forty feet behind them. A savage grin creased his face. "I'm starving." His mood seemed to have improved in just seconds. "I could sure go for some pizza."

James's ran a tongue over his lips. "My thoughts exactly," he said. "I love pepperoni."

"And a show," Jim added.

"That too," James confirmed.

Benny smacked them both on the shoulder. "Stop all your jibber jabber and pay attention," he said with a growl. "Screw the pizza. We got a job to do, so do not get sidetracked. You two have a hard enough time focusing."

Jim opened the door and started to get out, but Benny flashed out a hand and grabbed him by the collar. He yanked his nephew back into the car.

"What the hell." Jim's face turned red with anger.

Benny craned his neck and looked over his shoulder. "Shut the door and sit still for five minutes," he barked. "Don't be in such a damn hurry. We have to think this through, make sure there are no complications."

"Why?" Jim whined.

"Because I said so," he said.

James let out an amused giggle of sorts.

Jim pulled the door shut, pouting like a five-year-old child. "I thought we were going to take care of some business, maybe get something to eat on top of it."

Benny focused on Stark. "We will," he assured Jim, "if there is some left in the truck. I would rather he drop it off and get some money. Then we can buy our own food. We will wait until he comes back, after he collects the money for the stack of food. I could use some poker money."

Jim's head moved up and down. "And maybe get me some medicine for all this itching, yeah?"

Benny nodded. "Yeah, maybe," he said distractedly, "if you're lucky and get this done right."

"Cool."

"Make sure your gun is fully loaded."

Stark picked up four hot boxes from off the passenger seat and kicked closed the truck's door with a worn-out sneaker, oblivious to the dangerous eyes that spied on him from not so far away. He appeared happy, upbeat. He turned on the black asphalt and walked between two parked cars under a corrugated shelter that served as the building's carport, soon disappearing around a corner.

Ten minutes later, Benny spotted the deliveryman the instant he stepped out from between a brown station wagon and a small sports car, his hands now empty of boxes. He raised a finger and pointed at the only living threat to him and his liberty. "That's the guy, right there," he said to his nephews. "Now, go kill him."

His nephew James was first to react. He kicked open the door and practically leaped out of the car, hissing for his brother to hurry up and shoot the lousy bastard.

With the shotgun gripped in his hands, Jim got out of the car and ran alongside the passenger side of the Buick, heading toward the rear of the car with his head down. Benny spun around on the backseat of the car and watched his nephews in homicidal action. James had a fifteen-foot lead on his brother.

Theodore Stark's head turned toward the twin monsters running in his direction. His eyes darted back and forth, showing the same kind of fear displayed by a trapped animal. Terror marked his bloodless face as identical hulks, both twice his physical size, rushed at him with murderous intent blazing behind their eyes.

The scream of a child's voice pierced the confrontation only seconds away.

The crunch of metal, *chik-chook,* sliced through the high-pitched scream as Jim's hand slid up and down the shotgun and chambered a twelve-gauge shell.

Theodore's head jerked in the direction of a young girl running toward him, his eyes widening in horror at the sight of her waving her right hand in the air—a wad of bills crunched up in her tiny hand—and calling out for him, by name, to wait.

Her tiny legs feverishly pumped beneath her pink dress, blonde pigtails bouncing in rhythm to every slap her glossy shoes made against the pavement. Determination covered her youthful face.

Theodore raised his hands high and motioned for her to stop, screaming incoherent words at her to go back home, but she refused to heed his words and stayed on course to finish whatever mission she had planned.

Nausea gripped Benny's stomach, and he almost threw up at the unexpected addition to the calculus of premeditated murder. He was only seconds away from reaching a new low in his life as an incorrigible reprobate. In just seconds, he was about to graduate to child killer.

James pounced on the man like a rabid animal, slamming a huge fist into his face. Stark's head snapped to the side. Blood spurted from his face as he stumbled back on weakened legs, knees buckling. His mouth opened in a cry of pain. A second blow delivered to his torso twisted his body at an unnatural angle, doubling him over at the waist. Several ribs cracked loudly. His body struck the ground with a dull thud, blood dripping on the pavement with a wet splat. The child's screams escalated into horrified shrieks. He rolled over and waved a feeble hand for her to run away, but she appeared hell-bent ready to do whatever she could to help him. Her little hands balled up into fists. Tears smeared her face.

James's foot pulled back and then crashed against the fallen man's face, shattering bone and cartilage. A burst of maniacal laughter fell from his throat as he reached down and tore away the zippered pouch attached to the deliveryman's belt. He straightened up and barked orders at Jim, who now stood three feet away and leveled the shotgun at the sprawled man's head.

The young girl was closing the distance, shrieking wildly.

James pointed a finger at her. "Shoot the little bitch first!" he screamed. "No witnesses."

Despite the beating his nephew had just given him, bloodied beyond recognition and internally broken, Stark somehow found the ability to climb back onto his feet at the promised death threat shouted against the young girl. He lunged at the human beast holding the shotgun. Grabbing the end of the barrel and fighting with every ounce of energy in his body, he twisted his head around. "Run away, Wendy!" he screamed wildly, his face covered in blood, nose and lips visibly smashed against his face. "Get your daddy. Get help. I cannot hold him."

A middle-aged man suddenly appeared from around the corner of the building and ran toward the melee taking placing in the parking lot. He was yelling for someone, for anyone, to call 911 and the police.

A loud blast shook the windows of the apartment complex.

The full force of the twelve-gauge shotgun blast hit Stark point-blank in the chest, blowing him off the ground and back a full five feet. A dark pattern of gore quickly spread across the front of his tattered shirt. His body convulsed once, and he choked and coughed. Thick globs of blood spurted from his grimacing mouth, and his eyes fluttered weakly.

Benny's nephews danced a jig together and laughed at the unmoving man.

Benny stuck his head out the window, utterly repulsed by their cold-bloodedness. He had never seen such a demented sight. For the first time in his life, he truly understood the depth of evil. He waved for the boys to leave the girl alone and get back to the car.

His nephews exchanged quick glances, shrugged massive shoulders, and then ran for the car.

With tears streaming down her chubby cheeks, the young girl kneeled next to Stark and pulled his head onto her lap. Her chin quivered. "Why?" Sadness strangled her voice.

In the distance, sirens echoed, signaling the rapid approach of police cars.

The blue Buick Skylark raced away, leaving a trail of rubber on the ground.

The past few days had been grueling for Detective Lomax, and he would have been more than willing to attribute all the recent craziness in the city to a full moon, had one actually appeared in the night sky. Unfortunately, to his chagrin, the current state of murders, robberies, and random mayhems committed in the district was just routine.

When Captain Johnson had first covertly assigned him to the unofficial task of what he considered investigation "Rat Patrol," Lomax had believed that his search into Callahan's personal life would lead to no real mind-blowing surprises. All government officials were corrupt on some level. Far from naive to the inner machinations of government and the agents through which it functioned, the seasoned detective expected to find the usual evidentiary facts that proved what he already knew—information that would invariably support chronic abuses of power by officials. Even though he had never condoned such illicit conduct by those holding positions of public trust, he'd expected to uncover minor drug dealing, and bouts of larceny. A chain of extortion here and there involving local businesspersons and unions normally rounded out the parameters of civic responsibility as generally acceptable behavior.

Lomax privately prided himself on never having accepted a bribe or partaken in any criminal activity outside the law, and none of the delusional reasons his fellow officers offered for falling prey to peer pressure did nothing to lessen his condemnation for such a corrupt practice. He was not blind to the amoral beliefs insidiously injected into the new world order. "Look out for number one" had become society's axiomatic mantra.

This was America, and it was every citizen's inalienable right not to help anyone. Everyone lied about whatever might cause an inconvenience. Everyone cheated over anything that might help get him or her ahead of the curve. "I gotta get mine" formed on the lips of those sinking into the venomous cesspool of belief that entitlements for doing nothing were the new American staple.

For these reasons alone, not excluding a short list of things that did not immediately come to mind, Lomax preferred working homicide. Cadavers did nothing of the former. Nor did they complain or talk back. They were quiet and harbored no expectations. In addition, other than the unlawful taking of a human life, the crime of homicide was relatively uncomplicated, certainly not complex by any stretch of the imagination. There was a victim and a perpetrator. The perpetrator usually had a motive—not always the most rational, of course—and had killed the one now wearing a toe tag down at the city morgue because he believed his victim had wronged him and deserved exactly what he got.

Contrary to the initial belief that he was wasting his time, Lomax's discomfort with his secret assignment escalated the deeper he delved into the long-ago rumors about Callahan's shady past and meteoric rise in the prosecution's office. Although he had not dug up conclusive evidence that directly linked the former district attorney to a crime, a fast-growing mountain of soft evidence buried underneath forgotten skeletons revealed lethal connections to notorious drug dealers and powerful figures in the criminal underworld. A list of curious alliances with the darker side of society soon piqued Lomax's sleuthing mind enough to continue his investigatory quest and uncover the bottom line. Lomax had always enjoyed a good puzzle.

Convinced that there was much more to find in documents stored away years ago, Lomax had decided to covertly pay a visit to the dusty halls of the basement located below the department's headquarters, where authorized personnel had stored hardcopies from decades past not yet transferred onto either microfiche or flash drive. To his dismay, he'd found thousands of matching banker boxes filled with documents that had lain dormant, stuffed with near ancient facts and figures, for years unattended.

With an exaggerated yawn of weariness that accompanied the mind-numbing hours he had so far spent sifting aimlessly through a cardboard jungle covered with cobwebs and skittering bugs of every disgusting type, Lomax tiredly tossed another manila folder on top of the metal filing cabinet. A brown mushroom of dust kicked up from the rusted metal, which caused him to sneeze for what he counted as the twentieth time since he had taken advantage of the naive clerk perched upstairs and sneaked into the unauthorized area inside the building. Lomax thanked his lucky stars that the young clerk was more interested in finishing his college homework than in serving as a governmental gargoyle guarding paperwork no one had cared about for years.

After clearing his sinuses against another bout of mucus, joined by a quick sleeve wipe over his face, Lomax fished out a different colored envelope from a large accordion folder stuffed in the back of an isolated cabinet marked "miscellaneous." He made a mental note to cross his fingers, hoping that something hidden inside would prove valuable to his unofficial investigation. Unlike the previous three tucked inside tan folds, this envelope was black and labeled with Walter Callahan's misspelled name on the front.

Come on, baby. Give me a lead.

Despite his best efforts to ferret out what now seemed like a long-buried truth down a bottomless rabbit hole, Lomax had still not found the common thread that linked the past with the present. His gut instinct screamed at him, urging him to continue his research, warning him that he was on a dangerous path. All he needed to find was a hard clue that decrypted the formula to solve the elusive riddle. He knew it was there to find, just waiting somewhere in the ink-stained pages. He could feel it deep down in his bones. Something about the crime scene at Callahan's residence still bothered him, and he could not shake the feeling that Captain Johnson had not disclosed everything to him—that he was holding back something critical. He had called Captain Johnson's office five times to ask him about the details of the case Callahan had prosecuted in the *People v. Trent H. Varus,* all he had received for his troubled effort was a lecture that he was barking up the wrong tree.

His voiced suspicion that Varus might somehow be involved in Callahan's death, that he intended to pay the man a visit for an innocent round of questions, had not gone over well at all. In fact, to his surprise, Johnson had become angry. He had even verbally threatened him, ordering him to look elsewhere—to stay away from Varus and ancient history that had nothing to do with the present. Lomax had known Callahan, had actually loathed him on one occasion or another, and people like him were far too self-absorbed to commit suicide. If his job as a detective had taught him anything, men who suffered from god complexes did not take their own lives. Such an act went against their very nature.

After six long hours of painstaking work in what barely qualified as an underground bunker, all he had managed to discover was that the former *also deceased* District Attorney Hendinson had assigned his newest recruit, Deputy District Attorney Callahan—a decision no doubt meant to sharpen his prosecutorial teeth—to prosecute all narcotics cases to the full extent of the law. Lomax could not help but grin at the irony of how the illustrious Walter Callahan had come to meet his maker. Slowly but surely, a few more things started to make a little more sense, but he still had far more questions than answers.

I know you and your office were dirty as hell! Lomax knitted his brow. *What am I missing?* He then noticed a date partially covered beneath flaking whiteout. *Why would anyone doctor a redacted document with this stuff and not use indelible ink?* He scratched at it with a fingernail, revealing the date October 2, 1996. *How could anyone screw that up? This does not make any sense.* He opened the file and read a curled-up yellow Post-it stuck inside the front cover that referred to paragraph eight. He frowned at the initials

"THV" scribbled across the yellow square. The name block for the investigating officer to sign read "Detective Michael Johnson."

Intrigued by the connection between the initials he identified as Trent Henry Varus and his current captain, Lomax turned the page to the next official report—a search warrant signed by the Honorable Judge Terrence Harper—and scrolled down to the second paragraph. His eyes widened, his blood running cold. He was stunned at the possible connotations. The same judge who had validated the warrant had also signed a grant of immunity from prosecution for fifteen counts of drug possession and distribution, including witness protection and relocation to a town he had never heard of, in exchange for Sam Herd's testimony against Trent Henry Varus for the first-degree murder of Mr. Morris Stokes.

Lomax tilted his head back, thinking back years ago, and took a deep breath, *I know that name ... but from where and when?* He reached up to scratch the top of his head, and then it hit him. The face of the man the name belonged to struck his memory with the force of a lightning bolt. *I got it!* A slow grin creased his face when he suddenly realized that he had just made the second connection. His memory of the details on the night that Detective Johnson had arrested and beaten Morris Stokes for drug sales was a little foggy. It was a night in his career that he had managed to push from his mind. The man's name now seemed to leap from the page, as did the petty drug dealer's screams of agreement to act as Johnson's confidential informant as Lomax watched his friend beat down Morris in a back alley with a pair of brass knuckles.

He lowered his head and read farther down the page, stopping at the second to last paragraph. There were two names listed below the terms of the agreement with the witness, a Sam Herd and Jerry Smith.

He turned the page. His eyes moved past paragraph three and froze. A set of withheld facts stared up at him in bold letters, mocking him and his entire profession. The veracity of each word practically leaped off the page.

"Oh, you sneaky bastards," he mumbled. He shook his head as the details slowly sunk in, appalled by what Callahan and Johnson had done to an innocent man. He knew Callahan had been a hungry upstart, but to destroy a man's life in the process of seeking higher office was unthinkable. His captain's motive for putting him on the unofficial assignment to work as his personal mole and report his findings off the books resonated with crystal clarity. Lomax now knew his captain had conned him into conducting a secretive investigation into Callahan's death as a means to discover any evidence that might connect him with a series of related crimes that spanned over two decades at comfortable distance, while maintaining a neutral position of plausible deniability of any involvement in corruption. It then occurred to him that Varus was a prime suspect. He did not know how he could connect him to a death that the coroner had ruled as suicide by overdose, but he knew that he had to keep his cards very close to his chest. Everyone was a potential enemy, particularly the man he had considered a friend. He then wondered if his captain equally qualified as a viable suspect. Lomax had never felt more alone, and he knew that he needed to find Sam … Jerry Smith … whoever they were, or he was. He was the best candidate to clear away the hazy fog that lingered over the entire case.

Although he may not have worked out all the details, deep down he knew Johnson had tricked him into doing the dirty work.

"I'm not going to get boxed in," he said with a grumble. "I don't know what all of you are up to, but I am not going down for any of this. I am no straw man, and I am far too close to retirement. I'm not getting screwed in all this!"

His cell phone suddenly burst to life and startled him. He fumbled with the paperwork, before setting the folder down to retrieve it from his pocket.

"Yeah, this is Lomax," he announced. "Uh-huh. I got it. I'll be right there, sir." He terminated the call with a click of the button.

"Game on!"

Lomax closed the cabinet, stuffed the folder behind his waistband, underneath his shirt, and headed off to another reported crime scene found at the long-abandoned industrial park located on the outskirts of town.

Thirty minutes later, Lomax pulled his car alongside an ambulance parked no more than twenty feet from the main entrance to the garage of a large, run-down building. Two paramedics sat on the back bumper, talking and smoking cigarettes. Neither man seemed in much of a hurry to do anything, least of all their job. He took a quiet moment and quickly perused the surrounding area before finally getting out of the car.

What the hell? He stuffed the folder under his seat to hide it from plain sight. *I might as well bite the bullet and get this over with, before I change my mind. A minute's peace is just not in the cards for me this week.*

He got out of his car and walked underneath a large, corrugated, roll-down sliding door that someone had left halfway up.

Inside the walls, police officers buzzed about the grounds in what looked like reckless abandon. Most of the officers acted more interested in gossiping among themselves over the crime scene and victim than doing their jobs.

Dressed in ragged clothing, a homeless man sat with hunched shoulders on the edge of a loading dock. Deathly pale and malnourished, the man wore a pinched expression on his dirty features that spoke untold volumes of his life on the street. Just the image of him sitting on the edge of the dock summed up what life must be like when it was defined by human misery, a victimized descent into a void with no end. His body language showed palpable fear of the two police officers standing on either side of him. His scrawny legs hung over the edge, his feet swinging back and forth. Lomax wondered how his tattered shoes stayed on without laces. Several team members from the crime lab were kneeling next to a small body twenty feet away. The petite redhead from the motel seemed to sense his presence. She rose at the noisy approach of his footsteps. She and a lone uniformed officer moved toward him.

Her eyes blazed with what looked like green fury.

Lomax nodded, uncomfortable beneath her penetrating gaze. "Hello again, Dr. Swanson," he greeted. He was glad to find her on the job.

A flustered look flitted across her eyes. She made a forced smile, brushing away a loose strand of hair from her face. "It's good to see you again, Detective Lomax, despite the awful circumstance." Her face pinched.

Lomax peered over her shoulder. "What do we have?" His stomach heaved just a little. At closer inspection, beneath the pile of caked on makeup, the victim's face belonged to a teenage girl.

"We have a definite murder, Detective."

"That's a positive?" As much as the fact pained him, young junkies overdosed in the worst places imaginable.

"Absolutely," she said.

He ran a hand over his pate. "Pretty girl," he said.

A morbid chuckle fell from the officer's mouth. "She ain't pretty anymore." He threw a thumb over his shoulder. "Life of a skank-ass hooker, am I right?" His eye winked at Lomax.

Swanson grimaced at the cruel comments.

Lomax looked at the officer with indignant disgust. "And how do you know that she's a prostitute, Officer?" he said with a slight growl. "Do you have some sort of special power none of us have?"

A look of uneasiness suddenly shadowed his face. His right toe moved over the ground. "Well ..." he stammered. His voice was nervous. "She's dressed like one, and her face is painted so much that she looks like a damn clown."

Lomax narrowed his eyes. "Oh," he began with a heated snap, "so your position is that prostitutes are less than human and deserve to be treated like this. Is that your stance on the law and human decency? Just murder them and throw them away like a piece of trash—that's all prostitutes deserve?"

His head drooped. "I didn't say that."

"I think you just did."

The officer raised his head. His eyes darted back and forth, giving him the look of a trapped animal. "I just meant—" The words caught in his throat.

Lomax lashed out and grabbed him by the back of his neck, squeezing hard enough to make it hurt. Swanson yelped at the unexpected act of aggression and backed away. She moved toward the body and kneeled to continue her work. He twisted his hand and forced the officer to look down at the dead girl.

"Look at her!" he spat, furious at his fellow officer. "She was a human being, a young girl with real feelings, and some murderous son of a bitch killed her for no good reason. She had a family and friends, and I bet they loved her." He tightened his grip, forcing a low groan to slip from the officer's throat. "You will show her respect. Do I make myself clear?"

The man's head jerked up and down. "Yes," he said. "I understand."

Lomax shoved him away. "Good," he said. "Now, get the hell away from my crime scene. People like you, especially officers, make me sick to my stomach."

The officer shot him a hateful glare, rubbed the back of his neck, and then walked away. A list of obscenities reached Lomax's ears.

He shook his head at the fading figure dressed in blue. *Asshole!* He craned his neck and refocused his attention on the group of techs circling the girl.

She peered up at him, a grim smile creasing her lips.

Lomax took a knee next to her, ignoring the perplexed looks on Swanson's team members' faces when they saw the tears in his eyes. He could not help his reaction, and he sighed at the sad sight of a young girl's life brought to such a brutal end. He cleared his throat, wondering what had happened to the world. No one was safe from its random cruelties. Even the lives of the most innocent hung in the balance. "I remember that you prefer to wait until after the lab results come in, but can you give me a cause of death or a time of death on the girl?"

Swanson pulled a penlight from the pocket of her coat. "Well," she began with noticeable reticence.

He laid a tender hand on her shoulder, attempting to assuage her guilt for breaking normal protocol. "It doesn't have to be exact, Becky," he offered in a soft voice.

She finally made a weak nod. She then continued. "Based on the evidence extrapolated thus far, I would have to say that the COD is a broken neck. I see no trace evidence of GSR or an exit wound. I would dare surmise that our murderer shot her in the back, possibly while she was running away from the shooter." She took a breath and continued with her analysis. "Additionally, based on lividity and blood pooling around the body, I believe the girl was shot at a distance greater than thirty feet and fell here, the place of death." Her face went blank.

Impressed with her forensic skills, Lomax decided to prod further. "Anything else?" he said. "I will take everything you can give me."

As if shaken from a daydream, the investigator shook her head. "Um, yeah," she said. "Though it was a paralyzing wound because it severed the spinal cord and would have inevitably proved fatal, the victim didn't die from the bullet."

He knitted his brow. "How is that?"

"Chain of evidentiary events," she said.

"Explain," he said.

She tapped her chin with the penlight. "Based on my preliminary findings, while the girl lay immobilized facedown on the ground, our killer moved behind her and snapped her neck with a ruthless twist to the right." She offered a quick demonstration with her hands. "I'd say that, due to the amount of trauma done to the neck, we are dealing with a male of at least a hundred and eighty pounds."

Lomax straightened up and scratched his head. He studied the layout of the terrain, attempting to evaluate and retrace the girl's final steps as she ran for her life. He wondered how she had ended up so far from the city, in an abandoned building, just south of armpit central in the first place. None of it made any sense. She did not appear to have any significant marks on her body, defensive or otherwise. *Someone she knew. Alternatively, someone she trusted.* He took a deep, calming breath and tried to imagine the involved parties. *Think, Erik. Think, damn you. The answer is right in front of you.*

Someone cleared his throat and shook him from his train of thought. He craned his neck and looked at three officers standing no more than three feet away.

"Excuse me, Detective," said the officer on the far left. The other two officers remained unmoving and silent.

"Yeah, what is it?" he said with a growl. "I'm a little busy at the moment."

His head tipped. "We may have a lead, sir." Doubt touched his voice. "But I'm not real sure how reliable the information is because our source is … well, to put it lightly, pretty snockered." He placed his thumb against his lips and tilted back his head.

Lomax met the officer's eyes. "Are you telling me that you found a witness to the murder?" His heart skipped a beat.

His face winced at the question. "Not exactly, sir." His head turned to seek aid from his colleagues, but they had already stealthily sneaked off like a pair of thieves in the night. With a low grumble, the officer faced him.

Lomax shifted his gaze just in time to watch Dr. Swanson place plastic medical bags over the girl's hands. "Did you find something?" he said. Despite how most of these cases went, hope that he would catch the monster before he struck again and murdered another innocent girl still filled him. People who committed such atrocities never stopped until someone finally put their evil to an end. "Maybe some evidence. I could really use some good news to boost my spirits. I'm having a lousy week."

She motioned for her team to begin preparations for removal of the body. "I'm not sure at this time." Her voice was noncommittal. "We haven't found any form of identification on her, but the girl has rather pricey dental work and acrylic nails. This one was very particular about her nails."

Lomax winced at her use of the past tense. "I noticed that too. Do you have an opinion?"

She continued, unabated, impervious to his interruption.

"The fact that two of them are cracked and broken is highly suspect." She held up her fingers, wiggling them. "The damage appears recent. I found dried blood around the cuticles of both hands, so there may be trace left by the perp." She sealed the bags around her wrists. "If I find anything, I will run it through the identification data bank and hope we get a match."

Lomax crossed his fingers for effect and then turned his attention back to the officer. "I apologize for the interruption, Pierce," he said. "Please continue." He motioned with his hands. "You were saying 'not exactly.'"

The officer gave a sharp nod. "Yes, sir," he said in a firm voice. "That is correct." He pointed at the raggedly dressed man. "Our witness, mind you that he is still sloshed, said he saw a dark car enter the building, heard a loud bang not long after it had stopped, and then watched it take off like a bat out of hell the same way it had entered."

"Is that right?" Lomax clucked his tongue. "I get the feeling he said a little more. What aren't you telling me?"

"Um," he began in a stammer, "yes, sir."

As a seasoned interrogator, Lomax had honed his skills to detect the signs when someone was struggling with something dangerous or controversial. He changed tactics, deciding to tread indirectly. "This must be very difficult for you, Officer Pierce."

He nodded.

Lomax further softened his demeanor. He had to keep the man on point. "Is there anything else you might want to add before I pursue this investigation?" he pressed in a diplomatic tone. "Anything you might have to add can only assist in getting this poor girl justice."

Beads of perspiration dotted his forehead. "The witness said the car was a police car," he said in a tight voice. The words spilled clumsily from his mouth. "He also said the man was dressed in a uniform."

Lomax scratched at the stubble on his chin, thinking and weighing the words. *Someone you know, or someone you trust?* His mind raced. Elements seemed to fall into place.

The forensic team lifted the body and placed it on top of a metal gurney, which distracted Lomax for just a second. They pulled a tarp over the girl's body. He turned and grimaced when one of her tiny hands fell loose from beneath the cover, dangling lifelessly over the side.

He shook his head, wishing he could erase the chilling image from his mind. Anger rose in him. "Try not to get personally involved in all of this, Officer Pierce," he warned. "Emotional attachment can get the best of you, drain you of life."

Pierce shook his head side-to-side, grimacing. "I'm a just little disturbed by all this." His voice sounded distant. "This is actually my first murder scene."

Lomax met his eyes. The sickly look of the man's face reminded him of so many good officers who had come and gone over the years. "Trust me when I say that it never gets easier." He now understood the officer's reticence to speak on the subject. Most police officers did not want to step beyond that thin blue line separating them as brothers in blue and traitors to their oaths by implicating another officer without having all the facts. "Do you find the witness's implication false, maybe even ridiculous?" He studied the man's face and body language for signs of deceit or subterfuge.

Pierce's lips pursed. "That is not for me to say, sir." Nervousness touched his voice, but his words resounded with honesty. "But I do find it troubling that one of us could be a viable suspect for something so terrible."

Lomax cocked an eyebrow. "Why does it trouble you so much?" he said. "There could be many other explanations." He shrugged. "Things happen. You don't think cops are above doing something sick like this, do you?"

The officer's eyes watered at the question. "I guess I haven't given that scenario much thought, sir." His tone sounded defeated.

Lomax nodded approvingly. "How is it that your witness came to be here in the first place?"

The harmless question seemed to calm Officer Pierce. "Evidently, according to him, he lives in one of the neighboring buildings," he said matter-of-factly. "I guess some of the generators left behind by the previous owners are still functional to run auxiliary power, and there is still running water. He said it is safe because there are no visitors, which is why he got up to look out the window when he heard a car drive into the structure. He also said that no one really comes here anymore, not in cars anyway, and definitely not during the week. Occasionally, some high school kids come here to get drunk, smoke a little dope, and have sex, but he hides upstairs until they leave."

"Sounds like a sweet deal for him."

"I suppose that is one interpretation."

Lomax forced a grin to try to keep the officer at ease. "Then why don't you just cut to the chase and tell me the rest of the details the man gave you," he said. "I'm going to find out anyway. This way, I will have an angle to work with the witness. I hate starting a round of questions from in the dark."

Pierce took a deep breath. "Our witness said the murder was pretty savage." His voice turned sad, pained. "He heard the girl scream while she was still inside the car. She then fell out the passenger side onto the ground. The man ordered her to get back into the car, tried to reach for her, but she got up and ran for the exit. The man dressed in a cop's uniform got out of the car, pulled his gun after she refused to come back, and then shot her in the back. She collapsed onto the ground, facedown. The witness could hear her crying and feel how scared she was. He didn't know why, said everything about the scenario was weird and creepy, but she never did try to get up and run away. The man walked up to her and then twisted her head around. He said he heard bones break from where he was watching."

Lomax pressed his lips together, thinking. "Was this man older, appearing in decent shape?" He ran his hand over his head. "Did he have brownish hair?"

Pierce shook his head, appearing grateful to have spilled his guts to the detective. "Not at all," he said. "He said the man was somewhere in his early thirties, in good shape, and that he did this weird thing with his hat." He ran his finger and thumb across the bill to demonstrate.

Lomax gave an appreciative grunt. "That's some pretty good work, Officer," he said. "Let's go talk to your witness." He pulled a small silver flask from his pocket when he got within ten feet of the homeless man. He waved off the other two officers.

The man hungrily licked his lips at the sight of the silver container.

Lomax took a seat next to him and patted his dusty shoulder. "Hello, friend," he greeted warmly. "What's your name?" He flashed an award-winning smile.

The man dragged a filthy sleeve across the salt-and-pepper hair shrouding his mouth. "Joshua." His voice was gravelly. "My friends call me Mummy Dust."

Lomax uncapped the flask and took a quick swig. "Would you care for a little taste of the spirits, Mummy Dust?" He held out the flask, winking at Officer Pierce.

His mouth opened into a hideous-looking smile, revealing two rows of broken teeth blackened by unknowable stains. "Indeed I would, friend." He grabbed it with a pair of brown gloves missing the fingers and took a hearty swallow of the fiery brew.

"I understand you saw one of those lousy police cars drive into this very building," he said in an airy voice. He motioned for Mummy Dust to take another gulp, which elicited a thankful nod and grin from the man.

Lomax leaned back and stretched out his back. "I have a wonderful idea, Mummy Dust," he said. "You seem like a real stand-up type of guy."

"I was a marine."

Lomax offered him a thumbs-up. "I got that from you," he said jovially. "Why don't we just sit, drink together awhile, and talk about everything you saw."

Mummy Dust gave a soft giggle and lifted the flask to his parched lips.

The next phase of Trent's plan to avenge the tragic loss of his family and set things right, a vow he had made decades ago, began two hours after sundown. His heart beat with the thunderous pound of a war drum, blood pumping through his veins. The taste of crimson vengeance was sweet as he thought about all the horrors he had seen and experienced and the emotional pain he'd suffered over the long years. His life had almost come full circle, and the time for reckoning was at hand—his for the taking.

I shall take my last drink from the font of revenge, and never again will I thirst to whet my need to suckle at the poisoned teat that is death.

Trent looked at his reflection in the bathroom mirror, barely recognizing the lethal eyes staring back at him with a cold deadness that revealed nothing but apathy for life. The three bodies lying on the floor behind him did nothing to derail him or cause him pause. He would follow through with his endeavor. What he had done, he had convinced himself over the time behind bars, life had compelled. He had relinquished choice, his free will, a long time ago, leaving nothing but an empty husk. He had finally reached the point of no return, and somewhere along his travels along the road to hell, darkness had enveloped him. He was now becoming that which he had once loathed. Calculation was now his mistress in which to bathe his tortured soul. Everything he had mapped out had progressed like synchronized clockwork, completely free of any glitches in the time it had taken him to bypass courthouse security systems and breach the inner sanctum ruled by judiciary officers. Surprised by the simplicity installed by the alleged experts in electronics, Trent had circumvented the alarms with relative ease. The only part of the long orchestration that had proved easier than his break-in without detection was subduing the bailiff and security guards.

Trent had spent hundreds of hours researching and noting Judge Terrence Harper's schedules and late hour activities. His right-hand man, Lenny, had provided every minute detail to fill in the blanks, verbally and in written form, leaving nothing out, per his orders. Lenny's inside information was quickly proving invaluable to achieve his ultimate goal.

Having studied everything Lenny had listed as critical, Trent soon discovered that two security guards—both aging and on the short road to retirement—worked the evening shift and that they roamed the desolate corridors in the dark and randomly checked doors unwittingly left unlocked, using flashlights to search rooms filled with expensive equipment. In past days, youthful vandals and graffiti delinquents had always proved irritating to courthouse staff, but those wayward ways had come and gone, now paling in comparison to the recent increase of juvenile offenders breaking in and stealing newly installed computers and other electronic devices utilized by the personnel. Costs soon skyrocketed at such massive property losses, which made it mandatory for the authorities to insert new elements into the equation—armed night watchmen.

Since many judges remained in their chambers long after regular courtroom hours, security guards maintained a haphazard vigil as they made their circuitous rounds in the building. All took special precautions so as not to disturb a judge hard at work on the next big case.

Trent had read on page three of Lenny's report that Judge Harper often worked into the following morning, that he spent at least four nights each week past midnight reviewing and researching legal briefs submitted to his court. Night security remained clear of his hallway most nights, because circulating rumors suggested that he had an incomparable mean streak, a foul mouth that would make a dockworker cringe, and a history for arranging employment terminations that exceeded twenty different personnel for distracting him while he was discharging his legal duties. No one dared to risk losing his or her job over a bad attitude or a silly misunderstanding.

Ten minutes after he had successfully dealt with the bailiff and security guards on duty, Trent stood just outside Judge Harper's chamber door. The light from inside the room crept from underneath the lower edge of the door. He rolled back the glove on his left hand and checked the time on his wristwatch. The items rattled around inside the duffel bag he clenched in his hand. A slow smile formed on his face; he was pleased that he was moving according to schedule.

I think it is now time for me to roll and put this thing to bed.

Trent placed his ear against the door and listened. The sound of someone turning pages reached his ears. He then scratched at the door with a gloved hand.

"Idiots," he heard from the other side of the door.

Amused, he knocked on the door with a gloved hand. The dull thud sounded like the beginning bell to round three. "Come and get some," he whispered.

"Go away." Trent recognized Harper's voice.

Trent pounded his fist against the door five times. The door shook violently.

Harper growled from the other side of the closed door. "I'm coming, damn it!" Fury spewed from his words. "Stop all that infernal banging, you miscreant. I hope you like standing in the unemployment line, you bucket-carrying troglodyte."

The click clack of locks sounded, and then the door practically flew open. Judge Harper stood in the doorway, his hands planted on both hips.

Trent flashed out a gloved hand and viciously snatched him by the throat. The muscles in Harper's face went instantly slack, his pallor turning sickly white. Instant recognition flashed behind his aged eyes.

Trent grinned malevolently, savoring the powerful rush between life and death gripped in his hand. It took all his inner strength not to simply twist and break the man's neck. "Hello, Terry," he said with a throaty growl of disdain. "Did you miss me?"

Harper's face winced against the crushing stranglehold that threatened to cut off his air. "I—" An increase of pressure on his neck choked off the rest of the sentence.

Trent rushed forward, squeezing down on the judge's throat even harder, and threw the object of his hatred against the side of the heavy desk. "Day late, dollar short, pal," he said with a sneer.

Harper struck the hard wood with a dull thud and yelped in pain. His body bounced off the unforgiving mahogany, and he stumbled to the floor. He rolled over, clutching at his lower back. "Security." The word tumbled from his mouth in a grimacing whimper.

Trent pulled back a booted foot and kicked him in the abdomen. Harper's body jerked and he let out a sharp squeal. He curled up in a fetal position and puked up his late-night snack. Trent set the duffel bag on the desk and glared down at the man now coughing and wheezing for air. *Don't you dare even try to think this is over, you stinking son of a bitch! Far from it, pal. We are just starting to get reacquainted.*

Harper's chin jutted out. Tears filled his eyes. "Secur—" Another merciless kick to his midsection stilled his wagging tongue.

Trent hovered above like a bird of prey on the hunt, disgusted at the sight of the man who had cost him everything a wonderful life had to offer. Fury burned in his heart and mind. He was angry, angry at the man on the floor, angry with himself, angry at the entire world, and he wanted the judge to feel every ounce of his bottled-up wrath. For too long he had remained lost in a sea of black, drifting along a current of despair and hopelessness, floating in and out of the unknowable shadows that now defined his empty, loveless existence.

Now reality had opened his eyes, pried them wide open, and his now deceased brother-in-law had been instrumental in shedding light on the immutable truth. He had no choice but to question his destiny. Did poetic justice or a bizarre twist of fate now sum up his life? Neither choice comforted him.

For years, Trent had believed that Judge Harper was a good and decent man, truly devoted to truth and justice while on the bench, and that he had violated his judicial oath by making decisions contrary to law during the course of his trial only because he had genuinely thought Trent guilty of murder. He had actually come to find a sliver of comfort in the idea that Harper meant only to protect the public from a vicious killer. Such an excuse might not serve the ends of legal justice, but the explanation certainly met the criteria measured under factual justification. Judge Harper's sentence had been an act of desperate desire to protect the innocent—to prevent a catastrophe. Sometimes people compromised their beliefs and violated their oaths to see justice done against those where physical evidence is too weak to prove what they knew to be fact.

However, the revelations unveiled by Sam had cruelly stripped him of his last shred of dignity, a misbelief that had shrouded him in blissful ignorance. Everything he had come to trust and believe had turned out to be nothing but a scurrilous lie of epic proportions. His desire for revenge now burned hotter than ever.

Judge Harper forced his body to a seated position, his face twisting in agony. "What do you want?" Arrogance spilled from his voice. A small trickle of blood ran down his chin. "Do you have any idea who I am, who you have attacked, you stupid bastard?"

Trent chuckled softly, amused with the man's misplaced moxie. "Still a pompous ass, I see," he said. "Don't try to play dumb with me." He started to wag a teasing finger in the air. "The question that should most concern you is how well you remember me." He unzipped the bag and looked Harper directly in the eye.

Harper averted his eyes, shivering. "I-I don't know what you mean."

Trent smirked. "That's cute," he said. "I'm willing to bet that you remember exactly who I am, and I aim to prove it. I saw it in your eyes when you opened the door." Bitter resentment coursed through him. "And don't even think about yelling for help. I promise that no one can hear you."

Harper's eyes flashed back on him, glowering with a hateful snarl. "You'll pay for this, you lousy bastard!" He spat the words with unadulterated hatred.

"That's better, Your Honor." Trent reached into the duffel bag and withdrew three utility belts and matching hats worn by Harper's bailiff and the two security guards assigned to work that night. A can of mace and a black nightstick remained attached to each of the belts. Three holsters held Smith & Wesson .38 revolvers. Trent straightened up and tossed three shiny badges at the judge.

"My God!" Harper's feet kicked at the badges, and he pressed his back against the desk. "What have you done?"

Trent snorted his derision. "I did what I had to do," he said. He had never despised anyone as much as he did the coward now on the floor cringing. "I learned over the years that some evils are necessary, and I didn't think you would come out to play if I asked nicely."

His eyes went wide as saucers. "You killed them, didn't you?" His voice was a tremulous shriek. "You murdered them in cold blood."

Trent withdrew a semiautomatic handgun equipped with a perforated cylinder. "Oh, come on, Terry," he said comically. "Don't act so surprised. After all, at sentencing eons ago, you called me a filthy murderer, an animal, a monster unworthy of life. You said that I should take my evil carcass to prison and die there." He cocked his head to the side and grinned. "Don't you remember that part, Your Honor?" He pointed the gun at Harper's heart. "I just became the product of my environment." He took an over exaggerated bow. "Thank you."

Harper's hands flew up in front of his face. "Wait!" he screamed. He then looked around his chambers, desperation marking his face. "If you let me go, I won't tell anyone. It will be between just the two of us, I swear." Sweat beaded the skin below his nose. "I promise."

Trent broke out in laughter. "Prison made me mean and crazy, not stupid." He lowered his aim and pulled the trigger.

Pft.

Harper shrieked in pain and reached for his destroyed kneecap. "Oh, God!" He peered up with teary eyes, his weathered features twisted in agony. "Puh-lease."

Trent took new aim, slightly to the left. "God isn't here, and I don't think he helps filthy bastards," he said. "But I can help take your mind off what ails you." He pulled the trigger for the second time.

Pft.

Judge Harper howled even louder and clasped the other knee. "Aaaaaah."

"Hurts, doesn't it?" he quipped.

Harper's body tipped over onto the side, and he wept miserably. He rocked back and forth. Blood covered his hands. "No more, for God's sake. Please stop this madness."

Madness? You have not begun to feel the misery I plan on delivering. You are still getting off easy.

The judge's body convulsed on the floor. "I'll do anything."

Trent sneered at the hypocrite who would dare invoke the Lord's name for undeserved mercy.

"Please, stop."

Trent scratched at his head with the butt of the gun, feigning contemplation as if he was considering the vacuous offer. "Anything, you say?"

Harper's head nodded feverishly, while he still clutched both shattered knees. "Yes! Anything you want. I have money. I can give you money."

Trent continued to scratch his head with the butt. "I kind of already have money, lots of it in fact," he said offhandedly, wrinkling his nose. "Huh. Could I use some more?" He shook his head. "Naw, I think I'd rather just keep shooting you. It's fun." He retrained the gun and fired a third time.

Pft.

Harper screamed anew, writhing on the blood-spattered floor, his right arm now wriggling freely on unattached bone in the elbow joint. His pleas grew shallower.

Filled with indifference for the man who had condemned him to a private corner of hell for decades, Trent moved closer and struck the judge on the head to get his full attention. "Excuse me, Your So-Called Honor. I now have some questions for you." Just for the fun of it, he bopped him on the head again. "You will answer, or I will just keep shooting you." He moved his face within a foot of Harper's. "Do you understand the words coming out of my mouth?"

"Uh-huh."

"Is that a yes?" He placed the barrel of the gun under Harper's chin.

"Yes, yes, that's a yes." A deep groan marred his words. "I understand."

"Splendid," he said. "Now we are getting somewhere." He walked over and sat down in a nearby chair. "You see, that wasn't so difficult. Not if we have cooperation." He crossed his legs. "Now, I'm going to ask you a series of questions, Terry. If I don't believe your answer, I am going to put another bullet in something else." He pointed the gun. "Probably your other elbow. After that …" He shrugged. "Who really knows? Maybe I will put one in your balls, one nut at a time. Maybe I'll do to you what I did to your little friends pretending to be cops."

Harper's body shrank on the floor, horror masking his face. His eyes spoke tortured volumes, no doubt wondering if his tormentor had done unspeakable things to the other three men. His eyes darted to the duffel bag, probably wondering what kind of instruments used for inflicting the type of pain and suffering found only in a Wes Craven movie Trent had hidden.

Trent removed a small cell phone from his pocket and held it up for Harper to see. He hit record. "This is the oral deposition of Judge Terrence Harper." He turned it toward the judge. "State your name for the record."

Harper hesitated.

Trent pointed the gun at his crotch. "I won't ask again."

His chin dropped to his chest. "My name is Judge Terrence R. Harper." His voice was shaky with pain.

"Do you state and declare upon your oath that the statements made by you during this deposition are true and correct under penalty of perjury?"

"I do."

"Do you know who I am?"

"Yes."

"What is my full name?"

"Trent Henry Varus."

"How do you know me?"

"I was the presiding judge during your murder trial many years ago."

"Do you and did you know the recently deceased District Attorney, then Deputy District Attorney Walter Callahan, who prosecuted the case of *People v. Varus*?"

"Yes."

"Do you know Captain Michael Johnson, then Detective Michael Johnson, the lead homicide detective assigned to the case of *People v. Varus*?"

"Y-yes," he stammered. Nervous perspiration broke out heavily across his face. His eyes now appeared lazy, unfocused.

"Do you know Gary Kirkpatrick, the defense attorney during the case of *People v. Varus?*"

"Yes."

Trent changed legs. Vindication rose in his heart. "Did a time arrive when you, the deputy district attorney at the time, the homicide detective, and the defense counsel met in your chambers to discuss the future of the Varus case?"

His breathing grew labored, his tongue running over dry lips. "Um … yes."

Trent grinned, satisfied so far. "Did the four of you conspire to insure that Trent Henry Varus was in fact convicted of murder in the first degree?"

His face tightened, skin paling. His eyes widened. "How did you—"

Trent raised the gun and silenced him. "I'm asking the questions!" he snapped. "How I found out is inconsequential and irrelevant to this deposition, so answer the question."

Harper nodded. "Yes."

Trent narrowed his eyes, suspicious. "Yes, what?"

"Yes, the four of us conspired to ensure you, Trent H. Varus, were convicted."

"Do you deny that you did indeed know for certain that Trent H. Varus, namely me, was factually and legally innocent of the crime for which the four of you conspired to convict me?"

A heavy sigh fell from his mouth. "No, Varus," he mumbled. His voice sounded defeated. "I don't deny that all of us knew you were innocent."

Trent leaned back in the chair. His heart fluttered in his chest. The great weight of a burden he had carried seemed to slip from off his shoulders for the first time in what felt like a lifetime. He had waited years to hear those magical words, affirmation that he was innocent and not out of his mind. No matter how any defendant might get a conviction overturned or reversed, no one ever believes it is because of innocence. Everyone just assumes some legal technicality or loophole let slip free the guilty party, when in fact there is no such thing as a technicality or loophole in law. The authorities conjured up the vapid reason to mislead the ignorant masses, and the asinine words of the general population, "It's not a perfect system, but it's the best one in the world" always made him want to puke. He thought people that naive should be statutorily legislated as criminals.

Tears of redemption rolled down Trent's face. *Finally, after so many years, I have an admission of truth.*

He turned his eyes back on Harper. "Judge Harper, in your own words, I want you to describe what the four of you agreed upon to set up Trent Varus and secure his conviction for the crime of murder, a crime you have readily admitted you knew he was innocent of." He leaned forward and drilled his eyes into those of Harper, stealthily reaching behind his belt for the handle of a knife.

Harper angled his eyes upward and looked at Trent with what looked almost like shame. Exhaling, his chest moved up and down. His face spoke volumes. The decades-old charade had reached an end. There was nowhere to run, nowhere to hide. It was over. He was over.

With a pained gasp, Harper pushed up with his good arm and straightened his body against the desk. He cleared his throat. "This is what I know," he said.

Trent remained seated as Judge Terrence Harper revealed a saga that spanned years, rarely moving his body or averting his eyes. He was both appalled and fascinated as Judge Harper vividly described the systematic means he and his coconspirators had used to decimate every nuance of his life. Trent felt his commitment to visit everyone involved etch further into a destiny not yet fulfilled.

Soon, everyone would pay for what he had done.

CHAPTER 13

Having arrived at the vacant lot next to the city's only Starbucks fifteen minutes after Snapshot called him, as previously ordered if Trent Varus deviated from his business routine, Dominique Cieo raised a pair of high-powered binoculars and stared with dead eyes from the passenger side of a nondescript, late-model station wagon parked across the street from the courthouse. A throwaway cell phone rested on the seat beside his left leg. Stoic and emotionless, he had waited patiently in hope that Trent would stay on course and things would progress on schedule, according to a plan he had set in motion years prior to this day.

His chilling, thousand-yard stare missed nothing. Trained and methodical in everything he did when focused on a job not yet finished, Cieo had never experienced defeat. Pride and professionalism refused to allow failure. His one-track mind compartmentalized each intricate detail relevant to accomplishing his goal, pushing aside all things not connected, and he did not welcome distractions of any sort. Flawless best described his preferred execution on matters deemed business related.

Snapshot, who had alerted Cieo to Varus's anticipated move to next seek out Judge Harper and make him his third victim, sat rigid on the driver side of the station wagon, silent and unmoving. He was no doubt content to sit in solemn quietude and wait for his employer, a ruthless killer, to resume the brief conversation they had started when Cieo had first entered the vehicle.

Local traffic on the two-lane street had dwindled over the past twenty minutes to only a few sporadic cars traveling north and south. The low number of pedestrians that currently walked up and down the sidewalks on either side of the street matched the number of those driving, which made his surveillance on the huge structure and the prowler moving around behind its walls that much easier.

Cieo squinted. A slow grin crept across his cruel, thin lips. Darkness always seemed to nurture his scarred soul, joined by another seductive taste of envy that whetted his voracious appetite for the hunt he had counted on for quite some time. There was nothing like it on earth. He had hunted virtually every kind of beast that had walked, crawled, and slithered at one time or another, all proving little challenge for his honed skills. There was nothing more satisfying than stalking and killing a man. Above all, man was the most lethal creature on the planet, often proving more cruel and savage than ever believed possible, and his ability to reason made Cieo's homicidal trade a far more challenging and infinitely more interesting hobby than any other he'd undertaken. In all his years of taking human lives with guns, knives, or garrotes, very few men had ever impressed him as a worthy opponent. He had hunted some of the best murderers on the earth, successfully killing all without incurring so much as a scratch.

Soon after the desert explosion had taken place, Cieo had realized, whether he liked it or not, that his secret recruit—so secret that even Trent still remained in the dark about his induction into the criminal life to serve as a necessary tool for Cieo's ultimate endgame—was quickly proving extremely skilled. The temptation to join in on his student's mission and take an assertive hands-on approach, rather than observe from the distance, niggled incessantly at the back of his mind. He had always prided himself on being a doer, not a casual observer hidden away behind the shadows, where it was safe and sanitized. He could not help but wonder what marvelous things churned through his unwitting protégé's mind while dispensing the only form of justice at his disposal on the corruption that had ruined his life.

Time and place secures rational thinking. Cieo took a deep, contemplative breath, reminiscing the first time he had taken a human life. *Patience and disciplined self-control serves as the master to compartmentalize all emotional investments.*

Finally, Cieo made a low grunt and rested the binoculars on his lap. He stole a quick glance at the time on his wristwatch. "Once again, exactly how long did you wait before you called me?" He craned his neck to the left and turned black eyes on Snapshot.

A lightning-fast wince flickered across the smaller man's face, and he jerked away from the darkness people claimed embodied Cieo's raw essence. Cieo narrowed his eyes, aware that Snapshot had reacted the same way everyone did whenever trapped in closed quarters with him. No one had ever taken the time to explain why his presence affected people on such a primal level, not that he actually cared.

Cieo moved his left hand to the cell phone, tapped it with a finger. "Speak," he ordered. "We may be only minutes from critical mass here, so I need to know how long he has been in the building. Time and distance equates efficiency and effectiveness."

Snapshot's throat constricted, fear apparent in his eyes. "Fifteen minutes, sir." His voice pinched. His eyes darted away from the man who represented death incarnate. "I considered calling you sooner, but I wanted to make sure he entered the building and didn't have a change of heart at the last second." His Adam's apple bobbed. "Sometimes people get squeamish."

Cieo's facial features remained passive, unchanged, as he let the feeble explanation sink in. True to form, he had harnessed all control over his feelings, substituting them with logic and rationale. "So, you played it safe, weighed the odds before committing?" he said, pursing his lips ever so slightly. "You can't have believed Varus would not see this through once he breached the alarms."

Snapshot's face grimaced at the question. "I wanted to be

thorough and certain, sir." Strain tugged at his voice. "I am aware of your policy about errors." His voice caught in his throat. "I have heard that there are not second ones."

Cieo nodded. He turned his eyes back on the building across the street. "Do you think there is a chance that he knows you followed him here?"

"No way in hell," he said. Belief in his words showed on his face. "I attached a GPS tracker on the car's chassis two days ago, the same day you hired me to maintain a surveillance on him, so I did not have to stay right on his tail. He can't have made me."

Impressed with the man's foresight, Cieo growled his pleasure. "Smart and thorough," he said. "I like that in the men I hire."

Snapshot's shoulders shrugged. "I'm just good at what I do."

"So it seems," he said. "Did you get the pictures of him sneaking into the courthouse?"

His head bobbed. "Just as you instructed, sir," he said in a conspiratorial tone. For the first time since Cieo had gotten into his vehicle, a sly grin formed on his mouth. "He didn't see me, but I did see him. You can count the hairs on his head."

Again, Cieo nodded. "Excellent work," he said. "I must say that I am most pleased with your work and the work of your computer expert."

"He is one of the best, if not the best," Snapshot said.

"I am especially awed with how he hacked into the mainframe of the witness protection program's database and leaked the location and information on the snitching bastard Jerry Smith to Varus," Cieo said. "His tactics of utilizing the data banks of the Internal Revenue Service to infiltrate and deliver the intelligence was an ingenious bit of cryptic software manipulation and maneuvering. The work is most impressive, if I say so myself. At least the intelligence gathering done by the government and corporate America under the Patriot Act isn't completely worthless to the private sector." He smirked at the irony of the sordid affair. "We must love our government and its insistence on invading everyone's personal space." He paused. "By the people, for the people, of the people," He shook his head in disgust. "Give me a break!"

A look of confusion covered Snapshot's face. "I guess," he offered lamely. "I don't have a political position. I just do what I'm paid to do, sir."

Cieo wrinkled up his nose at the smell of complacency. "Fair enough," he offered. "I can respect that, I suppose."

"Thank you, sir."

"Is there anything else you have to tell me, something that might prove interesting?" he said, cocking an eyebrow. "How is our mutual friend Captain Johnson doing?"

A snicker fell from Snapshot's lips. "You guessed everything right, sir." Humor peppered his voice. "He and that dirtball prosecutor contacted me about looking into Varus's whereabouts at the times you predicted. We met at a small diner to talk about all things Varus related. A different jerk-off cop was with them by the name of Barry Markinson."

"Markinson, huh?" he repeated. "Did you run him for me?"

"Of course," he said, pointing at the glove department. "A copy of his file is in there. He is unimpressive. However, he does have a checkered career; evidently, this particular officer likes to smack his wife around. She has had several trips to the hospital. No charges ever filed."

"I can't imagine why," he said sarcastically.

"Yeah, a real prince of the city," he said.

"What did you tell them in answer to their questions?"

"Exactly what you told me." His voice was mechanical. "I tossed a lot of bread crumbs in hope that they would pick up on a couple of them and go down the rabbit hole."

"Good," he said, "but did you follow my instructions and inform Captain Johnson that Detective Lomax had paid a visit to that dope fiend defense attorney Gary Kirkpatrick?"

Snapshot nodded, smiling.

Cieo grinned and continued. "Did you tell him that he tried to pump him for information on the Varus case from years ago, about his suspected connections?"

"I did," he said.

"How did he react?"

"In a nutshell," he began, "nervous and then angry."

"Excellent," he said. "I like nervous and angry. The combination creates mistakes in judgment." He rested his chin on his fist. "And how is that cockroach Benny Maldonado? What about those genetic misfit nephews of his?"

Snapshot ran a hand over his face. "That's a whole different level of insanity." His voice took on a bizarre tone. "They're holed up in a flea-bitten motel, using it as some sort of hideout. It's the Motel 6 on the corner of Pine and Ash, a real dump. Those three are circling the drain."

"I figured as much," he said. "Have warrants for their arrest been issued?"

"I don't know." His voice quavered. "Something funny is going on with that whole situation."

"I don't doubt it," he said. "Things are about to get even funnier."

Snapshot's brow wrinkled. "How's that?"

Cieo ignored the question. Instead, he picked up the cell phone and dialed Captain Johnson's personal number. He waited for three rings and then smiled when he heard a grouchy voice answer.

"This is Johnson. Who is this?"

Cieo winked at Snapshot, allowing Johnson a few seconds to stew in the silence that separated them.

"I won't ask twice!"

"Tsk, tsk," Cieo teased. "Do you realize the hour and what we can do to you and yours?"

"Who is this?" A note of apprehension infiltrated the words. "What do you want?"

Cieo cleared his throat. "You exercise very poor phone etiquette, Mr. Johnson," he said in a silky smooth voice. "Has anyone ever told you such? There is never a reason to be rude to those who call."

A frightened squeak came from Johnson's voice. "I apologize, Mr.—"

"Do not call me by the familiar over the phone," he warned in an eerie monotone. Cieo had made it abundantly clear on several occasions that he was the last of God's creatures anyone wanted to anger, having forced Johnson to personally witness the sadistic extent to which he would gladly go to deal with a perceived problem. "I do not trust open lines with legally sensitive issues."

"Of course," said Johnson. "I understand."

Cieo chuckled. "You see, that is progress," he said. "Nevertheless, we, my employer that is, is now frankly a little concerned about this overzealous detective you so myopically assigned to investigate some very interesting cases that involve our mutual associates. In particular, we have grave concerns about his inquiries into the recent developments of the investigation my employer specifically requested that you independently conduct outside the one orchestrated by Internal Affairs."

"I-I don't understand." His voice stammered. "I have a lid on this thing. Nothing is at risk—I swear."

"Are you certain?" he said, adding a touch of doubt to the words. "He is proving rather shrewd, uncannily intuitive."

"Yes, I am sure!"

Cieo could almost smell the burning rags that Captain Johnson used for a brain. "Then why does this detective seem to think our associates might have knowledge of your old friends' activities?" he said with severity. "I have it on good authority that a lawyer by the name of Gary Kirkpatrick has spoken about a shady past best left alone. I do not react well to difficulties."

"Wh-what are you saying?" Johnson's voice was tremulous.

"We find this unwanted intrusion into our private lives rather unsettling, Mr. Johnson," he said matter-of-factly. "I do hope that you can appreciate our situation."

"I assure you that everything is completely under control."

"*Control* is the operative word, my dear captain," he said. "Whatever this Varus issue may be, we want you to see that it does not create discomfort for us. We do not like drama. Trust me—you will not like things if we become disenchanted with your ability to cleanly rectify things."

"I have everything handled."

"Do not force us to call in a sweeper," he said. "We are believers in scorched earth policy."

"That will never be necessary."

"Pray that it isn't."

"Uh-huh."

"Now, what about this Lomax fellow?" he said. "Clearly, he must have some sort of premise for asking such specific questions about your Mr. Callahan and meeting with this defense attorney? We do not believe in coincidences, and we do not like complications."

"Perhaps he is just fishing."

"We do not believe this is the case," he said with an edge to his voice. "The others he has asked about worked in tandem with Mr. Callahan. I know that you know these gentlemen rather well."

"Which gentlemen are you referring to?"

"I do not discuss such things over the phone," he chastised. "Suffice it to say, they are close acquaintances, if you will."

"Did he say in what capacity?"

"Not over the phone."

"Was my name mentioned?"

"That was my inference."

"If there is a problem at all, I promise to take care of it as soon as possible." The words came out with a small squeak.

"Be sure that you do."

"Lomax has hinted that someone on your side spoke with him." Johnson's voice was low and uncertain. "Could that be possible?"

Cieo paused to give the illusion that he was considering the question before answering. He recognized a desperate attempt to curtail the subject. "What was said that led you to believe such was done?"

"Lomax told me he has an informant." His tone lacked conviction. "He thinks this informant will drop names."

Annoyed by such a sophomoric attempt to distract him from the real issue, Cieo switched the phone to his other ear. "I see," he said, speaking the words exceedingly slowly for effect. "I will look into this matter immediately and then deal with it posthaste."

"Is there anything else that can be done to prove that I have these things under control?"

"As a matter of fact, there is something you may do for us that will indebt me to you," he said, finessing the most important part of his plans into the conversation. He needed to set the stage properly and force his heart's desire to the surface. "If you are unable to do this for me, then we will understand that some things—"

"Just name it," Johnson interrupted.

"Are you certain?"

"Consider it done."

Cieo said nothing for several seconds.

"Are you still there?"

Cieo cleared his throat before speaking again. "Do you know a Mr. Benny Maldonado?"

"Huh?" His voice sounded confused. "Benny Maldonado? Why would you want anything to do with that low-life loser?"

"The question is whether you know him, Captain Johnson," he said. "So, do you?"

"Um, yeah, I know who he is." His tone reflected his lack of understanding. "May I inquire as to why?"

"We would like for you to apply a little pressure on this Maldonado person to go after Varus and force him to back the hell up," he said.

"Why?" His voice came out with a whine. "Back up from what?"

"That's our business."

"Maldonado may be a little reluctant to go after Varus," he said. "I'm pretty sure they go back a few years as friends. They may be a bit estranged at the moment, some sort of falling-out, but they have history."

"Can you do this for us or not?"

"All I can promise is that I will try."

"Captain Johnson, it behooves you to do whatever you can

to convince this Maldonado person to silence Varus," he said. "Obsolescence does not have a long life expectancy in our line of work, as I am sure you well know."

"Do you want me to threaten him?"

"Threats are for amateurs, people lacking adequate brain capacity to reason a viable solution," he said sternly. "I am sure Mr. Maldonado has the means with which to handle this situation. His nephews are quite handy in a pinch, are they not?"

"What are you saying?" Johnson's voice took on a fearful edge.

"I'm just thinking out loud, my dear captain," he said. "If you are so inclined to assist on this issue, I believe you will find Mr. Maldonado and company at the Motel 6 located on the corner of Pine and Ash." He winked at Snapshot. "They may be a bit on the dangerous side, so you may want to take a few of your trusted men with you."

"How do you know he's at that location?" Worry touched the captain's words. "Even we don't know where they disappeared to."

Cieo snickered coldly into the phone. "Nothing happens in this town that I do not know about," he said. "I am everywhere, watching, listening. One never knows when life may come to depend on a shred of information. I suggest you get moving before they do."

"I will handle this for you tomorrow night, sometime around dinner," he said. "I will need a little time to gather the right men for the job."

"I thought you might," he said. "And the Kirkpatrick issue?"

"I don't know where he is at this time."

"I believe you will find Mr. Kirkpatrick at the Club Nouveau around midnight," he said. "He frequents that place."

"If he is there tonight, I will speak with him on the matters we have already discussed." A new strength filled Johnson's voice. "However, Gary Kirkpatrick is a bit of a wild card and—"

"He will be there," Cieo said, cutting the captain off before he finished the sentence. The last thing he wanted to hear was some sort of lame excuse or alibi for something that had not yet come to fruition. "I am well aware of Mr. Kirkpatrick's extracurricular activities, and he has never turned down an invitation from a beautiful woman."

"Then consider it done."

"On behalf of my esteemed employer, I thank you for this disclosure and your assistance on these matters." Cieo clicked off the cell phone and laid it back down on the seat.

Snapshot shifted in the seat.

Cieo craned his neck and looked at Snapshot. "Something on your mind?" he said. "If you have something to say, please do not pull the shy act on me now."

"How long have you been keeping tabs on Varus?" His voice was low, careful.

"A very long time," he admitted. "Varus does not realize it yet, but he has the ability to give me something I want. He lost it once, but he can get it back if he reaches out and takes a chance." He took a deep breath, daring to hope that he might reunite with the last of his family for the first time since childhood. "I just need to put a little pressure in the right place, force a confrontation, and leave a desperate man no choice but to use the only hidden weapon in his arsenal that will forever alter my life for the best."

Snapshot's brows knitted. "What are you talking about? You are talking in riddles."

"I am talking about dreams, lost, not forgotten," he said. "And I want one of them back."

Snapshot lifted his hands and rubbed at his temples. "How did you know that Varus would take the bait and move on the judge?" Something about the way he asked the question created an air of intrigue between them. "It sounds like you have seen it coming for a long time."

Cieo smirked with mirth. "Eyes and ears, my friend," he said, his voice crisp and filled with confidence. "I have them everywhere, on the street and behind prison walls. There is no such thing as useless information, and my people have kept an eye on him at my behest ever since a few unsavory characters decided to make him a patsy to take the heat and clean up their mess."

"I understand that," he said, "but there seems to be more involved. You sound like you actually like this guy."

Cieo considered Snapshot's words for several seconds, thinking before he spoke. "How long have we've known each other, Xander?"

A frown crossed Snapshot's face, no doubt a reaction to the uncommon use of his first name while in the middle of a job. "A long time," he said. "We were friends when you first stabbed that kid in the playground for hurting your sister."

Cieo smiled at the only man who had never tried anything shady on him. His sister's screams as he plunged his pocketknife into the bully's neck still haunted him when he felt alone in the world. "I remember that day as if it were yesterday," he said. "I still remember how you tried to take the blame for me. You are perhaps the only man in the world I actually trust."

"The jerk got what was coming to him," he said with an angry growl. "Everyone knew how protective you were over her, and he should not have grabbed her and made her cry. I still remember when the cops showed up, yanked her out of your arms as if you were some sort of monster, and then took you away in their squad car."

Cieo nodded. "Which is the prime example of why I do not condone the victimization of innocent people," he said. "Life is hard enough, and none of the hardworking people need our garbage on top of their problems. It is just bad business. Nevertheless, even after the world turned completely against him at nearly every level, Varus still refused to submit. Deep down, I do not think we are so different. He had lost everything—his wife, his children, and his freedom—for decades. Yet he still refused to stop fighting for his life. I cannot help but admire him and his inner strength. The man does not seem to know how to quit or fail. Any man unwilling to lie down and take a beating has always intrigued me. Currently, in an era where everyone claims entitlement and victimhood, such a person is truly rare. Most people just lie down and die when life gets too hard. Moreover, I figure a man like Varus is not likely to forgive and forget so easily.

I find those traits rather useful. With a little criminal education and a push in the right direction, a man like Varus can serve as a valuable asset to someone like me, which is why I paid a few prisoners on the sly to provide him with the necessary tools to serve our needs."

"Is that why you brought me into this life?" Snapshot's voice was unsteady.

"I'm sure such had something to do with it," he said. "You are loyal and tricky, and you do not faint at the sight of blood. Do we not pay you well for your services? Do you not live a lifestyle that exceeds that of most people?" He shrugged. "You simply leased your mind, body, and soul to us for money. Do you now harbor regrets? If you remember correctly, I never did force my will on you or your decision."

"I have no complaints."

Cieo waved the words off with a sweep of his hand. "Did you bring the materials I requested?" he said.

"Everything you wanted." Snapshot reached behind the front seat and retrieved a leather satchel. Cieo took the bag and quickly rifled through its contents. He found a pair of neoprene gloves, two surgical scalpels, a bone saw, a heavy-duty cleaver, four thumbtacks, a couple of paper clips, and four yellow Post-it notes with the words scribbled on them per his citation individually sealed inside plastic baggies. He then nodded. "Everything seems to be here. Good job."

"Do you want me to remain here and wait for you?"

He shook his head. "No. I will not be coming back to the car. I have made other arrangements. I want you to stay here until Varus exits the building. Make sure you get plenty of pictures as he comes out of the building, and then you can go home for the night."

"Are you sure?" His nose wrinkled up. "You don't want me to follow him from here?"

"No," he said flatly. "Just bring me the pictures tomorrow morning, and I will have fifty thousand waiting for you."

"I can keep a tail and follow him tonight, see where he goes from here."

"Absolutely not," he said with a growl. "Stay away from him. The last thing I need is for him to think someone is onto him. I already have a good idea where he is going tonight." He opened the car door. "Just get some good shots of him coming out, and go home. Only then is your job for today done."

He tucked the satchel under his arm, stepped out of the car, and headed toward the side of the building. His stroll was calm and casual, and he whistled his favorite Phil Collins song.

For the past hour, Trent had remained seated in the farthest corner booth in the smoke-filled nightclub, staring past the twirling dervishes on the dance floor and across the room at his former defense attorney Gary Kirkpatrick. Bitter disgust filled him as he watched the man standing alongside a wall next to the door of the club's pathetic excuse for a kitchen in the bent-over position snorting thick rails of cocaine spread over a vanity mirror. The picture conjured up a thousand words. How a man directly attached to the legal profession—many times serving as the only advocate to defend an accused client whose life hung precariously in the balance—could sink so low in the sewer, Trent had no clue. Just the thought that the man now playfully sprinkling his brain with mind-altering fairy dust, and had probably partied in a similar fashion while working on his case, made him sick to his stomach.

Trent ground his teeth together in anger, thinking about all the savage things he wanted to do to Kirkpatrick but that limited time would not allow.

Rage soon joined his disgust in an unholy marriage of dark and ugly emotions, and it took all his self-control not to simply sprint across the room and strangle Kirkpatrick for every able-bodied partier in the club to witness. The mere image of the man who had worked in nefarious tandem with others to destroy his life now debasing his own existence only increased his hatred for all those involved in his undoing.

The pounding volume of the music continued to ring painfully in his ears.

Two other men Trent easily recognized as Captain Michael Johnson and Special Prosecuting Attorney Sebastian Crue sat together on the far right side of the table. They had situated themselves nearly four feet back, as if they were trying to distance themselves from the illegal activities of an attorney whose once unblemished reputation and glory days in the courtroom had long vanished.

Trent hissed through his teeth. "You worthless reprobate," he muttered under his breath. "You conspired to murder my family for dope? Are you kidding me?" He rubbed at his eyes to clear his vision of the creepy dope fiend standing less than a hundred feet away, practically shoveling a narcotic up his nose.

Time had not been kind to his onetime defense attorney. What little remained of his silver hair appeared unkempt and knotted. His face was wrinkled and desiccated like a worn-out catcher's mitt with sunken eyeballs. His outdated suit was tattered and terribly faded. Out of the three men grouped together, only Kirkpatrick seemed to have aged so poorly.

Oh, how the mighty have fallen!

Trent had watched Johnson and Crue slide through the double doors guarded by a huge bodyguard and enter the club nearly a half hour earlier. Neither man had appeared remotely pleased to be in such an environment as they headed into the crowd, taking a direct route toward the other side of the building. A look of business had marked their unsmiling faces as Johnson sliced through the crowd, shoving and pushing at men and women to keep the sweaty masses away from him. His partner, Crue, had kept close on his heels to avoid a similar unwanted collision.

Only minutes after the two men had finally taken a seat at the same table occupied by Kirkpatrick had their facial expressions transformed into something visibly lethal. Their reactions made it abundantly clear that they were furious at the man ingesting drugs without shame right in front of them. Johnson had pointed an accusatory finger at Kirkpatrick several times during a heated discussion between the three men, but the defense attorney seemed undaunted by the exchange, opting instead to use his nose as a vacuum to suck up the white powder that had spilled onto the table from an overturned sandwich bag.

Johnson had pounded a fist on the table a few times in a vain attempt to gain Kirkpatrick's attention, but all the man had done was busily snort more drugs and grope the tantalizing flesh of his female company.

Trent assumed the argument had something to do with Kirkpatrick's refusal to hide his nasty habit from them or the other customers wandering in front of the table.

Men and women of all ages—some women dancing with other women, while some men danced with other men—writhed against one another on the hardwood floor like oily eels in orgiastic rhythm to the music.

Everyone danced drunk or stoned, more than likely both.

Repulsed by the surrounding atmosphere and the loud music blasting at merciless decibels that only added to the sexual frenzy within the four walls, Trent cringed inwardly as Kirkpatrick raised his head from the table. He watched him dip his fingers into a glass containing some kind of alcohol and then sniff at their tips in an apparent attempt to moisten the thrashed tissue that lined his nostrils. Trent knew that it was a trick some of the old-timers had used back in the eighties, a time when drugs, booze, and loud music were all the rage in nightclubs for the rich and aimless. For the party animals' intent on destroying their young lives before they even got started, such nightly antics had served as the great American pastime.

Two women barely clad in skintight dresses that left very little to the imagination—a buxom blonde-haired woman and a brunette who looked underage for such a club—sat laughing on either side of the failed defense attorney. Each woman eagerly slid a hand up and down the inside of his thighs, playfully bumping his crotch while holding what Trent thought were rolled up dollar bills to use as straws for the next offered line. He figured the lifestyle enjoyed by his former lawyer had cost him everything a beautiful life had to offer.

Hearing the rumors had been one thing, but to actually see the man that had promised him freedom in action felt like a sucker punch to the gut. Nothing could have made it clearer. His lawyer had obviously sold him and his family out to maintain the status quo of enjoying a party that never ended.

A young server wearing a pair of purple leggings, paper-thin material that advertised every curve and fold of her tight body, approached his table. Her body blocked his view of Kirkpatrick. Her upturned mouth formed a seductive grin. Her eyes sparked with a glassy hazel.

Trent set down his glass, reclined back against the cushion, and ran a hand over his freshly bleached blond hair. He righted the pair of glasses that accentuated the light brown contact lenses he had put in to complete the necessary task of disguising his natural features under the blinking lights of the club. The vintage clothes he wore were indicative of an older man desperately trying to cling to an age that had come and gone twenty years earlier, which he had intended to make him appear all the more harmless in the chaos that would soon ensue in the club's pandemonium.

The server held up an electronic pad, tapped the glowing screen with a long fingernail, and looked down at him with a bored expression on her painted face. Her nostrils flared, sniffing several times at the air.

"Would you like another drink, sir?" Her voice was that of a teenage girl, squeaky and high-pitched. She had to shout through the cacophony for him to hear.

Trent leaned over to the side and looked around her narrow body. The blonde and brunette now had their heads lowered to the mirror, straws sticking from their noses. He cleared his throat, straightened up, and nodded. "Yes, sweetheart," he said in a fake British accent. He tapped the glass on the table. "I'll have another one. Please, make it neat this time."

Her face took on a faraway look, as she shifted her eyes over to the glass holding only ice cubes. She leaned forward, wrinkling up her nose in a grimace. "I'm sorry, sir." She pointed the device at the glass. "But could you please remind me what you had. We are really hopping tonight, and I can't seem to remember much of anything." Her nose flared again, eyes watering. "My memory isn't working real good tonight, definitely not part of one of those beautiful mind things."

Trent pursed his lips, wondering how much time would pass before someone discovered her overdosed body dumped in a dumpster. He reached out and pushed the glass across the table, sliding it closer to her, and laid a twenty-dollar bill next to it. "Please, just bring me another Mai Tai," he said. "Forget the neat; make it heavy on the ice."

She tapped her finger on the glass of the electronic pad. "Will there be anything—"

A woman stepped out from the crowd of dancers and tapped her on the shoulder, interrupting her. His server's neck craned to the left, and an unfriendly grin crossed the other woman's face. "Yeah, Margaret," the server said in an irritable tone. "What do you want?"

"Phone call for you, Denise," Trent heard the woman called Margaret say with similar attitude.

His server's head bobbed her understanding. "Thanks, I'll be there in just a second."

Margaret spun with a huff and disappeared back into the crowd.

His server's attention returned to him "Just the Mai Tai, sir?"

Trent nodded and gave a thumbs-up to avoid having to yell.

Denise trailed after Margaret.

Trent returned his attention to Kirkpatrick, who had just kissed the blonde-haired woman on the mouth, before turning around and heading toward the back of the club, where Trent knew the restrooms were located.

Kirkpatrick vanished into the wave of sweaty bodies.

Johnson and Crue had turned their anger on each other and were busy shaking their heads at each other, appearing caught in an argument Trent had no chance of overhearing. The women still sitting at the table continued to chop up small rocks of cocaine with a razor blade and take turns on the mirror.

Trent grinned at the opportunity that had finally presented itself to him, knocking loudly on his door. *I got you, now, you son of a bitch!* Victory was now his for the taking. He felt it down into his bones.

He hurriedly scooted along the curved seat of the booth and got out from behind the table. The timing was perfect. Those in the throes of physical undulation were oblivious to anything outside their blissful circle, unwittingly providing him the necessary cover of sexual chaos. His patience had finally paid off, and he could hardly wait to see the look on Kirkpatrick's face when his long-forgotten past stabbed a vengeful blow into his arm. Pure adrenaline rushed through his body, with the powerful impact of the strongest aphrodisiac known to man, now that he was back on his fourth hunt to collect another long overdue payment from a man who had lived on borrowed time long enough.

On the prowl through the crowd, Trent rose up on his toes and caught sight of Kirkpatrick's head moving past the sea of hair. He trailed after his intended target, stealthily meandering through the mass of heads whipping about their necks in synchronized orbit to the thrash of their frenzied partner.

Time has run out on you. You want to dance, you have to pay the band.

He withdrew a thin pair of latex gloves from his pocket and slid them on as he continued to navigate his way across the floor, narrowing the distance between him and Kirkpatrick with every step. His eyes never wavered from the top of his target's head. Faces blurred as Trent moved past one couple after another, certain the dancers focused only on their next move and the one made by their partner. The intensity of the flashing lights dangling from the ceiling, spinning in a kaleidoscope of bright colors, created a near dizzying effect that rendered everyone on the dance floor incapable of seeing anyone's face clearly.

When Trent finally made his way to the other side of the dance floor, he turned right and circumnavigated the outside perimeter in close tow of Kirkpatrick, who turned left under a glowing sign that read "Men's Restroom" and disappeared behind a door.

Trent stopped just outside the door, surprised to find no line to visit the facilities. He turned and took a quick survey of the immediate area. In an ocean of nondescript faces and personalities, no one gave him a second glance, all attention enraptured by those still dancing to the beat. Johnson and Crue were still sitting at the table, angrily pointing fingers at each other, still obviously arguing over something to which he was not privy. The music sounded even louder in his ears on this side of the club. He reached into his shirt pocket and withdrew an insulin needle commonly used by diabetics.

Trent entered the bathroom, squinting under the bright florescent lights that traveled down the length of the ceiling. A dozen porcelain sinks lined the wall on the left, a row of bathroom stalls on the right. A dozen urinals attached to the far wall from where he stood rounded out the facilities. Black and white tiles checkered the floor. The stench of marijuana and Turkish hash filled the air, layering the atmosphere inside the restroom with a smoky haze. Men and women moaning in sexual pleasure came from behind the locked doors of the stalls.

He grumbled his disgust with the entire situation, grateful that no one was using the sinks or urinals.

"Come on, Joey," a female voice said from behind one of the stalls. "It's all good. I like it hard. I want you to slap and choke me while doing me hard! Use the popper on me if you want. If you won't do it, then I will find someone out there who will. It's all the same to me."

I bet Dad is just so proud.

Trent swallowed his discontent and walked down the length of the stalls, stealing a quick look into the empty space between the door and wall in search of a lone pair of feet. He found what he was looking for behind the seventh door, readying the syringe filled with a cocktail of heroin and cocaine, a lethal combination referred to as a speedball.

He knocked on the door. "Excuse me," he said in a phony British accent. "Is someone in there? I need to use the loo."

"Take a hike, you limey bastard," the familiar voice of Gary

Kirkpatrick said from behind the door. "This one is in use. Try the next one."

Heavy grunts coming from several stalls grew in volume, and someone was now banging on a partition wall that separated the stalls. A screech of female voices cried out in a mixture of demands and pleasure, followed by the sound of men groaning and cursing aloud at their sexual partners. A loud slap of skin against skin cut through the gale of moans and only seemed to feed into the frenzied lust behind closed doors.

Trent kicked the stall door open and rushed past the door. The stunned look on Kirkpatrick's face as he sat on the toilet staring up at him brought an instant grin to his face. Nothing had ever felt as satisfying as standing only a foot away from the man sitting helplessly on the crapper with a wad of toilet paper clutched in his hand. He slammed the needle into Kirkpatrick's neck and depressed the plunger, emptying the contents in less than a second. He yanked free the needle, dropping it to the floor, next to the toilet.

The deadly combination took effect immediately. Kirkpatrick's legs and arms jerked several times. Spasms wracked his body, foam forming at his mouth and running down his chin.

His arms soon fell loosely at his sides, the wad of toilet paper slipping from between his fingers. Then his body went completely still; his head drooping lifelessly, his chin on his chest.

Trent stepped from out of the stall, closed the door, and walked toward the exit. He placed his hand against the door, paused, and then craned his neck. It was clear that nothing could interrupt the debauchery behind the row of doors, because those having sex and doing God only knew what in the other stalls paid no attention to what was happening outside their hedonistic world. No one had missed a beat to continue his or her quest to seek the ultimate form of physical pleasure.

He pushed open the door and headed straight for the exit. The last thing he saw right before leaving the nightclub was Johnson and Crue leading the two women by the hand toward the dance floor.

CHAPTER 15

Lomax stepped out of the bathroom and frowned. He was surprised to find that only a skeleton crew remained on duty inside the precinct—two janitors dumping trash, a few secretaries working on computers and dropping documents on their coworkers' desks, and a lone desk officer. He stretched out his arms and burped, wondering what had happened during the twenty minutes he had spent in the bathroom ridding his stomach of a soured ham and cheese omelet he'd known better than to eat. It occurred to him that everyone in the department was probably doing something incredibly stupid, like celebrating another lousy birthday for some jerk who did next to nothing in the neighborhood of work to earn a slice of cake. Lately, it seemed that everyone had been born in the same crummy month. It was no coincidence that he had stopped counting his birthdays. His last dinner date had thrown a glass of cheap wine in his face and kicked him in the balls for insulting feminism on his special day.

He took a seat at his desk and retrieved a bottle of Pepto-Bismol from a secret stash he kept in the drawer. He took two big swallows of the pink liquid, drained it of its contents, and again burped, praying that it would cure his upset stomach. His day had not started well. The days were starting to blend into one long stretch of dead body after dead body. The only thing missing in his busy week was another massive headache. A case of diarrhea was just one meal away.

Lomax tossed the bottle in the trash can next to his desk, leaned back in his chair, and closed his eyes.

Someone in the room knocked on a desktop and disturbed his sought-after solitude. He slowly opened his left eye and looked in the direction of the interruption.

The precinct's desk officer stood only a few feet away. His face appeared strained and exhausted. "Excuse me, Detective." His voice sounded equally tired. "Is something wrong?"

Lomax closed his eye. "Why are you bothering me, kid?" he said with a slight growl. "I don't come over to where you work and pester you."

"Um, shouldn't you be at the courthouse?" he said in a pinched voice. "I'm fairly certain that the orders were clear."

Lomax yawned. "Why would I be at the courthouse?" he said. "I'm not scheduled to testify, or anything else." He waved the desk officer off with a hand. "Go away."

Feet shuffled about the floor.

"Why are you still here?"

His throat cleared. "Something major is going on at the courthouse." Nervousness now touched his voice. "The captain ordered all essential personnel to report at the courthouse effective immediately."

"Uh-huh."

The desk clerk continued. "You do realize that the mayor of the city has placed courthouse security on high alert and issued an executive state of emergency decree that ordered the structure and all surrounding buildings on full lockdown status, don't you?" His tone turned severe. "All state and county employees, including other personnel and civilians, received orders not to leave the premises. The mayor has promised swift and harsh punishment against anyone attempting to violate the order. In addition to those forced to remain indoors, the decree denies everyone situated outside all access into the structures without written clearance by Captain Johnson."

Lomax lowered his arms and lazily smacked his lips. "That's great, kid, but he didn't order me to do squat, so I'm happy to sit here and guard my phone," he said gruffly. "Now, go away, kid. I'm busy thinking up stuff here."

The officer grunted his disapproval. "Whatever," he said. "I'm just passing the message along. That's all."

Lomax cracked an eyelid and watched the officer walk back to his desk, snickering softly.

The phone on Lomax's desk suddenly chirped to life.

With a smirk of disdain on his face, the officer peered up and then lowered his eyes back to the paperwork on his desk when Lomax caught him in the act of spying.

He stared at the ringing phone as if it were a venomous snake ready to strike. He did not need special powers to know the caller's identify. His spider senses tingled. His stomach rumbled with acidic irritation. He winced and then farted.

His phone continued to ring.

Lomax snatched up the receiver. "Yeah, Lomax here."

An angry voice screamed over the phone and forced him to pull it away from his ear. "Are you still at the damn station?"

Lomax caught the desk officer watching him. This time a knowing grin that smacked of perceived vindication marked the young puke's face. Lomax glared a warning for him to mind his own business. "Yeah, I'm at the station!" he yelled back into the phone. "Isn't that where you called?"

"Don't be a smart-ass your whole life." The phone vibrated in his hand. "Where the hell were you, and why aren't you here? I gave specific orders for everyone to get their asses to the courthouse."

Lomax tightened his fingers around the receiver. "Well, hell, I was in the damn can, taking a dump. No one told me jack!" He nodded absently, rolling his eyes at how pathetic his excuse sounded.

"Do you know how pissed I am at you?"

"I'm sure you are, Captain," Lomax said.

"Now, get your ass down here on the double."

"All right," he said. "I'll be down as soon as I can." He ground his teeth together.

"Not soon," he shouted the words. "Get down here right this damn minute, now!"

"I said, all right," he shot back. "I'm leaving now, right now." He slammed the receiver down on the cradle with a crash.

Startled yelps of surprise came from the secretarial pool of women.

The desk officer was tapping his pen on his desk. "I told ya so." His voice mocked Lomax.

Lomax waved a dismissive hand through the air. "Shut your ass up, kid," he snapped tiredly. He rubbed at his temples, groaning miserably.

The mountain of work that had plagued him since Callahan's death was now wearing heavily down on him. He had not slept since, and his temper was growing thinner by the hour. Even his thinking was becoming clouded. Experience told him that something would have to give soon. No one could go on forever without sleep, and he was now running on pure fumes. The deeper he looked into the man's past, the more his concerns grew. Several names of highly questionable people continued to show up in hundreds of documents, narrowing the field of dangerous players directly involved with more than a hundred serious crimes.

The well-known defense attorney Trent Varus was among the leading characters in a playlist that read for volumes. He had finally finished reading the last of the files maintained on all those directly and indirectly involved in a drama that had spanned the better part of two decades. Varus may have had motive to seek revenge on those involved with his wrongful prosecution, but he had not found one shred of physical evidence that linked the lawyer to any crime. He did not need much to get a warrant—probable cause the immemorial standard—but he did need more than a gut instinct to curry favor. Judges did not validate a legal warrant with the I-got-a-feeling approach. Another problem Lomax found with trying to bring a case against Varus was that Callahan's death had been officially ruled a suicide. The coroner's report had been quite clear on that issue.

The only name in the documents that seemed to pop up more than Varus's was that of his old friend Captain Mike Johnson, another character woven into the web of crimes that did not set well in the same gut that implicated Varus.

Lomax's intrigue escalated to the third degree when he discovered a common thread shared by both men that went by the name of Benny Maldonado, the sleazy club owner whose illicit past only added more spice to the ingredients.

"Are you okay, Detective?"

Lomax stood up and headed toward the door. "This damn job isn't what it used to be," he said over his shoulder. The last thing he needed was more drama at the courthouse. "There are too many politics and shit." He kicked open the door on his way out.

The moment Lomax rounded the corner in his beat-up Ford and saw the pandemonium flooding the streets outside the courthouse, there was no doubt in his mind that it was going to be one of the worst days in his career. The dull throb of a headache birthed itself at the back of his head.

He parked in the middle of the street and got out. *I really don't need this shit today.* He started to walk toward the stream of yellow crime scene tape that stretched across the street. His stomach gurgled in violent unrest. *I wonder if it is too late to tender my resignation and try my pen at writing cheap crime novels for a living.*

Outside the monolithic building, a madhouse was taking place in the street. Rumors had already spread like wildfire among the spectators watching the frantic government response teams scurry on jackboots about the street. Speculation and conjecture ran rampant from the mouths of those standing behind yellow tape. A line of police officers dressed in combat gear and armed with semiautomatic weapons stood just inside the marked perimeter, leaving little doubt that a dire situation had occurred behind the walls. All personnel on scene acted ready and willing to shoot anything and anyone deemed a threat. Mass panic seemed practically inevitable, clouding everyone's common sense and judgment. The word *terrorists* slipped from the mouths of those standing in relative proximity to the vicinity.

A dozen media vehicles from every major network in the country had already staked their claim to a piece of concrete or grass, depending on their arrival time, and headquartered either in the middle of the street or along the sidewalks. Camera-toting lackeys busily chased after those carrying the microphones, in hope of getting an exclusive sound bite and becoming the envy of all other competitors unable to keep up with the hungriest reporters.

On his way to the center of the storm, a reporter craned his neck. His eyes widened in recognition of Lomax when he got within ten yards of the yellow tape. He fell on him with the appetite of a famished buzzard on a fresh carcass. Others soon joined his fray, rudely pushing, and fighting each other for an advantage to hurl the first set of questions in the detective's direction. They unceremoniously shoved microphones in his face. Hands grabbed at his arms, and reporters shouted their demands to know the truth.

Lomax struggled to push past the inquisitive masses that swarmed around him. "I don't know," he commented drily to no one in particular. "I just got here."

"Can you tell us if it's terrorists?" an indiscriminate voice yelled at him.

Lomax fought to keep his temper in check. "I don't know!" he snapped heatedly. "I just got here. They don't tell me shit."

"But you're the police," another voice yelled from the crowd.

"So what," he shot back. Lomax yanked his arm free of a groping hand. "It's not like I have a friggin' Magic 8 Ball, and I'm no genius."

A middle-aged reporter unexpectedly jumped directly in his path and rudely shoved a microphone in his face, which struck him on the chin.

"What are you hiding?" The reporter's face turned beet red as he screamed the words at him. Spittle flew from his mouth and hit Lomax in the eye. "The people have a right to know, you fascist pig!"

Lomax placed a firm hand on the reporter's chest and shoved him back into the swell of the crowd. "Get the hell away from me, you damned parasite!" He forced his way through the mass of bodies.

The reporter tripped and fell hard on his backside. He glared up at his cameraman and shouted out claims of police brutality to the viewers with a gleam in his eye.

Filled with a new level of disgust for the press, Lomax flashed his badge at the standing sentinels dressed in blue, ducked under the yellow tape, and then moved toward a cluster of men huddled together.

Captain Johnson stood with his hands shoved deep into his pockets, the mayor directly on his right, Internal Affairs Officer Biggs on the left. A representative of the FBI sat not far behind the three men, his presence apparently offered only in an observatory role. The captain turned and smiled at Lomax's approach, waving him over with a hint of anxiousness.

Lomax cringed inwardly. *Uh-oh.* He dreaded a confrontation with a man whose reputation had fallen under a very dark blanket of suspicion over the past few days. *This is not a good sign for me. They always smile before they screw you over.* He put on his best fake grin and picked up his pace.

Johnson moved toward him like a cat on the prowl and threw out an enthusiastic hand in greeting. "Erik, damn am I glad to see you." His tone was uncharacteristically friendly. "Please, come with me; walk with me. I want you to meet the mayor."

Lomax reluctantly accepted the captain's hand and eyed him coolly with suspicion. Something was definitely amiss. Johnson was not the happy-go-lucky type. "I've met the mayor before," he offered in a low, unimpressed voice. "I didn't vote for him." He looked over Johnson's shoulder.

His features pinched. "Well, uh, then come and meet him again." The captain's voice stammered. He draped an arm over Lomax's shoulder and guided him over to the small flock of men.

Lomax stole a quick glance over his shoulder at the crowd of malcontents, sadly realizing that he preferred their company to that of a bunch of hypocrites. Johnson's hand slapped him on the back several times as they narrowed the distance.

"Mr. Mayor, I'd like to introduce you to Detective Erik Lomax." His voice was jovial, another contradiction to the man he had known for years. "He's the best homicide detective this department has ever produced."

The mayor held out a dainty hand, flashing a peroxide-bleached smile meant for television. "It is a pleasure to meet you, Detective Lomax." His voice reeked of political salesmanship. "I have heard a lot of great things about you."

Lomax shook his hand. "Yeah," he said in a tight voice, remembering exactly why he disliked the slippery man, "from whom?"

The mayor's face pinched, clearly flustered by the detective's lack of etiquette to accept a vacuous compliment. "Excuse me, Detective?" His hand pulled back. "But I do not believe your query is apropos to the current situation."

"What the hell is 'apropos'?" Lomax grumbled.

Biggs and the FBI agent snickered under their breaths.

The corners of Johnson's mouth curled up at an almost freakish angle. "Don't you just love this guy, Mr. Mayor?" The look on his face signaled his desperation to intervene before Lomax responded with another crude remark. His hand patted him on the shoulder as a familiar warning to keep his mouth shut, while maintaining a sycophantic grin. "He is such a card. He keeps all of us laughing down at the precinct."

The mayor gazed at the two men with lidded eyes. A faint sneer formed around his thin lips. He removed a wet nap from his suit pocket and dabbed effeminately at his hands. "Yes … well, very well, Captain Johnson." His tone was trite. "I just hope you and your man Friday here can resolve this terrible situation both cleanly and quickly. I am counting on you making an arrest on this unseemly matter in the very near future." He tossed the used wet nap on the ground, eyeing Johnson critically. "Do not disappointment me. Am I understood?"

"Of course, Mr. Mayor," the captain said in a subdued voice. "I've got my best man on it."

The mayor turned and left in obvious search of another reporter.

Lomax stared daggers at the mayor. "Shit, Captain, why are you sucking up to that political prick?" he growled. "He's already laying groundwork to blame the department if something goes wrong."

Johnson spun on his heels, his eyes glaring at Lomax. His nostrils flared. "Shut the hell up, Erik! Do you have any idea what has happened? Do you even have a clue?"

Lomax shrugged. "No," he said in a neutral tone. "I didn't get the memo, but I suspect someone killed another someone, and that's why I'm here. Same shit, different day, no biggie."

Johnson's body shook in anger. "Some maniac murdered the Honorable Judge Harper." His eyes went wide. "Some crazy bastard out there in the city cut off his head."

Lomax whistled softly. "No kidding?" he said. "Damn, I guess that sucks for him. Doesn't it?"

Johnson's mouth fell agape in shock. "Do you have any idea what this means?"

He flipped a hand in the air. "Yeah," he said. "The judge is dead because someone chopped off his damn head, duh." He checked his pockets for some aspirin. "That's a lot better than the rumors floating around the unwashed masses that terrorists are in town and ready to blow some shit up."

Johnson's face went slack. "What in the hell is wrong with you?" he said, incredulous. "What this means is someone has struck an attack at the very core of our way of life and the very system our—"

Lomax fished out a small bottle and shook it hard enough to make the pills rattle, cutting the captain off abruptly. "Give me a break," he said with a growl. "Save the preaching for the television cameras. Judge Harper was a hateful old bastard, and he's been screwing people over for the past twenty plus years while hiding behind his cloak of immunity. If what you have said is true, then Harper probably screwed with the wrong person and got what was coming to him. I cannot say that I am all that surprised by how he ended. He was no better than the hardworking people in this city, so lay off the plea for sainthood." He popped the top and poured five white pills into his palm, tossed them into his mouth, and chewed.

"You can't be serious."

Lomax continued. "Quite frankly, I'm surprised more of them aren't shot down in the street like dogs." He tossed the empty bottle to the ground. "Don't misunderstand me, captain. I don't condone the act, but I do understand how someone can feel like there's no other way to get justice." He looked at Johnson with a curious eye. "You can relate to this, right? Sometimes bad people screw good people, and then the good want a little payback."

"You're crazy."

"No, Captain," he said matter-of-factly. "I'm quite sane. The only difference is that I can recognize the warning signs. People are getting sick and tired of big government pushing them around." He pointed a finger at the crowd. "Just look at them. Look at all those vultures waiting for some little tidbit of news. Do you really think any of them give a rat's ass about some dead judge? Once they know they are not in danger, all they will want is the gory details, nothing more. Morbid fascination moistens the mental gears of the bored. I'd be willing to bet dollars to doughnuts that most of them will probably think the judge had it coming one way or another."

"We got a dead DA and now a dead judge." Johnson's eyes narrowed. "You don't think that there might be a connection?"

"I think you are missing a major fact that severs your connection," he said.

"Which is?"

"Callahan was a suicide, not a murder." Johnson blanched, and Lomax grinned, and then he added, to see how his superior reacted, "But I'm looking into that as well."

His brows knitted. "You are looking into what, exactly, Erik?" A slight tremor entered Johnson's voice.

"The facts underlying Callahan's death." He paused. "You do remember Trent Varus, don't you?"

The blood seemed to drain from his face. "What does Varus have to do with any of this?"

"Nothing," he began calmly and then added, "at least not yet. If there is a connection, I will find it. Of course, it will be easier to connect the dots with the next one. Then I can triangulate and narrow down the suspect or suspects."

"What are you talking about?"

Lomax held up three fingers. "Everything happens in threes," he said. "I doubt our guy … or gal is done."

"For your sake, you better hope he's done."

Lomax thought it tactical to test the waters once again, suspecting the captain was involved in what was happening in the city but not sure how deeply. He had never been a believer in coincidences. "I can't help but wonder if anyone from the Viscotti crime family has taken any interest in what goes on down at city hall," he said, slipping the notorious name into the conversation just to see whether his captain took the dangling worm.

Sweat broke out across Johnson's forehead. "Just focus on what we have in front of us for right now, Erik," he said. "I don't want you to go poking around in places that have nothing to do with the current investigation. Let me worry about Dominique Cieo."

Lomax pressed his lips together. "I didn't say a word about Cieo," he said in an almost teasing manner. He weighed his options about mentioning Benny Maldonado to see how his captain reacted but then thought it prudent to keep that information secret for now. He did not know exactly what the captain was hiding, but he suspected it was much more than what he had found in some dead file forgotten years ago. Everything would fall into place soon enough.

Johnson quickly regained his composure. "His name was

implied," he said. "Focus on this case and the facts that revolve around it."

"Very well," Lomax said. "Now, I will find who killed the judge and arrest him." He nudged past the captain. "Please excuse me while I go do my job." He walked toward the steps of the courthouse, leaving in his wake what he had perceived as a very nervous Captain Johnson.

The atmosphere of the hallways inside the courthouse was far less robust than outside the doors; in fact, it was morose and darkly cold. Those who had been assigned to the slaughter area stood along the walls, anemic and listless, their faces sullen. No one appeared remotely interested in wandering anywhere off their posts. Few officers spoke a word of encouragement or anything else. *Grotesque* and *obscene* were the common words that apparently summed up the grisly crime scene, and the Post-it notes left by the killer had struck a primal nerve in the men and women on duty, punctuating the sickness of the mind responsible for such a horrendous act of violence.

When Lomax reached the end of the hallway, he tried to speak to several officers standing nearby to get directions to Judge Harper's chambers, but only one man standing in the rear of the group responded to his query. Without looking away from the floor, the officer jerked his head to the right with a sickly groan, mumbling incoherent words under his breath.

Lomax rolled his eyes and went left. *Friggin' pussies.*

Detective Erik Lomax had worked homicide longer than any other detective in the department, having personally investigated most of the grisliest crimes ever committed in his once fine city, and yet nothing in his years of crime fighting had prepared him for what he found when he entered the chambers of Judge Terrence Harper.

An involuntary gasp of revulsion escaped his lips at the bizarre presentation of gore left for those in law enforcement to find. Two officers stood on the left side of the room and held wet rags over their mouths, their eyes wild, their complexions a distinct shade of green. They looked worse than the men and women standing outside the room in the hallways.

His stomach lurched. "Lord Almighty," he mumbled, aghast. Nothing in his past had come close to what he now faced. The sight and smell of dead flesh and blood threatened to overwhelm his senses. "No one mentioned that four people had been murdered. I thought it was a single, just the judge."

One of the officers slid the wet rag away from his mouth. "Brass thought it better to keep those details quiet from the press until we have something positive to offer," he offered with the forward jerk of a dry heave. His face turned a deeper green. "I … Oh, God—" He recovered his mouth and ran from the room.

Lomax stepped farther into the chambers, hesitant. "Yeah, I can see why," he said to no one in particular. "This is now the worst I have ever seen. I don't know what I was expecting, but this isn't it."

A thick layer of congealing blood covered the top of the desk. Morbidly situated so they faced the door, four severed heads rested on each corner. The killer had ruthlessly gouged out their eyes, and their severed tongues and ears now lay in a small pile in the center of the crimson pool. Tiny drops of blood dripped from the desk and hit the floor with a faint splat. A small, plastic baggy stapled to each forehead contained a piece of paper with writing on it. There was no sign of bodies in the room.

Lomax grimaced. *Got a live one here, and he does not faint at the sight of blood.* He craned his neck at the groan of the other officer, who violently heaved once and then darted from the room to join his partner.

Shrugging at the understandable sound of men retching around the corner, Lomax turned his attention back on the severed heads and leaned forward. He had to squint to read the scribbled words in cursive left on the notes through the transparent packaging.

The first read, "Hear No Evil." The second read, "See No Evil." The third read, "Speak No Evil." Attached to Judge Harper's forehead, the fourth read, "Article III."

He backed away and looked about the room. If his memory was correct, that particular article had something to do with the constitutional provision about a judge holding office in good behavior, and he figured only someone familiar with the law would know.

"Hmmm," he muttered. His revulsion instantly transformed into morbid fascination with everything in the room and how each detail related to the mental state of the perpetrator. "Someone went to a lot of trouble to make a point." He marveled at the overall setting of the murder. The personal methodology utilized only seemed to confirm his initial opinion that the murder of Judge Harper was personal and probably an executed vendetta. How the other victims worked into his scheme as an act of revenge, he did not know. He suspected it was safe to assume that they had simply been at the wrong place at the wrong time.

The first officer returned. His hand held a new rag to his mouth.

With a low grunt, Lomax bent down and studied the separate bloodstains in front of the desk. "Tell me, Officer." He paused, craning his head to look at the man. "Who are the other three vics? Do you have an ID on them?"

He moved the rag away before speaking. "One of them was Harper's bailiff." His voice was dull, virtually lifeless. "The other two were night security guards. All three have worked here for more than two decades. The bailiff had been with Judge Harper longer than the others."

Nodding absently, Lomax took a knee and looked at the floor. "I see," he said in a faraway voice. "And where are the bodies?" He waved for the officer to come closer.

The officer took two steps forward and kneeled. "Three of them have been located in the public bathroom." His voice strengthened. "We are still looking for Judge Harper's body."

He nodded. "Uh-huh."

"So, what do you think?"

Pinching the bridge of his nose, Lomax climbed back to his feet. Trent Varus was the first name that popped into his head, but he knew that the ghastly savagery involved in these murders did not support him as a likely candidate. He had spent hours reading the criminal file and psychological profile on Trent Varus, and he had found nothing in any report that labeled him as a violent sociopath—quite the contrary in fact. In his professional opinion, only someone raised in violence with a murderous past was capable of committing such callous brutality. "I think someone is extremely pissed off, and the judge did the pissing off," he finally said.

"So, we meet again, Detective Lomax," a feminine voice said from behind his back.

Lomax turned and offered a crooked smile. "Well, hello, Dr. Swanson," he greeted. "You really have your work cut out for you on this one."

She set her forensics kit on the floor and motioned for her team to enter. "Yeah, well, a girl's work is never done." Her voice was light and flirtatious. "No rest for the wicked, so I guess I was a real bad girl in another life." She snapped on a pair of gloves. "You should stop by the lab later. We managed to get some trace off that young girl's fingernails. You know the one—the girl from the warehouse murder."

"Thank you, doctor," he said. "I'll be sure to do that." He ambled toward the door. "I have to go check out the three headless stiffs in the crapper, so I'll try to stop by after dinner. Please, do not feel obligated to wait. I also have a lot on my plate, but I will stop by at first chance."

She stepped to the side, grinning at him. "Sounds like a plan. Just keep in mind that I might be here for a spell, because I haven't even gotten to the bottom parts of these guys."

He shot a quick look at the desk. "Point taken," he said grimly.

She wriggled her fingers inside the latex. "Nice to see you again," she said to him.

"Ditto," he said.

He then headed back down the hallway in search of the bathroom, where he expected no surprises other than three corpses without skulls attached to their necks.

CHAPTER 16

After Jim had killed the man who could have placed him at the motel, Benny had reluctantly agreed to let his sadistic nephews push the envelope to the extreme and go on a criminal rampage the city had never experienced, their crimes ranging from robbing bank tellers to well-known drug houses to unceremoniously killing anyone who got in their way.

Deep down, although the three of them were all that was left of their blood-related family, Benny harbored no delusions that his nephews would turn on him like a pair of vipers and do what they wanted without him or his unsolicited blessing, if push came to shove. Ashamed of his unwillingness to sever the last two ties that bound him to his sister's past, he mentally crossed his fingers and hoped that neither boy came back.

To his chagrin, Benny had sat in a ramshackle motel on the far outskirts of town and watched the television while waiting for his insane family to return from their newest crime spree. The news reporting their violent escapades had spared no details describing the unidentified assailants and their insatiable lust for death and destruction. It made no difference that the authorities withheld from the media the perpetrators identities, because Benny knew that Jim and James were responsible for the homicidal rampage, leaving a bloodstained path of fatally stabbed and gunshot bodies scattered along the neighborhood streets.

After his nephews returned from what they had jubilantly referred to as a party run like they had not experienced since the last time they had paroled from state prison, Benny went to the cabinet and removed the only bottle of alcohol left on the top shelf. He shuffled over to the sink and unscrewed the cap, taking a healthy swig of Jack Daniel's. He stared at the residuals of his last remaining family with teary eyes as they took their positions in the cramped space of the room. The three women they had picked up along the way only made things worse.

His nephew Jim now sat on a tattered couch, squeezing a thick wad of cash held in his right hand. Several fat sacks of dope rested on a table in front of him. Thick rails of cocaine, crystal meth, and heroin lay across a large mirror he had ripped from off the motel wall. Two women sat on either side of him. His arms draped over their emaciated shoulders. All three of them were busy watching a third woman on her knees as she greedily performed oral sex on him in apparent hope of earning another promised turn on the mirror in return for her expert services.

His other nephew, the one he considered the brains of the outfit, now sat at the kitchen table. His focus remained solely on satisfying his own deadly pleasure. For reasons Benny had never learned, James did not share his brother's proclivity for having sex with multiple partners at the same time, particularly women who accepted money or drugs in exchange.

Earlier, Benny had heard one of the women offer herself to James in exchange for a few hits on his new pipe. She had rubbed her breasts against his arms and playfully grabbed at his crotch, trying almost every trick in a whore's unwritten handbook to entice his nephew to play ball with all three, but James had grown furious and shoved her away, toward Jim. Then James had made it clear to everyone in the room that he did not share his dope, especially with some disease-riddled coke whore who would do anything with anyone for a line or a shot of crank. He had also warned the women not to get between him and his sack, that his brother Jim handled that part of the arena. His rules of riding bareback while giving a good hard spanking served as his only prerequisite in the book of love.

Benny ran a tired hand over his face as he watched James

bring the flame shooting from a butane torch to the crack pipe's bowl stuffed tight with three grams of rock cocaine.

A grin of pure pleasure marked James's face. "Now this is what I'm talking about," he mumbled.

Small tendrils of smoke slowly swirled within the large bubble. The musical crackle of narcotic and glass brought an enthusiastic sparkle to James's eyes.

Benny turned away with a groan of disappointment and then winced at the sight of the women seated under Jim's arms leaning over his lap and kissing openmouthed. A childish giggle slipped from Jim's lips.

My family is a bunch of sickos!

Jim's head turned. "Hey, bro," he said excitedly. "Come on over here. You have to check this out."

With an angry grunt, James slapped his hand against the dark vial to knock loose a stuck rock of cocaine. "I'm a little busy here." His hand slapped harder, clearly impatient. "Damn it!"

The women's breathing grew labored, as their hands busily wandered over each other's body. Without breaking their lip-lock, the women moved their hands upward and began to unbutton the other's shirt, pushing the thin fabric from off the shoulders, and exposing ample breasts and hard bellies. Sensual pants of pleasure resonated from their throats and filled the room. Their tongues collided in darts of fury, coiling around each other like a pair of slippery eels.

Jim's fingers snapped. "Would you put that thing on hold for a minute and come watch this." His eyes widened in wild wonder. "You can smoke that crap later. This is happening right here, right now, right on top of me."

James's hands froze; he glared at his brother. Annoyance covered his face. "What?" His lips curled up into a snarl. He held the vial up to the light and squinted his left eye. "What in the hell do you want me to watch that is so interesting?" The crazed look on his face made him look as if he might lose control of his temper at any second.

"Girl on girl action, bro," Jim said, his voice turned giddy.

"They are going to get it on right in front of me, maybe on top of me, and you're going to miss it if you don't get your dope fiend ass over here before it is too late."

James's hand twisted the cap to seal the top of the vial and shook it hard enough to break up the rock inside. "How nice for you, dummy," he said. His interest rested only on the contents inside the vial. "I don't give a fat crap about two nasty twats licking each other. I have better things to do. If you are so concerned about me, you can always just make a movie or something. I will catch it later. Maybe you can do a documentary about venereal diseases, Spielberg."

Jim's arms squeezed the women against his chest. His legs rose up and locked around the back of the head of the woman pleasing him with her mouth. "Hey, that's a great idea." A huge smile broke out on his face. "I like that picture."

James's head jerked up. A frown formed on his face. "Huh? What's a good idea?"

His hands pried the women apart. "How about it?" he said. "You want to make a movie and get freaky on film?"

The women exchanged what appeared to be curious looks, before looking at Jim. "Sure," they said in unison. "Why not film us?"

Benny groaned at the counter as he listened to his nephews bicker back and forth, wondering how two grown men could possibly be so stupid. Their lives were spiraling down to earth in a fiery inferno, and all they could think about were drugs and sleazy women. He had never wished more for a way out of the twisted tapestry he had woven than at that moment. It was clear that his nephews were going to be the death of him, if he did not find a way to escape from them and they continued to live the life they'd chosen to lead.

The woman on the left ran a hand down the length of Jim's chest. "Do we get more dope?"

Jim nodded, smiling. "All you can smoke, snort, and shoot."

"Those tramps aren't getting their filthy hands and noses on any of my sack," James said with an angry growl. "It's mine, so don't any of you forget that."

Benny straightened up and glared at them, feeling his last shred of patience snap. "Would the two of you just shut the hell up and stop arguing," he said heatedly. "We have a serious situation here, and nothing about it is going to turn out well if we don't figure out something."

James's eyebrow cocked to the side. "Lighten up, Uncle Benny." His voice had a humorous undertone. "We're just taking a break, and doing what we want while things calm down out there. We'll be back on the street in no time, raising hell and taking names."

Benny widened his eyes at the idiocy he had just heard. "Are the two of you shittin' me?" he said. "You can't be that thick. How can any brain handle that much stupid?"

A deep chuckle came from Jim, who threw a thumb over his shoulder. "Ignore him, girls." The words fell lazily from his mouth. "He's just an old grouch and doesn't know how to have real fun." His finger tapped the busy fellator on top of her bobbing head until she stopped and looked up at him with bloodshot eyes. His member slipped from her mouth.

"Huh?" Her voice was slurred.

Jim's hand wagged his erect member at her, smacking her on the chin. "Do you feel like making a movie, girl?" His fingers ran through her hair. "I'll make you a star."

Her nose wrinkled up. "Do I get more dope?"

His eyes rolled, sighing. "Yeah," he said in a bored voice. "Everybody gets more dope. That includes you too, honey." Her head nodded, and his hand pushed her head back down. "You may continue."

"No one's getting their greasy dick beatin' mitts on my dope!" James's hand came down on the table with a crash. "To hell with those nasty bitches."

Benny crossed his arms across the counter and dropped his chin against them, staring at the two morons in action. "I give up on the two of you," he whispered. "You are both hopeless."

"I wasn't talking about your dope." Jim flipped off his brother James, apparently unmoved by his uncle's words. "No one is going to touch your damn sack."

"Better not."

"Relax, I got this covered."

"You don't even have a camera."

"I'll get one."

"From where?"

"That's my damn business."

The cap on the vial broke off in James's hands, and the rock sprang free, falling to the heavily stained carpet. "Shit!"

Benny rolled his eyes as he watched the smarter of the two drop to his knees and crawl across the floor in search of his next high.

Benny's shame threatened to bubble over. "Would you get off the damn—"

A hard pound on the motel door reverberated throughout the tiny room.

All three stopped what they were doing and turned at the noise. The room fell dead silent.

Another hard pound came from the door.

"Police!" a voice yelled from behind the closed door. "Open up. This is a raid."

A loud explosion erupted and blew the door wide open, nearly blasting it from the hinges. Led by a large man carrying a transparent shield held outstretched in front of him, a half dozen officers armed with drawn guns rushed into the room, ordering everyone inside to get down on the ground. Their numbers split up once they had cleared the threshold, half going after Jim, the other half James.

Benny threw up his hands and watched the melee unfold in front of him. "I'm unarmed," he shouted. "Don't shoot."

Captain Johnson followed his men, walking into the room with a cocksure attitude. "We won't." His eyes looked right at Benny, a mischievous grin forming on his hard features. "I have a whole different plan for the three of you."

Jim's head jerked upward, curling up his lower lip in hatred when the first of many officers rushed into the room. "Come on and get some, you lousy sons of bitches!" He looked like a complete lunatic intent on killing everyone running at him. "Let's get their asses."

His massive hands shoved the women sitting on either side of him, and he growled crazily as they flew screaming wildly over the sides of the couch, crashing their heads against the cheap pair of matching lamps. With a size thirteen shoe, his legs kicked out and smashed his foot into the face of the girl kneeled between his legs, knocking her into the charging officers. Her hand grabbed at her destroyed nose, and she cried out in pain as she crumpled underneath the rampaging feet of those dressed in blue.

With the agility of a much smaller man, Jim's torso twisted as he nimbly leaped over the back of the couch. Three officers tackled him in midair and wrestled him to the floor.

Benny made to move toward his nephew to help, but Johnson slowly shook his head as an obvious warning not to get involved. His hand slipped down to the butt of his .38 revolver, tapping the burnished wood with a finger.

"Get the hell off me, you stinking pigs!" Jim screamed. His body writhed against the weight of three grown men, two of whom were trying to yank his muscular arms behind his back to secure the cuffs around his thick wrists.

"Stop resisting!" an officer barked.

Jim's elbow jerked back in a flash and smashed into an officer's face. The officer cried out in pain.

"Screw you, you piece of shit!" Jim's head craned, and his teeth latched onto a leg.

Another officer hollered, and a hand slapped at the back of Jim's head. "Get him the hell off me. He's chewing through my leg."

"Stop resisting, asshole!" All three were now shouting orders.

Jim's head twisted about his neck. "I'm warning you, pigs." His eyes widened in a mixture of fury and fear when they came to rest on his downed brother, who was lying facedown with his wrists cuffed behind his back. One officer had a knee firmly planted in the back of James's neck. A second sat on his back, straddling him like a small horse. A third sat on his legs. A huge gash zigzagged over the top of his right eye.

He looked dead.

"Give it—" an officer began, but the howl from the damned that came from Jim silenced the room.

Jim's head whipped back and forth, breaking the spell. "What did you do to my brother, you bastards?" His body arched, pulling his arms and knees underneath it. "I'm going to kill the whole damn bunch of you."

"We need more backup!" the officers yelled.

Despite the weight of several men on his back, Jim's arms pushed with all their might. His body rose from the floor.

"Holy shit," an officer shouted. "This bastard's stronger than shit. Someone stun this big son of a bitch before he kills one of us." Their numbers bounced up and down, pummeling him with fists, to no avail. His body continued to push away from the floor. "Or just shoot him."

Jim's hand snatched one of the officers and dragged him to the floor. He grinned madly at the sound of garbled gasps as he choked the life out of the officer. "You killed my brother. Now, it is your turn."

Cowering in the corner, away from the carnage, the three prostitutes were screaming uncontrollably.

The officer's hands grabbed Jim around the wrists and struggled to pull his fingers loose. "H-help," he managed to squeak. "I can't breathe."

With a snicker, Jim tightened his grip around the officer's throat. "Do you see God yet, punk?" Spittle flew from his mouth.

The officer's face started to turn blue.

"I'm going to grease your monkey ass for killing my brother."

A fourth officer leaped on Jim's back and wrapped his arm around his neck, but Jim just laughed at his feeble attempt to choke him out.

The sharp sound of crackling electricity filled the room.

Four officers armed with fully charged Taser guns stepped forward and shot multiple darts into Jim's lower back and shoulder. His head jerked up, and he shrieked like a wounded animal. His hands slipped from the officer's throat, his head lolling to the side. A grimace of pain crossed his face.

The officers lowered their arms, looks of relief now covering their faces. His arms started to buckle, and they made a slow approach.

Suddenly, as if jolted awake by some invisible force, Jim's arms straightened back out with a snap. His head shook, as if his homicidal impulse had just flipped into overdrive. His face whipped around, eyes smoldering in bitter hatred at the officers. "That hurt, you shits." His voice was eerily calm. "Come here and get some more."

The officers again hit him with electrical charges, this time with longer bursts.

Jim collapsed, rendered unconscious and finally harmless.

The officer still trapped beneath Jim's weight yelled out for assistance, trying to roll the unconscious man off his body. Red welts were already starting to appear around his neck. The other officers involved in the life-threatening scuffle were either sitting nearby on the ground or standing against a wall, taking a moment to catch their breaths. Perspiration covered their ashen faces.

The sergeant who had taken no chances and clubbed the first suspect on the floor with his nightstick sauntered casually over to where Jim lay out cold over his newest recruit on their team and peered down at Officer Eddie Carter. "How're you doing, Mr. Ed?"

Eddie's struggle ceased against the immovable object crushing down on him. "Everything's under control, Sarge." A hint of pain entered his voice. "But I've been better."

"It's a good thing they aren't triplets, huh?" he said. "We would have needed a whole helluva lot more cops." His eyes roamed over the tired faces of his men before he continued. "Now correct me if I'm wrong, but wouldn't it be a good idea to drag poor Eddie from underneath this shaved yeti and get some steel restraints on the big bastard before he wakes up to strangle all of us to friggin' death."

Benny started to say something but then thought better of it. He figured it was probably wiser to simply wait and see how things played out. There was more going on than met the eye. The captain had not conducted this raid in the normal fashion. He could feel that something was up. He shifted his gaze over to where Johnson leaned up against the wall. The captain motioned the sergeant with a slight jerk of his head.

The sergeant stepped in front of the girl with the broken nose and pointed a finger at her. Her face looked as if a truck had smashed into it. "You," he said, "talk."

Her eyes glared through the swollen folds around her bloodshot eyes, which were already blackening.

"We didn't do anything." Her voice was a nasal murmur. "We just came to party with these guys. We got nothing to do with what's going down here."

The other two girls kicked their friend in the shins.

"Shut up, Stacy," said the blonde-haired woman.

Stacy's head whipped around. "But—" Another hard kick to her shins shut her mouth.

The brown-haired woman's head shook. "We don't know what this is about or who these guys really are, so shut your ass up." Her tone was severe, which left no doubt as to which of the three was in charge. A strange sort of street wisdom sparked behind her eyes. "We're not saying a word, cop. We demand a lawyer."

Stacy nodded. "Yeah, that's what I meant to say. I want a lawyer."

"Me too," said the blonde-haired woman.

The sergeant's shoulders shrugged. "I thought a couple of pros like you would." His tone was snide. "In this case, that's probably a good idea." He waved a hand to the only officers not assisting with carrying the twins out the door. "Take these women downtown and book them for prostitution and drug possession." He made a slight bow at the waist. "Ladies, perhaps a few felony charges might help loosen your otherwise busy lips."

Stacy flipped her middle finger at him. "Screw you, Five-O." Her voice was razor sharp. "You wish you could get into some of this stuff."

The sergeant's eye roamed over the motley trio. "No thanks," he said smugly. "I can't afford the deductible on that much penicillin."

Benny grew warm around the collar when Johnson pushed away from the wall and motioned for him to remain right where he stood. *This cannot be very good for me.* His heart beat harder in his chest. Sweat stained his shirt. Nothing in all his years on earth had ever made him feel so helpless, and the thought of spending the rest of his life behind bars for multiple murders was his worst nightmare now realized. Out of options, Benny had nowhere to run and hide. His life was over. Four-time losers did not get a fifth chance; of that he was most certain.

Johnson's hand flicked out at the remaining officers still hanging around for no apparent reason. "I want everyone out, now!" A vein bulged in his neck. "That means you too, Markinson," he warned. "I want to talk to you later, so don't wander off too far. Mr. Maldonado and I have something to discuss."

With a huff of malcontent, Officer Barry Markinson shot an angry set of eyes on Benny. "Why can't I stay?" His voice was petulant. "Benny and I have a little history, and I think it would be best if—"

Johnson pointed a finger at the door, his eyes smoldering. "Out!" Johnson took a step toward Markinson. His hands balled into fists. "If I wanted your opinion, I would beat it out of you. I'm going to need you to do something for me a little later, so go outside, and sit by the curb."

Barry Markinson's eyes narrowed into two pinpricks. "Fine," he said with a grumble. "I don't even know why we're giving this scumbag the time of day." He turned and hurried out the door.

Benny frowned after Barry stomped out of the room. "What's going on?" he said. "Am I under arrest?"

Johnson motioned to a chair with his hand. "Do you want to be under arrest?"

He licked his lips, nervous, and then he took a seat. "I don't understand," he said. "Do I need a lawyer?"

"I wouldn't think so … at least not yet." Johnson's voice was slow, careful. Arrogance emanated from him. "I have it on good authority that you and an attorney by the name of Trent Varus are friends. Is that true?"

Benny furrowed his brow at the unexpected change in the conversation. "I know Trent, yes," he stammered. "We were close a few years back, but now we are kind of estranged. We haven't talked in quite some time."

Johnson's lips pursed. The right corner of his mouth tilted upward. "Nothing irreparable, I hope."

Paranoia tugged at Benny's gut. "No, nothing that bad," he parried. "What does Trent have to do with anything?"

"We'll get to that in due time, Mr. Maldonado." Johnson held up a hand. "What would you say to making a deal with me, with us?"

"What kind of deal?" He sensed a setup. "You're not making very much sense."

"Can you control those two boys of yours?"

Benny nodded. "For the most part, yes," he said. "They will do what I say, as long as I keep them on a short leash."

"Fair enough," he said. Johnson visibly relaxed. "The deal is this. I will let all three of you go, in exchange for sending your nephews on a little job to pressure Varus into backing off."

Benny blinked, dumbfounded. He knew the captain was holding back something critical, but whatever it was did not matter. He had no other choice except to accept, and the captain knew it. "Backing off from what?" he said. "Do you mean to kill him?"

Johnson seemed to think over the questions for several contemplative seconds before answering. "I'm not at liberty to discuss the finer details with you, and I definitely don't want you to kill him. That would create the very situation I am trying to avoid. Something like that would bring far too much attention. I want it done quietly, without witnesses. With your colorful past, I'm sure you know all sorts of ways to get people to back off, even leave the city on an extended vacation." He paused, and then added. "If your boys roughed him up, maybe put him in the hospital for a few days to cool down his jets, I would not object. The bottom line is that I need you to buy me a little time. I'm in the middle of something, and I don't need problems."

"How much time do I have to make a decision?" he said.

He glanced at his wristwatch. "Five seconds." His tone left no room for discussion. "Are you in? Or do I haul all of you down to the jail and put the three of you away forever? It's all up to you."

"When does this pressure need to be applied?"

A vicious grin of victory creased Johnson's face. "As soon as possible, preferably tonight," he said. "But don't try anything at his home or at his office."

Benny rubbed at his temples. Everything was getting complicated. "Then where and when?" he said. "Can't you throw me a damn bone? The more I know, the cleaner all of this can be."

"You're right," he said. He removed a slip of paper from his back pocket and a pen from his shirt pocket and quickly scribbled down an address and time. He held the paper out. "You will find him here. The time is more of an approximation, so you will just have to wait for him to show up. I can do only so much."

Benny snatched the paper from his hand, frowning at an address he instantly recognized as that of Markinson's residence. He stuffed it into his pants. "Then I guess we have a deal."

Johnson's hand swept through the air in a gesture to leave the room. "Then let's get to it, Mr. Maldonado."

Benny stopped at the open doorway. His nephews were standing next to a squad car, rubbing at their bruised wrists with freed hands. Nothing in their playful attitudes toward the officers now joking with them about what had happened less than a half hour ago evidenced any hard feelings for one another.

Everybody is friggin' crazy these days.

Benny faked a smile and walked over to gather his psychotic

family. Just the idea that Captain Johnson had predicted his response with enough certainty to take the restraints off Jim and James gave him gooseflesh.

He knew right then that he would send his nephews on the job alone, while he returned to his club and waited for word of the outcome.

CHAPTER 17

At five minutes after ten o'clock, Trent pulled over and parked alongside the curb in front of the Markinson residence. He let the car idle for several minutes, which allowed him a moment of much-needed quiet time to think about all the potential circumstances he had shared with Lisa Markinson over the phone an hour ago. Sympathetic to her fears, he had spent most of the conversation trying to reassure her that everything was fine and that he was paying close attention to her wayward husband.

Despite his attempts to assuage her terror, the worry in her voice, bolstered by panicked claims that Barry Markinson may have cruised past their house several times during the day, struck a nerve in his confidence that he could protect her from a violent police officer. She had calmed only after he'd promised to come and see her at her house. He realized that her situation was different from that of most abused wives, and he did not wish to take unnecessary chances. Shattered relationships brought out the worst in people, and he had read her husband's personnel file. Nothing in the documentation read favorably high on Markinson's ability to cope with stress or control his temper. Acts of aggression peppered the papers of those he had arrested over the years. Men in general did not receive rejection well, police officers even less so. Their masculine egos rarely went unscathed during divorce proceedings, particularly when the wife put her former husband's pride and manhood on display during trial in front of complete strangers. Compounding this volatile scenario, the threat of physical attack usually escalated if the wife genuinely appeared happier with finally having the opportunity to move on with her life without him, free to date other men. A husband sued by his wife for divorce often made a point of drifting in and out of her life, sometimes looking for a chance to beg forgiveness and plead with her to take him back, while others served as opportunities to hurl threats and seek revenge.

Trent turned off the ignition and got out of the car. Dressed in a three-piece Armani suit, he ran a hand over the pants to smooth out the wrinkles. The night air felt fresh in his lungs as he stretched out his arms and looked up at the small sliver of moon in the picture-perfect sky. Several stars shined like tiny diamonds. The soft sound of approaching footsteps distracted him from the seductive peace found only in the late evening hours. He dipped his chin and turned around, offering his best toothy smile.

Hobbling from the house across the street, an elderly man was clumsily heading in his direction. He wore a heavily coffee-stained wife-beater T-shirt, a pair of partially moth-eaten pajama bottoms, and a fuzzy pair of mismatched slippers. From the look of things, Trent thought the man should have burned the ugly ensemble long ago. With every third step, the man would hoist his drooping bottoms up with one hand, while using the other to pull down the shirt that refused to keep his hairy stomach from poking out.

Trent pressed his lips together to stifle a laugh. *I guess he's not the fashion police.* He shut the car door with a soft click.

The disheveled man's hand flashed out in a friendly manner when he got within arm's distance. A grizzled smile formed beneath the thick moustache that covered most of his mouth. "Hello, mister." His voice was warm and aloof. "May I help you? We don't get visitors in this neighborhood at such a late hour. We're a lazy bunch around this block."

In an instant, Trent summed up the nosy neighbor approach with unblinking eyes. His weather-beaten face defined busybody. He neither accepted the hand nor responded, recognizing the man as harmless and nothing more than a concerned person looking out for his tiny corner in the universe. Instead, he simply waited for the man to start speaking again.

His brows knitted, and he threw a thumb over his shoulder. "I'm Ted." His voice was less enthusiastic. "My wife, Maggie, and I live across the street." The fingers on his outstretched hand wriggled.

Finally, Trent accepted his hand and gave it a firm pump. "No, thank you, Ted," he said, grinning. "I'm Trent, an old friend of the Markinson family. I'm just stopping by for a quick visit before I head out of town on some business." He slid his hand free.

Ted's eye widened. "What kind of work do you do, Trent?" His voice was inquisitive. He jerked his thumb at his chest. "I dealt in plumbing supplies for years, and that is a major rat race, if I ever did see one."

Trent gave a quick chuckle. "I bet it was, Ted," he said. "I'm afraid mine isn't nearly as chaotic."

Ted leaned forward, as if expecting his new friend to elaborate. His eyes blinked a few times, frowning when Trent did not offer anything more on the subject. His lips pursed. "Oh, well, okay then." The words rolled clumsily off his tongue. "Have a good visit and a good night."

Trent offered a halfhearted tilt of his head. "Good night to you, Ted," he said. "It was a pleasure to meet you." He then turned and walked toward the Markinson's front door, leaving Ted in the middle of the street to gawk in his wake.

"Excuse me, Trent," Ted's voice said from the street.

Trent stopped at the curb and turned around. "Yes," he said. "What can I do for you?"

A door opened in the house directly across the street, and a woman suddenly appeared under the porch light. Her gray hair was poorly rolled up in thick curlers, and she was dressed in a shabby robe that looked like it had a bad case of the mange. She was waving a worn slipper at him. "Teddy, will you get your hairy ass back in here before you catch your death of pneumonia." Her voice reminded Trent of a mad banshee he had seen on a television show. "I'm not wet-nursing you if you get bedridden.

I'm done with all that." His wife looked a lot meaner and tougher than the old man who still stood in the middle of the street.

Grumbling his discontent at his wife, Ted turned on his heels and headed back to where his wife shook the slipper. "I'm coming, you old crone." His volume now matched hers. "Stop naggin' me, for Christ's sake. I ain't deaf. I was talking to my new friend."

"You ain't got no friends, you old fool!" With an evil cackle of the damned, she disappeared back into the house.

"No thanks to you, you old biddy!" His voice turned into a defeated grumble. "You chased 'em all away." Then Ted disappeared into the house, followed by the slam of the front door.

With a shake of his head, Trent turned back around and resumed his trek to the front door, which opened when he reached the porch. With a huge smile plastered across her face, Lisa took five quick steps across the threshold, grabbed him by the hand, and then practically dragged him inside the house.

Trent let out a startled yelp as his client quickly ushered him across the floor and into what he assumed was the living room. The force of her nimble fingers surprised him. Her grip felt like bands of iron, far stronger than her tiny frame had led him to believe. She gave him a sparkling smile, giggled like a schoolchild, and guided him over to a nearby chair, where he finally took a seat and stared at her, stunned at the difference in her attitude from the one she'd displayed when he had first met her.

Trent shifted uncomfortably in the chair. *Well, this is certainly odd, unexpected. I thought she would be a mess.* He grimaced.

Lisa spun on her heels with the grace of a ballerina. "Thank you for coming by, Mr. Varus." Her voice was strangely bubbly, giddy even.

He crossed his legs, wondering if she might not be suffering from some kind of nervous breakdown. Her mood shifts seemed far too erratic. He licked his lips. "Excuse me, Mrs. Markinson," he began uneasily. "Are you feeling well? You seem a little … off."

Her twirling suddenly stopped, and she stared at him open mouthed for the count of two. "Am I feeling well?" she shot back.

"Are you kidding? I feel great!" Her hand flashed out and took his into hers. Her fingers squeezed his hand a final time, before releasing it. "I saw my sister for the first time in years today, spent the whole day with her, and we plan on doing it again tomorrow."

"That's nice, Mrs. Markinson," he said. "I'm glad to hear you are doing so well."

"Mr. Varus, whether you realize it or not, you are saving my life."

Trent felt his face grow warm, embarrassed by the compliment. "I-I don't know about all that," he stammered. "I'm just glad I was able to do something for you." He then added, "If for no more reason than peace of mind."

"And thank you for sending Lenny as our bodyguard." A huge grin forged matching dimples on her cheeks. "No one was going to mess with us with that giant around, not even my lousy husband," she said. "He and my sister, Maureen, really hit it off. I never thought anybody that big could be such a squishy teddy bear."

Trent smirked. He could not wait to pass that particular description forward to his man. "Teddy bear, huh?" he said. "I'll be sure to let him know that the two of you approve. I just hope he did not get in the way. He can be a little clingy at times, especially when on a job that really matters to us."

Her hand went to her chest, followed by an emotional gasp. Her eyes practically lit up. "And that is why I knew you were my knight in shining armor," she whispered. "Your modesty is so refreshing—no pretentious attitude or hostile arrogance. Be still my heart." Her eyelashes fluttered. "And please, call me Lisa."

Trent nodded. "Um, okay," he agreed. "So, Lisa, what is it you wanted to see me about? As much as I do enjoy your company, I sensed your fear, something that you did not want to discuss over the phone." He did a quick survey of the room. "Is something wrong? Did your husband violate the order?"

Lisa's face suddenly pinched, blanching. Pain creased her porcelain features, shifting in the chair and hugging herself. "I don't want you to think that I'm being silly or anything." Her throat strangled the words, and she swallowed with visible difficulty. "I just get this weird feeling when I'm home, like Barry has been poking his head around the house and watching me … or something."

He sat up, now deeply concerned for her safety. Nothing he had heard sounded good. He had come to trust his clients' instincts, no matter how ridiculous they might sound to someone else. *Lenny was right.* Barry was a professionally trained police officer who would be able to maintain surveillance unnoticed, unlike an amateur armed with a notepad and a pair of binoculars.

A grave look clouded her face, and she shuddered.

"Is this just a feeling, or have you, either you or your sister, actually seen him?" he said, refusing to turn a deaf ear.

Her shoulders lifted. "It's more of a feeling, I guess." Her voice was soft, barely audible. "I actually haven't seen the creep. Maureen said she got the same feeling. The only time we didn't feel anything was when Lenny was walking between us down the street."

Trent needed only to study her face a minute before recognizing her words as truth. Of course she and her sister had every reason to feel paranoid, but he also knew that just because the sisters hadn't actually seen him did not mean Barry was not stalking them, hot on their trail, just waiting for an open chance to pounce and do damage. Documented evidence proved that Barry Markinson was an extremely violent man, which did not come as any real shock. Law enforcement was inherently violent. However, what did surprise him was that every victim who had filed an initial complaint against him for excessive force had inexplicably withdrawn it for undisclosed reasons. Trent suspected bribery—threats and coercion if the former proved toothless—which served as standard operating procedure in most departments in the larger cities.

He suddenly stood up and fished his phone out of his jacket, her eyes following his every move. He punched in a series of numbers.

"So, you believe me?" Her voice was one of amazement. "You

don't think it's just my imagination, that I am just hearing and seeing ghosts in the machine?"

Trent held up a silencing finger. "Hello," he said into the receiver when Lenny's familiar growl came from the phone. "It's me."

"Yeah, boss," Lenny's voice said over the speaker.

"Are you on him?" he said.

"He's in my sights as we speak." His voice resonated with confidence. "The creep isn't going anywhere without me knowing it. I'm all over him."

"Any sign of threat?"

"Not at the moment, boss," Lenny said in a deep voice. "He's just doing the weirdo thing, that's all. I will fill you in on the details later. How is Mrs. Markinson?"

He shot her a quick smile, nodded. "She is fine, Lenny," he said with a smirk. "Try not to worry about her."

"What do you want me to do?"

"Nothing for now," he said, thinking. "Just keep close tabs on the guy, make sure he doesn't try to sneak over. How close is he?"

"Near enough to tap her," he said in a worrisome tone of voice. "But don't worry, boss. I am on him like a maggot on trash."

"Keep it up, pal," he said. "I'll pick you up in a few." Trent furrowed his brow and clicked off the phone. He looked at the frightened woman. "Don't you worry, Mrs. Markinson. I predicted this. My people are the best and will keep a close eye on him and make sure he doesn't get near you … ever."

A look of stunned disbelief suddenly shadowed her face. "I don't get it." The words slipped from her mouth in a soft whisper.

"I'm sorry," he said, perplexed by her statement. "You don't get what?" He hoped that he was not reading too much into her sentence.

"Why are you doing this?"

"It's my job."

Tears welled in her eyes. "It's more than that, isn't it?"

He felt the blood drain from his face when she bit down on her lower lip. His thoughts drifted into the same emotional sea that had once threatened to drown him in its murky waters. The mask of tearful fear that now swept over her face reminded him of his deceased wife's face at sentencing decades ago. He averted his eyes, afraid to see the same reflection of pain in her watery windows that spoke volumes. Words failed him. Some wounds simply cut too deep. He lowered his chin halfway to his chest. Guilt gnawed at him for failing to answer such a simple question.

"Aren't you going to answer me, Trent?" Her voice was soft, caring. "It's okay. It's safe. I know what it takes to get past the nightmares."

He met her eyes. "There are things that can never be reconciled," he said.

Her eyes sparked with a conscious look of understanding as she gazed at him in silent wonder. "Then I'm not the only one who has lived with pain, am I?" She spoke with what sounded like aged wisdom. "I can see it in your face, in your eyes, when you don't think anyone is watching." Her eyes were downcast in what he thought might be shame. "Thank you, Mr. Varus. I'm sorry to have bothered you so late at night over nothing."

Her words pierced him, her insight into a starved soul impeccable. "Please, Mrs. Markinson, don't you give that a second thought," he said gently. "It's my pleasure, and I want you to feel free to call me whenever you feel the need … or feel scared. That's what I am her for." He smiled lopsidedly at her.

Trent jerked back when she rushed over to him and unexpectedly wrapped her arms around his body, squeezing him tightly with a sigh. "Thank you for looking out for me." Her voice was a quiver. "I was so scared that he was coming back to kill me."

He stroked the back of her head, now truly moved by her gratitude. "It's okay, Lisa," he said, hoping the use of her first name might calm her. "Everything is going to be fine. We will take care of you."

Her arms released him, and she wiped at the tears running down her cheeks. "I know you will." Her voice strengthened. "I trust you."

At a loss for words, Trent turned away from her and headed out of the house. He shut the door behind him and moved on quick feet to where he had parked his car.

Trent made a sharp U-turn and drove back down the street the same way he had come. He then made a left-hand turn at the first corner, pulled alongside the curb, and waited patiently for the second phase of his plan. He had promised Lisa Markinson that he would keep her safe and take care of everything that involved her husband, Barry, a solemn vow that he would keep at all cost, and he refused to disappoint her. He craned his neck and grinned at his insurance policy.

Less than a hundred feet away, an enormous figure of a man leaped off the roof of a garage across the street. His massive body nearly eclipsed the small slice of moon as he fell to earth from the sky. He hit the concrete below with a dull thud. His knees barely bent from the strain of his bulk falling from such a height.

Trent peered down at his watch and nodded appreciatively. He rolled down the window, grinning at one of the only two men in the world he had ever truly trusted. *My boy Lenny is a real pro.*

The three hundred-pound Lenny lumbered toward him on sneakers that looked like matching snowshoes, gently lifted a leather strap over his head, and pumped a camera fitted with a telephoto lens into the air that marked their combined victory.

Trent waved him over. "Come on, Lenny," he urged. "Get in so we can get the hell out of here before anyone sees you or me hanging around the area like a pair of burglars. We don't need some neighborhood watch pest calling the cops on us."

His huge head nodded, and he picked up his pace to a slow jog. He slid into the passenger side of the car, bumping his head against the upper doorjamb with an audible thump. "Ow!" His hand wound the strap around the camera and tucked it safely in a large case.

Trent dropped the car into gear and raced off down the street. Neither man said a single word until they were several blocks away. He headed toward the main drag of the city.

Trent broke the silence. "So, our little cop friend actually showed up, huh?" he said.

A snicker slipped from Lenny's mouth. "Oh, yeah, boss." His tone dripped with disgust. "He showed up just like you thought he would. I got some excellent shots of the little creep from the top of our client's house. He couldn't see me, but I saw that little piece of weird crap hiding in the bushes across the street, the same one that old man came out of."

Trent navigated the road, careful to obey all traffic laws. His thoughts filled with distress. Officer Markinson's bizarre actions went beyond the usual type of spouse stalking. He frowned, not liking any of what he had just heard. "How long do you think he'd been hanging around?"

Lenny's hand rubbed the stubble on his lantern jaw. "I'd have to say at least a couple of hours." His face tensed. "He wasn't wearing a coat, so I'd have to say that he got there before it started to get cold."

Trent winced. "He saw me drive up?"

"He had to have," Lenny said in a stern voice. "I saw him write down your license plate while you were in the house, after the old man went in to fight with that wife of his, and then he took off down the street. My best guess is that he parked his car around the corner to avoid detection. I know he didn't just walk here from only God knows. If so, then he's probably planning something. He looked like he was in a hurry to get somewhere fast."

Trent rubbed at his chin. "I see," he said.

His head shook. "No, boss, I don't think you do." His voice turned serious. "The creep had a gun on him."

Trent shrugged. "I'd expect him to," he said. "He is a cop."

"An armed cop hiding in the bushes across the street from his house, watching his wife," he said with bitter distaste. "The combo isn't a good mix."

"Do you think he's dangerous—that he might try something soon?"

"He was in a hurry to get somewhere. I just have a strange

feeling that he was in a hurry for a specific reason. There was purpose in what he was doing, which only makes things worse."

"How so?" Trent turned left on the next street and looked into the rearview mirror. "Whatever is bothering you, just spill it."

"There's the sister, and he can carry—" Lenny began, but Trent threw a thumb over his shoulder and silenced him.

Trent craned his neck and looked at Lenny. "Don't look now, but we definitely have company," he said. "They pulled out of a driveway and snuck behind us after I picked you up."

Lenny's hand reached under the seat and removed two large-caliber handguns. "How many do you count?" His hand worked the slides and chambered a round in each of them. He set one of them in Trent's lap.

"I think there are two of them, one car," he said in a grave voice. The last thing he wanted or needed was to get into a wreck or a gunfight with a pair of idiots. "They're driving a blue Buick, two cars back, on the left."

"Do you have any ideas why they're on us?"

"Not yet," he said. "There could be a lot of reasons, but I figure there is only one."

"Someone put them on us?"

"That's what I'm thinking."

"So, how do you want to handle this?" A hint of excitement slipped from Lenny's voice. A slow grin creased his face. "You're the lawyer, so it's your call."

Trent pursed his lips, thinking things through. "For now, we'll keep to the plan and meet with your pickup, see if they follow us or not," he said. "I want to make sure they aren't just trying to rob us. They may have just seen the car and picked a shot on a couple of wealthy suckers."

Lenny did not look convinced. "You don't believe that for a second, do you?"

"Nope," he said.

"And if robbery is not the case?" His voice sounded as dubious as the look on his face.

"Then just follow my lead," he said. "If they are armed, then we take them down. Now that I think about it, what you said about the sister has me a little concerned. As soon as we figure out what's going on here, I want you to go over to her house and check on her. This just seems a little too coincidental."

Lenny's hand tightened on the gun. "That sounds like a plan to me." His head bobbed. "Let's rock, boss."

Trent pulled into the parking lot of a liquor store, where the men had agreed to have Lenny's partner wait inside a brown sedan. His partner stuck his arm out the open window and waved just as they parked three stalls away.

"What's up?" Lenny's partner yelled out the window.

Trent heard the loud roar of the Buick's engine only seconds before it recklessly turned right at a high rate of speed into the parking lot and careened wildly toward them.

Lenny's partner pointed a finger at the vehicle speeding toward them and hollered a warning.

Trent grabbed hold of the gun on his lap. "Get down, Lenny!" He screamed right before the Buick slammed into the back of his Jaguar with a deafening crunch of metal. The force of the impact drove them forward into the retaining wall that separated the liquor store from the parking lot, crumpling the front end of his car. Glass shattered from the windshield and side windows, sprinkling the interior of the car and the blacktop outside.

With a loud growl of anger, Lenny's body straightened up in the front seat. Several small lacerations made by flying glass marked his face and neck. His arm smashed into the side door and forced it open, shouting, "You worthless sons of bitches!"

Trent threw open his door and crouched behind it. He knocked out a couple of large chunks of glass that remained of the window with the gun clutched in his hand and then draped his arm over the top of it, ignoring the tiny shards stabbing at him through the material of his shirt. "What in the hell is this?" His head was pounding in pain, having struck his forehead against the steering wheel. A sticky wetness slipped into his eyes. He blinked it away and took careful aim at an enormous man climbing out of the

Buick on his side with a shotgun in his hands. "They have guns, Lenny," he yelled. "It's not a robbery. Shoot the lousy bastards!"

A second man, the duplicate of the first, was now also climbing out of the other side of the Buick, holding the same model of shotgun as the other killer.

Trent heard the blast of a twelve-gauge shotgun, followed by the sound of shattering glass on his left. The report of Lenny's Colt .45-caliber handgun responded less than a second later. A loud grunt of pain and curses came from where the destroyed Buick sat stalled and smoking under the hood.

The gigantic brute on Trent's side of the vehicle was now standing in the open, just beyond the safe coverage of the car door, and leveling a shotgun on his position. "I'm going to kill the whole lot of you, you stinking bastards." The brute's baritone voice reeked of vengeful wrath. "You just shot and killed my brother Jim."

Trent pulled the trigger.

The brute's head whiplashed back at the explosion of gunpowder, a huge red hole now marking the entrance of the bullet. His body dropped to the ground like a sack of wet cement.

Trent got to his feet and looked over the top of his mangled car. "Lenny, are you still with me?" he called out. "Are you hit? Talk to me, big boy. That's an order!"

With a huge grin of relief on his bloodied face, Lenny popped up from the other side and held the camera case up. "I'm always with you, boss." His voice was jovial. "And we still have the camera intact."

Despite the attempt just made on their lives, Trent started to laugh at the ridiculousness of his friend's words. He wiped tears out of his eyes. "You do know that you're friggin' nuts, don't you?"

Lenny laid his gun on the top of the car. "It takes one to know one." His fingers picked at glass fragments clinging to his clothes. "So, what do we do now?"

In the aftermath of the attempted assassination, small crowds of people started to form around the perimeter of the parking lot, wide-eyed and mumbling to one another about what they had just witnessed.

"How's your phone, Lenny?"

"In the car, smashed into a thousand pieces," he said.

Trent grimaced at the spectators, reached into his pocket, and took out a broken cell phone that had no doubt served its last purpose. He dropped it to the ground with a clatter, and then peered up at an elderly woman clutching an oversized purse against her chest. Fear covered her pale face. He took a step toward her, but then he stopped when she moved away, her eyes now wet with tears.

"Excuse me, ma'am," he began in his softest tone, "but would you please call the police. As you can see, my phone has seen better days, and my partner's isn't working."

Several men and women lifted their cell phones into the air and yelled that they had already notified the authorities and told them what they had seen the killers try to do.

Trent looked at Lenny and grinned. "Well, that definitely wasn't any fun," he said. He dabbed lightly at the painful lump forming on his forehead, wincing. "I don't like people shooting at me, and I definitely don't like steering wheels smacking me in the face." He looked at his finger and frowned at the spots of blood.

A snicker slipped from Lenny's mouth as he busily wiped at the bloody cuts on his face with the bottom of his shirt. "So, now what do we do, boss?"

"There's nothing much we can do, pal," he said, "but sit and wait for the authorities to show up."

"Sounds like a plan." The shirt slipped from his fingers. "And after they're done questioning us?"

"I want you to head over to Maureen's house and check on her," he said.

His brows knitted. "You don't think I should go now?"

Trent shook his head. "No way in hell," he said. "I'm not about to make things worse by taking off. If one of us took off, and nothing happened over there, we would be up shit creek. We do not need a warrant issued for leaving the scene of a crime. We are not any good to our clients if the cops lock us up in the county jail. Besides, the investigating officers won't take long. We have at least thirty witnesses, and the crime scene speaks for itself. We will save time if we just go by the book."

"When you're right you're right," he said. "As a former cop, you'd think I'd be better at sticking to procedures, no matter how much I think they get in the way."

The two men then walked toward the crowd of people, smiling at each stunned face, and took a seat on the curb. Lenny's partner got out of his car and joined them.

The screech of approaching sirens echoed along the streets only minutes after they had settled on the perfect spot.

CHAPTER 18

Benny had always been one of those fierce men who thought nothing good in his life could ever be mistaken for luck. His refusal to leave anything to pure chance had contributed to his staunch belief that something positive happened only if forced. In his experience, something for nothing was a ridiculously asinine concept, which simply did not occur. Moreover, no one had ever beaten him in the long game.

When the stakes were high, Benny was a gambler only in name, his fingers nimble, his mind sharp as a whip at the table. For more years than he cared to count, he had practiced perfecting his poker skills, and he considered five-card draw one of his greatest passions. His developed intuition and ability to calculate the odds at a moment's notice, to play the percentages, and to read the other players' tells rivaled that of any professional in the world. Benny thrived on the adrenaline rush from beating his competitors and taking cold hard cash from their pockets. Increased riches never failed to sweeten the art of the deal.

When Benny flipped over the fifth card dealt to him and stared down into the painted eyes of the fourth royal lady gripped in his hairy hand, the magic of making another round of easy money sent his greedy spirits flying higher than he'd ever remembered. Tonight he was on a hot streak like never before, drawing inside straights and right colored cards to polish a perfect flush. Life had never felt so good, and there seemed that nothing could stop him from bleeding the other men dry at the table. He wondered if the card gods had finally decided to take a shine to him after all the long years of abandonment. The dealer had dealt him nine pat hands in just the last hour, and even his firm belief that lady luck did not exist began to come into question.

He sat up in the chair, face stoic. His mind focused on stripping the remaining chips from the other players' short stacks as he slowly fanned out his cards.

The four players who filled chairs spread around the felt-covered table clearly found the poker playing experience this night far less pleasurable. Large beads of sweat peppered the confounded looks on their strained faces. One by one, heavy loss after heavy loss, each player's mood worsened as his once proud stacks of chips dwindled to little more than pocket change in less than three hours.

Benny peered up from his family of queens and studied each face of his card playing foes in search of more tells. His cocksure attitude had only needled their taut nerves, and their nervousness over the current hand practically screamed across the table at him. In a tactical ploy to make them sweat even more, Benny folded his cards together and laid them facedown with a silky elegance. It was a tricky move meant to intimidate.

A guttural groan fell from the mouths of two players.

Benny moved around several large stacks of chips, wondering how long his poker friends would wait before someone finally complained. He looked at the center of the table. "That's a lot of moolah out there, fellas." He looked across the table at Bill Thompkins.

Dressed in a low-cut evening gown, her spiked heel bobbing in rhythm to what looked like thinning patience, Tabitha sat in a plush leather chair directly behind Bill. Her face showed an angry mask of bitter contempt as she nursed a mixed drink and watched the game's progression with nothing short of open hostility. She voiced her opinion on several occasions as to how ridiculous it was for the men to squander time and money for no other reason than to drink booze and screw their friends out of hard-earned cash.

Over the years, at least a hundred violent episodes had occurred. A few men had actually shot each other across the table for cheating; even more had utilized a hidden buckle knife or switchblade for payback.

Severe beatings in the back alley had become commonplace. Although Benny knew how deeply Tabitha hated the sight of blood—bullet holes, stab wounds, and broken bones only painful reminders of her sadistic brother's antics in a world she had denounced long ago—none of his promises to stop the attacks had staunched the flow of blood in the club's secret room.

Benny continued to scan his competitors' faces, only stopping when his eyes for the third time came to rest on Tabitha, who sat with her legs crossed and busily tapped a manicured fingernail against the side of her glass. Her eyes narrowed. Her jaw clenched.

He grimaced. *Oh, man, she looks pissed.*

With the mutual consent of his most serious poker playing associates, who had not so surprisingly insisted upon inflexible rules each time they met at the same table, Benny had agreed to schedule a high stakes game on the first of every month. The group had also unanimously appointed Tabitha as the liaison between the main room of the club and the secured private room, where the five men gathered monthly to gamble.

He smiled in response to her frosty glare and then laughed aloud when she stuck her tongue out at him and took a heavy swallow of liquor. Forgotten were thoughts and concerns about his nephews handling business on the street; those worries had taken a backseat to a string of winning hands that would provide enough cash to put his business back in the black.

"Come on, Benny," Bill said to him in an impatient tone. His fingers were playing with his small stack of chips. "Are you in or out?"

Benny picked up his cards. He cut them several times before he looked at them. "Patience, my friend," he admonished in a patronizing voice. "I'm trying to find my mojo, so don't be in such a hurry to give me the rest of your money." He rearranged his stacks of chips. "I got all the time in the world."

A man by the name of Carl Triskins took a long drag on a cigarette and exhaled. "Man, come on, Benny." Irritation resonated from him. "We don't have all friggin' year. This isn't rocket science. Are you going to fold, call, or raise?"

Benny winked at him. "Easy, C-man," he said smoothly. He approximated the other players' remaining chips and pushed several stacks forward. "I'll see your three thousand … and raise two more." He leaned back and waved Tabitha over.

Seated on Benny's left, Marvin Gates stared at his hand. His head shook slowly. "No way did you get another pat hand." His eyes drifted up from his cards. "You have to be bluffing. No one is that damn lucky."

Watching Tabitha sashay over, Benny shrugged his shoulders and grinned at his longtime friend. "Then call my bluff, old man," he said. "But it'll cost you to see these babies." He paused to let the insult sink in a little deeper, and then added. "Yup, it will cost you plenty, if you're wrong."

Marvin's hands enveloped his chips, hesitated, and then finally pushed them to the center of the table. "To hell with it. I'm all in," he said.

Carl followed Marvin's play.

Bill went all in too.

The fourth man, Brian Zinner, appeared less eager to bet against Benny's unnatural lucky streak. A heavy scowl of deep concentration clouded his face as his eyes looked from his cards to Benny's grinning face and then dropped back to his cards. He seemed to have reached an impasse.

Benny motioned for Tabitha to bend down, and then he whispered his gratitude for her hanging in there, saying that he needed his beautiful lucky charm.

A single knock came from the only door to the room, and her head spun around.

Five faces tensed at the unexpected interruption. Hands reached into their coats for weapons, ten eyes riveted on the door.

Benny ground his teeth together. The air grew thick with paranoia. *This better be good!*

"Damn it," Tabitha whispered.

Benny took immediate control of the situation and raised a calming hand. "Relax, you guys," he said. "It's probably just the bartender." He moved to stand up and then stopped. Suspicious eyes focused on him, their hands still hidden inside the fabric of their coats.

Marvin's head shook in a slow manner. "You know the rules, Benny." His voice turned lethal. "No one comes in or goes out in the middle of a hand." His eyes shifted to Tabitha, softening. "Only Tabby can go out and handle stuff. That is the agreement we pledged years ago."

Benny settled back into the chair. "You're right, Marvin," he said. "My mistake, and I apologize to all of you."

Tabitha slipped her finger into her drink, stirring the cubes in the glass. "Gentlemen, please," she began in a sensual voice, "there is no reason to get all worked up over nothing. I will just check to see what's up through the trap." Her finger slid free from the glass, and she ran it over rosy lips. "That is, if that's okay with you boys?"

As if hypnotized by her seductive actions, their hands pulled free from the flaps of their coats and simultaneously motioned for her to handle the situation.

Fluttering her eyelashes, she walked over to the door, and then slid open a small panel, exposing half a man's face on the opposite side of the door.

"What is it, Danny?" Her voice filled with annoyance. "You know we aren't supposed to be disturbed while this door is locked."

"I know, I know." His voice was scared and erratic. "But I have a message for Benny. It's important. Believe me; I wouldn't bother any of you, especially him, if it weren't. I know the rules."

Her neck craned, and her eyes met those of the five waiting men. Her head turned back to where Danny's cycloptic eye peered back through the small opening. "Are you sure it's an emergency?" Her volume lowered. "I like you, Danny, but if you're wrong ..." Her voice trailed off, seeming to let the words hang in the air.

His eye narrowed. "I know," he said, "but the guy on the phone said that I had to tell Benny immediately—that Benny would want the heads-up because his failure to get things done the right way is now on him."

"What does that mean?"

"I was told to tell him to his face."

"Tell him what, exactly?"

Benny knocked on the table. "Tabitha, what's taking so damn long?" he said. "I don't like riddles, so just get rid of him. We're in the middle of a hand, and we don't cater to interruptions."

She faced him. "Danny says it's an emergency." Her voice now had an edge. "Some bonehead told him to pass a message along to you."

The men's eyes glared at Benny.

He shook his head. "Can't it wait?"

Her face pinched. "He seems pretty nervous." Her voice grew tight. She turned back to Danny. "Just give me the whole message to pass along, pal, before you end up shot."

His face pressed against the small opening in the door. "It's about the Maddock brothers and the job Benny put them on. The dude said everything went bad and that Benny better clean up the mess real fast."

Her head whipped around. "Danny says it's about Jim and James and some job that didn't go right." A frown formed on her face. "Does that mean anything to you?"

In an instant, four poker faces blanched at the names. Everyone in the room was aware of the brothers' reputation for unsolicited and unprovoked violence. Two men seated at the table had lost half their pinky fingers to Jim, after he'd bitten the tips off and spit them down the garbage disposal over a paltry fifty dollars.

Benny slapped a hand against his forehead, aghast. *What did those two oafs do, now? I should have known better than to have them handle Trent. What is this going to cost me?*

Marvin's cards slipped from his fingers, and he stood up from the table. His eyes were wild. "Those two aren't coming here, are they?" His voice turned into a squeak of fear. "I don't need their kind of shit today."

Carl's fingers pinched the bridge of his nose. "No offense, Benny, but those two are just flat crazy, and I don't want to be anywhere around them." He held up what little remained of his pinky finger. "Been there, done that."

Benny waved off the comment. "None taken, C-man," he said gravely. His patience with his incorrigible nephews had now reached an end, and he was really going to lay into them when they showed up with another one of their lame excuses. "I've tried to help them after my sister ran off, but those boys are just not right in the head." He tapped the side of his head with his cards. "Broken toys upstairs are all they have. They're junkyard mean, probably because their father was a triple-rated prick."

Marvin's head dipped. "Was that before or after they killed him?"

"Who knows, Marvin," he said. "They just don't care about anything or anyone, except each other. I think they tolerate me only because their mom is my sister."

A gleam of curiosity sparked in Marvin's eyes. "So, where's your sister?" he said. "You never talk about her."

"Who knows?" Benny looked at them. "Long gone years ago," he said. "She could be dead for all I know." Benny tossed his cards on the table. "Look, fellas," he said. "I know it's against the rules and such, but can we finish the game later? I really should go see what they've done. Whatever it is, I'm sure it's horrible."

Everyone exchanged a quick glance, and each man nodded his head.

Benny forced a strained grin. "Thanks a lot, fellas."

Brian's cards hit the table. "No sweat, Benny. I'd just like to get the hell out of here before they show up."

"That goes double for me," Carl said.

Everyone headed for the door, Benny bringing up the rear.

Out in the main room of his beloved Mousetrap, Benny

escorted Danny over to a far corner and questioned him about everything he had learned about his nephews.

Five minutes later, despite the few tears that threatened to well in his eyes, Benny did not altogether feel sad that the last of his family had died in a gunfight. Instead, all he felt was relief that someone had finally done him a favor and killed them. Their attempt to kill Varus rather than follow his explicit instructions to simply apply pressure and make him back off as directed by Johnson was the only reason they had died. His only regret was that they had failed to do as told, a debacle that now placed his life in jeopardy.

After Benny told Danny to go home for the day, he turned in search of Tabitha, who was sitting at the bar and watching him through the reflection of the large mirror behind the bar. Shame now filled him. He felt dirty and unclean for what he was about to do. Nevertheless, she was his last hope, his only chance to get out from under the deadly mess he had created by living a life of crime. He saw the heightened curiosity in her eyes, which shined from the reflective glass with sparkling intelligence. She would do anything to help him, and he knew that he did not deserve her.

Her ability to read people had always impressed him—skills so perfected that she was like an emotional savant—and he had done nothing but selfishly use her special gift against her, manipulating her loyalty and innate need to protect and save him. He knew she had no possible way of truly grasping just how much power she possessed to save his life, or end it, with a simple word, but soon everything he had kept secret from her would bear its soul. All his powerful lies would cruelly pierce her heart with an arrow of lost love unwittingly forsaken into a darkness in which he had forced upon her.

"Tabitha, would you please come over here," he said. His eyes were downcast as he shuffled over to a nearby chair. "I need your help on something rather personal."

With a look of pleasure at the opportunity to help on her face, she hustled over to where he sat and took an opposite chair. "Whatever you need, Benny," she said in a perky voice. "Your wish is my command."

Benny gave a pained chuckle. He lifted a finger. "First, my dear, you cannot ask any questions," he said. He paused, thinking, and then added. "At least not right now, okay?"

Her brows knitted. "O-okay," she stammered.

Benny shifted in the chair, growing far more uneasy than he had anticipated. "I need you to get in your car and drive over to see an attorney for me by the name of Trent Varus," he said clumsily. "Now, my dear, he may get really pissed because I'm kind of breaking a deal we made a long time ago." He grimaced. "But it cannot be helped."

"I don't understand."

He removed a business card from his wallet and handed it over to her. "His home address is written on the back," he said. "It's late so, if he's not in the office, you have to go to his house."

Her hand took the card, and she looked it over, squinting at the fine print. "Why have I never met this man before?" Her voice was inquisitive. "You already have a good attorney, who has done right by us. What's wrong with Harold?"

He put a finger against her lips. "No questions," he said. "Remember?"

"I'm sorry," she said. "Please, go on." She set the card on the table. "Why can't you just call him?"

Fear shot through him. "No!" he said unintentionally louder than he had intended. "You have to talk to him face-to-face, no phones. He does not like them. Hell, he's not going to be too thrilled that you're coming to see him."

"Why?"

He waved off the question. The less she knew the more effective her presence would prove. "Just don't be shocked if he turns three shades of white."

"Okay, no phones." Her reluctance touched the words. "What do you want to me to tell him?"

Her compliance made him relax a little. He took an easy breath. Johnson would never forgive another failure. "Just tell him that Benny needs to dig into the favor bucket a little deeper and that I need to see him as soon as humanly possible."

Her eyebrow cocked to the left. "And he'll know what I'm talking about?"

He nodded. "Trust me, dear—he'll know," he said. "If he tries to blow you off or have you escorted out of his office because he doesn't believe you, just tell him it's Tabby Cat."

A look of confusion flitted across her face. "My pet nickname will make him listen?" Her voice quivered with suspicion. "I don't understand. You're the only one—"

Benny flashed out a silencing hand. "It does not matter," he said gruffly. "He will know exactly what is meant, and that is all that matters right now."

"Okay, if you say so." She picked up the card, slid it underneath her brassiere, and stood up. "But it is a little late for him to be in his office, don't you think?"

He looked up at the clock. "M-maybe," he stammered. "But all he does is work. If the office is closed, go to his home. He will definitely be there. If I remember correctly, it is his second workplace. He has no life."

"That's it?"

"Yup, that's it."

"Then I'm off to see the wizard."

"Good luck."

Tabitha grabbed her car keys and left.

As Benny watched his adopted daughter walk across the floor, a modicum of guilt tugged at him for not disclosing the identity of the man. She and Trent were not the strangers he had led her to believe, for he was just one more hidden clue to a past of which he rarely spoke. He had spent years with the man inside a cell and knew all his soft spots, his most vulnerable one that of his love for Tabitha Verelli.

CHAPTER 19

Trent dropped his pen on the desktop and rubbed at his tired eyes. He had spent hours at the desk in his home office upstairs drafting several pretrial motions for two of his clients facing armed robbery charges. Though the warrant lacked the usual specificity required under the law, he presupposed his attempt to cripple the state's case before it got started was DOA. The presiding judge had a reputation for denying most Fourth Amendment claims based on the principle that the police had acted in good faith, an assertion normally buttressed by eventual discovery.

He stifled a yawn. *Well, boys, that's all she wrote. The only thing standing between you and ten years in the clink is a Hail Mary. I doubt it's worth the paper it's—*

A knock came from the front door downstairs and interrupted his train of thought. He jerked his head around, wondering who could be traipsing around his quiet neighborhood and banging on doors. The last thing on earth he wanted to deal with was an unwanted visitor.

Now what? He groaned. *I do not need any more drama.* His morbid quest had proved exhaustive, and all he wanted was to crawl into bed and sleep for a week. Seven days of unconsciousness seemed like the best solution to replenish his depleted energy reserves since exacting revenge on those responsible for ruining his life.

Lack of sleep was not the only thing adding stress to his life. More questions with even fewer answers haunted his every thought. Some of the many details Lenny and his client Lisa Markinson had revealed about her husband Barry lurking around the house continued to nag at him, filling him with dread and suspicion as to what might happen next. Officer Markinson's menacing behavior had devolved into something dark. His actions had drifted off the predictable coordinates on a map normally followed by a jilted husband. There was something off about the whole situation, inherently dangerous, and he now feared more for everyone's safety. The attempt made on their lives in the parking lot had left him with the indelible impression that only one small part of the story had come to life—the first loop in a long chain of mysterious events—and that something terribly sinister swam just below the dark waters, beyond his ability to see clearly.

After the police officers on scene had finished debriefing the three of them about their version of events, Trent had directed Lenny and his partner to sit outside their client's house and wait to see if her husband returned to the house. He was not willing to take a chance that Officer Markinson would not use the attack as an opportunity to direct full attention on his wife, Lisa. He knew the sick mind of a jilted husband carried with it unshakable focus. With nothing to gain, the three of them had agreed to withhold details about the Markinsons from the police, unanimously figuring it wiser to leave Lisa and Barry out of it. Which officers, if any, could be trusted was still unclear.

Trent had never been one to believe in coincidences. The fact that Officer Markinson and the men who had tried to kill them just happened to be on the same block at the same time was just a little too convenient for his taste. There had to be some sort of connection.

Another round of knocks came from the front door, harder, louder, and more insistent.

Trent got up and headed downstairs to answer the door. "Hang on," he yelled. "I'm coming, so stop pounding on my door." He crossed the foyer, growing annoyed at the interruption.

The knocks turned to a loud pounding, followed by a boom

that sounded like someone had just kicked the door with a pair of combat boots.

"Stop banging on my door," he yelled again. "And you better not my put boot prints on my damn door."

A woman's voice yelling at the top of her lungs on his porch sounded like someone scratching a chalkboard. The doorbell suddenly sprang to life.

"Knock that shit off!" He pressed his eye against the peephole. "What do you want?" He was surprised to see that the irritating voice belonged to such a beautiful woman.

"I want to come in." Her voice was insistent, demanding. "I need to talk to Trent Varus."

He kept staring at her through the peephole, secretly admiring every perfect curve of her body. Her hair was long, flowing like waves of spun silk. "Why?"

"That's my business."

"Who in the hell are you?" he said.

"My name is Tabitha." Long fingers ran through her hair, dabbing at the other side of her head with a palm.

"Tabitha, who?" he said. He was not about to open the door for a complete stranger. Life experience had taught him that women made the best assassins. They were clever and always disarming.

"Tabitha Verelli, bozo," she said in a petulant voice. "Now, are you going to let me in or what?"

He paused, taken aback by the name. He watched as she rose on her tiptoes and moved her face near the peephole. Words failed him.

"I hope you're getting a good gander, you pervert," she snapped at him. "If you will just open the damn door, then we can talk."

He backed away from the door. Fear that another part of his romantic past he had cut loose years ago had inexplicably found him created an aura of paranoia. Suspicion raced through his mind. The adage "Trust nothing of what you hear and only half of what you see" came to mind. If what she said was true, her sudden presence had just added a new complication into the formula of his chaotic life. "I-I don't know you," he stammered. "You should not be here. What do you want?"

"I already explained all that." The pitch in her voice increased. "I need to speak with Trent. If you will just open the door, then I am fairly sure that—"

"So speak!" He emphasized the last word as a demand. "No one is stopping you. I'm a busy man, and you don't need the door open to hear me." He took a step forward and looked through the peephole. Her tenacity brought a grin to his face. She was definitely a fiery woman.

"I didn't drive all the way over to your stuck-up neighborhood, and fall asleep in my car because you weren't here when I first got here, just so I could talk to a damn door!" Her foot kicked the door with a ferocity that reminded him of his wife. "You better open up, or I'll kick this mother chucker off the hinges."

"Hey!"

Her foot continued to kick at the door. "Look, asshole," she yelled at him. "Benny sent me here and I'm not leaving until I talk to you!"

He pulled his head away from the door with a sharp jerk, stunned to hear his former cellmate's name. His muscles grew taut, his pulse increasing. "Benny," he repeated numbly. "What the hell does that bipedaled fungus have to do with you being here, and what does he want now?" He narrowed his eyes, though she was on the other side of the heavy oak door. His mind raced for an explanation. "He still owes me a good chunk of money for that flophouse bar of his … Some partner he is."

"Um … I don't know anything about that," she stammered. "I didn't even know he had a partner."

I don't need another complication.

A cough cleared her throat. "If you didn't believe me or refused to open the door, he told me to tell you that it's Tabby Cat."

Trent stared at the door, dumbfounded. His heart pounded in his chest, fear coupling with desire to open a door that had remained closed for many years. "How do you know Benny? Are you his daughter?"

"Benny doesn't have any kids," she said. "I'm more adopted than anything else."

"Do you have my money?"

"He just told me to say that it's Tabby Cat. He said that you would understand. I sure as hell hope so, because I certainly don't."

Trent slid the deadbolt free, unlocked the door, and then opened the door. "I am Trent," he said.

Her feet made a nervous shuffle in reverse, and her eyes darted to the left and to the right in what looked like a search for a safe escape route.

"T-Tabitha," he stammered in a breathless voice. Just the vision of her standing no more than a few short feet away nearly stole his breath. His heart beat faster inside his chest. "Is it really you?" He wiped tears from his eyes. "I apologize for my stupidity."

A look of bewilderment flitted across her face. "I—"

He lunged at her, startling her into silence, and wrapped his arms around her. "Oh, how I've missed you." He tightened his hold on her.

A small cry slipped from her throat. "Do I-I know you?" Her voice was a shudder.

He kissed her on the cheek and moved his hands to her shoulders, extending his arms. He gazed into her eyes with affection so deep that she averted her eyes. "Not in so many words," he said, "but you kept me sane and saved my life, Tabby Cat."

Tabitha's hand flashed up and knocked his hands away from her shoulders, and she twisted her body to the right. Her hand rose in the air. "Don't call me that!" she snarled. "Benny's the only one allowed to call me that."

He tilted his head. "And Henry," he said softly. "You do remember Henry, don't you?"

Her body seemed to grow rigid at the name. Tears welled in her eyes, pain flooding them.

Trent reached out for her, but she jerked her body away from his touch.

"Are you ..." He let the words trail off.

She wiped away the tears with the back of her hand. "Did you know Henry, Mr. Varus?" Her voice quavered.

Her question took him by surprise. He stared at her, confused. "I'm sorry, but I don't understand," he said. "What do you mean, did I know him?"

Her eyes narrowed. "I mean, did you know him?" She spoke harshly. "It's a simple enough question."

He frowned. "Of course I know him." He placed a hand against his chest. "Tabby, it's me," he said. "It's me. It is Henry. I'm Henry."

Her eyes grew wide as saucers, and she staggered back on weak knees. "That's impossible." Her voice was faint, barely audible. "Henry's dead." Her knees appeared on the verge of giving out completely as her body sagged toward the ground.

Trent lunged forward and caught her right before she hit the hard concrete. *I got you, Tabitha, and I will never let you go again.* He scooped her up into his arms, gently cradled her as he had imagined doing for so many years while wasting away in the dark, and then carried her into the house. He gazed down at her angelic face, remembering every loving word she had ever written to him during his most vulnerable times, when suicide felt as if it were the only plausible solution to the surrounding madness found only in prison. Her love was the only thing that helped heal the loss of his wife, Connie. It had made no difference that they had never met or exchanged pictures. Their relationship had gone far deeper than the superficial.

Two hours later, Tabitha awoke with a startled yelp. Trent adjusted the silver tray in his hands, balancing a crystal pitcher and matching cups sitting atop the polished metal. He then smiled when she sat up in his king-sized canopied bed. The cold compress he had placed on her forehead slipped down her face and fell atop the satin comforter that covered her from the waist down. Her eyes looked about the lavish décor and dipped down at her clothed body. A tiny sigh fell from her lips. Her eyes then rose to him. Her legs curled up to her chest, pulling the shimmering edge of the comforter up to her throat.

"Oh, good, you're finally awake," he said in a light and airy voice as he walked across the floor and set the tray on a nearby nightstand. "You had me worried there for a second." He turned on a lamp with a click. "You could have hurt yourself. I barely reached you in time."

Her eyes remained wary, the corners of her mouth drawn tight with suspicion.

Chuckling, he poured a glass of water. "You're still unsure about me, huh?" He held the glass out to her. "That's fine. I cannot say that I blame you. I certainly did not prepare for a visit from you. Here, please drink this."

The apprehension on her face intensified, shaking her head. "I'm not thirsty."

Trent sampled the water to allay any fears that she might have that he drugged the liquid. "It's just water," he said softly.

She accepted the glass and drained it. "What happened?" Her hand wiped away a few dribbles.

"You fainted," he said bluntly.

"Unlikely," she said. "I don't faint."

"Okay," he said mildly. "Then you passed out, if that makes you feel tougher."

A sly grin formed on her face. "It does." Her eyes swept over the room. "Where am I?"

"My home," he said, and then he clarified, "My bedroom."

Her legs straightened out. "Nice digs, dude."

Trent pulled a chair next to the bed and took a seat. "It's all right," he said drily. "It's a little too big for just one person though. I've been thinking about selling it and moving to a smaller place, somewhere near a beach maybe."

Her brows knitted. "Must be nice to have money," she said sharply.

He wrinkled his nose. "It's not a penalty, if that's what you mean," he shot back at her.

She held the glass out to him. "So, you're not married?"

He took the glass and set it on the tray. "No. I'm not married."

"But you were married, right?"

He smirked. "Are you testing me?"

"Why would you ask that?"

"You're a very clever girl," he said and then added, "And you already know that I was married ... a long time ago."

Her face remained passive, undaunted by his answers. "Divorced?"

He winced, shook his head. "Passed away," he said, morosely.

A flash of sympathy sparked in her eyes. "Do you have a girlfriend?" Her voice grew kinder.

He shook his head. "No. Not for a long time now."

Her lips curled up into a devilish smile. "Gay?"

He feigned amusement at her ploy to disarm him. "No. I don't think so."

She attempted to get out of the bed, but then she stiffened when he placed a hand on her shoulder and stopped her. Her eyes hardened.

"Sorry," he said in a tender voice. "But you should lie still a little longer just to make sure you don't get another dizzy spell. You were out for quite a while. I may not be a doctor, but that cannot be the healthiest thing in the world." He made an awkward grin. "Besides, you could fall and hit your head." He picked up the cold compress and used it to dab at her face. "You're safe here, Tabby."

Her lips pursed. "Please, don't call me that."

"Why not?"

"There are only two people in the entire world that ever called me by that name." Her voice was a whisper. "Benny is one. The other died years ago. His name was Henry, and I loved him very much."

A lump formed in his throat. "What makes you think Henry's dead?" he said with a guttural squeak.

Her body shuddered. "Benny told me he got stabbed in prison and died there, in the infirmary." Her voice cracked. Tears welled in her eyes at the memory. "Henry had made promises to me. He was a very special man. We wrote each other for years, nearly every day. He said that we would have a life together, after he finally got out of that awful place, that everything was going to be fine—our dreams come true."

He frowned. "That sounds terrible," he said.

She started to sob and then continued as if she had not heard him. "Then one day his letters just stopped, and that's when Benny told me that Henry got killed in some sort of race riot. It was the worst day of my life, and I think I died that day." She pressed her hand against her chest. "In here."

Trent leaned back in the chair, deeply troubled on an emotional level he had not experienced since Connie had died. "I see," he mumbled. "What else did he tell you?"

She sniffed back tears. "Why?" Her voice oozed with pain. "What difference does it make now?"

"I'm curious."

She drew in a deep breath, as if seeking an inner strength she no longer felt. "I know they celled together while Benny was serving his time for drugs." Her voice was choppy, strained. "Benny wrote me and told me all about his new friend—said that he was a real nice guy and needed a friend to write. He had always believed Henry was innocent, but that didn't matter because his appeals had tanked in the courts." A rueful smile shadowed her face. "After writing him for six months, I fell in love with him. The things he wrote to me were so beautiful, so profound, and he filled me with a hope that I had never felt. He was so caring, so genuine. His letters made me cry and laugh." Her hands trembled. "Starlight …" Her voice trailed off, and she cast her eyes downward.

Trent finished her words. "Star bright," he whispered affectionately in a thick voice. "I wish I could, I wish I might, wish upon this star tonight."

Her eyes rose, and she stared at him. A gasp slipped from her mouth. "How do you—" Her mouth fell agape. "Oh, my God, it really is you."

He leaned forward and took her hands. "Yes, Tabitha," he said. "It really is me." He kissed her fingers. Passion burned inside him. "Those words always spoke to us. Do you remember?"

A mixture of anger and hurt replaced the wonder on her face. "But how?" Her eyes narrowed. "The letters stopped coming. Benny said your appeals were over, and you were going to remain in prison for the rest of your life." She pulled her hands free. "He then said some dirtbag murdered you, out on that godforsaken yard."

Trent dropped his chin to his chest, ashamed of his part in the sham. "I didn't know he'd told you that I died," he said. "However, now a lot more things make sense."

"What does?" Her voice rose in pitch.

"After what I thought was my last chance in court failed, Benny thought it best for you to forget about me and move on with your life." He paused. "Granted, Benny was grateful I filed the brief that eventually reversed his conviction and loaned him the money he needed to open his club, but he contacted me a month after his release and told me that you were in love with me. He told me the only way you'd have a chance for a real life, for true happiness, is if I cut off all contact."

Her hand flashed out and slapped him across the face. "So, the two of you conspired to lie to me!" Her face turned red in fury. "You tricked me."

He nodded, and his shoulders sagged beneath the weight of her words. "It was an impossible dilemma," he said. "I didn't want to let you go, but I also didn't want to rain misery down on you. I was in love with you. You were everything to me. Benny said that you were loyal to a fault and would never leave me, no matter what."

She lifted her hand as if to slap him again. "Don't you dare justify what you did to me or defend that lying bastard!" Her voice rose to a shrill. "He said you were dead, murdered. I gave my heart to you, and you stomped all over it. I didn't even have a picture of you, not even a face to mourn."

Trent sighed. "I'm sure Benny told you that only to protect you," he said. "Maybe it was the only thing he could say to make sure you wouldn't try to track me down. You can't visit a dead guy." He smiled weakly. "We know just how resourceful you can be when it's necessary. You're a very clever woman, very savvy, monumentally tenacious."

Her face softened, lowering her hand. "But why didn't you contact me after you got out? I don't understand."

He was at a loss. Nothing he could say would make sense to her.

"Aren't you going to answer me?" Her voice was firm. "I deserve an answer. I deserve to know why the man I fell in love with ditched me like a second-rate prostitute."

He pressed his lips together. "It wasn't like that," he mumbled. "It was just that so much time had passed, and I was afraid you would never forgive me for cutting off all ties without an explanation." He bit down on his lip and then continued. "I was afraid that you had stopped loving me." He shook his head. "I don't think I could've handled that."

"Why?" Her voice softened.

He closed his eyes, thinking back to his life spent in a cage and the awkwardness he had experienced after his release. "What felt like years to you felt like only yesterday to me," he said, opening his eyes and gazing into hers. "The world moves forward, even if we are stuck in the past. After my wife died, I was alone for so long. Year after year, I thought about suicide daily. I think the only reason I did not just hang myself was that I didn't want it to hurt. Then you came into my life and breathed life back into me. I do not know how many times I reread your letters, dreaming about a life shared with you. Connie may have been gone, but God was giving me another chance at love. I never actually moved on. Even now, I live in the past, and I did not want to face losing you all over again. So, I took the coward's way out."

Her face flushed. "Damn it!"

She moved to get out of bed, but he pushed her back down.

"I almost forgot about Benny."

"Don't worry about him right now." He pulled the comforter up to her neck. "All that matters is you, us."

She pushed the comforter away. "You don't understand." Her voice rose in panic. "Benny sent me here because he needs help with something. I don't know the details, but it sounded important to him." Her head whipped about. "What time is it?"

He placed a finger against her lips and hushed her. "I'll go see him and take care of whatever needs to be done, if you promise to stay here and rest."

"But shouldn't I go with you?"

"I won't stop you if you want to come, but I would rather you stay here." He walked over to his walk-in closet, rummaged for his spare set of keys, and then set them on a large speaker. "I would like to have someone to come home to, and I doubt this will take very long. These keys are to every room in this house, so please make yourself at home."

"Uh, Trent ..." She corrected herself, "I mean Henry?"

He looked at her. Just the sight of her lying on his bed stabbed unbridled emotions in his heart. His love for her had not diminished in the slightest. "Yes?"

"Do what you can to help him, please."

He knew without reservation that he would move mountains for her, if only she asked. "Everything and anything," he said. "Cross my heart, Tabitha. So, where is he?"

Her legs stretched out. "At the club," she said, grinning, "And don't take too long."

"No longer than necessary," he said. "We have a lot of catching up to do."

"Can't wait," she said.

He turned and headed for the club.

❦

Thirty minutes later, Trent found Benny in the club's private office in back. He was sitting comfortably behind a desk with his feet propped up on the corner, his hands held behind his head. A lopsided grin creased his face.

He closed the door behind him and took a chair in front of the desk, smirking when the grin on Benny's face faltered. The chair creaked in protest of his weight. "She's not here," he said. "Tabitha is finally where she belongs, where she has always belonged since you first introduced us."

Benny's feet slid off the desk, and he sat up in the chair. "I sort of figured something like that might happen." A hint of caution touched his voice. "Your home, I suppose?"

Trent brushed at invisible lint on his pant leg. Something in Benny's demeanor pestered him. It seemed as if he was busy calculating something outside the topic of discussion. He scrutinized his body language. "Of course," he said finally. "Of all the people on this crummy little planet, you know how much I adore that woman."

Benny planted his elbows atop the desk. "I do," he admitted. "I wasn't sure if you'd be pissed at me for sending her to you rather than going myself, in person."

"Why is that?"

"I didn't want you to think that I was trying to manipulate you into coming here and helping me." Something behind his eyes seemed to darken, masking the truth behind the words. "I just hope she wasn't too ticked off at me when she found out the truth."

Trent scratched at his chin. Benny was up to something; he could sense it. "But isn't that precisely what you intended?" he said.

A faint chuckle came from Benny. "So, you're not mad at me?"

Trent waved off the question. "Naw," he said. "Tabitha's not mad either. She was initially." He then added, "But telling her that I was dead, killed on the yard was a little harsh. Don't you think?"

"It was the only way I could stop her from trying to find you. She would have never left you alone in that hellhole, and I did not want her contacting the others—especially that nightmare of a brother of hers—out of misplaced desperation. He is someone best kept at arm's length."

Trent leaned forward, intrigued by what sounded like a cryptic manipulation of words and their meanings. "That's sort of what I figured," he said. "Who are these others?"

His face blanched a warning. "No one you want to know," he said. "Trust me on that."

"What about this brother of hers?"

"The same," Benny said. "They are nothing nice."

"You have never really talked about your family," Trent said. "I have always wondered why you have kept that such a big secret."

"They are nothing to talk about." His voice grew tight. "Most of them are insane."

Trent leveled steely eyes on him. "They can't be any worse than the two scumbags who tried to kill me and Lenny in town, practically out in the middle of the damn street," he said sternly.

A brief flash of pain crossed Benny's face, his features pinching. His throat cleared. "When did this happen?"

Trent detected his failed attempt at misdirection. He decided to play along, unsure as to the old convict's motive. Benny was as slippery as they came. "Recently," he said. "They were camped out somewhere by my client's house and followed us."

His brows knitted. "What happened?"

"They died. We didn't," he said matter-of-factly.

"Didn't the police show up and question you?"

"Of course they did."

"And what did they say?"

"Not much," he offered. "The witnesses backed us up all the way. The two scuzzbuckets rammed into my car, they tried to kill us for whatever reason, and we shot them dead in the course of a gunfight. Apparently the men in question were wanted for a list of other crimes, including several murders committed around town over the past week." He shrugged. "Basically, the cops said 'no real loss' to the human race and that they were nothing but wild animals and got exactly what they deserved. The homicide cop, someone by the name of Lomax, might come by for a follow-up interview in a few days."

Benny's eyes glazed over.

Trent moved forward with the reason he had come in the first place. "Tabitha told me that you needed to see me about something." He spread out his arms. "Well, here I am."

"Right to the point, huh?" His words lacked the expected interest.

"You know me," he said. "Why waste time. Besides, you caught me in a good mood, so shoot."

Benny shifted in the chair. "I'm sort of in a financial crunch with the club ... taxes and whatnot, and I need to borrow some money to pay—"

Trent shot to his feet and interrupted him. "How much do you need?"

His eyes blinked stupidly several times. "Uh, what?" he stammered.

"How much do you need to bring you into the black?" Trent said.

A look of shock washed over Benny's face. "Well, I ... am not exactly sure," he stammered. "I think maybe twenty thousand might get me over the hump and give me enough to hire a few new girls, maybe buy a couple of outfits for them."

Trent tilted his head at his former cellmate, a man with whom he had spent years locked in a cell and once considered a close confidante. "I'll have thirty thousand transferred into the club's account as soon as I get in touch with my financial adviser," he said. "You can use the additional ten thousand for ancillary services, if necessary. There are always additional expenditures involved in business, and I'd prefer you to have a little more financial latitude."

Benny rose from behind the desk, frowning. "Why are you doing this for me?"

Trent smiled at him. "Because Tabitha asked it of me," he said. "I will never deny her anything."

"I don't know what to say, Trent," he said, "except thank you. You have been a good friend to me."

"Try to relax, Benny," he said soothingly. "There is never anything so broken or wrong that cannot be fixed. Guys like us have to stick together."

His face pinched.

Trent opened the door and left, leaving Benny to stare after him.

CHAPTER 20

Lomax leaned his head over the steering wheel and groaned in exhausted misery. He had to struggle just to keep his weary eyes open and focus on the road ahead. His preliminary investigation into the courthouse massacre had so far uprooted next to nothing as far as identifying a bona fide suspect and/or suspects. He had theories aplenty. Cause of death was a given. Persons of interest were far too many to apply either inductive or deductive reasoning, because no one, not even the other judges in the building, cared one iota about "some grouchy old bastard" who had brought only shame on the bench—an opinion everyone seemed to share.

The crime scene investigators had taken every precaution to preserve the area and any evidence inadvertently left behind by the culprit, but not one member on the team had found a single shred of forensic evidence in the now dead judge's chambers.

His options were nonexistent.

Whoever had murdered the four men had taken special precautions to cleanse the room with professional efficiency and had completely wiped down the room with chemicals found in the janitorial storage rooms, including every book, chair, and pen. Even Judge Harper's fingerprints and those of his assigned bailiff were gone.

Lomax stifled a yawn, stuck at a macabre crossroads between two violent crimes as he now headed toward the crime lab to speak with Dr. Becky Swanson about the trace evidence she had discovered underneath the fingernails of the murdered girl from the warehouse. He did not require much to pursue either case, but nothing to go on epitomized the very essence of stagnation.

What have I gotten myself into now?

Everything about his life over the past week had turned surreal. His whole reason for existing on the planet distastefully revolved around death and mutilation in one way or another.

Still, something about the courthouse murders felt off, as if he had overlooked a valuable ingredient to a bubbling cauldron of murder and mayhem. His instincts tugged at him. No matter how many times he ran the same scenario through his head, he had a difficult time imagining how a single man could breach security and decapitate four men without alerting anyone. No one was that efficient. He had read the guards' rotation schedules that mapped out their nightly rounds at the top of each hour, and nothing in the documentation allowed a lone man the time or opportunity to conduct such time-consuming savagery. Judge Harper's body—that a rookie officer had discovered in a downstairs trash bin—had sustained several gunshot wounds in multiple appendages, which Lomax inferred as motivation for the judge to answer the perpetrator's questions. Several lacerations and deep puncture wounds Lomax recognized as method incisions evidenced his theory that someone highly skilled had tortured Judge Harper for information. The blood pooling and spatter along the floor supported a forced conversation between the killer and victim.

Lomax dug a palm into his blurry right eye to clear his vision. All he wanted to do was drive home as fast as his clunker would carry him and crawl into bed for a month. The grotesque scene at the courthouse still haunted him, and his investigation into Callahan's life had become a complication he no longer wanted or needed. The surrounding events of Callahan's death and the people he had connected in *People v. Varus* provided him with little recourse other than to believe that someone in authority had pressured the coroner to rule the DA's death a suicide to cover up premeditated murder. The answer as to *why* anyone had done so had eluded him at every turn.

Lomax pulled into the parking lot of a local gas station, one of his favorite stops for snacks and drinks of a varied sort, and drove around back and parked. Today, he needed a quick infusion of caffeine.

A super jumbo cup of hot coffee would cure everything.

His cell phone burst to life.

Oh, no you don't! He waited until the ring tone died and got out of the car. *I'm on break for the next ten minutes.*

He walked across the parking lot and entered a small grocery store annexed to the filling station. He gave his usual greeting to the elderly man working behind the cash register. "Hey, Jo-Jo," he said in a friendly but tired tone. "How're you doing?" He laid his money on the counter. "Gas me up."

Jo-Jo's lip curled up into a crooked-toothed smile, complete with squinting cataract-afflicted eyes. "I'm okay, Maxie." His voice evidenced too many years of smoking cigarettes. "No offense, but you look like a beat-up sandbag washed up from Hurricane Katrina." He chuckled at his joke and then began to cough from dying lungs long riddled with emphysema.

"Thanks for the vote of confidence, you old coot," he said. "You're all heart and sound like a million bucks." He smirked. "Why don't you go get me some snack cakes before you hack up one of those black alien things on the counter."

"Screw you, copper." Another fit of congestive coughs pummeled Jo-Jo's lungs. His hand dove into his back pocket and retrieved a small handkerchief. He dabbed at a few small specks of blood on his lips. "I've not smoked in ten years, and they're killin' me anyway. I should've never quit my sticks. Now I'll just die miserable, alone, and unwashed at my funeral."

Lomax nodded. "Yeah, that's a bitch," he said. "Quite frankly, I kind of envy you. There isn't much worth living for in this crap hole of a world anymore. The world is made up of shit with feet. I kinda wish I was dying."

A deep grunt came from Jo-Jo's diseased lungs. "Yeah, it's pretty bad these days," he said glumly. "No one's got respect for nothin' these days—not life and not property." He snatched the money off the counter and rang it up in the register. "Same thing for ya, Maxie?"

Lomax waved his hand through the air. "Um, well ... Yeah, maybe just a small tweak," he said. "Give me the decaf stuff."

Jo-Jo's whole face crunched up. "You're shittin' me, aren't you? Trying to play old Jo-Jo for a fool, are ya?"

"'Fraid not, buddy," he said. "I have just one stop to make, and then it's off to bed. I don't need anything messing with my sleep tonight. I'm way overdue for some z's."

Jo-Jo laid the change on the counter. "I got a new pot of that opossum stew from this morning, so hang on for just a second."

Lomax's phone suddenly sprang back to life, startling both men. Jo-Jo's hand covered his emaciated chest, grimacing. His face turned pale.

Lomax rolled his eyes. *Damn it to hell!*

"Lord have mercy on this poor old man," Jo-Jo squeaked. "That thing damn near stopped my ticker."

Lomax stepped away from the counter. "Excuse me, Jo-Jo." Against his better judgment, he turned for a little privacy and answered the phone.

Jo-Jo let out another round of violent coughs, waving for Lomax to pay him no mind.

He brought the phone to his ear. "What!" he snapped with a growl.

"What the hell kind of answer is that?" Captain Johnson's voice barked. "You sound like my friggin' ex-wife."

"I stand by my statement."

The captain's throat cleared over the phone. "We got another bad one, and I need you to come in and take over the investigation." His voice was grave. "It's one of our own."

Lomax hunched his shoulders at the thought of handling another murder. "I can't," he protested. "I'm doing a follow-up. Then I'm—"

A loud screech interrupted him. "Screw your follow-up! Did you hear what I just said? It's one of ours."

Lomax gritted his teeth. He did not care if the vic was the

president of the United States. His body ached, and his eyesight had diminished from exhaustion. "I understand that, sir, but I need to get some sleep," he pleaded. "I've been up for two days straight, and I'm seeing shit. I'm running on the last bit of fumes."

"Then use those fumes and bring your methane-burning ass in here."

"Can't you pass this one to another detective?" he begged. "I'm not the only one in this stink-ass city."

"You are right now!"

Lomax dropped his shoulders. "But—"

"No buts." Johnson's voice left no doubt that the subject was not open for discussion. "Are you going to make me issue a formal order?"

"Um, no," Lomax said with a grumble.

"Good. Now get your ass over to a Miss Maureen O'Shay's home. Her address is 1435 Armin Street."

"Who the hell is that?"

"You'll find out when you get here."

"Well, shit, Captain," he argued. "I need to—"

"Get your ass over here!" He gave a wicked chuckle after finishing his sentence. "If you need reminding, Erik, don't forget that you're my bitch until one of us retires."

Lomax shook in fury. "All right," he said. "I'll be there."

"When?"

Lomax tightened his grip on the phone. "I said I'll be there," he said heatedly. "Five, maybe ten minutes. Can I at least get a cup of friggin' coffee before I look at some other dead asshole?" He snarled. "Is that okay with you?"

"Make it fast. We're burning daylight."

Lomax clicked off his phone, removed the battery, and then threw it in the trash can by the door.

Jo-Jo was busy wiping down the counter with a rag reeking of ammonia. His eyebrow cocked to the side. "Is everything okay, Maxie?"

He ran a hand over his head. "Aw, shit, Jo-Jo," he mumbled miserably. "Some guy killed some other guy, and now I've been assigned to investigate the damn thing. I am so sick of seeing stiffs. I spend more time with the dead than the living. The worst part is the dead give me less headaches."

Jo-Jo's lips pursed. "It's a crazeee world." His head shook, clearly saddened by the news. "Folks always killin' folks just ain't right."

Lomax grunted. "You better give me the morning's hard stuff," he said. "It looks like I'm going to be up till the cows come home."

Jo-Jo's feet shuffled over to the far end of the counter. His hands snatched up a jumbo size cup and filled it with coffee the shade of ebony. He snapped on a lid and passed it over.

Twenty minutes later Lomax pulled his car alongside the curb and parked across the street from Maureen O'Shay's home. A wave of relief coursed through him when he found that only two unmarked cars were present. The last thing his thread-thin patience needed was another circus of vapid performers bumping into him and trampling all over his crime scene.

He snatched his steamy cup of coffee and climbed out of the car. *Maybe this won't be so bad after all.* He then ambled across the street and up the serpentine walkway to the front door, stealing a sip every third or fourth step. *In and out.*

Oddly enough, someone had inexplicably left the front door cracked open. He pushed it open and stepped into a modest foyer. "Hello," he called out. "Is anybody home? It's me, the cop who can't get any damn sleep."

A familiar voice called out to him from somewhere in the back of the house, "In here, Erik."

He took a deep swallow of coffee, casually strolling in the direction of the voice. He shoved his free hand into his pocket, his eyes roaming over bits of furniture and artwork on the walls.

Where in the hell is everyone?

Again, the same voice called out to him, "Back here."

Lomax blindly walked into the center of the alleged crime scene. He stopped just inside the bedroom and frowned at what he saw. The situation appeared far worse than he had anticipated, and the hair on the nape of his neck stood on end. The atmosphere was thick with tension. As far as he could tell, only five people appeared to be present in the house. There was no sign of a victim. The woman who sat gently sobbing on the bed did not look remotely familiar, but Lomax recognized everyone else in the room. Captain Johnson, Special Prosecutor Crue, and Officer Biggs from Internal Affairs stood on one side, while a familiar man who dwarfed all of them remained sitting on the bed next to the woman. It was a bizarre selection of men, and the fact that none of them were speaking struck a paranoid cord in Lomax's spine. All fixed cold eyes on him. He set the cup on a nearby dresser to free his hands.

Lomax met Lenny's discerning eyes, and he nodded in professional courtesy at the only man he actually trusted in the group. "Hey, Lenny," he greeted warmly. "Long time no see. What's it been, three maybe four years?"

Lenny's features remained stoic. "Closer to four, I think," he spoke in an uncharacteristic monotone. "It's good to see you again, Erik. How have you been?"

"I've been good," he said.

Captain Johnson rose from his squatted position and took three quick strides toward Lomax. His hand shot out. "I'm glad you could make it, pal."

Lomax looked down at his hand with distaste. "It wasn't as if I had a choice," he said bitterly. "You made it clear that I get over here ASAP, or else."

Johnson's hand fell to his side, his face tightening. "Fair enough," he said. "We have a potentially major problem here."

Lomax narrowed his eyes, saying nothing. He studied the man's chiseled face, and he no longer felt like an ally.

"Did you hear what I said?" Johnson's voice squeaked on the last word.

He clenched his jaw. "I heard you," he said. "I'm standing

right here, right in front of you." He shifted his eyes when Crue made an aggressive step forward, his eyes beady like a hairy rat's.

"Hello, Detective. I'm—"

Lomax threw up a hand and silenced the special prosecutor in midsentence. "I know who you are, so save your breath," he said crisply. "I'm not a total miscreant." He then looked at Biggs. "And I know who you are as well, so spare me the bullshit. What I don't know is why all of you are here, at a supposed murder scene."

The three men shot each other surreptitious glances.

Lomax moved back into the doorway and crossed his arms over his chest, so that he could move his hand a little closer to the firearm cradled in a shoulder holster.

The muscles in Johnson's jaw writhed. "What's the matter, Erik? You seem a little tense." His eyes moved down at the splayed fingers near his gun. A knowing grin crept on his face. "Is something bothering you?"

"Just tired, Captain," he said. He jerked his head at the bed. "So, who's the woman?" He watched Johnson move next to her and place a hand on her trembling shoulder.

"This is Maureen O'Shay." Her shoulders cringed beneath his touch. "She was attacked by a piece of trash, almost raped and murdered in her own house."

Lomax dared to step a little farther into the room, while maintaining a watchful eye on everyone. "I thought you said someone was killed," he said. "Where's the attacker? And where's the body?"

Johnson's finger pointed in Lenny's direction. "You'll have to ask him."

"As you probably already know, Eric," he began in a no-nonsense tone, "after I quit the force, I started working as a private investigator and part-time bodyguard for a defense attorney by the name of Trent Varus."

Lomax nodded. "Yeah, I've heard of him," he said noncommittally. "He's supposed to be one of the best criminal defense attorneys around, isn't he?" His mind raced at the possibility of another piece of the puzzle falling into place. He then added for effect, "And a former convict."

"That depends on your definition of a convict." Lenny's voice took on a defensive edge. "His conviction was reversed based on new exculpatory evidence and government misconduct." His deadly eyes shot at Crue. "He sat in prison for a couple of decades for nothing. He was innocent."

Crue's chin lifted in defiance, his eyes glaring at Lenny. "Innocence was never actually established by Varus." His tone was razor sharp. "The courts found that the remaining evidence did not meet the 'reasonable doubt' standard to affirm his conviction."

"That's lawyer mumbo jumbo bullshit, and you know it," Lenny retorted.

A wry grin formed on Crue's face. "Whether you like it or not, there is a huge difference, pal." Venom filled his voice. "He's a killer turned lawyer, and now he defends the scum of the earth."

Lenny rose from the bed and started toward Crue, his face now red with rage. "You little piece of shit!" His cantaloupe size hands balled into fists. "I should smash you into next week for lying about one of the nicest guys I've ever known."

Crue's head dipped into his shoulder, abjectly cringing away from the behemoth. Fear filled his eyes. Lomax took two quick strides and placed his hand on the giant's chest to stop him from doing something he would later regret. With a comical look of enjoyment on his face, Johnson merely stood to the side.

Lomax tried to give Lenny a shove back, but he failed to budge the man. "Easy, Lenny," he said soothingly. "You don't want to bust up a DA, do you?" He shot a quick look at Crue, who ducked away with a visible shudder.

A large grin creased Lenny's face. "As a matter of fact, I do."

"If you lay one apish finger on me, I'll have you arrested for assault," said Crue.

Johnson's head snapped around. His face was a mask of irritation. "Shut the hell up, Sebastian, before I clock you myself!"

Lomax focused his attention on Crue. "Can we forget your

personal problems with each other for just a minute and talk about why I was called in on this?" He looked at Maureen, concerned about her mental state.

She seemed to have become a by-product of the situation. "Has anyone even bothered to think of the woman by calling for medical assistance? I don't know what in the hell happened here, but she is obviously traumatized."

Johnson's head shook. "Not yet."

Lomax kneeled in front of her. "Why in the hell not?" He turned his head to Lenny, who met his eyes and crossed two massive arms over his chest.

"I tried to call for medical help, but Captain America here told me to wait until after you got here." His voice was a guttural growl, eyes blazing with hatred. "I told him that she was in shock, but he didn't give a damn about that."

Lomax lifted his hand to brush a loose strand of hair from the woman's eyes, but she let out a startled gasp and instinctively pulled away from his touch as if burned by a flame. He sensed Lenny move behind him, placing a hand on his shoulder.

"I think she's sinking into a deeper shock, Erik." His voice dripped with sympathy. "She's been through one helluva ordeal. That freak show tried to kill her." He got down on one knee and smiled at her. "It's okay, Maureen. Erik's one of the good guys. I'd bet the farm on it."

Her chin slowly rose as she reached out to Lenny. His hand enveloped hers.

Lomax got to his feet and placed his face within inches of Johnson's. "If you don't tell me what this is about right now, I'm taking her out of here," he declared. Nothing could possibly justify such cruel treatment of a victim. "This is ridiculous."

Johnson's eyes turned vicious.

Lomax sneered and jerked his head at Lenny, who scooped Maureen up in his arms. His expression dared any of them to try to stop him.

"Thanks, Erik," he said with another growl, this time lethal. "The first man who tries to stop me will end up like that broken piece of shit in the bathroom." He started for the door, but Crue stepped in his path.

"You can't just leave with the victim, you damn ape!" His finger waved in front of Lenny's face. "You are interfering with a criminal investigation."

"I'm warning you, little man," Lenny spat. "Get out of my way, or I'll move you."

Crue's eyes shifted to Johnson. "Aren't you going to stop him, Captain?"

"Let him go," said Johnson. "We can talk to her later, if need be. We have more pressing things to worry about right now." He then walked toward the bathroom. "Come on, Erik. It's just easier to show you. I've wasted enough time, so just follow me."

Lomax grinned when Lenny took one last look around and then pressed forward. Crue barely got out of his path before the bigger man trampled over him.

Inside the bathroom, Lomax stopped dead in his tracks at the sight of a naked man lying akimbo on the cold floor, face down in a fresh puddle of blood.

What in the hell is this? He watched Johnson tiptoe over to where the body lay and scratch his head. *Where are his clothes?*

Lomax did a quick study of the scene, perplexed by everything he saw. Things now made even less sense. "Captain, would you mind telling me why you have not called an investigatory team and why those two monkeys are here with you? This is not normal procedure."

Johnson's neck craned. "It's not that easy, Erik," he said, and then kicked the corpse in the head. "This piece of shit is Officer Barry Markinson. He's a decorated cop who tried to rape and kill his wife's sister." His face pinched. "There's a disturbing history behind all this."

Lomax frowned, wondering how much uglier things could get. "You're talking about the woman in the other room?"

"That's the sister."

Lomax decided to tread lightly. "Is that why the prosecutor

and the joker from IA are here?" he said and then added, "because of this dead cop?"

Johnson gave him a slow nod, seeming to weigh just how much he should admit. "I thought it pertinent to bring them in immediately."

He now felt certain that Johnson had a hidden agenda, another thread revealed in the tapestry he was trying to unravel. "Okay, that makes sense." He preferred to placate until he learned more. "But why are you so adamant about bringing me in on this? The department has plenty of detectives for this type of case."

"Because you're the best, beyond reproach, and I need you on this case to avoid potential fallout."

His captain was definitely holding out on him. "I see," he said drily. Warning bells went off in his head. "So, what happened?"

"According to Lenny, Markinson was trying to drown the woman in the tub when he busted through the door and saved her. He killed Markinson during a struggle. Evidently Varus thought the sister might be in danger, so he had Lenny keep an eye on her." His head cocked to the side. The corner of his eye ticked. "What can I say? The damn lawyer was right."

Lomax winced. "Jeez," he whispered. "She's lucky to be alive."

"Very."

"Has the sister made a statement yet?"

Johnson's face tightened. "No. Lenny refused to let her speak, said she had lawyered up with Varus."

Lomax chuckled. "As a former cop, Lenny knows the ropes," he said. "You didn't find it odd that he told her to lawyer-up, did you?" He pointed at the dead body. "After all, your dead dude is a cop, and Lenny knows cops protect other cops, no matter what they do."

His nostrils flared at the insult. "Under the circumstances, no, not really," he said. "The woman was pretty freaked out and wouldn't even look at me."

"Why would Markinson flip out and attack his wife's sister?" Lomax was at a quandary. "It seems to me that he would go after his wife."

"Evidently the wife is suing him for divorce, and the court issued a TRO." His voice turned bland. "You know the routine. Besides, Lisa Markinson, that's the sister, had protection."

Lomax whistled. "That'll do it all right," he admitted.

"The evidence is fairly clear and supports self-defense, but …" His voice trailed off.

Lomax shot him a curious look. "But what?" he said. "You can't just sweep this under the rug. I mean, shit, we got a naked, dead cop on the floor of a bathroom. Some things just cannot be spin-doctored."

Crue's head suddenly poked through the small opening of the door. "So, is he on board?" He spoke with a nervous squeak. "Biggs is getting impatient and isn't willing to wait much longer, Captain. I need an answer."

Lomax leered at Johnson. "On board with what, Captain?"

Johnson's head spun around, his face livid. "Damn it, Sebastian, you idiot!" With incredible swiftness, his captain moved toward the door, placed his calloused hand on Crue's face, and then shoved him out. "I haven't told him yet, so get the hell out of here."

Lomax wrinkled his brow, "On board with what?" His suspicions rose to new heights when Johnson sat down on the toilet and looked at him with dead serious eyes.

"It's like this, Erik." Indelible frankness touched each syllable. "Sebastian and I think it would be beneficial to the department if we portrayed this as more of an accidental death of a police officer, perhaps even a he-gave-his-life-in-the-line-of-duty sort of thing."

Stunned at the perverse prospect of cloaking a murderous rapist with a heroic act, Lomax felt heat rise from his neck and fill his cheeks. "You mean lie, don't you?" He spat the words like poison.

A disgruntled gasp slipped from Johnson's lips. "Markinson's dead, and the woman isn't hurt too bad, so to speak." The words tumbled out clumsily. "We see nothing to be gained by advertising what happened here today. There's just bad and worse." His shoulders shrugged. "You know how politics work."

Astounded, Lomax looked at him with wide eyes. He jerked a thumb at the bedroom. "And that prosecutor thinks this is the right course of action?"

The captain ran his tongue over his lips, "Actually, it was his idea."

"Does IA know this?"

Johnson nodded, somewhat leery. "Yeah," he said. "That's why Biggs is here."

Saddened at how things had declined over the years, Lomax shook his head. "So, he is willing to go along with this sham?"

"He and his department are in full agreement." His hands lifted. "With Markinson now dead, prosecution is moot. The facts can only reflect negatively on the force. There are a lot of good men and women sworn—"

Lomax threw up a hand and stopped him from finishing the sentence. "And what about the woman attacked by this mongrel?" he said angrily. "Doesn't she matter at all?"

He tensed when Johnson rose from the toilet. His face flushed in response to the questions. "Don't be a sanctimonious ass, Erik," snapped Johnson. "Of course she matters, but this is the world we live in. To get along, you go along." His lips pursed, and then he continued. "The truth of the matter is she will never get the kind of justice she wants or deserves. I ran down the alternative to Lenny. He has at least agreed to take our offer to Varus."

"That's corruption!" he said, outraged, and then added, "Obstruction and interference with the administration of justice."

"In this unique case, we believe it is necessary."

"So, Varus knows about this?" The hairs on the back of his neck prickled. He now smelled a rat, a real stinky one.

His right shoulder lifted. "Sort of," he admitted with apparent reluctance.

"Then why isn't Varus here?"

"Lenny took care of that for us."

"How?"

Johnson's eyes rolled in his head. The look on his face now showed the first signs of genuine aggravation. "He called Varus before we got here to let him know what happened." His voice was deadpan. "Varus told him to call the police and report the crime. You were out doing whatever, so I intervened on your behalf and came here personally. I notified Crue and Biggs on the way over here. Lenny made another call to Varus after we arrived and assured him that everything here was good—that he could handle things on this end for now." His tone turned petulant. "A defense attorney on sight with us and his client's sister could attract the sort of attention I would prefer to avoid."

Lomax stared at him, bewildered, wondering how much the plot would thicken before everything blew up in their faces. "What does the woman get in return for her silence?" he said. "What about the victim's sister?"

"You're like an old dog with a damn bone." His eyes closed and opened. "The victim keeps quiet about all this and lets us attribute his death to line of duty. In return, while sparing her sister the indignities of questions, interviews, and so forth, the wife will collect on the husband's full benefit package." His Adam's apple bobbed. "Lenny seems to think Varus will be disgusted with the proposal, but he will acquiesce and do what's in the best interest of his client and her sister. I've checked, and the Markinsons carry a butt load of debt."

"So, what do you need me for?" he said. "It sounds like the three of you have everything figured out among yourselves."

"We need a detective from homicide division to conclude the case for legal effect."

Lomax felt his guts churn in revulsion. "You mean … a straw man?"

Johnson corrected, "A partner."

Lomax mumbled under his breath. He needed a hot shower to wash away the scum. "And I'm your man, huh?" he said bitterly. "What's the COD?"

Johnson's finger pointed at Barry's corpse. "It's all right

there and speaks for itself." His tone reflected no respect for the dead. "Markinson hit his head and suffered a broken neck while struggling with a perp burglarizing his sister-in-law's home."

Silence filled the space between the two men.

"Can we count on you, Erik?"

Lomax wondered what drove a man so deep into immorality and corruption. "Don't you and Varus have a nasty history?" He hoped to elicit another tell.

Johnson's face remained stoic. "You might say that," he said. "But that was a long time ago."

Impressed with Johnson's ability to remain passive, Lomax snickered softly. "You were involved in sending him to prison for years, weren't you?" he said.

"Did your homework, did ya?" Johnson's face flashed a hint of dangerousness.

"Something like that," he admitted. "I am a detective, and my job is to detect stuff." He paused to give the implied threat time to sink in, and then continued, "It seems that a few of the people connected to the Varus case a couple of decades ago have, well, sort of, died … violently."

The captain's eyes seemed to darken. "Things happen," Johnson offered in a calm tone of voice.

"Like the witness in the case getting blown to smithereens out in the middle of nowhere?"

"Exactly," he said. "What's your point?"

"Dead judge and dead DA," he said.

The corner of Johnson's eyes grew taut. "What are you trying to say?"

"I'm trying not to say it."

"Just ghosts in the machine, Erik." His voice turned casually light. "Don't get offtrack. Focus on the matter at hand. Callahan killed his coward self, and the judge—" Again, he shrugged his shoulders, and then he added, "Well, that's up your alley."

Lomax sighed, exasperated. "If you can get Varus to go along with everything, who am I to stand in the way?"

A huge grin of satisfaction formed on Johnson's face. "Perfect!"

His voice was jubilant. "I'll tell the others and let you take care of business here." He slapped his hands together. "I'll call in forensics."

Lomax kneeled next to the body, turning his attention on the corpse after Johnson hurried out of the bathroom to spread the news. "Do what you have to do," he called after him.

CHAPTER 21

Trent exhaled deeply from mental exhaustion and rolled back over to where Tabitha lay next to him, naked. Her beautiful smile vanquished the stress his conversation with Lenny had created and filled his heart with renewed vigor.

Earlier, when they had made passionate love together, her eyes had sparkled with a vitality that had mesmerized him, pulling him closer to a heaven in which he had refused to believe years ago.

He propped himself up on an elbow and greedily devoured her physical form with hungry eyes, which tempted his libido to ravish her fleshy essence once again. Her indescribable beauty defied natural perfection. Her lustrous hair fanned out across the black-satin pillowcase like the feathers of a proud peacock, reminding him of the wonderful works of art hanging on the walls of museums, where streaks of pure light radiate from a face whose eyes pierce the human heart with love and kindness.

He leaned over and inhaled her feminine scent, smiling when she suddenly sat up in bed and looked down at him with eyes brimming with pure pleasure. He had never wanted anyone to devour him as much as he did while under her hypnotic stare in that moment.

Her lips puckered. "Are you going to tell me what that was all about?"

Trent forced an innocent smile to try to put her mind at ease. Nothing in his life had ever felt so perfect, and he did not wish to ruin it. "It was just Lenny," he offered, flippant. "He gets easily excited over things and whatnot."

Her demeanor looked unconvinced. "Who's Lenny?"

Trent maintained his contrived smile. "He's just a guy who works for me from time to time," he said as he reached out to caress her cheek. Her hand lashed out and slapped it away.

"Don't do that!" Her voice was rough, demanding.

He frowned. "Do what?"

"Play things off like they're nothing." Her mannerism intensified, as if she sensed something amiss. "Benny does that bullshit, and I'm not a moron." Her nose wrinkled. "Is something wrong? You didn't act like it was nothing on the phone."

He winced at the sting of words. "Naw," he said. "We have just a couple of unforeseeable bugs in a plan, nothing all that serious. Everything is fine, just a glitch."

"Do you have to leave?" Her voice took on a darker tone. "It kind of sounded like you had to go somewhere."

"Not just yet," he said. "You worry too much."

"And you don't seem to worry enough."

"I don't want to show up too fast," he countered. "It could look a little funny for a conscientious objector. Besides, he's a big boy, smart too, and he knows what to do."

"Then why would you advise him to call the cops?" It was obvious that she did not believe most of what he was telling her. Her eyes began to mist. "Why would he and Maureen invoke client-attorney privilege?"

"I can't talk about that, Tabby," he said with conviction. Her suspicious walls began to close in on him. "You know why, privilege and professional relationship."

Her lower lip quivered. "Have I done something wrong?" Her hand wiped at a tear rolling down her left cheek. "If I said or did anything that—"

He placed a finger against her lips and hushed her. "God, no," he said softly. Guilt tugged at his heart for misleading her. "You can do no wrong in my eyes." He took a deep breath. "It's just—" He arrived at an impasse that severed his train of thought. The last thing he wanted was to build their relationship on a foundation of lies. Either he trusted her or he did not. Without trust, true love could never survive. Middle ground in a monogamous relationship, he knew, did not exist.

Her hands pulled free of his; her face showed hurt. "Just what?" Her voice cracked. "You're starting to scare me."

Trent rolled onto his back and cradled the back of his head on laced fingers. He stared up at the ceiling. "It's just that so many things have happened—things I never believed possible," he said, treading gently on a virtual path of jagged rocks. The collected experiences during a person's life defined his or her essence in the present. "And now I'm not quite—" He craned his neck and looked at her. Today was the first day of his new life.

Her brows knitted sharply. "You're what?" Her tone demanded an answer. "You're what? Just say it."

Trent blinked back tears. The past, present, and future seemed to combine intangible forces all at once and crash down on his consciousness.

Her finger poked him in the side. "Say it or get out of this bed!"

"I'm afraid!" he blurted out. "Is that what you want to hear? I'm afraid I'm going to lose everything all over again—that I'll lose you, lose this, and eventually lose us." His voice cracked on *us*. "I cannot lose you, Tabitha. Not again, not ever."

Her head jerked back, her face a mask of confusion. "Why would you say that?"

Tears rolled from the corners of his eyes. "I just couldn't let things go, could not let what they had done to my wife, to my family go unpunished," he admitted grudgingly. "I gave in to the darkness, allowed it to consume me, and now I may have jeopardized us and everything we now share. In my anger, I lashed out, and I may have decimated the future."

"What are you talking about?" Her voice was tender, inquisitive. "What did you do?"

He shook his head. Guilt gnawed at the pit of his stomach. "I betrayed the memory of my wife, Connie," he whispered. "She would never have condoned what I've done in her name. The loss and pain had just eaten me up, and I never thought of how my actions would mock everything on which she stood. I wasn't thinking. Anger and hatred had become my masters." He sniffed back tears. "She was such a gentle soul. She detested violence, and she didn't deserve what they did to her."

"No innocent deserves bad things to happen to them," she said. "Sometimes terrible things just happen; life happens."

He continued, unmoved by her vacuous explanation. "For so long, I never thought I would get a second chance for real happiness, for real love, and now I feel guilty for loving you, like I am betraying Connie somehow."

"Even though I never met your wife, I am sure she would want you to find love again and be happy." Her voice carried with it a gentle inflection. "She sounds like a wonderful woman, so I doubt she would want you to be alone, drowning in a past that made you miserable."

"If you knew everything about me, what I've done, the triple life I've begun, I doubt you would believe the things you are now saying to me," he said.

"You're not making any sense." The words tumbled clumsily from her. "There is nothing you can say or do to make her love you any less … or me for that matter. I am with you today, tomorrow, forever. It's now you and me until the end."

He shook his head. "You can't know that," he said in a pained voice. He widened his eyes when she pushed up from the bed and nimbly climbed on top of him. "You don't know what I've done."

Her long legs straddled his body, her hands pinning his shoulders to the bed. Her eyes bored into his. "Don't you dare tell me what I know and what I don't know." Her body trembled in anger. "I love you with every molecule of my body, and I will fight to keep you. There is nothing I will not do for you; so don't you dare treat me like some kind of snot-nosed schoolgirl!" She snapped. "I am not exactly the innocent girl next door, and I've seen shit that would make even you turn a sick green with disgust."

"It's not that simple," he protested.

"The truth is always simple."

As he looked up into the intensity burning behind her eyes, feeling the soft caress of her hair against his chest, Trent felt a tightening in his chest. The words of what he had done refused to spill from his lips.

Her fingers tightened on his shoulders, digging into his flesh. "Just tell me, so we can get past it!" Inner strength poured from her words. "Either tell me, or get out of this bed right now."

Trent felt as if his heart would break into a thousand pieces.

"Tell me!" She spoke the words as a demand. "You never know, maybe I can help with whatever it is."

For several silent seconds, Trent merely stared at her. He now recognized an unspoken commitment in the reflection her eyes cast. He belonged to her, and she to him. They had become one in heart, one in mind, and one in soul.

God help me!

"Speak!"

Finally, his tongue loosened.

"You are safe with me," she promised. "You can tell me anything without judgment."

He took a deep breath. "I've killed men, murdered them in cold blood," he admitted, "in prison and after I got released."

Silence filled the space between them.

Her eyes blinked, appearing dumbstruck. Her lips parted. A slow smile then formed on her mouth. "Is that it?" Her voice stammered, resonating incredulity. "That's the thing that was driving you so crazy?"

Trent's thoughts went in a hundred different directions, shocked by her lack of reaction to such an admission. "Didn't you hear me?" he said. "I just told you that I have murdered men, killed them dead."

Her eyes rolled. "So what," she said in a carefree voice. "I would have been surprised if you hadn't. Prison is not exactly the most conducive environment to make people nicer. I grew up with people who have killed other people most of my life." She smirked. "Have you met my extended family? Everybody in my life is a maniac."

"So, you're not disgusted or repelled by what I just told you?"

Her head shook. "Do you love me?"

"What kind of question is that?" he mumbled. "You already know the answer to that question."

"It's a simple enough question," she said. "Do you love me?"

"You know I do," he shot back at her. "I love you so much that it's clouding my judgment."

"Then say you love me."

"I love you!"

Her hands pushed off his shoulders, her back straightening. "Good," she spoke with finality, "because I love you too. I am not about to take any chances in losing the love of my life over some sort of testosterone-induced bullshit. I've been walking through life like a damn zombie for years, doing things I'm ashamed of for much longer than I would ever care to admit." Her head shook. "But none of it mattered because nothing in life mattered." She inhaled deeply. "Now it does, so don't you dare try to send me back to that life." Tears pooled in her eyes. "Don't you dare do that to me, do you hear me?"

"Yes, I hear you, Tabitha," he said, thinking, "but it's complicated, and I don't want to get you involved."

Tabitha's slender arms stretched toward the sky before she folded them behind her head, lifting her heavy breasts. Her face shimmered, aglow with sensual intoxication. Her hips twisted, grinding against him. "I am already involved, so tell me what I can do to help. It would be a mistake to underestimate what I can do for you. If I cannot help, then I ask you to let whatever unfinished business you think you have left fall to the wayside, so we can begin our lives together."

He placed his hands on her hips, kneading her flesh with his fingers. "And if I can't let it go?" he said.

A purr slipped from her throat at his touch. "Do you trust me?"

"Trust you in what?"

"For anything," she countered, "about everything."

Her thighs squeezed him, and he gave a quick nod. "Yeah, I trust you." He frowned. "Where is this coming from?"

"Would you ever lie to me?"

Her sex moistened warm against his skin. "What is this?" he said distractedly.

"It's about trust," she said, increasing the pressure against his aching crotch. "If we are going to be together, forever, I have to know that you trust me, that you know that I trust you, and that you will never lie to me ... again."

He clenched his teeth. "If this is about me not breaking my promise to Benny and—"

Her hand flashed down between his legs, silencing him. "No!" Her hand began to stroke his member. "It has nothing to do with that. I am not a moron. I understand why Benny told me that you were dead and why you agreed to go along with him."

He lifted her off him and set her down beside him. He recognized a verbal dance when he heard one. "What are you trying not to ask me?" he said. "You keep around the edge without going for the bite."

Her tongue ran over her lips. "I want to know how you lost your family," Tabitha finally said. Her face paled for just a second after she spoke. "Specifically, I want to know about your wife. I want you to talk to me. I want you to share with me the things you have been through and have never told me. I want no secrets between us."

A sharp pain shot through his chest. "Why in the world would you ask me about my wife now?" He dropped his chin on his chest.

Her hand rested on his chest. "It's okay," she said. "You can tell me. I can only imagine how much it must eat you up inside. You need to talk to someone, so why not me?"

He looked at her with blurry eyes, anguish tearing into his soul. "You don't understand," he mumbled in a barely audible voice. "It was all my fault."

"What happened to her?" Her voice was soft and loving.

"She died," he muttered, miserable, and then added, "they died."

Tabitha's body reflexively jerked back, eyes now wide. "Who's 'they'?"

He closed his eyes tightly enough to squeeze tears from them. "My wife and child," he said, deadpan.

Her hand reached out, but he cringed away. "How did they die?"

"It was over twenty years ago," he continued. "I was housed in the southern reception center at the time, waiting for staff to classify me for designation. My wife …" He exhaled. "Her name was Connie. She was coming down to visit me. She was bringing our child."

"That's nice," she whispered.

"You think so, huh?"

Her lips pressed together in befuddlement. "Isn't it?"

Trent opened his eyes. "On the way down, if I am to believe a word from the so-called authorities, some lowlife tried to carjack her. The scumbag thief shot Connie and Howie." He began to weep softly, reliving the event all over again.

A small gasp fell from her throat. "Oh my God," she said in a horrified voice. "Benny never said anything about a kid."

Trent straightened his back against the headboard, struggling to regain control over his emotions as he continued in a drone-like voice. "I sat in the cell all day, on my bunk, swinging my legs in anticipation, and waited for staff to call my name over the intercom." He hissed. "But it never came. I waited all night and then again all the next day, never taking my eyes away from the door. Eventually, two days later, I think, I finally collapsed from stress and exhaustion. I don't really remember anymore. Much of those days are little more than a painful blur." He shuddered. "All I remember is the guards waking me from a dead sleep and telling me that my family had been involved in an accident—that my family was dead. No one would answer any of my questions. The sergeant said the chaplain would be by to see me, and then he just left. The chaplain never did come, and the guards refused to let me use the telephone. When I refused to stop demanding the phone, they pepper sprayed me, stripped me down to a pair of boxers, and threw me in solitary confinement on suicide watch. I remained there, stuck in a concrete box, freezing and emotionally destroyed, for over a week."

With tears streaming down her cheeks, Tabitha's mouth quivered in sympathy to the horror suffered at the hands of a bloodsucking prison system. Trent opened his arms to her, forcing a weak smile. The look on her face spoke of her helplessness to exorcise the demons still haunting him from a merciless past. He was grateful that she did the only thing within her power to keep the cries at bay—she crawled into his arms and verbally vowed to protect him from anything and anyone from this day on.

CHAPTER 22

From the quiet solitude inside his parked car, Benny sat in the front seat and stared numbly out the side window at Trent's house. His mind was racing in feverish turmoil, desperate and lost in the irreconcilable conflict between remaining loyal to his longest living friend and saving his own skin from a madman more than happy to remove it from his bones one scrape at a time. Trapped in a snare created by his selfish design, he recognized that the impossible had happened. He had never thought his current predicament possible. Greed and desire to live another day now left him stuck in a quagmire from which he could not escape.

The disastrous news he'd received from Johnson of Markinson's inconvenient death had changed everything for Benny. The unforeseeable event had left him completely vulnerable to summary disposal in a local dumpster and powerless to refuse the tyrant secretly running the city from beneath its underbelly.

Benny had no delusions as to how Dominique Cieo would rectify disobedience. The enforcer was, without measure, the most vicious man he had ever had the misfortune of crossing paths with. The last example Cieo had made in front of him to prove a point—the subject a young upstart trying to move heroin along the strip without first seeking permission—had left a lasting impression. Benny shivered at the prospect of meeting a similar end. The kid's torture was the worst thing he had ever witnessed, and he wanted his appendages to remain right where God had intended them, attached to his body.

Sorely convinced that he had only one option if he wanted to save his own life, Benny finally opened the car door and stepped out.

Sorry, Trent, he thought. *I got to look out for number one. It's nothing personal, just business. The man's vile evil scares the bejesus out of me!*

He made his way to the front door and rang the bell. He turned and took a visual sweep of the immaculate landscape. His nerves had been shot to hell since he'd hung up the phone. He trusted nothing and no one at this point. The rattle of locks coming from the other side of the door caught his attention. He turned just as the door swung open.

Dressed in a man's robe and a pair of matching slippers several sizes too big for her petite feet, Tabitha pushed the door all the way open and stepped into clear view. Her eyes sparkled with a vigorous life of happiness he had not seen in a very long time. Her pouty lips curled up into a huge smile that engulfed her entire face. Hair slightly mussed, she squealed in wild delight at the sight of her Uncle Benny standing on the porch. She ran at him, arms splayed apart in a wide arc, opening and closing her fingers in hungry anticipation.

Surprised by her girlish antics, Benny instinctively took two quick steps back in retreat. He had never seen her actively demonstrate such affection.

Her voice chirped excitedly, "Oh, Uncle Benny!" Her arms tightened around him. "I'm so glad you are here."

Benny pulled her head down into his shoulders and cringed in expectation of her punching him for lying to her for so long about Trent's death. Her tears of joy splashed his neck, and he felt himself melt in the embrace of the woman he had considered his daughter for two decades.

Again, Tabitha shrieked her happiness. "I can't believe how great everything is!" Her arms twisted him back and forth. "I owe you everything. I love you so very much for bringing him back to me."

Her words struck him deep, piercing the core of his heart. He had not planned on such a reception from her. A new level of guilt tugged at him for what he had already placed in motion. He tried to hug her in return with equal enthusiasm, but he found it difficult. Nothing could ever cleanse his soul of such hypocrisy.

Tabitha's embrace broke off, and her eyes gazed into his. Her whole face alit with the love only a daughter feels for her father.

Benny lowered his eyes in shame. *What have I done?* Death was too merciful for him.

Tabitha's hands pulled the robe tighter around her waist. "What are you waiting for?" Her voice was crisp and vibrant. "Trent's been waiting for you. He has everything ready for you." Her eyes danced brightly. "So much has happened, and we have great news to tell you, so hurry up and get in here." She turned and ran back into the house, yelling at the top of her lungs for Trent to hurry up and come downstairs because Uncle Benny had finally come home.

Benny lumbered into the house and shut the door behind him, watching Tabitha bounce on her toes in the center of the large foyer, smiling ear to ear. Her neck craned, and she pointed at the top of the stairs, where Trent appeared and waved a friendly hello down at him.

Benny raised a hand and gave the halfhearted wave of a hypocrite and traitor. *I am such a friggin' Judas!*

Tabitha sprinted across the floor and bounded up the stairs two at a time, meeting Trent at the top. His arms wrapped around her.

Benny grimaced. *She is going to kill me three times before I hit the ground.*

Trent's face beamed with happiness. "I'm glad you finally made it, Ben," he said, guiding her back down the stairs.

Benny furrowed his brow, feeling worse than ever. "Sorry for being so late," he mumbled. "I got kind of hung up on some stuff I needed to take care of."

Trent's arms slipped free from her shoulder, and he held out a hand. "Don't give it a second thought, old friend," he said. "You're here now, and that is all that matters."

Benny felt his heart leap into his throat. His friend had never acted aloof in front of him, so at ease, practically giddy. It was as if she had miraculously transformed him into a completely different person. He no longer seemed dark and threatening.

Could he love her that much?

The answer to his question disturbed him greatly as he reached out and accepted Trent's hand.

His brow knitted. "Is something wrong, Ben?"

Benny forced a smile. "No. Not at all," he said. "I suppose you're right. I'm here. You're here. She's here." He slid his hand free. "In the grand scheme of things, I guess that is really all that matters."

She nuzzled her head against Trent's shoulder, grinning, and then added in a soft purr, "And that's all we need."

"I have the documents compiled and ready for you to sign upstairs, Ben." Trent's eyes shifted to the antique clock on the wall. "They're in my office. We can take care of this in just a couple of minutes."

Benny motioned with his hand. "Then lead the way."

Trent planted a kiss on Tabitha's check. "Would you mind confirming our flight plan, while I take care of this stuff, dear?"

She beamed at him. "Not at all," she said. "I'll take care of everything." Her lips formed a pout, and then she added, "But what about our news? Don't you want to share our wonderful news with him?"

Benny's stomach did a flip-flop. Surprises had never boded well for him. Feelings of his betrayal intensified, even though he did not know what the couple was about to tell him. He dared to ask, "Are you going on a trip?"

Trent's hand ran over the top of his head. "Something like that," he said.

Nervous energy coursed through Benny. He shifted his eyes back and forth. His life threatened to spiral out of control.

"We're going on an adventure," Tabitha piped in.

Benny's throat constricted. The happiness on her face scared him down to his marrow. "When are you leaving?"

"We're leaving tonight," she chirped. "Trent chartered a private plane for us, just us."

Things were about to get far more difficult than he had anticipated, and Benny struggled to maintain his composure. "What time are you leaving?" Time was growing shorter with every tick of the clock.

Tabitha's eyes narrowed. A look of puzzlement replaced the joy on her face. "Midnight," she offered. "Why?"

"Where are you going?"

Her smile returned. "We're going to—now get this—the Virgin Islands." Her voice was bubbly. "I've never been there." Her shoulders lifted. "Actually, I've never been anywhere."

Benny felt his face flush. "Why? What's the big damn hurry?"

Tabitha's head turned, her eyes pleading with Trent, who then grinned and nodded. Her hand flashed up. Benny stared at the sparkling diamond ring on her finger. "We're engaged!"

Benny's blood turned cold in his veins at the announcement. He blinked several times, stunned and speechless for what felt like forever. His whole world came crashing down on him in an instant. *This cannot be,* he thought. *It's ridiculous, reckless, impulsively so! No one is that damn reckless or stupid.* His mind drew a blank for a nanosecond. *I'm dead friggin' meat!*

Their eyes stared at him with awkward expressions on their faces.

A slow growl rose in Benny's throat. "What?" he snapped. "You can't be serious?" He glared from one to the other, silently demanding one of them to tell him the punch line.

Trent took a short step toward him, protectively placing his hand in front of Tabitha. "And why not?"

Benny threw his hands into the air, exasperated. He had heard all he could stand. "You barely know each other," he said. "You just saw each other for the first time."

"So," Trent's voice was sharp.

Benny wondered if his longtime friend had actually lost his mind in the aftermath of prison life. "*So*," he repeated, flabbergasted.

Her hand pushed Trent's away, and she moved closer. "Yeah!" Her face was red. "So what?"

"This isn't like you, Trent," he said. "You are not an impulsive guy by any stretch of the imagination. I know you better than you know yourself, and you're a planner, not a fly-by-the-seat-of-your-pants type."

Trent's arm reached out and pulled Tabitha's body against his chest, his eyes narrowing. "I think you have forgotten the fact that we were writing each other for years, exchanged thousands of pages, and we know all we need to know. I love her. I've loved her for years."

Benny sighed, searching for a way out of an impossible dilemma. "Look," he began, holding his hands out in a pleading manner, and then finished, "I don't mean to say you don't love her, but why are you in such a hurry? You need to give it some time, really get to know each other."

Trent's face twisted up, incredulous. "Give it some time?" Disgust filled his voice. "Are you kidding? Trust me, Ben—I know all about giving things time. I am done with putting my life on hold and giving everything time. My life has been on hold for decades, and now I am ready to finally live."

With discernment, Tabitha's eyes seemed to study the situation. Benny recognized the look she was giving him as the same one she gave whenever questioning his true motives for doing something with which she did not agree. He averted his eyes and focused on Trent. "So, when are you coming back?" he said in a begrudging tone.

"We're not coming back." Trent's words cut straight through his heart like a sharpened knife.

Benny swallowed with difficulty, his mind racing.

Trent's hand then playfully spanked Tabitha on the backside, which made her jump and giggle with mirth. "Would you please go and check our flight schedule?"

She darted from the room, her giggles fading in the distance.

Benny stared after her in disbelief. It felt as if someone had just mule kicked him in the gut. He turned after she disappeared around a corner and leered at Trent, his nostrils flaring in anger. "What in the hell do you mean, 'We're not coming back'?" He spat out each syllable with intentional slowness.

"Can't we talk about this later?" Trent's hand patted him on the shoulder. "Let's take care of the paperwork first."

Benny allowed Trent to escort him. "But why aren't you coming back?" he said morosely. His feet felt as if they weighed a thousand pounds as they ascended the steps that connected to the long hallway leading to Trent's private office. His fear of forever losing Tabitha nearly overwhelmed him.

Upstairs, Benny followed Trent past the office door and sidestepped next to a massive bookcase that ran down the length of the wall. Its shelves supported numerous volumes of legal books. Out of the corner of his eye, he watched Trent unhurriedly move around a large mahogany desk and take a comfortable seat in the custom-made chair stationed behind the enormous structure of wood. He picked up a manila folder from off the top of the desk and held it out to him. Benny did not attempt to accept it, choosing instead to ignore it, so Trent let it drop to the desk.

"What did you mean when you said you're not coming back?" He had never wanted a question answered so badly.

"Back on that again, huh?"

"We never got past it."

"Everything you need is in the envelope." Trent leaned back in the chair. The leather squeaked.

While running a finger along the smooth wood edges of the expensive bookcase, Benny walked toward the far wall, stopped, and then indiscriminately plucked a volume from the second shelf. He cracked it open and began thumbing through the pages.

"Is something on your mind, Ben?"

Benny snapped the book shut. "You've done very well for yourself, haven't you?" he said bitterly, wondering why life came so easy to some men. "You got just about anything a man could ever want." He turned angry eyes on Trent. "You've got the money, the beautiful home, and now you have Tabitha." He returned the book with a shove.

"I suppose you might say that." Trent spoke the words evenly. "But it didn't come without a heavy price. I've paid a hefty sum—no shortcuts or easy ways in for me." His finger pointed skyward. "And I worked my ass off for everything you see."

Benny moved toward the desk and picked up the envelope. "Perhaps," he said noncommittally, taking a seat in the nearest chair. "Are you going to answer my question or not?"

A bored look shadowed Trent's face. "About what?" His voice now sounded tired.

Benny opened the envelope and removed the documents. "About not coming back," he said with a note of hostility as he perused the enclosed papers.

"We discussed it, Tabitha and I, and we decided that we want to begin a new life together, free from all the ugliness of the past." His voice was matter of fact. "No looking back, only forward."

Benny signed the documents and slid them back into the envelope. "How very nice for the two of you," he said sharply. "But don't you mean *you* decided?" He set the envelope back on the desk.

"No!" Trent's voice was firm. "I mean, *we* decided. I would not make a unilateral decision for her or ever force my will on her. You know this to be true."

Benny sneered at him. "That sounds—"

A soft knock on the door interrupted him.

The door opened without invitation.

Tabitha's head poked through the opening. "Okay for me to come in?"

Trent's face lit up. "Yes, yes, come in."

Benny looked at her, scowling. Her eyebrows pinched together. She moved behind one of the other chairs. Her eyes roamed in a downward angle, and then she frowned, appearing flustered by something she saw.

"Did you get confirmation?"

Her head nodded.

Benny followed her eyes, took a nervous gulp of air, and then quickly smoothed out his pant leg to cover the exposed gun fastened inside an ankle holster. He looked up and offered her an awkward smile, hoping she would not make a big deal out of him carrying a gun outside the club. He still had one more job to do.

Concern covered Trent's face. He seemed to have noticed the tension between them. "Are you all right, Tabitha?"

"Um, yes," she said in a faraway voice. "We're supposed to be at the hangar at midnight."

"Great!" Trent beamed with joy. "I can't wait."

Benny feigned a grin, praying they did not see through his charade. His life expectancy looked bleak, and all his prearranged plans were quickly falling apart at the seams. With no arrows left in his quiver of schemes, Benny decided to risk it all and switch tactics. He jumped to his feet and slapped an open palm on his leg. "This calls for a boy's night on the town," he said, ignoring the disturbed look on Tabitha's face. She had an uncanny knack for unearthing his hidden agendas. "What do you say, Trent? Can the man giving away the bride buy his best friend's last drink as a bachelor? You can't expect me to let you run off and get the old ball and chain attached to your ankle without a proper send-off, can you?" He forced a conspiratorial wink to sell his last-minute idea.

Tabitha's lips formed a thin line of mistrust. Her eyes clouded with dark suspicion. "I don't think we…" Her voice trailed off, and she shifted her eyes to Trent.

His eyes sparked with interest. "Whatcha got in mind?"

He stole a quick look at his watch. His only chance was to trick Tabitha into staying back on her own volition. Her eyes were now drilling into him. "How about the three of us have a drink at the club?" he offered. "Let's say we meet there in a couple of hours."

She glowered at him. "But I still have a lot of packing to do, and then I—"

Trent's hand rose and interrupted her. "Then that's perfect." The words spilled from his mouth.

Her hands went to her hips. "How's that?"

Benny jumped on the opportunity. "The two of us can have a boy's night out, just two old cellies sharing a couple of drinks together for old time's sake," he said. "It'll give us time to say good-bye the right way."

Tabitha did not appear convinced that it was such a good idea. "I-I don't know," she stammered.

Benny thought fast to disarm her growing suspicion. "You can join us down at the club after you get done with all your packing," he said.

"Sounds like a plan to me." Trent removed a set of keys from the desk drawer and dangled them from his fingers. "Hey, Ben," he said.

Benny craned his neck. "Yeah," he said, just as Trent tossed him the keys.

"Why don't you move in here and keep an eye on the place for us."

Benny stared at the ring of keys, the blood draining from his face. He took a quick look around the room, admiring the expensive decor he could never hope to afford if he lived several lifetimes. "You mean for me to live here?" he said.

Trent rose from behind the desk, made his way around it, and then draped an arm over Benny's shoulder. "Sure." His voice was cheerful. "Why not? We go way back, and now we're practically family." He winked in Tabitha's direction, which brought a smile of gratitude to her face. Her lips mouthed silent words of *thank you*.

Stunned at the offer, Benny blinked back tears. "I-I don't know what to say," he stammered. "I, um, never thought you—" The rest of the sentence caught in his throat.

"Say you'll move in and take care of the place for us," Trent said and then added with a happy laugh, "free of charge, of course."

Benny squirmed in his own skin. "O-kay," he said with a squeak when Trent patted him on the back.

"That's what I want to hear," he said. "Come on, Ben, I'll walk you out. I have to stop by the office and make sure everything is taken care of on the lease."

Benny watched Tabitha move behind the desk and take a seat in the chair, wondering what she was doing. "Aren't you going to follow us down, Tabitha?"

Her fingers coiled around the phone. "You two go and have fun," she said. "I have a few phone calls to make before I start all that packing."

He started to say something more, but Trent practically pulled him out of the office.

CHAPTER 23

Lomax placed his hands against the panes of matching glass doors and wearily pushed his way through the science division's entrance inside the laboratory building annexed to police headquarters. He cursed his bad luck, wondering if the fiery little redhead, Dr. Becky Swanson, had not given him up for dead and finally gone home.

Just one last stop, and it's off to dreamland.

The hallways were as desolate as the parking lot out front. Only a lone receptionist sitting behind an elongated desk at the end of the hallway offered any hope that someone bothered to show up for third watch work. Even at a distance, he could hear the elderly woman prattle on the telephone without missing a beat in her conversation.

Behind him, the glass doors shut with an audible *whoosh* and *rattle,* alerting anyone within thirty feet that someone had either entered or exited the central corridor connected to the main lobby.

In an instant, the woman stopped talking and looked up. Her eyes squinted over the rim of vintage glasses that slid down a nose resembling that of a parrot and hung at the tip.

With a snide huff of malcontent, she wrinkled her nose in apparent distaste and swiveled around in her chair, rudely turning her back to him. She renewed her raucous chatter into the mouthpiece.

Soured to a new level with his day, Lomax ground his teeth together and dug deep to find enough strength to see things through to the end. Her contemptuous act to discourage him from approaching her desk and asking questions failed to work her intended magic on him.

He sneered, unperturbed. *Lazy old bag!*

With a quick hoist of his pants, Lomax dragged himself on exhausted legs across the immaculately polished tiles and stopped in front of the counter. He drummed his fingers on the cheap Formica, grinning when the woman visibly shuddered and tightened her shoulders around her ears at the noise.

Her lips continued to flap like a windsock in a storm, which made it abundantly clear that she did not intend to help him.

Lomax cleared his throat, obnoxiously loudly to get his point across the counter.

Still she refused to respond, other than a disapproving grunt coming from her yammering mouth.

Taking a deep breath, Lomax counted back from thirty. *Mellow out, Maxie,* he thought. *Remember what the doctor said about your blood pressure.*

"What'd you say, girl?" The woman's voice screeched into the phone. "Leon cussed like that at you. Who in far corn does he think he is? He ain't no God's gift to no one."

Lomax stopped at the count of fifteen. His blood began to boil, so he decided to take a different approach with the woman he now viewed as the sea hag on the Popeye cartoon. He tapped the counter with his knuckles. "Excuse me, ma'am," he said in the most pleasant voice of his arsenal. "Could you please—"

Her brow arched in irritation. "All visitors must fill out the visiting questionnaire." She then tossed a clipboard of papers on the counter.

He frowned. "Yeah, but …" He was at a loss for words.

"But nothin'!" she snapped rudely. "Can't you see that I'm on the phone?" Her finger pointed at the paperwork. "Read it. Learn it. Live it."

He struggled not to lose his last thread of patience. "I think you misunderstand why I am here," he said.

She made an exasperated grunt, pushed the glasses back up her nose, and then rolled her eyes. "Just let me know when you've finished filling out the paperwork." She turned back around and resumed her conversation over the phone.

His last nerve snapped. He was tired, overworked, and underpaid, and he was in no mood to tolerate nonsense from a woman circling the drain of the secretarial pool in the last stages of her golden years. He took out his gold badge, stomped around the end of the desk, and spun her around in the chair so she faced him. A startled yelp fell from her aged lips, her eyes peering up at him in fear. He held his detective's shield only inches from her face, flaring his nostrils.

"I've tried to be nice, you old bag, but I can see good manners are wasted on you," he spat. Spittle flew from his mouth and dotted her glasses.

She cringed beneath his glare. "I-I'm sorry, sir." She spoke in a frightened stammer.

He shoved his badge back into his pocket. "Shut up!" he said with a heated growl. "I'm done acting nice. Now tell me. Is Dr. Becky Swanson still here, in her lab?"

She made a quarter turn and hurriedly shuffled through a large stack of directory papers with her free hand. "Well, um, I," she began clumsily, her lips trembling. "I have to check the sign-out sheet."

He snatched the phone from her hand and slammed it on the counter. "She's forensics, you halfwit," he said. "Just tell me if she's left for the day."

Her fingers continued to rifle through the clutter. Panic sparked behind the lenses. "It was just …" Her voice trailed off.

Lomax groaned. "Never mind," he said with a huff. He turned and circumnavigated her desk. "I'll just find out myself." He then headed down the main corridor that led to the science departments, craning his neck to the left and to the right.

A dozen doors lined the walls on either side of the grand corridor. Except for a faint light seeping into the hallway from one of the rooms located at the far end of the long hallway, no sign of life existed anywhere else in the immediate area. Still, Lomax checked each closed door on his way toward the lighthouse.

Lomax leaned against the open doorway and smiled when he found Dr. Swanson busy at work. Her innate tenacity was obvious as she obsessively went from one microscope to another, expertly exchanging slides and scribbling down her findings on a small notepad hanging from a chain draped loosely around her neck. Her lab coat appeared several sizes too large for her body, dragging lightly across the floor.

Uneven and frayed around her wrists, the sleeves looked as if she had cut the white cloth short enough with a pair of dull scissors to allow her dainty hands free to work.

Chuckling softly under his breath, he wondered what was going through her head. She looked like a woman possessed by something visible only to her. He crossed his arms over his chest, content to watch her shuffle over to a centrifuge resting next to a large microscope and press a button that stopped it from spinning.

With gloved hands, she plucked the test tube from the carriage and transferred a sample of its contents onto a sample slide.

"Come on, baby." Her voice sounded like that of a young girl egging on a friend. Her fingers secured the slide under two metal clamps, while dancing a little jig, and then peered through the dual lenses. Her hands twisted magnification knobs, grinning. "Come on. Talk to momma." Her hips swayed in rhythm to music heard only in her head. "Ah-ha, gotcha, mother fu—"

Lomax made a grunt and interrupted her.

Her head whipped around, squinting in his direction.

He moved away from the doorway. "Such a little potty mouth, Dr. Swanson," he said teasingly.

Her palms dug into her eyes. "Who in the hell …" A sheepish grin formed on her face when recognition of her visitor registered in her cleared vision. Her cheeks blossomed scarlet.

He took a few more strides into her inner sanctum, looking

around the otherwise vacant laboratory. "With a welcome like that, no wonder everyone left the building," he said jokingly.

Her hand ran down the front of her lab coat, as she moved away from the table. "I apologize for my unwarranted outburst." Her voice sounded embarrassed. "I don't get many visitors down here."

He waved a nonchalant hand through the air. "Please, doctor, don't concern yourself," he said easily. "I've heard far worse in just the last hour."

Her face returned to its former color. "Okay," she began and then added, "thank you." Her brow furrowed. "How long have you been watching me?"

"Not long," he said. He then threw a thumb over his shoulder. "The sea hag was giving me the business out front."

A quizzical look flashed across her face. "Who's the sea hag?" Her eyes suddenly lit up when it dawned on her who he was referring to. Her hand lifted and stifled a giggle. Her fingers parted to allow her lips to move freely. "Oh, you mean Mrs. Hughes."

"I guess," he said as she peeled off a pair of surgical gloves, dropped them in a hazardous material bin, and then walked over to the sink. "She's, um, well, pretty horrible."

"I supposed she can be a real bear until you get accustomed to her." She washed her hands.

Lomax took a seat on a nearby stool. "Not to get off topic, but something was mentioned about finding trace evidence under the murdered girl's fingernails," he said. "Isn't that right?"

Her demeanor changed into one of strictly business. "Yes, that's right." Her tone now matched the seriousness on her face. She stepped over to a filing cabinet and opened the top drawer. Her fingers thumbed through several rows of files.

He ran a hand over his pate. *Come on, doc, I need you to give me something I can work with.* He silently prayed for direct evidence that would lead him to the young woman's killer.

Her hands suddenly froze.

Lomax cocked his head. "Is something wrong?"

Her head turned in his direction. "Don't you already have a copy of my report on the girl?" Intensity blazed in her eyes. "We are talking about the warehouse murder, aren't we?"

"Why would I have a copy of your report?" he said. "I just got here."

Her hand fished out a file and then used it to fan her face. "Well, yeah, I understand that." She seemed flustered by something unsaid. "Captain Johnson came by earlier and picked up the file on the warehouse case. He said he was picking it up for you, because you got hung up on some other case and might not be able to make it over here anytime soon."

"For me?"

"Yeah. For you." Her lips thinned. "It is your investigation, isn't it?"

"The captain was here?"

She nodded. "That's what I just said." Her voice was impatient. "He came here, to my office." She scratched at her head. "I guess there's a first time for everything."

He straightened up on the stool. The hair on the back of his neck stood on end. Warning bells went off in his head. She had to be mistaken, he thought. Picking up evidentiary materials from a lab was well below a captain's rank. Johnson's ego would never permit him to do fieldwork.

Her eyes stared at him.

"When was he here?"

"Earlier," she said. "I didn't check the time."

"How much earlier?"

Her brow furrowed. "Is something wrong?"

"Are you sure it was Captain Johnson who came here?" he said.

"That's what I just said," she said. "He said that you asked him to swing by and pick it up because you were up to your neck investigating some dirtbag stabbed to death in the manager's office of some rundown motel or hotel … Which one, I can't remember."

"Did he give this dirtbag's name?"

"Of course he did," she said irritably. "I had to label the physical evidence he submitted to my lab from the crime scene." Her eyes suddenly grew wary. "Why?"

"What is the name?"

"Ely Barnes," she said to him. "He was some bum who worked at some sleazy hotel place." She pointed a finger at a large cup preserved in a plastic bag lying on a stainless steel table. "According to Captain Johnson, he found that large coffee cup at the scene of the crime, next to the body, and he wanted me to check it for fingerprints and do a battery of DNA testing. For some reason, he believes that cup will reveal the murderer's identify."

His blood ran cold. He moved toward her and grabbed the file from her hands. Pieces of the puzzle were now falling into place faster than he could have ever imagined, and the picture they would show once finally placed together was his. He would recognize the cup Jo-Jo had given him out of a lineup of hundreds. He had to move or risk losing everything. His so-called peers were out to get him. "How is it that you have a file if the captain came in here earlier and took it with him?"

Her hands dropped to her hips in a display of petulance, and she glared at him. "I don't understand what you are implying," she said, "but I assure you that I don't like any hint of misconduct or incompetence."

He tapped the file with his finger. "Where did this come from?" He opened it and quickly perused the pages until he found the highlighted section marked "Evidentiary Forensics." He searched for the DNA results.

"Just for the record, Detective, I made it a habit years ago to make my reports and findings in triplicate, sometimes more if the case merits special attention." Her voice was now angry. "I gave the captain a copy. I never part with an original. You can call it insurance to keep everyone honest."

Lomax continued to scan the documents. "Did you mention that fact to Johnson?"

"I don't explain myself to anyone." Her aggression escalated. "Not to him and certainly not to you."

Lomax peered up from the paperwork. His detective's paranoia went into overdrive. "Did you?" he pressed.

She seemed to sense his fear. Her eyes widened. "I-I saw no reason to tell him the report was a duplicate." Wariness clouded her face. "Why would I?"

"So Johnson believes he has the original?"

"Yeah, I guess so. What can I say? He didn't ask."

"What did the two of you talk about?" he said, attempting to probe deeper in hopes of discovering something more hidden beneath the surface.

Her face twisted up in confusion. "Nothing much," she offered lamely, pursing her lips. "There was not enough time to discuss the findings, because the prosecutor kept bitching about being in a big hurry to leave. If memory serves, I think they mentioned something about seeing somebody before you." She shrugged, as if in apology. "I wasn't paying that much attention to either of them at that point. I'm swamped in here."

"Sebastian Crue was with Johnson?" His mind raced. More things were adding up for him.

"Well, yeah," she said. "Didn't I mention that?"

"No. You didn't." Lomax stopped reading at the bottom of the page. "Excuse me, but is this report accurate?"

"What kind of asinine question is that?" She sounded offended. "Of course it's accurate. I'd bet my career on it."

"Why is Barry Markinson's name written on the report?"

"I ran the specimen of trace extracted from under the girl's nails through the DNA data bank, and his name popped up." Her voice was bland. "The sample belonged to him. I figured he must have been one of the officers at the scene—that he stupidly screwed up and accidentally tainted the scene. Some of you never remember to be careful or put gloves on before you handle evidence, especially cadavers before the medical teams bring them in for autopsy. It happens more often than you might think, and it really messes with our results."

"Did you notify Internal Affairs about this?"

Her brow wrinkled. "Over cross contamination?" Her voice expressed additional confusion. "No, of course I didn't." She then added, "I didn't have to. IA called me."

Lomax felt his heart skip a beat. "IA called you?" he repeated.

Her chin jutted. "Uh, yeee-yah!" The look on her face made it clear that she was tired of his questions. "That's what I just said."

"Who from IA?"

"Some pissant tea bagger by the name of Biggs," she said.

Stunned even more by the unexpected implications now involved, Lomax felt as if a seven-foot monster had just sucker punched him in the stomach. "Did you find anything linked to someone by the name of Varus?"

He knew he was reaching for an invisible straw.

A scowl marked her face. "'Varus'?" she said in a faraway voice. "Who's that?"

"Just some guy," he said.

"A possible suspect?"

"Evidently not," he said glumly.

Her face suddenly lit up. "You don't mean Trent Varus, the defense lawyer, do you?" Her head shook. "I don't understand what you are getting at. About the only thing I told that jerk was that I detected faint traces of chloroform around the mouths of those decapitated at the courthouse."

He narrowed his eyes. "The chemical that knocks you out cold?" he said.

"In layman's terms, yes," she said. "Why would—" As if something had just clicked at the back of her mind, her hand flew to her mouth.

Lomax snapped the folder shut, struggling to maintain a calm composure. "Is there any chance, no matter how remote, the results are wrong, that it's not Markinson's DNA?"

Her eyes met his with stern conviction. "No damn way in hell, Erik!" Her voice was adamant. "I ran the tests myself, and I don't make first-year, rookie mistakes."

Lomax believed her with every fiber of his body. Fury swelled within him. *Those lousy, no-good sons of bitches are setting me up on everything!* he thought, curling his mouth into a rabid snarl. *They sat right there and lied right to my damn face. They knew Markinson was a murderous bastard, and they tricked me into covering up their dirty work ... and then there's that effing cup.*

Her throat cleared in distress. "Are you okay?"

He held up the file. "Can I keep this?"

"Sure. It's just a copy. I have the original locked away."

He rolled up the file and stuffed it in his back pocket. "Good," he said. "Keep it that way, and don't tell anyone about the copies." He reached out and grabbed her by the shoulders, shaking her to hammer his point home. "You have to keep your mouth shut about this. Do you understand?"

She let out a small squeal and nodded.

"Do you have somewhere other than home to stay?" He now feared for her safety. The others would no doubt consider her a loose end. Her body crumpled underneath his rough grasp, and she started to cry.

Again, Lomax shook her when she did not respond right away. "Please, listen to me," he begged. "I'm not crazy. Markinson killed the girl at the warehouse and possibly many others that I don't know of yet, and that cup you have in the plastic bag was planted by Johnson. I may not have all the details right now, but Johnson and Crue are trying to cover everything up, making me the fall guy in all this. I don't know why or how, but Internal Affairs is also involved. There is no telling what they might do to hide whatever they have done. I'm sure it's something awful. My gut tells me it is a whole helluva lot more than some dead runaway. The girl is probably just the tip of the iceberg."

Tears streamed down her face. "Wh-what?" Her voice was a whispered stammer of terror. "You can't be serious."

He loosened his grip. "I wish I wasn't."

Her hand ran under her nose. "You're serious?"

Lomax scribbled down his address on a piece of scrap paper, removed his house key from his pocket, and handed both of them over to her. "I want you to go to my house and stay there until you hear from me," he said. "Do not answer the phone or the door for anyone but me." He placed a gentle hand under her chin. "Do you understand what I'm telling you?"

She nodded.

"Now, I want you to think hard," he urged. "Do you remember if they mentioned who they were going to meet or where they were going to meet the people? This is extremely important, so please try to remember. Everything might depend on it."

Her eyes closed. "What was that name?" She muttered the words aloud, as if hearing herself speak would help draw the name from her memory. "Was it called the Bear Trap?" Her head shook off the words. "No, that's not it. What about the Tourist Trap?" Again, her head shook, now visibly straining to recall the name. "No." A grin creased her face. "I know … it was … the Mousetrap?" Her eyes opened. "It's called the Mousetrap, Erik. They were going to meet at some place called the Mousetrap."

Lomax pounded a fist into his palm with a loud smack. "That's my girl!" Victory was now possible, his for the taking. "I know the place." He started to turn away from her, but her hand flashed out and grabbed him by the arm.

"And where in the hell do you think you are going?"

"To that dive called the Mousetrap," he said. "Thanks to your wonderful memory, I think the last piece of the puzzle I've been shuffling around the board just fell into place."

Concern shadowed her face. "What makes you say that?"

"Benny 'Bones' Maldonado owns that place, and things just became a whole lot clearer to me."

Her eyes widened in fear for his safety. "Benny 'Bones' Maldonado," she repeated numbly, as if the words tasted of poison. "I've heard of him, and none of it is very good."

"If I'm right, he's a box of puppies compared to the rest of them," he said. "Even though I haven't connected him directly to any of the crimes, that attorney Trent Varus is somehow involved in all this. He may or may not be a serial killer of sorts, but I aim to find out. Too many people from his past are now dead and stinking. Though there are several inconsistencies in my theory, one thing seems to remain a constant, and Captain Mike Johnson is at the center of the storm I've chased since Callahan's murder."

"Murder," she stammered. "You think someone murdered the district attorney."

"I don't think nothing," he said. "I know it, deep in my bones."

"Oh my God!"

He slid her hand loose. "Now, I am going to make whoever is guilty of trying to destroy my city pay for what they or he did."

"You're not going alone, are you?" Her voice filled with fear. "You are going to call for backup, right?" Her eyes watered, as if struggling with some sort of irreconcilable dilemma. "I mean, it sounds incredibly dangerous to try to take these men down all by yourself."

He shook his head. "I can't trust anyone but you, Becky," he said. "For luck." He pulled her against his chest and planted a wet kiss on her mouth, muffling her words of protests.

Then he darted for the infamous strip joint.

CHAPTER 24

Trent pulled his car into the parking lot of the Mousetrap and gave an enthusiastic honk of the horn to announce his arrival. He frowned. It was odd to find the area outside the club's doors so quiet and empty of traffic. Not one customer's car sat parked in a stall, and a closed sign hung in a large, plateglass window next to the entrance. No one was loitering about, either drunk or sober. It was a mystery. Benny had never shut down his club for anyone or anything.

He parked in the reserved VIP space and turned off the ignition. *I guess he was serious about giving me a proper send-off.* As much as Trent appreciated the gesture, he already missed Tabitha's company. *I should have—*

A burst of loud music suddenly erupted from inside the building and distracted him from further mooning over his fiancé. He looked up and grinned at the ridiculous sight not more than twenty feet away.

Dressed in a tacky Hawaiian shirt, a pair of khaki shorts, and faded flip-flops, Benny stood on shaky legs in the open doorway of his beloved club. A stupid-looking smile covered his weathered face. He held a large, colorful drink in one hand, while clumsily waving to him like a lost tourist with the other. Drunk on his feet, it was clear that he had started the proposed celebration alone. Trent gave a hearty laugh and got out of his car.

While wondering how much alcohol his friend had already

consumed without him, Trent headed toward the short flight of stairs that led to the entrance.

A fool and his unlimited booze. Benny rarely got drunk. *This should prove interesting.*

Trent cleared the last step up and cringed when Benny staggered over to him and draped an arm over his shoulder. His breath stank of whiskey.

"Hey, buddy." Benny's speech was slurred. "Come with me to the Land of Oz." Somehow, to Trent's amazement, Benny managed to keep his sea legs and guided him through the open doors and across the reception room and hardwood dance floor. "I was beginning to wonder if'n you were going to stop by before you took my baby girl and flew off into the wild blue yonder." His body pulled up, swayed on wobbly legs, and stopped in front of the bar.

The magic of acoustics inside the room brought extra life into the music that flowed from liquid-cooled speakers.

A loud belch exploded from Benny. "I'm glad you made it down to see me, cellie." His arm fell free from Trent's shoulders, and he staggered around the end of the bar. He pressed his left hand against the polished surface of the bar, balancing himself as he slowly and unsteadily ambled to his intended destination. His fingers scooped up a book of matches and a lone cigarette lying on the bar.

Trent pressed his lips together, uncomfortable. "Are you all right, Ben?" He frowned when Benny lit up the cigarette, planted his elbows on the bar, and then leaned toward him.

A thick cloud of smoke engulfed his head. "What'll you have, Trent?" His hand flicked about the air. "I got it all—anything you can drink."

Trent intertwined his fingers. "How about a glass of your best bourbon," he said and then added, "neat."

"Uh-huh."

"Kind of quiet in here today, isn't it?" Trent looked around the club. "I thought there might be a crowd."

Benny's half-lidded eyes stared at him. He set two crystal

glasses on the bar. "I shut this sucker down, homeboy." His voice took on a darker quality. He reached under the counter and retrieved a bottle of his finest bourbon. "After all, it's a special night, and I didn't think we should be disturbed on such a momentous event." He glanced at his watch and then filled both glasses.

Trent raised his glass and gestured with a toast. "To you, Benny," he said sincerely. "You are perhaps my only real friend." He then took two healthy swallows of the fiery brew.

Benny's hand reached out and picked up the other glass. His face pinched as he swirled the glass in a tight circle and stared at the liquid with bloodshot eyes. "Do you mean that?" His voice turned solemn.

Trent took another sip. "Mean what?" he said.

"That I'm your friend." Sorrow masked his features. "That we're friends."

With a tiny chuckle, Trent set the glass on the bar. He had never known Benny to dwell on feelings. "I think you've had a little too much to drink." He tapped the side of his head with a finger. "The booze is fogging up your thinking."

His eyes appeared to clear up. "I haven't had that much to drink." His mouth hardened around the edges. "Do you mean it?"

Trent moved away from the bar and glared at the man he had known for more than two decades. "What in the hell has gotten into you?" he said sharply. Tension grew thick between them. "You are going up and down faster than a friggin' yo-yo on steroids. It's making me dizzy." He made his way to the other side of the bar. "Of course I mean it, you ass!" He pointed a finger at Benny and then at himself. "You … me … We're friends. Whether we like it or not, we are family, Ben. You are like a crazy brother to me, and I love you."

With downcast eyes and an expression that looked like hurt and shame, he whispered, "And Tabitha?"

"What about her?"

Tears welled in Benny's eyes. "Why are you taking her so far away from me?" He seemed to have aged years in just the last two minutes. "She is like my own daughter, and I don't have anyone else but her." He looked around the club. "I don't give a rat's ass about any of this crap. It means nothing to me."

Trent sighed. "Aw, hell, Benny," he said. "Is that what all this is about?" He playfully punched Benny in the arm. "You poor, dumb, drunk-ass bastard. I'm not taking her away from you. I'm taking her away from here, away from all the filth in this stinking city, so we can start a fresh life together." He paused, thinking about the best way to convince his friend of the veracity in his words. "You can come with us if you want." Benny smiled, and Trent added, "After the honeymoon, of course. I would bet money that she would be on board with you joining us. She loves your shot-out old ass."

"Are you serious?" he said, wiping the back of his hand under his nose.

Trent rolled his eyes. It felt as if he was talking to a three-year-old. "When have you known me to say something I didn't mean?" he said. "I say what I mean, and I do what I say. Always have, always will."

Benny's face suddenly twisted up as if someone had just slapped him across the face. Something seemed to register in his eyes. Again, his eyes dropped to his watch. He grimaced, eyes turning wild. "You have to get out of here, Trent," he said in a frantic voice.

"What in the hell is wrong with you?"

Benny's hand lashed out and grabbed Trent by the arm. "I really screwed up bad, and you have to get the hell out of here." His hand yanked on his arm. "Right now!"

Trent wrenched his arm free and spun angrily. "Damn it, Benny!" He smoothed out the shirt's wrinkles with his hand. "Are you on crack or something? I just do not understand you anymore. What has crawled up your nutty butt this time?"

"You just don't ..." His words trailed off, mouth falling open. His face paled to the pallor of death. His eyes focused on something.

Trent took a step closer to Benny, baffled by his unusual

behavior. "I just don't what," he prodded. The soft scrape of shoes coming from behind his back caught his attention. He turned and glared in hatred. A low growl rose in his throat as he measured two of several men who had destroyed his life and killed his family. He looked at the .357 revolver held in Johnson's hand and then at the duffel bag Crue's fingers held dangling next to his leg.

"He's trying to get you out of here before we showed up," said Johnson with a cruel snicker. "Just like all ex-cons, Benny jumped on the first chance to sell out his crimey at the first sign of trouble. It was all so beautiful, something right out of a movie script. We barely had to apply any pressure whatsoever to get him to switch sides and join the winning team."

"I'm sorry, Trent," Benny whispered in a sickly groan of despair. "I really screwed everything up. I just thought …" His words trailed off into a series of sad sniffles.

Trent opened and closed his hands, rage filling him. "Forget it, Ben," he said in an eerily calm voice. "We all do things we regret, and we're right as rain."

Johnson's lip curled up and formed an arrogant grin. "We couldn't have done it without you, Benny." His tongue stabbed out each syllable.

Trent took two steps toward Johnson, narrowing the ten feet that had separated them to eight feet. Desire for revenge burned inside him, flames of fury licking at his heart. He started to take another step forward, but Johnson's thumb cocked the pistol's hammer and stopped him in his tracks.

"Just say when," said Johnson.

Trent sneered. "You're a coward," he said through clenched teeth.

His eyebrows lifted. "That's one interpretation." He shook the gun. "But that doesn't really matter in the grand scheme of things, does it? I have the gun."

Trent looked at Crue, who was no doubt unaccustomed to physical confrontation. He chuckled at how small and pathetic the prosecutor now appeared to him. The large beads of nervous perspiration that dotted his forehead left the distinct impression that he was no doubt used to pulling strings from behind the scenes. Crue started to back up and allow Johnson to take the lead.

Johnson's head whipped to the side, and he shot a pair of angry eyes of contempt at his criminal cohort. "And where the hell do you think you're going, Sebastian?"

A stunned look crossed Crue's face. He set the bag down. He lifted his hands in a display of peaceful diplomacy. "Perhaps it would be best if I were just to wait outside, Captain." The words came out in little more than a squeak. "This is more your arena than mine, don't you agree?"

"You're not going anywhere, you little worm," said Johnson. "You're up to your damn neck in this, so get your ass over there and search them for weapons."

His face turned ghostly white. "What?"

Johnson's hand grabbed Crue by the collar and practically threw him over to where Trent and Benny stood. "You heard me!" He emphasized the last word to express how the man's cowardice sickened him. "Get your pencil-pushing ass over there and check them for guns. I have to do this right. I'm running out of people to do the damn legwork, so now you're up at bat."

"All right!" snapped Crue. He walked behind the two men and quickly patted them down for weapons. "They're not armed."

"Are you sure?"

"Yeah. I'm sure."

"Good," he said, motioning Crue with the gun. "Now get your ass back over here and do what we talked about." His eyes rolled after Crue nearly tripped over his own feet on the way back over to him. "Come on, stupid. Hurry up!"

With shaky hands, Crue removed a pair of gloves from his pants pocket, put them on, and then kneeled down to open the bag. He removed several large bags of cocaine and stacked them neatly on a nearby table.

Helpless to do anything while Johnson held him and Benny captive at gunpoint, Trent's mind raced as he watched Crue zip up the bag and then toss it to the side. Time was now his greatest enemy, and he needed to stall so that he could reason out a way for both of them to escape. He refused to lose Tabitha again.

"So, what are the two of you planning to do?" Trent said. "What's the dope for?"

"Come on, Varus, you're a very smart guy," said Johnson. "You can figure it out."

Trent jerked his head at Crue. "What about your pet monkey?" he said with a snort of derision to punctuate his personal feelings for the man. He hoped to goad one of them into making a mistake. "When are you going to dump his weak ass in the trash?" He offered a chuckle of provocation. "You know he's the weak link in your fast-shrinking crew."

A snarl appeared on Crue's face. "What did you call me?" He started to move forward, but Johnson's hand flashed out and grabbed him by the shirt.

The captain's hand jerked him back roughly. "Don't be stupid!" he quipped, winking a "nice try" in Trent's direction. "He's trying to bait you. Besides, Sebastian, Varus would tear you apart without batting an eye. There is a whole lot more to him than you might think. Isn't that right, Varus?"

Trent clenched his jaw. "If you're going to shoot, then just go ahead and get it over with."

"You've been a busy boy, haven't you, Varus?" Johnson's face turned hard. "Now, you're savage to the bone."

Benny's neck craned and looked at Trent with a furrowed brow, his expression quizzical. "What's he talking about, Trent?"

A comical expression flitted across Johnson's face, his eyes sparkling with genuine amusement for the first time since his arrival. Trent knew the sadistic captain was enjoying their shared secret, and he detested him for it. His chin then lifted in arrogance. "Varus knows exactly what I'm talking about."

Crue's eyes ticked; he was no doubt confused over the cryptic wordplay. "What are the two of you talking about?" He spoke in a strained voice. "What does Varus know?"

Trent leered at Johnson, bloodlust now filling his heart. Memories of his wife, Connie, and the terrified look in her eyes as she watched the bailiff cart him away to a steel cage rose from the ashes of long ago.

Vengeance screamed for satisfaction.

Johnson continued in an almost giddy manner. "Deep down, we're not so different, are we?" His nostrils flared. "Oh, sure, you may have been a real nice guy before prison, but now you're a vicious killer down to the marrow. Years of prison have that effect on most men, if they manage to live through it. All bloodthirsty killers are cold, calculating, and apathetic. I can see murder in your eyes. I see that same reflection every time I look into the mirror. I saw that look in your eyes when you started to walk toward me." The corners of his mouth turned upward and formed a cruel grin. "I bet the others saw it too, didn't they? No fear, only lethal intent."

Trent swallowed the urge to lash out and attack, pressing his fingernails into his palms hard enough to draw a few drops of blood. "I am done with all that." Trent ground his teeth together when Johnson playfully elbowed Crue in the side.

"Can't you just feel his anger, Sebastian?" Johnson sniffed at the air. "I just love it."

Trent took a step forward, jutting his chin. He no longer cared if Johnson shot him dead, as long as he got the chance to drag the bastard down to hell with him. "You ... him ... and those other lousy bastards killed my family and sent me to prison to die in a cage like some kind of wild animal with the dregs of humanity," he said. "What do you think any of you can do that hasn't already has been done a thousand times over? What ... kill me?" He laughed at the thought. "Threaten me with a good time. I could use the peace of mind that death brings."

Crue's eyes shifted to the gun in his partner's hand, widening at the implications. No one doubted the captain would fire. "He's crazy."

"Who isn't these days?" Johnson's eyes narrowed. "Yeah, we killed them. It was nothing personal, just business as usual." He snickered under his breath. "I thought our mule was going to turn state's evidence after the feds busted him for possession of a rather large amount of dope. That was the moron's first mistake. The agent he contacted in search of immunity for testimony made a call to me, as a professional courtesy. Law enforcement looks after its own. His second error was that he thought he was safe from us, that the agent would protect him. He was dead wrong, and someone had to go down for killing that cockroach. You can bet your ass that I certainly wasn't going to come forward on it."

Trent could hardly believe his ears. His knees grew weak under the weight of Johnson's words. "But how did you focus on me? Why would you pick me? I was nobody."

A snide smirk slipped from Crue's mouth. "After all these years, he is still stuck in the damn dark," he said. "How can someone so smart be so damn dumb?"

Trent remained concentrated on Johnson, who was the only real threat in the room. "In the dark about what?"

His eyes practically lit up. "The beauty of my plan," said Johnson. "We couldn't have done it without you and your beloved bride."

Trent gaped at him, dumbfounded by the mysterious claim.

With a small chuckle, Johnson continued. He now seemed anxious to explain the genius of his orchestration. "Do you remember your wife's participation in a lineup down at the jail?" His voice rose an octave. "It, of course, was decades ago. She made a positive identification on the lowlife who broke in and burglarized your home."

Trent nodded, following the man's scenario so far.

Johnson acted pleased. "Good ... good," he said in a condescending tone. "Unfortunately for you, our mule was doing business with that sleazebag, who then tried to make a deal for a lighter sentence, which was something we could not allow. We had already collected personal effects for forensic comparisons from your residence to use at the defendant's trial."

Trent knitted his brows. "But what does any of that to do with me?"

His hand lifted. "Patience, Varus," he said in a humorous voice. "I'm getting to that. You are going to love this part."

Trent growled. *Maybe I will make room for just two more.*

With renewed exuberance, Johnson pressed forward in unraveling his tale. "Of course, not all of it was properly documented and stored in the evidence room. My motto is always hedge, just in case I need to fill in the blanks to close a case fast. Motive and testimony from a reliable source always paints a perfect picture for the twelve stooges in the jury box. The arrest of your wife's loser brother for dope fit nicely into the mix, and your attorney's appetite for nose candy helped us to keep him in check. We had plenty of other things on that ambulance-chasing Kirkpatrick, and he was not about to go renegade and risk losing his license over something as expendable as a client. In his words, and I quote, 'They're a dime a dozen.'"

"And then you had to go and screw everything up for us by being prideful," interjected Crue. "All you had to do was take the deal."

Trent thought he might puke. "So, truth and justice never meant anything to either one of you?"

Crue sneered at him. "Don't be so naively ignorant, Varus." His voice filled with contempt. "Justice is an antiquated ideal hatched up by eighteenth-century dreamers who did not have the foresight to contemplate the cultural decline of this nation's future reprobates. The truth is that the only people that matter are just us, the active alter egos of the government. We are *the people,* and the individual civilian is simply something for us to manipulate and step on to climb the ladder of success and power. The alleged servants are now the master."

Trent shook his head in despair. "You cannot possibly believe that," he said. "If the individual is not protected from the collective powers of an abusive police force, then the masses are also in jeopardy, and this country is nothing more than a remnant of a once great society. No one is safe if the executive branch of government can summarily pluck the individual and capriciously persecute him. The king must also be held accountable to the laws."

"Perhaps you are right, Varus." Crue shot Johnson a curious

look, and then added, "But the individual has always been the one who has created change, and change is no longer welcome in our modern empire."

"That's just a bunch of fascist bull—" Trent began, but Johnson's hand wagged the gun in his face and stopped him from finishing his sentence.

"Let me tell you something, since you don't seem to be catching on." Johnson's voice turned feral. "People are free because I allow them to remain free. I can arrest anyone for anything I want, whenever I want, and I can make the charges stick no matter how weak the evidence. If anyone refuses to turn in his friends, his mother, his father, his own damn son, then I will make sure the system buries him forever. Everyone will say and think whatever I tell them. If I identify a man and say he's guilty, the jury will not even hesitate to question that fact. I can sell drugs, steal, rape, beat, and kill anyone I want and never risk going to prison because the district attorney will always support the police department." He slapped at his own chest. "I am the police!"

The ceremonious clap of hands came from somewhere in the shadows of the club.

Surprised by the unexpected intrusion behind locked doors, all four men craned their necks and gasped at the bizarre sight of five heavily armed men dressed in expensive suits moving toward them, slowly fanning out across the floor. Each held silenced weapons trained at the group in an obvious show of force and domination.

Trailing the squadron of beefy henchmen, Dominique Cieo stepped from around the corner and walked through the gauntlet of mobsters. His perfectly manicured hand gripped a small handgun fitted with a silver silencer. His charcoal, double-breasted suit was the ultimate complement to his graceful movements. His black eyes reflected death.

Johnson's face blanched in fear as he lowered his gun.

With not so much as a twitch in his face, Cieo stopped at a distance of ten feet. His cruel eyes missed nothing. "Such an eloquent and awe-inspiring speech, Captain Johnson." His voice scratched out each syllable with distinct bitterness. "So, is it your position that you, the two of you, can do whatever you want to me and my most trusted men?" His head cocked to the side. "Is that what I heard with my own ears?"

Crue's face turned white as a sheet.

A tiny mewl slipped from Benny's throat.

Trent studied the situation, watching and listening carefully to everything. Nothing about the man he had met at the shooting range seemed present in the man now standing in front of them with a gun in hand.

That man was pleasant, affable. The man leading the crew of obvious killers was void of humanity, chilling, and sadistic. He was both appalled and intrigued by the dual personalities that resided in Dominique Cieo's mind.

Finally, Johnson dared to take a small step toward Cieo. "Sir, I assure—"

Cieo flashed out a hand and silenced him. "Please forgive the interruption, Trent." His voice was now apologetic, sincere. "I do find bad form most distasteful, though it is a pleasure to see you again. I was hopeful that we would not meet again under such, shall we say, unsavory circumstances, but life can be a very funny thing." A grin tugged at the left corner of his mouth as he switched hands on the gun and held his now free one out. "These men are my most loyal and trusted associates."

Trent stepped forward and shook hands with one of the most dangerous men in the world. "The pleasure is mine, Mr. Cieo," he said. "I'm not sure of the purpose for your visit, but …" He let the words trail off.

Cieo's face now transformed into one of amusement. "Please, Trent, I would prefer you call me Dom or, if more comfortable for you, Dominique."

A disturbance erupted from the area of the back exit. All heads except Cieo's turned in the direction of the raucous noise. A few seconds later, two hulking mobsters emerged from a dark hallway. They were dragging a groaning man by the arms. They dropped him on his stomach with a dull thud in front of Cieo, who leaned over and peered down at the badly beaten man with no more compassion than he'd have for a dead cat lying in the gutter.

The mobster on the right held up two folders—one marked "Forensic Report," the other marked simply "Confidential"—and a gold detective's badge. He handed everything to Cieo.

"We found him in his car, Mr. Cieo." His voice was deep and surly. "He was watching the place with a pair of binoculars. He tried to resist." His chin jerked in Johnson's direction. "He's one of them, a cop."

Cieo held the badge up to the light, squinting with a hint of curiosity in his eyes. "Is he now?" He spoke with humorous inflection. He handed the badge back. "I find that rather interesting, Alfred. Why would a detective be outside and not in here with his friends?" His arm lowered. "I wonder why he has no backup. Tell me, was he alone?"

Alfred's enormous shoulders shrugged. "I'm not exactly positive if he is alone," he said.

A frown shadowed Cieo's face. "What does that mean?"

"There was another man on the street, but I don't think they were together," he said. "They were in separate cars, one in the parking lot, and the other outside it." His eyes turned on Johnson and Crue. "He had a badge too. Internal Affairs. Biggs was the name on his official identification. I think he was with these two. He had a mouth on him."

Seeming to enjoy a good mystery, Cieo's fingers rubbed at his chin. "Was?"

His head jerked at his partner. "Carmine broke his neck and tossed him in the trunk," he said matter-of-factly. "Like I said, the man had a mouth on him. We'll dump the body later."

Trent continued to watch and listen, wondering what new twists and curves still lay ahead for him to figure out as Cieo moved toward the groaning man and used his foot to flip him onto his back.

Severely bruised and beaten about the face, Lomax strained to turn his head and look up at Johnson with swollen eyes, his movements revealing thick cords of muscle and sinew. His breathing was a series of haggard wheezes; split lips parted to speak.

"You miserable bastard, Mike," said Lomax in a gurgling voice. "You killed my witness and set me up for his murder. You set up Varus all those years ago and murdered his entire family. You covered up the crimes of that murderous rapist Markinson. And all for what, huh? Was it for money?" His arms and legs struggled to get him back on his feet. "I will see you sent to prison for the rest of your corrupt life if it's the last thing I ever do." With a last shudder, Lomax's arms and legs finally gave out, and he fell flat on the ground unconscious.

"Do you know this man, Captain Johnson?" said Cieo. "His face is a mess."

A look of disgust appeared on Johnson's face. "He's a homicide detective," he said. "His name is Erik Lomax, and he's the one I sent on that secret mission of sorts."

"I see." His expression became one of contemplation. "Is he a good cop, or a bad cop, Captain?"

"I don't understand the question."

"I think you do."

Johnson's head shook. "He's just a relic from the past."

Trent cleared his throat. "I think this man is a good cop," he offered, in hope of possibly saving the life of an innocent man—someone who was just trying to do his job.

A wry grin touched Cieo's face. "What makes you say such a thing, Trent?"

"Call it a gut feeling."

"Me too," he said. "I trust my gut feelings."

Crue suddenly became livid. He started to take an aggressive step forward. His face was beet red. "Enough of this shit!" His hand shot into the air. "I'm the special—"

A muffled pop froze him in his tracks. His hands flew to his neck, he gasped for air, and his eyes bulged. Thin lines of blood leaked from between his fingers, before he crumpled to the floor in a lifeless heap.

Trent struggled to fight down the urge to laugh aloud as he watched Cieo shuffle his feet to the right and shift his aim at Johnson, who let out a small yelp of surprise and dropped his gun to the floor with a loud clatter.

"Don't shoot. I'm unarmed," he pleaded.

"Stupid man," said Cieo with disdain. His eyes peered at the two thugs who had dragged Lomax into the building. "Get rid of that body too."

"I hope you burn in hell!" Trent glowered at the dead prosecutor. "I hope it hurt." He then raised his chin and met Cieo's eyes. The man's face was now oddly aglow in what looked like fascination by the satisfaction derived from the summary execution of Sebastian Crue.

"I do not suffer men who overestimate their importance in life," said Cieo. "Their arrogance is normally misplaced, as is their ability to see the bigger picture and appreciate the nuances involved. Such men cannot possibly grasp the responsibilities carried by those in charge of men's lives."

Trent shifted his focus to Johnson, *If I have to go, I just hope I get to watch you take a bullet to the head and drop dead first.* He clenched his teeth together and awaited the inevitable, figuring he was equally disposable under the circumstances.

Then Cieo did the last thing Trent expected.

He lowered the gun, letting it hang against the side of his leg, and then turned his eyes on Trent. "I understand you spent a great many years in prison for a crime you did not commit."

Trent furrowed his brow, surprised by the reprieve from certain death. "Is that a question?"

His head nodded. "It is."

He pressed his lips together. "I spent more time in a cage than I care to count," he said.

"That did not answer my question."

The stress left Trent's shoulders as he stared into the eyes of the notorious killer. "No, I don't suppose it did," he said, "but I am finished with trying to plead my case of innocence. No one ever listened, so I don't see a point in repeating myself."

"How about saying it just one more time?"

"Okay," he said. "I did not kill that man so many years ago."

As if mentally weighing something unspoken, Cieo used his fingers to tug at his earlobe. "It is my understanding that you're one of the best, if not the best, criminal defense lawyers in this state." His voice took on a crisp edge. He took out the documents inside the folders and gave them a quick perusal, careful to keep a firm grip on the gun. "I've also been informed that you hate men like the captain here."

Trent mulled over the words for several contemplative seconds, wondering why the mobster was so interested in his personal life. "He and his friends killed my family," he finally said. His emotions churned in turmoil. Tears welled in his eyes. "They stole and destroyed everything I held dear."

The lines around Cieo's mouth grew taut, and Trent thought the man's eyes appeared to appreciate the veracity of the words. He then slid the paperwork back into the folder. "That does coincide with my information," he said. "It may seem impossible to you, but I too have suffered much loss in my life."

"I'm sorry to hear that."

Cieo's eyes darkened, turning hard and lethal. "Would you like to kill this man now?"

Trent leered at Johnson. Hatred welled in him like molten lava, fueling anger he had carried most of his adult life. "I would like that very much," he said and then added, "But I made a promise to someone that I would let the past go, forget what had happened, and move on with a whole new life."

His eyebrow lifted. "Is that the only reason you won't kill him where he stands?"

"Yes," Trent said. "It's the only reason that has any meaning to either one of us."

"Do you always keep your promises?"

"I try to do my very best to keep all my promises," he said and then added in a subdued tone, "if life will let me."

"Did you not promise to make your enemies pay for what they had done to you?"

Trent knitted his brow. "As a matter of fact, I did," he said, "but then someone very dear to me reminded me to think about what my wife would have wanted me to do. Connie was a gentle soul, and I know in my heart that she would not want me to kill in her name. She was better than that—better than me."

"That is very commendable, very wise, and very true," Cieo said. "I believe promises and vows are the glue that keeps everything together. This person must be very important to you."

"She is," Trent said. "She is everything in the world to me."

"Would you be willing to provide legal services for us, if they were necessary?" Cieo's voice remained stoic, unemotional. "We would pay you, of course."

Nervous tenseness tightened the crow's feet etched in Johnson's face. His eyes nervously ticked back and forth. His Adam's apple bobbed. "Hey, what's going on?"

Trent shifted his weight to the right when Cieo turned sleepy eyes on Johnson. Tension filled the air.

"Be quiet and do not interrupt us again, or I shall cut out your tongue and flush it down the toilet with the rest of the defecation," said Cieo.

Trent inhaled deeply, his pulse quickening. It was clear that the balance of power now rested solely in Cieo's presence and gun. He also knew that he had to tread lightly and not overestimate his unexpected change of fortune. There were far too many unknowns to assume anything. Something had provided pause in the killer's trigger finger, but that could change at any moment.

"I would be honored to defend anyone you ask me to defend," Trent finally said. Conviction filled his voice. "The enemy of my enemy is my friend."

"Ah-ha," chimed Cieo, clearly appeased by the declaration of solidarity. "That adage is one of my personal favorites."

"Are you insane?" shrilled Johnson. His face turned red with rage. "You can't make a deal with Varus." His eyes peered down at the dead man with a hole in his head. "He's a damn psychopath and a violent serial killer, and we can't trust him. He murdered our friends. He killed Callahan, and he blew our informant into kibble." His arms flew wildly into the air. "What about the innocents at the courthouse? He butchered all of them, chopped off their damn heads!"

As if amused by the questions and accusations, Cieo gave a hearty snicker. His head shook in what looked like an incongruent mixture of disbelief and disappointment. "I really thought you were smarter than all that," he said in a gruff voice, motioning with his hands for Johnson to lower his arms.

Trent jerked his head to the left and to the right, stunned to have heard that the men he had simply rendered unconscious with a chemical soaked rag had been mutilated and beheaded. His stomach churned with disgust, heart pounding in his chest. He had killed two men responsible for ruining his life and killing his family, but to have butchered men beyond recognition went far beyond his ability.

"What are you talking about?" Johnson's eyes widened.

A vicious sneer creased the lines around Cieo's mouth. "I'm afraid to say that your facts are based on misinformation, my dear captain," he said. "Varus didn't kill Judge Harper, and he certainly didn't murder any of his courtroom lackeys." The muscles in his jaw bunched. "Of course, if Harper had been left alone for any amount of time without proper medical attention, I suppose the miserable old bastard might have died of severe blood loss. Who knows? Who really cares? None of that matters now, anyway. He is now dead and of no use to me."

Trent blinked, stunned at the revelation. *I didn't kill them?* His lips parted when Cieo offered him a knowing wink. *What in the hell is going on?*

Cieo then continued. "The point is that I found Harper alive." There was now a gleam in his eye. "For reasons I am not going to get into at this time, Varus has intrigued me for years. I only vaguely remembered the case, but then he became of personal interest when I found out from a staff member at the prison who he was writing from his cell. However, that eventually cooled off for reasons that are none of your business, so I put him on the back burner until Callahan turned up dead."

Johnson's eyes narrowed. "But if you suspected Varus was coming after us, why didn't you give me a heads-up so I could deal with him and the situation swiftly, permanently?"

"Keeping you in the loop is not my job or responsibility," said Cieo matter-of-factly. "Besides, I did advise you to apply pressure to make Varus back off, and your idiotic response was to forcefully lean on stupid Maldonado here to betray his friend. He not so brilliantly sent those two miscreant nephews of his to kill him. They damn near ruined everything. I did not want Varus dead. I believed—still do, in fact—that he was in the right for going after all of you for what you did to him and his family. I harbor no ill will toward him for avenging his wife."

Trent craned his neck and stared at Benny, who dipped his chin on his chest in shame. Tears now filled both of their eyes.

Oh, Benny, why didn't you just come and talk to me? We could have worked something out. It didn't have to come to this!

A growl slipped from Johnson's throat. "But what is Varus to you?" His voice was curt. "He has nothing to do with our mutual business. He's an acceptable loss."

A smirk emanated from Cieo. "There are so many things far more important than business and money, you myopic fool. Varus was the key to everything I have wanted for a very long time, an emotional angle, and I was not about to let you or anyone else trample all over it." His eyes sparkled with life. "The man I met at the range was someone with whom I enjoyed talking, which made many things much clearer. I needed him to remain free, on the street, and out of the press, so I had one of my freelancers keep a watchful eye on him to make sure he did not make any amateurish errors, like leaving physical evidence behind. My eyes-and-ears guy called when he saw Varus break into the courthouse. Upon my arrival, my man filled me in on some of the grisly details. I then entered the building shortly after Varus apparently finished his business behind the courthouse doors. He had me curious, so I followed his tracks. I was not about to leave Harper alive so he could finger Varus at a later date, so I finished him off, along with the rest of his worthless bootlicks. Varus had only drugged the others with chloroform. I know that odor well, and I smelled it around their noses and mouths."

"So you killed Judge Harper to protect Varus?" said Johnson, incredulous. "Why would you do that?"

"My mantra remains no witnesses left behind," said Cieo, "so I cut off all of their heads and laid them out for public display on the geezer's desk to get a message across." His lips pursed. "You should have seen the look on Harper's face when I walked into his chambers and tossed their decapitated heads at him. He was lying on the floor, practically bawling his little pig eyes out over the whole situation. People cringe when faced with actual death—what it looks like up close. It made me sick to see a grown man weep like some kind of punk, so I put him out of his misery. He was old and weak and pathetic."

"What about Callahan, Kirkpatrick, and our informant?" A look of shock covered Johnson's face.

Cieo snorted with apparent disdain. "No loss," he said. "They were spent, obsolete."

"But they were our partners, and you knew Varus was coming for me next," he said. "He was coming for all of us."

Cieo's eyes sparked with intense intelligence. A strange aura of darkness seemed to encircle his head. "Correction, my dear captain," he began in a suave, cool voice. "They were your partners, not mine. Other than that backstabbing informant, those so-called partners were stealing from me. All of you have been pilfering my pockets for several years. This is why you opted to send this"—he pointed at an unconscious Lomax—"detective on a misguided adventure to investigate Callahan's death. It is why you assigned him to the current murder cases and why you drafted that Markinson creature into your ranks. My eyes-and-ears man had been monitoring all of you for months—tracking all your moves, locating bank records, and so forth. You were trying to find the money your partners had stashed in safety deposit boxes and other assorted places. You systematically did everything possible to cover up your involvement, leaving everyone behind as straw men."

"But—" began Johnson, but Cieo raised a hand and silenced him.

"Save your breath," said Cieo. "I am not a naive fool. The only reason I have allowed you to continue breathing is that you still had uses for me. Now those uses have reached their inevitable end, or so it seems. Your services are no longer necessary or required." His lips drew a thin line. "I believe the word *obsolete* best describes your current situation, and I never tolerate anyone stealing from me. Varus simply saved me the trouble of having to do most of the difficult legwork."

"You're insane!" Johnson shrilled. "I never stole anything."

"It's now time to take your medicine." Cieo's arm raised, and he shot Johnson through the eye. The captain's head whiplashed, and he crumpled to the ground. Blood seeped from the wound and pooled around his head. "Liar!" He flicked the gun at his bodyguards. "I cannot abide a thief or a liar. Dispose of him as well."

Trent stood unmoving as he watched two of Cieo's henchmen grab Crue and Johnson by the ankles and drag them away. Their nonchalant attitudes as they chatted back and forth over the dead bodies added a macabre element to the atmosphere, which strangely extinguished the expected euphoria he thought he would feel from watching the two men pay the ultimate price for their crimes. He brought his eyes back on Cieo, who lowered his gun and motioned for his crew of killers to holster their weapons and step back.

Appearing too stunned to move, Benny stared wide-eyed; a frightened squeak slipped from his mouth.

Nothing about the scenario made sense to Trent. People involved in the criminal underworld, he knew, did not commit heinous crimes in front of outsiders, and they certainly did not leave living witnesses behind for the authorities to interrogate. Despite his skill as an excellent litigator in the courtroom, lawyers were a dime a dozen.

Trent jerked back his head when Cieo took two quick steps forward and placed the barrel of his silenced gun against Benny's forehead. His eyes were severe and remorseless, savage doll's eyes.

"You were not included in part of the agreement." Cieo's voice was a guttural growl of condemnation. A vein throbbed in his neck. His eyes would freeze water. "This man's worth is negligible at best." He sneered. "Would you like me to shake this rat from off your neck?"

Trent shifted his gaze from Cieo to Benny, who was silently pleading for him to save his life. His throat constricted from taking a hard swallow; his chin quivered in obvious fear. He had never seen Benny so terrified.

"I can make it painless if that helps with a decision." His index finger tapped the trigger, as if anxious to pull it and end Benny's existence on earth.

Trent pressed his lips together. He needed no time to think anything over, for there was only one decision to make. After so much loss and pain, another murder, no matter how deserved, seemed unconscionable. His hands had already shed too much blood, and more spilled for the sake of vengeance served no purpose. Although Benny had betrayed him, Trent did not altogether blame the man he'd thought of as a close friend for such temporary weakness. After all, the club owner had tried to undo what he had set in motion and save his life. Of all people, Trent knew fear often drove people into doing stupid things, and he was not about to make another mistake by letting Benny's murder possibly come between him and Tabitha. For better or worse, she did love the old sleazebag. He had made a promise to her that he would not allow any secrets or lies between them, and he was not about to break it. Everything he now did would set the rhythm for every day that followed.

Trent sighed at the irony created by his mess of a life. *No matter what, Benny is still family.* He reached out and placed his hand over the gun. *I have no choice.*

Black eyes turned on him, life failing to flicker behind ebony irises. The corner of Cieo's mouth twisted into a malevolent grin that offered no warmth, only cruelty.

Trent applied more pressure for him to lower the gun. "Please, don't kill him," he said softly. "He's the only family I have left in this crummy world."

Cieo's hand refused to budge. "So, you will take responsibility for him and his future actions?" His tone sounded more like a demand rather than a question.

"Yes."

Cieo gave a slight nod and slid the gun back into the holster. "You have a true friend, Mr. Maldonado, and that is truly a rare gift," he said in an emotionless voice. He then took a seat in a nearby chair. His hand flicked dismissively into the air. "The two of you are free to go. Do not give me reason to regret my benevolence on this day. Please leave the keys so my men can lock up after we have finished."

Trent nudged Lomax with the tip of his shoe. "What about this man?" he said. "Certainly he deserves something better than what the others got."

His eyes flashed with a hint of curiosity as to why Trent would bother to concern himself with the life of a cop. "I am afraid that his fate rests within himself and the answers he provides." His legs crossed. "Police work is a noble business, but that business is only as noble as the man or woman wearing the badge. I have no personal grievance against this detective, and he is of no threat to us. If he is a good cop, then he shall live. If not … He did not come here for me." His jaw clenched. "I must warn you that you should not concern yourself with irrelevant matters, Counselor. I shall be in touch."

Trent took the hint and started to drag Benny toward the exit.

I have to know.

Then he stopped in the middle of the dance floor and looked over his shoulder. Something Cieo had said to Benny a few minutes ago now niggled at him, and he wanted just one more answer to a question he needed to ask. He knew that he might never get another chance.

Benny reached out and grabbed his shirt when he made to go back where Cieo sat with a gun lying atop the folders on his lap.

"Is something wrong, Trent?" Benny said with a faint squeak.

Trent waved him off. "Naw," he said distractedly. "Go on ahead, and I'll meet you outside by the car."

Benny's brow furrowed. "Are you sure?"

"Yeah," he said. "It's fine. I will be only a minute or two."

"Okay."

After Trent watched Benny disappear around the corner, he then walked back over to where Cieo sat alone watching his men hoist Lomax to his feet.

"Is there something else on your mind, Trent?" Cieo's eyes sparked with humor.

He nodded. "Just one thing, I suppose," he said.

"I thought you might have another question," he said casually. "I can't say that I'm surprised."

"You do not mind?"

A smile formed on Cieo's face. "Go ahead and ask your question." His voice was friendly. "You may not realize it at this time, but I owe you a very large debt of gratitude." His fingers laced over the gun and folders. "Family means everything to me."

"What did you mean when you said Benny was not included in the agreement?"

Cieo seemed to relax as he cleared his throat. His pallor took on a warm glow Trent had never before seen on the man's face. "Tabitha really loves you," he said with a note of affection. "She was worried about you, worried that you had gotten into something dangerous and way over your head."

Trent felt his heart leap into his throat. "T-Tabitha," he murmured in a stammer. "What does she have to do with any of this?"

Cieo's face beamed at him. A faint laugh fell from his lips. "She has everything to do with all of it," he said, leaning back in the chair. "Benny is a tricky man, but Tabitha is actually quite brilliant, way outside his league. I had to manipulate a half dozen people and several situations that left her with only one choice to protect you. My gamble to convey that you were in danger worked better than I had anticipated. She loves you so much that she actually reached out to her only brother just to make sure that you were kept safe from whatever might threaten you."

"You manipulated her," he said.

"Love is a treacherous emotion."

"Aren't you worried that I might tell her what you did to trick her into calling you?"

"You won't."

"Why wouldn't I?"

"You would never hurt her like that."

Trent looked at him, thinking hard. He knew the man was right.

Cieo's hand pressed against the expensive material covering his chest. "Tabitha is my baby sister, and there is nothing on this planet I will not do for her." His eyes watered. "She was one of my greatest losses, one of my most treasured things in the entire world, and you helped bring her back to me."

"So, all of this is all about her?"

"Everything is and always will be about her," he said serenely. "Knowledge is power, and power creates the unlimited security to earn the money necessary to pursue more knowledge, which ultimately creates a vast and infinite loop to rule over all." He winced. "But none of it means anything without her, my only sister."

Trent wondered if he had reason to worry about all the potential implications now involved with having a dangerous man such as Dominique Cieo in the life of the woman he loved. "So, what's the agreement?" he pressed.

His hand lifted. "Only that she calls me brother again and accepts my calls," he said. "I miss her. Even bloodthirsty killers love their baby sisters."

"Does Benny know?"

His eyes turned frosty. "Yes, of course he knows." Bitterness touched his voice. "But Tabitha has not spoken to me in years, so there was no reason for him to ever mention anything about our relationship. Truth be told, she thinks I am a monster. Who knows? Maybe I am. I have done terrible things over the course of my life, and she wanted no part of my world. She refused my help and my money, called it blood wealth." He held out the folders. "If you truly want to put the past behind you and move on to a future with her, I recommend that you take these and burn them. The documents inside explain many details you may not know about why Johnson and his ilk did what they did to you."

Trent accepted the paperwork. "Thank you," he said. "I believe I will rely on your judgment."

"Don't thank me yet." Amusement tugged at Cieo's voice. "You just may have made a deal with the devil himself." The corners of his eyes smiled. "Congratulations on your new life. You will find Tabitha waiting at the airport for you, so good night. I always wanted a brother."

With the fresh scent of freedom filling his nostrils, Trent stepped outside the club and stared up at the shining stars in the night sky. Tears of joy welled in his eyes. No longer did he feel the burden of the past weighing down on him. After so many years of silent torture, his time for renewed celebration of life had finally come—a miracle that had seemed unattainable through all the pain and suffering he had incurred for as long as he could remember. Trent now finally felt free and at peace. It was a beautiful night for new beginnings, for a second chance at life, and just the idea of squandering another precious minute without his new love was offensive. He looked into the parking lot and smiled at the ridiculous sight of Benny standing on the bumper of his car and pumping his hands into the air, sharing in his aged friend's sentiment.

I am in love, and I am reborn.

Trent then headed toward his new and exciting destiny, where Tabitha awaited him with a warm mouth and open arms.

ABOUT THE AUTHOR

K. R. Lugo graduated from law school in 2001. He is also the author of *Schism, Prey for the Soulless,* and *Dream Kill*. Lugo and his wife, Alisa, live in Nevada.

Printed in the United States
By Bookmasters